FROM A HIGH TOWER

The Elemental Masters,

Book Ten

MERCEDES LACKEY

DAW BOOKS, INC.
DONALD A. WOLLHEIM, FOUNDER

375 Hudson Street, New York, NY 10014

ELIZABETH R. WOLLHEIM
SHEILA E. GILBERT
PUBLISHERS

www.dawbooks.com

First Printing, June 2015

1 2 3 4 5 6 7 8 9

DAW TRADEMARK REGISTERED
U.S. PAT. AND TM. OFF. AND FOREIGN COUNTRIES
—MARCA REGISTRADA
HECHO EN U.S.A.

PRINTED IN THE U.S.A.

DEDICATION:

To Oklahoma and especially the people of Claremore, home to poetry, comedy, bold change, and kindness. Oklahoma was part of the Wild West, and it brings us all adventures even now. Thank you for being good to me and to our household. We may be weirdos, but we're your weirdos.

Foreword

I don't normally write a foreword for the books in this series, but this time I thought I'd give you all a little warning. In this book, I'm going to be heavily referencing an author utterly unheard of in the US: Karl May. This 19th-century German writer of American Westerns is the bestselling writer of *all time* in Germany. His books, particularly *Winnetou and Old Shatterhand, Old Surehand,* and *Old Firehand,* are still widely in print. Many movies have been made from them (mostly using the Czech Republic as a stand-in for the American Southwest, and Italian actors as Native Americans). There are Karl May Festivals all over Germany every year, where avid fans watch reenactments and plays based on the books and dress as their favorite characters, not unlike Western-themed, outdoor versions of American SF conventions. Karl May mania has created over a century's worth of fans just as rabid as any would-be Jedi or Trekker.

Karl May's closest contemporary counterpart is probably J. K. Rowling, but it remains to be seen whether the popularity of Harry Potter will persist for 150 years, as the popularity of Winnetou has in Germany.

I have no explanation for this. We're not exactly talking Shakespeare, here. Karl May literally writes *himself* as the hero of the *Old Shatterhand* series. The books themselves are incredibly self-indulgent; May's heroes never, ever put a foot wrong. *Old Shatterhand* is such a powerful puncher that he levels his opponents with a single blow; never having faced a grizzly before, he kills one with a knife; never having seen a buffalo, he takes down an enormous bull with a single shot to the heart! Winnetou is the noblest of "noble savages," and is so accurate in predicting the movements of his enemies that you'd suspect psychic powers. May strongly encouraged his readers to believe that *he,* personally, was the hero of his works, despite never once having set foot on US soil, much less gone as far as the West, a fact that is painfully obvious to anyone who reads the original German or the one good translation I was able to find. He wrote in the first person, named his hero "Charlie" (the English version of Karl), then dressed as Charlie and encouraged all his fans to assume Charlie's adventures were his own. And yet hundreds of thousands of Germans read and reread the books obsessively, and no less a personage than Albert Einstein said that the adventures of Winnetou and Old Shatterhand brightened his childhood.

Perhaps the explanation is the simplest possible: despite the defects (and they are many), and despite an egotistical self-aggrandizement that led him to dress like Old Shatterhand, and even commission a rifle that replicated the "magical" 25-shot carbine the hero carried (although I have no clue whether or not the thing ever actually worked), Karl May wrote a rattling good story. If he was a "hack," remember that the definition of a "hack" is this: a strong, dependable horse that can always be relied on to get you where you want to go.

There are worse things to be.

Prologue

BLESSED Mary, it is bitter. Friedrich Schnittel did not take his coat off after closing the door to the single room he and his family inhabited in a ramshackle building on the inaptly named *Gartenstrasse* in Freiburg. There was no point in taking it off. It was only a little warmer inside than it was outside. The single room, with its peeling wallpaper and single window with rags stuffed in every crevice, was mostly heated by the bodies of his family, when all was said and done.

His eight children crowded around him, waiting to see what he would produce out of his coat, but they knew better than to clamor at him. And they knew better than to grab for the loaf of day-old bread, the head of cabbage, and the little pot of rendered fat that was all he had to show for an entire day of work stacking crates of wine. He passed these treasures over their heads into the hands of his heavily pregnant wife, Maria. Eight pairs of eyes followed the food with longing and hunger. Maria sat down beside the hearth on a tin bucket, and propped a piece of chipped tile on her lap to use as a cutting board. The cabbage wasn't very good, or very large, but Maria chopped it fine and added every bit, including the stem, to the pot over the tiny hearth. Meanwhile, Friedrich sat down on the bit of ruined masonry that he used for a stool on the side of the hearth opposite her. They didn't have any furniture to speak of; if they'd had anything, it would have been broken up and added to the fire long ago. The only reason they had anything at all to burn was because three of the four oldest children spent all day scavenging every bit of wood or crumb of coal they could find within walking distance of their home. They were good at it, finding even the smallest scraps and the thinnest twigs, but they were competing with many others in similarly impoverished circumstances.

The eldest boy had a different task: he took whatever jobs people would give a nine-year-old boy, which in the winter, wasn't much.

Friedrich stuck his feet, shod in his cracked, rag-wrapped, and ill-fitting shoes, so close to the tiny fire that if the flames had been enthusiastic he might have been in danger of scorching them and surveyed his family with the eye of despair. Eight children, six boys and two girls, all of them clad in every scrap of clothing they possessed, all of them staring at his wife with desperate longing as she cut the loaf into ten absolutely equal pieces and scraped a bit of the lard over the surface of each piece. All of them with the pinched, slightly grayish faces of those to whom hunger was ever present, and soap unheard-of. *Dear God,* Friedrich thought, sadly. *Oh, dear God, why did You make Maria so . . . fertile? I know that You have told us to be fruitful and multiply, but surely You meant that for wealthier men than me. . . .* The Priest at Saint Martin's Church said that it was a blessing that they had so many children, and that none of them had died, but Friedrich could not see how it could possibly be a blessing to have so many children when not one of them could get a full belly no matter how hard he worked.

Especially not in the winter, when they needed full bellies the most.

Maria looked up at him sharply, as if she had gotten wind of his thoughts. But then she looked back down at her task, which was no easy one, slicing so carefully through the bread so as not to waste a crumb and carefully apportioning the lard so that everyone got the same tiny amount. When she had finished, she carefully—almost reverently—handed it over, slice by precious slice, into the out-stretched hands. Then she protected her hand with her threadbare skirt and lifted the pot off the hook, took her own battered cup, and apportioned one cup of the cabbage soup to each of nine bits of abused tin or chipped pottery that the children passed her. When she had given Friedrich his, she lifted the kettle and poured out the rest—exactly a cupful—into her own vessel.

They all ate slowly, carefully, dipping the bread into the broth and taking tiny bites and then, when the bread was gone, drinking what remained, and chasing the little bits of cabbage remaining with fin-gers and tongues until the vessels could not have been cleaner had they been scoured. Maria sent Pieter, the oldest, for the bucket of water in the corner, refilled the pot, and hung it back over the fire. They would all drink hot water if they got too cold, and to ease the complaints of still-empty stomachs.

While they were relatively warm, and had *something* in their bel-lies, the children all piled together on the heap of rags that they called a bed, made of rags too small to be patched into clothing or too coarse to wear. In moments they were asleep. Maria sighed, and rubbed her belly. "I wish it was summer," she said, sadly. "I long for green things and vegetables to eat. I feel I will die without them. Ramps! Oh, if only I could have ramps!"

Friedrich winced. Of course she would crave what she couldn't have. Vegetables in winter? Other than cabbage and potatoes, they were dearer than meat. When she had been pregnant in the summer, she had wanted meat, which they couldn't afford at any time, and pickles. Now in the winter, she craved green things. But . . . this time was a little different. This time it seemed to him that her face was thinner than before, and more strained, and that there was a fever-ish, haunted look about her eyes. Was she voicing more than her usual complaints and cravings? *Could* it be that this time bearing the child would kill her?

And then what would *he* do? He couldn't work and watch over the children at the same time! Panic rose in his throat, though he kept his face stoic.

"Rampion," she said wistfully. "Oh, for a heap of rampion."

Unable to bear any more of this, or the frightened feeling in his belly, he stood up, abruptly. "I'm going back out," he said gruffly. "By now everyone has cleared out from the winter market. I might find some cabbage leaves or onion tops, or maybe some spilled oats or barley." He turned without another word and went out the door. As he closed it, he glanced behind, through the closing door. She was sitting there, still rubbing her swollen belly. He tried not to feel angry with her, but it was hard. What was he supposed to do? Conjure up food out of nothing? It took almost everything he could earn just to keep a roof over their heads!

It was dark now, but that was all the better so far as he was concerned. No one would see him rummaging in the fouled straw left after the farmers at the winter market packed up their remaining wares and beasts and left. He was no longer too proud to hunt for the old discarded cabbage leaves, or even, if the light was good enough, pick through the straw for grain the hens might have left. Thanks be to God, there was a full moon and the snow was thin. That made foraging easier.

But before he reached the market square his attention was diverted.

He thought he saw a flash of light where no light should be, on the other side of a wall that surrounded what had once been a fine old house that was now as rundown as any other place in this slum. No one lived there, to his knowledge, and it had been boarded and locked up for as long as he and Maria had lived in this neighborhood. But behind that wall, it occurred to him, was what was left of a garden. And even a garden long-deserted might have things still growing in it that were worth salvaging. Roses bore hips that made good tea, and might give Maria some strength. There might be herbs. Maybe at one time there had even been vegetables, and some might still be there, half-wild. Perhaps there were withered apples.

The thought was father to the deed. He found a place where he could scale the garden wall, and in a moment, he was over.

He realized as he dropped down the other side that the "light" he had seen must have been the full moon reflecting off a glass witch-globe in the center of the garden. But that was not what caught his attention.

No . . . what caught his attention was that somehow, some way, this garden was not a useless garden full of half-choked flowers and weeds, but—a *vegetable* garden. And more than that, it was a vegetable garden that was cultivated, and as full of produce as if it was harvest season. By some miracle, there was not so much as a flake of snow on the ground, nor were the plants frost-killed and rotting.

There were squash, kohlrabi, and beans, onions, kale and cabbage, carrots, Brussels sprouts, and beets and turnips. There were peas, potatoes, radishes, leeks, parsnips, and the rampion that Maria craved! He felt nearly faint at the sight of so much food.

There was no sign of life in the house . . . and he did not hesitate for a moment at the theft he was about to perform. *My children are starving. And no one has* touched *this garden. It would be a sin for it to go to waste and freeze and rot.*

An hour later, he was over the wall again, wearing his coat and jumper only, with his shirt over his back stuffed full of vegetables and serving as a sack.

Maria wept when he spilled out his bounty on the hearth; wept, and gathered it all in, marveling and looking up as if to say something. But he didn't stop to answer her questions, for this was an opportunity that might never come again, and while he had moonlight, he was going to steal as much as he could. After all, he had already *stolen;* the sin was committed, the deed was done, and he thought that *how much* he took really didn't matter at this point. How was it the old saying went? *Might as well be hung for a sheep as for a lamb.* By the time the moon went down, the children were awake again, and there were vegetables stacked everywhere in the room, and herbs hanging upside down in bunches from a string knotted between two nails on the wall. The kettle of hot water now held more vegetables stewing away merrily, and potatoes baking in their jackets in the ashes, and they all went to bed again, exhausted, but knowing that, for the first time in more than a year, they would wake up to something to eat.

In his dreams he continued to fill his shirt and bring out more food. But in his dreams, it wasn't only vegetables he was looting; when he pulled up beet and turnip tops, there were loaves of bread and even a sausage or two attached to the greens.

But then, he almost always dreamed of food. The children probably did, too. At least when he woke to the first light this morning there was something to fill his stomach.

He would have very much liked to have lingered over his breakfast of roasted potato the way the children did, but he was well aware last night might have been a fluke. Surely, whoever had planted that garden was going to notice and take measures to protect it. So when he went out in the thin morning light to see if there was work again at the vintner, he detoured by the old house, fully expecting to find that he had been mistaken—that it *was* inhabited, and the occupants were now incensed over his raid on their garden.

But the shutters on the street side were all closed and locked, and it was silent as only an empty house could be.

He still didn't believe in his luck. Perhaps they didn't awaken in the morning as poor people had to. He passed on; he could not count on a second night of raiding. This was only a brief moment of luck, surely.

He did find work that day, though not at the vintner, but turning a manure pile at the stable. It was filthy, stinking work, but he didn't care; besides his pay, he managed to get his hands on some coarse burlap grain sacks that had the seams ripped open. Truth to tell . . . he hid them under his coat to sneak them out, since even a sack that could no longer hold anything was worth something, but he doubted that anyone would miss them in time to connect their disappearance with him. He had also taken the time to chip some salt from the block that the horses licked and fill his pockets with it. Salt was salt, the vegetables would be even better with salt and herbs, and he had eaten worse than horse saliva.

He tried not to think about how easy stealing had suddenly become . . . then resolved to repent of it as soon as he could. But right now . . . well . . .

I have starving children and a wife who may not live to give birth unless I do something.

He arrived home with his burden of burlap, bread and little pot of lard to open the door to the unaccustomed aroma of cooking. Instead of sending him out to look for an odd job, Maria had sent Jakob, the eldest boy, out farther afield to find wood. Once again, potatoes roasted in their jackets beside the fire, and the kettle was full of chopped vegetables. His children looked at him with hope instead of desperation, and there was a little color in Maria's cheeks.

He had made another detour past the house and its walled garden—and there was still no sign of life. He resolved to loot as much as he could tonight.

When he went out at moonrise, he had with him real sacks now, since Maria had managed to sew them up again, and Maria had come up with clever ways to store the rest of the bounty during the day, sending the three eldest besides Jakob out to forage in the rubbish. Baskets with broken bottoms could still be filled as long as you didn't move them. Pots broken in half could be tied up with foraged twine to hold peas and beans. Since he had pulled things like onions and beets up whole, she had used an old country trick and braided the tops together so they could be hung on the wall, on bent nails painstakingly straightened with a stone and a brick.

When he returned that night, it was with even more of the garden's bounty. And any regret he was feeling died when he returned to see his children sleeping peacefully, not whimpering with hunger in their dreams.

It was the third night of his raids on the walled garden, and he had lost some of his caution. There still was no sign, none whatsoever, that there was anyone living here to notice his depredations. He had stopped watching over his shoulder, or even paying attention to any-thing other than pulling up root vegetables without damaging them. It was hard, cold work, even though the soil in this garden was some-how soft and unfrozen. And he didn't want to break even the tiniest bit of root off his prizes.

So when he heard a low, rumbling growl at his shoulder, it came as a complete and utter shock.

It came again: a feral, warning growl that made every hair on his body stand on end.

He froze, his heart in his mouth.

He didn't dare look. His breath puffed out in the frosty air, reflect-ing the moonlight, and he stared down at his grimy hands, at the enormous turnip that was half-dug from the cold, soft soil.

The growl came again, louder.

Overwhelmed with panic, he slowly turned his head and looked up from the turnip he had almost unearthed to find himself sur-rounded by three huge black dogs, two on one side, one on the other. They eyed him menacingly, and the one at his left who had alerted him with its sinister growl uttered yet another terrifying rumble.

"I should be very interested to hear whatever excuse you have for robbing my garden," said a cold female voice behind him. "I might even let you stammer it out before I give my dogs the order to deal with you. Turn around. Let me look you in the eyes."

Still on his knees in the cold earth, he slowly turned.

Behind him, her face clear in the moonlight, was a tall, hawk-faced woman in a long black cloak, her dark hair severely braided and pinned tightly around her face. She had her arms crossed over her chest and stared down at him icily. "Well?" she prompted. "What sort of fairy tale have you to tell me?"

He opened and shut his mouth several times without any words coming out. But then . . . his panic got the better of him, and he fell apart.

He groveled. He babbled. He wept without hope that he would get even a crumb of pity from her. He really didn't know what he was saying, although he certainly went on at length about Maria and the children. He begged and pleaded, he cried shamelessly until he was hoarse. She said nothing. And finally, when he had repeated himself far too many times and ran out of words, she stared down at him in the silence while he waited helplessly for her to set the dogs on him, call for the police, or both.

I am going to be savaged. Then I am going to prison. Maria will die, and the children will starve.

"Well," she said at last. "I am actually inclined to believe you." She looked down at him for another long, cold moment. "And I am not an unreasonable woman, nor am I inclined to make your children suffer for your sins. It is clear that they will probably all starve without you to provide for them. I would not care to have the deaths of children on my conscience. Perhaps I can think of some way you can repay what you stole."

He began to have faint hope. Perhaps . . . perhaps she would let him go? He looked up at her and clasped his hands under his chin, trying to look as prayerful and repentant as possible. "Anything!" he blurted.

But she was not finished. "A bargain, then. You owe me, Friedrich Schnittel. You owe me a very great deal. But I won't have you thrown in prison. In fact, you can come here and gather what you need for your family every day, on condition that you repay me."

"H—" he did not even manage to get all of the word *how* out before she interrupted him.

"You have—or will have—something I want, just as I have something you want. So, this is the bargain: you may continue to help yourself to this garden. I would prefer that you come at night, so that I don't have other thieves coming to steal from me, and you might as well keep coming over the wall as well, since you are so good at it. Then, when your wife gives birth to this new child, you will give her to me." He opened his mouth to object. She stared at him with her lips compressed into a thin line. "Don't try to barter with me. It is this, or I set the dogs on you and have the police take what is left of you to prison. What will it be? Will you feed your eight children and your wife for the trivial price of a baby that is likely to die anyway?"

Well, what *could* he say? If he refused, what would Maria and the children do but starve? What good would it do him *or* them if he suddenly decided that selling the baby was wrong? "Very well . . ." he said, slowly.

She smiled, as if she had already known he would say as much. "Take what you have. Come back tomorrow night. I'll even leave sacks for you."

And with that, she turned on her heel and stalked back into the house, her dogs preceding her. They all went in via the kitchen door—which showed not so much as a hint of light—and she closed the door behind her, leaving him chilled and drenched with sweat on the cold earth of the garden.

It was not an easy birth.

When it was over, Maria lay too exhausted to even move beneath a heap of every scrap of fabric that could be spared to keep her warm, and the new baby girl had been tightly wrapped and was being held by Jakob near to the fire. Friedrich was just glad Maria had had three weeks of good food before the birth; he really didn't think she would have survived this one without the extra nourishment. She'd gone into labor the previous afternoon, and it had gone on until well after sunrise.

He was just as tired, since he had served as midwife. He was slowly eating vegetable soup and drinking herb tea, his first meal since she had gone into labor. And he really wasn't thinking of anything else when the knock came at the door. Before he could say anything, his second oldest, Johann, jumped up to answer it.

And fell back again, in astonishment and fear, as the terrible woman in black and one of her dogs pushed their way in.

She closed the door behind her and surveyed them all with an icy glare.

The children all froze in terror; the tall woman was no less forbidding and formidable in broad daylight than she had been by night.

The dog didn't growl, but he didn't have to; he looked like a black wolf, which was more than enough to make the children try to inch back until they were squeezed into the corner farthest from her.

All but Jakob, who remained where he was, by the fire, the baby clutched in his nerveless hands.

Before Friedrich could utter a word, the woman looked around the room and spotted Jakob and the baby. In four strides she had crossed the room, then bent and snatched the baby out of Jakob's arms.

"I've come for your part of the bargain, Friedrich Schnittel," she said. "And now I'll be gone."

And with that, she turned, stalked out the door, and left.

Maria fell into hysterics, of course—he hadn't told her about the bargain. When he explained, she only became more hysterical, weeping and pushing him away until he just gave up trying to reason with her, and, for lack of anything else to do, made sure the children were all fed. As they all ate, she cried herself into a sleep that was less sleep than collapse, and he stared at her white, tear-streaked face and wondered where the girl he had fallen in love with had gone.

When Maria awoke, she refused to speak to him. After a while, he got tired of the silence and decided to make another visit to the garden. The terrible woman had not put an end-date on *her* part of the bargain, and he was determined to get as much out of it as he could.

He was beginning to resent Maria's attitude. The woman had been right, after all. If not for the food, Maria, the baby, or both probably would have died. And what about the eight *other* children? Didn't *they* warrant some consideration too? Didn't they deserve to have full bellies for once? Wasn't one baby likely to die anyway worth bartering away to save the lives of his living children?

At this point, he was a little drunk on exhaustion himself, and a little reckless. And he went in—if not *broad* daylight, certainly just before sundown. By the time he got over the wall, he was . . . not exactly seething, but feeling far more the victim than the victimizer. And it occurred to him that if he could just get a glimpse inside that house, perhaps he could see that the baby was being treated in a manner far better than he and Maria could ever afford, and perhaps that might make the foolish woman see reason.

But as he approached the house—he noticed that the kitchen door was slightly ajar.

That's . . . odd.

He made his way carefully to the door, and when nothing came out of it—especially not an enormous, possibly vicious dog—he pushed it all the way open.

Nothing. And there was no sound in the house, at all.

He ventured inside.

The kitchen was utterly empty. And so was the next room. And the next.

The caution ebbed out of him, and he began to prowl the entire house while the light lasted: all the rooms, downstairs and the two stories above. No furnishings, only a piece or two, like the great bed in one of the bedchambers, which would have been impossible to move. No sign that anyone had lived here, except for the absence of dust.

As he stood there in the empty house . . . a plan formed in his mind.

There was a gate to the garden; he had always come and gone over the wall, but now, he ran to it and forced the rusty lock and latch open. Then he ran back to his little room.

By this time, he was somewhat incoherent, probably wild-eyed, and talking like a madman. But that was no bad thing . . . the children looked at him with bewilderment and fear and did not ask him questions. With words and a few blows for those too stubborn to obey immediately, he gathered up the children and all of their meager possessions, forced Maria to her feet, and drove them out the door, down the street, and in through the gate.

At this point even Maria looked afraid of him and kept any objections to herself.

He locked the gate behind them all and herded them in through the kitchen door. "This is our home, now," he said sternly. "At least it is until someone comes to tell us differently."

The children made up the bed of rags and straw for Maria again, and she crept into it, shivering.

Once the family was installed in the kitchen—which alone was three or four times the size of the room they *had* been living in—he left them there, instructing Jakob to make up a fire with the plentiful firewood that was already there. Then he ran back and forth until he had brought all of the food that they had cached, and their old room was scoured bare of anything remotely useful, down to the smallest of rags.

Then he returned to the deserted house, locked the gate behind him, and joined the rest of his family in their new home.

Yes. Their home. For it had come to him, as he had seen this empty, echoing house, why should it go to waste? It had been untenanted for as long as he could remember. If that woman came back she could easily evict him and his family, but in the meantime, why should they not save the rent money and live here, where the garden and its bounty were easily accessible? Why not?

Maria was terrified at this new version of her husband, who had gone from stealing turnips to "stealing" an entire house . . . and truth to tell, he was not displeased with this. At least it stopped her from reproaching him.

The strange woman never returned to her house.

And Maria never forgave him.

1

GISELLE leaned out of the window of her room at the top of the tower and drank in all the spring fragrances being carried up to her on the breeze. Her room had the best view of any in the former abbey, and she often wondered who had been the tenant back when the complex had been inhabited by the Sisters of Saint Benedict. The abbess herself? Or perhaps it had been a room devoted to communal prayer?

Probably the abbess, she decided. It would have been a good place from which to keep an eye on the entire abbey. Mother said she had no idea why the abbey had been abandoned for so long, to the point where only the tower had been inhabitable when she had first taken it over, and only because the entire tower was built of stout stone. That had been long before Giselle had been born. By the time Mother brought her here as an infant, the tower had been completely renovated, all the other buildings had been reroofed with proper, strong tile, and the building attached to the tower itself, which had probably housed the nuns in their little cells, had been converted into spacious living quarters for Mother. Only the chapel remained in ruins. Mother never explained why she had not rebuilt the chapel, but then, why should she have? It wasn't as if she and Giselle needed a church.

There were four windows in Giselle's tower room, facing precisely in the four directions of the compass. Giselle preferred the view from the east window, which looked out over the valley meadow to the forest beyond, and to the mountains beyond that. Probably, back when the abbess had lived here, there had been nothing to keep out the winter winds but simple wooden shutters, and only a charcoal brazier to huddle over to keep out the cold. Mother had changed all that. There were proper glass windows *and* shutters in all the windows now, and a good fireplace on each floor of the tower.

Giselle wondered if dwarves had done the work. She'd never seen any here, but then, the work had been completed before she ever got here. Since it had all been stonework, it would have been logical for Mother to have made a bargain with dwarves to accomplish it. Mother was an Earth Master, after all, and dwarves were Earth Elementals.

I certainly can't imagine her allowing ordinary stonemasons here.

The nearest village—and it was a very small one—was over two days' ride away, in the next valley over from the abbey. You couldn't even see it from the top room of the tower. Giselle had never been there herself, only Mother, driving the cart out to get the things they could not produce for themselves and coming back again days later. Still, it wasn't as if she could be lonely. Not when she was surrounded by all the Elementals of her own Element, Air.

There were three of them here in the tower room with her, since she had flung open all four windows to the winds. Sylphs, who generally looked—at least to Giselle—like lovely, mostly naked women with wings. These three were all longtime friends of hers. One had the wings of a moth, one of a dragonfly, and one of a bird. They wouldn't give her their "true" names, of course, even though they trusted her, so she called them Luna, Damozel, and Linnet. Linnet was perched on the lantern hung from the peak of the roof, Luna was in the west window, and Damozel dozed on the mantelpiece. Generally when Mother was gone, she had one or more of the sylphs with her at all times, which was a great comfort. When she had been *very* little, there had been one of the Earth Elementals, a brownie, who had acted as a kind of nursemaid when Mother had to leave, but she had not seen old Griselda for many years now. It wouldn't have been wise to entrust the safety of a baby or a young child to the sylphs; they were well intentioned, but easily distracted. Even now, there was some sort of Earth Elemental who tended the chickens, the cow and the goats when Mother was gone, but Giselle had never seen it. It might have been a gnome; they were very shy. Eggs and milk simply appeared in Giselle's kitchen while Mother was away.

There were other sorts of Air Elementals than the sylphs, of course. There were great ones, like the Four Winds, dragons of the Air, and Storm Elementals, and according to the books she had studied, there were djinns of the Air and tiny pixies, and all manner of bird spirits. Giselle had more than once, especially in winter, watched the great Storm Elementals playing in the clouds. Sometimes in vaguely human shape, and sometimes as powerful vortices of wind and cloud, she had marveled at them until Mother had made her close the windows and the shutters. "Don't attract their attention yet, my little rampion," she would murmur kindly. "They do not know how to play gently."

Mother was right, of course. Elementals were not all as trustworthy as brownies or as fragile as sylphs. You had to know your magic, had to be a Master, before you dared have dealings with the Greater Elementals. At fourteen, Giselle was only just beginning her serious studies. It would be years, maybe decades, before she dared to make contact with one of the Greater Powers of Air. If she ever did.

"Why would you want to dance with the Great Ones?" asked Luna, lazily. Giselle turned away from the window to meet the eyes of her ethereal companion. *"They are too serious. They do not know how to have fun."*

She had to giggle at that. The sylphs didn't seem to know how to do anything *but* have fun.

Luna's wings waved lazily back and forth as she smiled at Giselle. She had lovely white moth wings that glowed as if they were made of moonlight—the reason that Giselle had named her "Luna" in the first place. *"I hope you never forget how to have fun. So many magicians are always dour and serious. So tiresome."*

"I'll try not to, Luna," Giselle replied. With a glance backward at the vista from the window, she left the three Elementals lazing about her room and went down the stairs to the lower levels of the tower. Unlike the sylphs, she couldn't live on air alone, it was past breakfast time, and she was hungry.

Mother always had meals precisely on time, but when she was away, Giselle tended to eat irregularly. There was a tiny little kitchen on the bottom floor of the tower, a miniature version of the bigger one that Mother used. Mother said the big one had been the "refectory kitchen"—Giselle guessed that was where the sisters of the abbey had done all their cooking. It was certainly huge, but Mother said she liked lots of room when she cooked. And, indeed, perhaps that was because in the fall and winter, she often cooked large batches of things that could be kept in the freezing cold of the cold-pantry and would not spoil, and in the summer and a little in the spring, she put up huge batches of jams and jellies, preserved fruits and vegetables. She even cured whole hams of boar and venison!

Even when it would have been convenient, Mother did not seem to use her magic very much, at least not when Giselle was around.

Luna left her window and followed Giselle all the way down into the kitchen, which was unusual. The sylphs didn't care for the enclosed room, which was only illuminated by lanterns and high slit windows at the ceiling. But it seemed that Luna's curiosity was overcoming her distaste for walls this evening. She perched out of the way while Giselle cut herself some bread and cheese and filled a little bowl with pickles. *"Where is the Mother?"* Luna asked, as Giselle poked up the fire in the little hearth and held the bread and cheese on a toasting fork over the coals to melt.

"She went to Fredericksburg," Giselle said, keeping a careful eye on her food.

"Why?"

Being with the sylphs, Mother said, sometimes with exasperation, was like being with a little child. Once they decided to converse, they often had never-ending questions, and often questions they had asked before, since it was hard to keep their attention on anything for long. Giselle didn't mind.

"There are things that we need that we do not have and cannot get from the forest or our garden, our chickens, our bees, our little cow, or our goats," she explained patiently. "Flour and salt and spices and sugar. Books. Cloth. Needles and thread."

"You could get them from the villages."

"Mother doesn't want to do that. She'd really rather the villages around didn't know we were here. She says it's dangerous." Mother had explained some of the dangers; it seemed that the villagers hereabouts were not as accepting of magic as in other places in the Black Forest, perhaps because there were no members of the *Bruderschaft der Förster*—the Brotherhood of the Foresters—nearby. And truly, given some of the dangerous, even *evil* things that Giselle had seen in the forest while roaming there under Mother's protection, she could understand why they would fear magic. "Besides, she wants to make sure my father and mother and siblings are still all right."

"Why?"

That question made Giselle pull a face, for she didn't really understand it herself. "She says it's an obligation. That once a magician interferes in the lives of people, the magician has to make sure her meddling wasn't for the worse."

"Is it? The meddling."

The cheese was just melting and Giselle pulled the bread back, noting that it was nicely toasted on the underside. "I suppose not. She says he's still living in the old house she bought. He's got a job as an under-gardener for rich people somewhere in the city, so he gets the vegetable and herb seedlings when the rich garden gets thinned out. So he's keeping *her* garden producing and feeding the family." She made another face. "All those children! I think it would be *horrid* to be one of nine. Nine! You'd never get any attention! And before Mother took me from him, they hardly ever got food. Now at least they can eat."

Luna nodded wisely. *"Because he is making the garden of the house grow."*

"Not as well as Mother did, of course, but *he's* not an Earth Magician. He can't grow vegetables in midwinter." Mother did that even here, though she was discreet about using her power and kept the interference with nature to a minimum. Giselle knew why, of course. When you used power, there was always the chance that you would attract things, and those things weren't always—or even often—friendly. The sylphs were here because she had invited them. There were other things that could, and would, come uninvited. Mother had been freer to use her power in the city, because most of those things avoided cities and their high concentrations of people and poison, iron and steel.

"So you would never go back—"

"Ugh! Never," she said emphatically. "Mother *loves* me." Of that, she was absolutely sure. "That . . . man that was my father, he couldn't possibly have loved me if he just *gave* me away like that!"

Luna was silent for a long while as Giselle savored her cheese-and-toast. And then, she said, *"Hunger makes desperate choices. You have never gone hungry."*

Where did that come from? Giselle wondered. She didn't even know if sylphs *could* hunger.

"That may be so," she said, feeling stubborn. "And it is true I have never known want. But I do not think that a man who loved his child would give it away for the sake of a wagonload of vegetables, and I don't really understand why Mother feels obligated to him."

Luna only smiled. *"When will she return?"*

Giselle consulted the calendar. "At any hour from today on," she said, feeling a happy thrill of excitement—for there would certainly be new books, and perhaps some beautiful new fabric to make into new clothing, and the treats that Mother always brought back from the city. Mother's Earth Mastery could allow her to grow amazing things, but she could not grow exotic spices, and she could not grow chocolate. Giselle's mouth watered at the thought of chocolate.

They could have done without the fabric, Giselle supposed.

Mother was very patient, but she said herself that she was not patient enough to spin her own thread and weave her own cloth. She had taught Giselle how to do both, but . . . Giselle was not very patient at all. To be honest, it was very hard for her to just sit and do handwork; she found it terribly tedious.

But—books! She hoped there would be a new Karl May book! The ones set in the Orient were very, very good, but the ones set in America, in the Wild West, were *superb!* Old Surehand, Old Firehand, and especially Winnetou and Old Shatterhand. She could not get enough of Winnetou and Old Shatterhand. Especially Winnetou and the other Indians. She wondered what it would be like, to be an Elemental Master on the plains. What the Elementals would look like. They were different in other places, she knew from her studies. And what would it be like to stand in a place where the horizon was flat, where the land was flat for as far as you could see, and not hemmed in by mountains?

Luna brightened. *"Will there be new ribbons?"* she asked. Giselle smiled. The sylphs loved to play with ribbons, and would wear them to shredded tatters, twirling them about and using them in games of tag. Mother always made a point of bringing bolts of ribbon back from her trips to the city.

"Of course there will be new ribbons," Giselle promised. "Mother would never forget you." Luna clapped her hands in glee.

Giselle finished her meal and went back upstairs. She didn't much care for the kitchen either, it was so dark, and so close. But she had to cook her food somewhere, and when Mother was gone, she was locked into the tower.

She took the stone stairs that spiraled up the tower wall two at a time; there was nothing like a handrail, but she had been scampering up and down these stairs since she was old enough to toddle, and it never occurred to her to feel fear.

This tower had four levels. The bottom was the kitchen, and had been her bedroom as well until she was old enough to safely navigate the stairs. The next level was the library and workroom, where she took her lessons and learned her magic. The third level was the storeroom, where everything was kept that wasn't a book, and the final, top story was her bedroom. Besides her bedroom, none of the rooms had anything but slits for windows.

She breathed a sigh as she got to her own room and the wide-open windows again. So did Luna. The sun was just setting, and the view from the tower was particularly glorious tonight. The very air seemed full of golden light, and the long shadows cast by the trees across the meadow were a deep, deep amber.

Damozel woke up, stretched and yawned. Linnet flitted down from the lantern and landed beside the west window. Her fellow sylphs joined her.

"We will see you at dawn, magician," Luna said, as the other two took turns balancing on the windowsill before launching themselves out onto the evening breeze. She did not wait for an answer; sylphs lived very much in the moment, and seldom waited on human politeness.

Sylphs could flit about at night, of course, but the ones that did tended to be shy and secretive and seldom visited Giselle. Giselle leaned out of the window to watch her friends soar up into the clouds. She often wondered if they slept up there, and if the clouds were as comfortable as they looked.

She remained leaning out of the window, dreamily watching the sunset and twilight stealing over the forest. From here, it looked so peaceful, and near the abbey, it actually was, but all sorts of things could be lurking deeper into the trees—

"Hello up there!"

A deep voice called from just beneath her, startling her and making her jump, yelp and nearly hit her head on the top of the window frame. Her heart beating wildly, she looked down to see that there was a man standing just beneath the window. A man . . .

She knew what a man was, she'd met at least three when members of the Bruderschaft came to consult with Mother. But none of them had been nearly this handsome. Or young.

Because he certainly was younger than any man she had seen before. She wasn't very good at estimating ages, but she didn't think he could be more than a few years older than she. He was blond, his hair pale in the twilight, with a wonderful face, like a warrior in one of her books: clean-shaven, square jawed, with a fine brow and clear eyes. She couldn't tell what color they were in this light but she thought, given that he was blond, that they were probably blue.

"I'm very sorry, I didn't mean to startle you!" the man said, pulling his hunter's hat off and clutching it at his chest.

"How did you get down there?" she asked, telling her heart to calm down. It didn't, but at this point she suspected that had more to do with the man's handsome features than the fact that he had startled her.

"I came around the east side of your tower," he said. "I'm a hunter, I'm very quiet. I didn't even know there was anyone living here until I saw you at your window. I apologize for frightening you!"

She smiled down at him as he peered earnestly up at her. "Apology accepted. It's all right, really, no harm done." She felt an odd shyness and found herself tongue-tied. What to say to a handsome young stranger? She had no idea.

He seemed under no such burden. "I thought I would come survey this part of the world before hunting season begins," he continued, and shrugged. "Too many others in what used to be *my* forest. Time to move on."

"Oh," she managed, resting her chin on her hands so she could look down at him more easily. "I don't know anything about that." After all, the men of the Bruderschaft, although they were hunters, were not *primarily* hunters of game. It was the evil things of the forest that they hunted . . .

"But what are you doing, out here in the middle of the wilderness?" he asked, putting his hat back on his head and tipping it at a jaunty angle.

"I live here, with Mother," she replied.

He shook his head. "I cannot imagine living alone in such a remote place. What do you do with your time?"

She had to laugh at that. "We work, of course! There are all the animals to tend, the garden to care for, food to make, clothing to sew, cleaning to do—what do you think we do? Gaze out of tower windows all day?"

"And here I thought you were a princess, who only had to do just that!" he replied, with an ingratiating smile. "May I come in to see your tower?"

"When Mother gets home," she replied truthfully. "She locks the door when she is gone, and she has the only key."

"Doesn't she trust you?" He frowned.

"She doesn't trust the things in the forest," she corrected him. "I don't mind."

"Hmm. Well, there are gypsies in the forest, and tramps. She's probably wise." He nodded sagely. She smiled.

"You haven't told me your name," she pointed out. "I'm Giselle."

"And I am Johann Schmidt," he replied, and swept off his hat in a flourishing bow. "At your service. Shall I tell you all about myself?"

She felt herself coloring all over again. "Oh," she replied. "Please!"

Johann stayed until moonrise, then bowed again and took his leave, promising to come back on the morrow. Giselle could not remember ever having been so excited at the prospect of something, not even when learning new magic. After all, her magic had been a part of her for as long as she could remember, but handsome young men were things she had only read of in books, and a handsome young man standing beneath her window for hours just to talk to her was something entirely new.

The men of the Bruderschaft that had visited Mother had not had much time for her; she understood that, of course, to come all this way to this remote part of the Black Forest, deep in the mountains, they must have had very urgent business indeed. They certainly had no time to spare for idle chat. To have another person besides Mother interested enough in her to regale her with tales was wonderful.

To have that person be a very handsome young man was intoxicating.

After Johann was gone, she spent a long time just dreamily staring up at the night sky, for once not watching for the shyer and more elusive sylphs and other Air Elementals that only came out at night.

In the morning there was no sign of Johann Schmidt, not from any of the four tower windows, and with a feeling of disappointment, she went about her usual chores. Of her particular sylph friends only Linnet turned up, and she seemed listless, and soon left.

The milk was set out in pans to rise; she skimmed off the cream and put the separated milk and cream in the "special" pantry where things were not allowed to spoil. Giselle made herself something to eat and had her breakfast up in her room with a glass of milk she had set aside. There still was no sign of Johann.

As listless as Linnet had been, Giselle turned over pages in the history books that Mother had left her to study. Truth to tell, she didn't think she was a very good scholar at the best of times, and right now, with vague discontent standing between her and the pages, she wasn't making much headway with them.

So she set the books aside and turned to another tedious chore, which at least had the virtue of requiring attention without concentration.

She unwound her braids from her head, unbraided them, and began combing out her hair.

This was a far different task for her than it was for Mother. Giselle's hair grew at a rather astonishing pace.

Right now, it was roughly twice as long as she was tall, unbraided, and when Mother returned it would be time for her to cut it again. There was an entire chest full of locks of hair as long as Giselle was tall. Mother said this had something to do with her magic; certainly the smaller of the Air Elementals, the pixies and other little things she had no name for, had something to do with it. Mother was no help there, except to call them *elber*, sort of generally. Some of them looked like very tiny sylphs, some like fantastic winged creatures that were part insect, part human, and part plant. They all liked to play in her hair when she unbound it; she let them, because they untangled it as they went.

The rate at which it grew varied. It could grow as much as a foot in a week, though only rarely. It generally grew about a foot a month, which meant she had to unbraid it, comb it out, and rebraid it at least once a week. Washing it took almost half a day.

Mother used to joke that she should just let it keep growing and never cut it, saying *then you could let yourself down out of the window by your own hair.* As a child that had always made her giggle.

As usual, as soon as she took her hair down and began to unbraid it, the little Air creatures turned up, showing none of Linnet's listlessness. She was very glad for their help, because when it got to its current length, it was practically impossible to comb and braid without their help. Today they made a game out of it, as if her locks were the ribbons of a Maypole, and did most of the work for her.

They had gone, and she was pinning up the coiled braids on the top of her head, when she heard a melodious whistle that sounded nothing like a bird just outside the west window.

Hastily she stabbed the last hairpin in place and practically flew to the opening, and laughed with delight to see Johann Schmidt standing there below. He looked even handsomer in the sunlight, and his eyes were, as she had suspected, a vivid blue.

He swept off his hat to her as he had last night, and now she could see he was dressed in hunting gear of loden green wool, just like the men of the Bruderschaft wore. She wondered for a moment if he might be one of their number—

But he wasn't wearing the silver Saint Hubert badge they all wore on their hats. Instead, it was a fanned cluster of pheasant feathers in a silver holder.

"Good morning, fair maiden!" he said, cheerfully.

"It's nearly afternoon," she corrected, perhaps more sharply than she had intended, but she was vexed with him. Hadn't he promised to be here? And how long had she waited for him? Hours and hours!

"So it is. I don't suppose you could spare a bite to eat?" he replied, without seeming to take any notice of her temper. "I looked about, but there doesn't seem to be a friendly inn hereabouts."

She relented immediately. "We've plenty to spare," she said truthfully. "I shall bring you something."

He was still calling his thanks as she turned and made for the stairs.

When she came back up, she had a small basket with a sausage, some cheese, an onion, and a couple of boiled eggs in it. Bread was something they *didn't* have a lot to spare of, since flour was one of those things that Mother had to go a long way to get. And she wasn't certain how to get milk down to him; they had cups and pitchers of course, but she was going to have to lower the basket down to him from the window, and she was afraid that the cord she had would break, or the milk would spill.

But he didn't seem to be discontented with her offerings; he took them out of the basket and placed them on his handkerchief, which he spread out on the grass, then sat down and took a flask out of his pocket. She pulled up the basket as he waved at her.

"Shall you dine in your window while I dine below, fair one?" he asked, taking a swig. Since that seemed like a good enough idea to her, she got milk and bread and butter and ate that while he cut off chunks of sausage, cheese and onion and washed them down with whatever was in his flask. As he ate, he regaled her with tales of his hunting, and she listened raptly. The men of the Bruderschaft who had visited had never talked about hunting ordinary creatures, only things like werewolves and other malignant or cursed spirits. Stalking bears, wolves, and stags certainly sounded just as exciting, at least as Johann told it!

They spent the entire afternoon in that way, him telling her story after story of his life—which seemed *much* more interesting to her than her own was—and her listening. Time seemed to pass far too swiftly, and when he began to hint that his luncheon had been several hours ago, she hurried down to the little kitchen and came back again with a hot dinner of bratwurst and sauerkraut, since that was something she could heat quickly, with strawberries from the garden for dessert. He thanked her handsomely, and when he was finished, sent up the plate and fork in the basket. "And now again, I will take my leave of you, fair Giselle," he said with a bow. "There are dangers that only come out of the forest by night, and since I am alone and do not have the eyes of a cat, I had best seek the protection of my shelter. It would be different, of course, if you could offer me your roof as well as your food—"

"I can't," she interrupted him mournfully, thinking of how pleasant it would be if only he could stay, and continue to regale her with tales at the fireside. "I told you, Mother has locked the doors. I can't let you in."

"Then I shall bid you good night, and return on the morrow." He bowed to her, and strode off around the side of the tower. She ran to the other window, but he must have been walking close to the wall of the abbey where she couldn't see him. So frustrating!

But it had been a wonderful day, and he *had* promised to come back. She could hardly wait for morning!

She awoke to the sound of her name being called from below, and flew to the window, her braids nearly tripping her, as she hurried to answer him. She stuck her head out of the window—she had left it open to the evening breeze last night, and one of her braids slithered over the sill and dangled down above his head.

He laughed, and pretended to jump for it. She giggled—he couldn't reach it, of course. As long as it was, the end was still a good twelve feet above his head, but he looked so funny, like a kitten with a string, trying to snatch the end out of the air.

She pulled it back up and he mock-frowned at her. "Temptress! I hope you are prepared to feed me breakfast in exchange for teasing me with a way to climb up to you!"

"Of course I am!" she promised, and ran down to the kitchen without bothering to change out of her nightdress first.

She wanted to impress him, so she made a *real* breakfast: sliced

ham, beef, tongue, three kinds of cheese, some of the precious bread
(toasted over the fire, since it was getting a little stale), and generous
dollops of butter and jam in a little bowl. His eyes lit up when he saw
the feast in the basket. She tied the string to the shutter hinge so she
could leave the basket down there with him until he was finished,
and raced off to change and get her own meal.

When she returned to the window, he looked up at her and
snapped his fingers as if he had suddenly had an idea. "I know what
we can do!" he said, and laughed. "If you cannot come down, I will
come up!"

She stared down at him, baffled. "How?" she replied. "The stones
of this tower are like glass, they are so smooth. There isn't enough of
a chink between them for a bird to catch his claw."

"This!" he said, tugging on the string that was tied to the basket
he had just put the plates back into. "I shall go back to my shelter and
bring my rope. I can tie it to your string and you can pull it up. You
needn't even try to find something to tie it to that will bear my
weight—just tie it to the middle of a fireplace poker."

She laughed at how clever he had been. Of course! The poker was
made of stout metal, and was longer than the window was wide.
Once his weight was on the rope, the poker and the stone of the
tower itself would hold him. "Why didn't we think of this before?"
she said. "Oh, do run back to your things and bring the rope!"

He saluted her and ran off. She pulled up the basket, let down the
string again, and took the basket to the kitchen, then waited impatiently at the window for his return.

It seemed an age, but eventually, Johann appeared around the
bottom of the tower with a coil of stout rope over his shoulder. He
tied one end to her string, and she hurried to pull it up and make it
fast to the poker. She guided the poker in place as he pulled slowly
on the rope, and once he was satisfied it was wedged properly, he
scaled the side of the tower with all the skill of a practiced mountain-
eer. Before she was really prepared for it, he was perched on the sill,
then jumping down into her room.

"Well!" he said, smiling. "Here I am at last."

And then . . . the smile began to change. From cheerful, it turned . . . cruel. His eyes grew cold, and instinctively she began to shrink away from him. "Y-yes," she faltered. "So you are."

With growing alarm, as she realized that she didn't much care for the feral gaze he was bending on her, she realized he was much taller, and very much stronger than she was.

"Now, I ask myself," he said, advancing on her as she backed up a step at a time until her back was against the wall. "What kind of a girl meets a man in her nightdress? And what kind of a girl lets a man into her bedroom after only three days of acquaintance? I think it is the kind of girl who knows a great deal more about men than she lets on. And maybe that is why her Mother locks her in, to keep her from any more of them."

She stared at him in shock, the blood draining from her face, unable to move.

"So I think that I will give her what she wants, yes?" And with that, he lunged for her. She was so transfixed with horror that she couldn't even move, and he slammed her against the wall of her tower room.

She screamed then, and tried to fight him, as he pinned her against the wall with one arm and ripped her blouse open with the other. She kicked at him as he stared at her breasts greedily, and with his free hand, groped up her skirts. As her boot connected with his shin, hard, he swore, and backhanded her so hard her head bounced off the wall and, for a moment, she knew only blackness.

When she could see and think again, she found that she was pinned in her bed, her hands tied to the bedpost, and her skirts up around her neck. He was kneeling between her legs, and she screamed again, and kicked and kicked—she was, at least, keeping him from doing anything more than trying to pin her legs down, but she knew that once he managed that—

Her mind was on fire with terror, so much so that every part of her that was still free had new strength and she writhed and screamed and kicked like a creature possessed by a demon.

Her sylphs were flying around and around him, trying futilely to pull him off or beat him with their tiny fists. But he ignored them as if they weren't there—because, of course, to him they were not. She kept screaming and kicking—he kept cursing and trying to secure her legs.

The sylphs were screaming too, and then, suddenly, outside the tower, the sky darkened, plunging the room into gloom. A moment later, lightning lit the room in flashes and thunder shook the tower. He glanced up, startled, and she redoubled her efforts. As if echoing her actions, more lightning crashed down around the tower, and a great wind tore through the windows and whipped violently through the room.

And then, with no warning, and out of nowhere, a staff hit him in the side of the head, knocking him away from Giselle and off the bed.

In the light of near-continuous lightning, skirts and cloak billowing in the wind, a veritable Valkyrie armed with a staff that she wielded expertly stepped between Giselle and her attacker. Johann scrambled to his feet, pulling a knife from a sheath at his waist, snarling.

"Get away from her, you bastard!" shouted Mother, her face a mask of fury in the lightning flashes, her hair loose and whipping around her. *"Get him, boys!"*

It was Johann's turn to shriek as Mother's three black shepherd dogs avalanched up the stairs, leapt on him and attacked him, tearing gashes in his arms, savaging his legs. The knife fell from his hand. Blindly he threw himself toward the window, arms reaching for the rope he had left there—

The rope that wasn't there anymore.

With a howl of terror he balanced for a moment in the window, when a single thrust of Mother's staff sent him tumbling into the storm.

The dogs howled their victory as Mother turned to Giselle, who was still reeling from the shock of her sudden rescue.

Mother didn't bother with trying to untie Giselle; she picked up Johann's abandoned knife from the floor, slashed the cords holding her wrists and gathered Giselle into her arms. Giselle sobbed with relief and hysteria as Mother soothed her, stroking her hair, saying words Giselle barely heard.

"Oh, my little rampion, my little darling, I meant for you to never, ever be hurt. That is why I kept you here, to keep you safe. When the gnomes told me there was a strange man here, I started back as fast as I could," Mother sobbed, almost as wrought up as Giselle. "I nearly killed the horse getting here. There was no one nearer than me to help."

Giselle sobbed in Mother's arms as the storm outside abated until, as the last of the thunder faded away and light returned to the room, she fell asleep, exhausted.

When she awoke, she heard voices below. Her face ached, and the back of her head had a huge, painful lump on it. As she pushed back the covers, she could see that Mother had put her into her night-gown, but that there were scratches and bruises all over her arms and legs, and her wrists were raw with rope-burns. She felt her eyes grow hot with tears and dashed them away, reminding herself that Johann might have beaten her, but Mother had saved her before he had done—*that*—to her. Or murdered her. As narrow as her escape had been, it had still been an escape.

There were definitely three voices down below, and all three of them were familiar. Mother, and two of the Bruderschaft—Pieter Meinhoff and Joachim Beretz. Resolutely swallowing down sobs, determined to fight through all the horrible feelings coursing through her, she slowly dressed, grateful that the clothing she had been wear-ing was nowhere to be seen. She never wanted to wear that blouse and dirndl again.

She made her way slowly down the stairs, ending at last in the kitchen, where Mother and her guests were sitting at the table, talking and drinking. Old Pieter was facing the stairs and was the first to see her; he stood up, and the others turned and saw her stand-ing hesitantly halfway down the last flight.

"Come join us, *Liebchen*," said Pieter. "We were just speaking of your future."

Pulling her shawl tightly around her, she descended the rest of the stairs and perched on the empty stool at the fourth side of the table.

For a while, they talked around her, and she learned that Pieter and Joachim had brought the wagon and the supplies Mother had been forced to leave behind. She learned she had been asleep around the clock. And that there was a reason why Mother had kept her all alone here.

An Air Master—and it had been plain to Mother that Giselle was going to grow into Mastery—was at her most dangerous and unpredictable in the years of adolescence. Strong emotions, which could call up powerful magic, were not matched by equally strong control, as evidenced by the terrible storm she had summoned while Johann was assaulting her, a storm so powerful that lightning and wind had felled nearly a hundred trees in the forest around the tower, and that storm had barely been at half its full strength when it died. So Mother had kept her isolated and happy, while she *learned* control.

"I should have also taught you how to defend yourself," Mother said mournfully, speaking to her directly at last. "But I was so sure this place was so far away from everywhere, and had such an evil reputation for haunting, that no one would venture near. . . ."

Pieter reached out to pat her hand. "Never mind, Annaliese. We can't change the past. We can fix things now." Now *he* turned to Giselle. "That is why Joachim and I are here now. We are going to teach you these things. Not only how to use your *powers* to defend yourself, but also weapons, or anything that can be used as a weapon." His expression turned fierce. "No man will dare try to touch you, for you will have his guts on the floor before he can take a step."

"Pieter—" Mother said, looking at him with wide eyes.

"Well? It's how we taught you, Annaliese," Pieter said, unrepentant. "And it's easier to explain to the constable how a blackguard ended up with a cracked skull from a broom handle or a knife in his liver than it is to explain how he was lightning-struck inside a building! The first is understandable. The second is witchcraft."

Slowly, as they talked, and told her what they were going to teach her, the terrible, fear-filled tightness inside her ebbed. There were no remonstrations, no accusations that she had brought the attack on herself. Or rather, the only remonstrations were from Mother, who accused *herself* of failing to prepare Giselle adequately for the dangers of the world.

They talked for hours and hours . . . through two meals that Giselle had been sure she would never be able to eat, yet managed to devour once she got the first bite past the lump in her throat. She told them everything that had happened. They assured her again and again that nothing was her fault, until at last, she finally believed it. They talked until she was yawning and couldn't keep her eyes open.

She took her leave of them then, and slowly climbed the stairs to her bedroom. But as she reached the second floor, she heard something that made her heart nearly stop.

"Do we tell her the bastard disappeared?" Pieter asked.

"What would be the point?" Mother replied, and said a bad word that Giselle had never heard her say before. "He won't be back. My Elementals will see to that. Why make her live in fear?"

"Good point," said Joachim. "I just—wish we knew where he'd gone."

2

THE small church was simple, very dark, and very quiet. The altar had been decorated for St. Walburga's Day, but of course it was the far less Christian celebration of Maifest had the attention of the citizens of Mittelsdorf and the surroundings, and who could blame them? Food, drink, dancing and music and contests were far more attractive than a Mass.

She put a pfennig in the charity box, took a candle, and lit it for Mother. Not that Mother had been in any sense religious—in fact, Giselle didn't know if Mother had even been *Christian,* let alone Catholic—but Pieter and Joachim, and many of the Bruderschaft were, and some of that had rubbed off on their student.

Besides, she doubted that Mother would have objected to having candles lit for her.

She knelt for a moment in a prayer, although she was altogether certain that, whatever her beliefs had been, Mother was certainly in some sort of Heaven. The loss of her still ached, even though she had been stricken with pneumonia and carried off within days a year and a half ago. Pieter and Joachim had been with her, or she was not sure how she would have borne the grief. One of the last acts of Mother's

Earth Elementals had been to make her a grave in the abbey yard and cover her over; when that was done it was only the brownies that tended the house, garden and chickens, and the faun that watched over the goats that remained. It was only at that graveside farewell that Giselle had learned how old Mother really was—*at least* a century, according to Pieter. That had been almost as much of a shock as Mother's death.

She rose and turned to go, to find there was a priest coming up behind her, an inquisitive look on his face. "Is there anything you need, my son?" he asked. Giselle smiled.

"No, thank you, Father," she replied. "I just wanted to light a candle to my mother's soul."

The priest peered a little more closely at her—no doubt because she was a stranger to his church—and then his face lit with recognition. "Ah! You are young Gunther von Weber, who won the shooting contest! That was most impressive. One of the finest exhibitions I have ever seen!"

Giselle laughed a little. "I suspect my dear mother had a hand in my victory, Father. And perhaps the dear Virgin too, although I would never be so blasphemous as to pray to win."

The priest beamed his approval of such sentiments. "Well said, as well as well done. But you are very young to be so skilled."

Again, Giselle laughed. "I learned to shoot my rifle as soon as I was able to hold it to my shoulder," she replied—which was close to the truth anyway. The rifle that now seemed like an extension of her arm had been heavy enough to unbalance her when she began under Pieter's tutelage. "Mother and I were alone, and knowing a single bullet stands between you and a bear that wishes to kill your goats or root up your garden is powerful incentive to become skilled."

Not quite true, because Mother didn't need mere *bullets* to safeguard her property from animals, but it was an answer that made the priest nod with more approval.

"Well, I will not keep you from your well-earned celebration," the priest said, and sketched the sign of the cross between them as

Giselle bowed her head for his blessing. "Go with the good God, my son, and prosper."

Giselle left the church, blinking a little in the sunlight, and made her way through the Maifest crowds slowly, having to pause every now and then to accept the congratulations of one or another of those who had seen the shooting contest. Mittelsdorf was too big to be called a village anymore; "town" was more appropriate, so the Maifest was fairly large, and the shooting contest prizes well worth competing for. Of course she hadn't signed up for the contest as "Giselle"; no one would ever have allowed a female to enter. She was disguised as a young man with her hair cut short, and ironically, in her typical hunter's gear of worn loden green wool, she could have been the younger brother of the hunter "Johann Schmidt" who had attacked her six years ago.

Or perhaps not. Her attacker had been dressed in a much finer and far newer version of her own hunting gear. The shabby, bastard cousin, perhaps.

She called herself Gunther von Weber, and what brought her here to Mittelsdorf was what had brought her through a string of five towns and villages so far this month: the prize money for the shooting contest.

Right now there were a lot of stall owners trying to tempt her to part with some of that money. The town's only inn was overwhelmed with customers, far too many to feed, and there were plenty of stall owners taking advantage of that. The scents of grilling sausage, of hot pretzels, of roasting chicken, and of fresh pastry assailed her on all sides. And if she'd been inclined to indulge herself in other ways, there were drink tents set up with Maiwein and Maiboch, and plenty of peddlers with temptingly pretty things. She could even have bought some of those pretty things without anyone blinking an eye as long as she invented a sweetheart she was buying them for! But she was determined to keep her money in her pocket . . . and she was just glad that it was tradition for the villages and towns hereabouts to stagger their Maifests all through the month so that she could take advantage of as many shooting contests as possible.

When Mother had died, suddenly, leaving her with no idea of where the money had been coming from that had kept them supplied with the things they could not grow for themselves all these years, she realized she had taken all that for granted. Mother had merely gone off with the horse and empty cart and returned with everything they needed several times a year. Nor had Pieter and Joachim any notion of where that money had come from. When they'd all sat down together to discuss Giselle's future, both the old men had scratched their heads at the question.

"Obviously she was well enough off to buy that house and then just give it to your family," Joachim had said, doubtfully. "But where that money came from, where she hid it, and what you're to do now, I haven't a notion."

"You could come move to the Lodge and join us," Pieter had offered.

But she had shaken her head vehemently at that. She'd visited there enough times to know that living in the old, tree-shadowed building, with its many tiny, dark rooms and small windows, would quickly drive her mad. She needed air and light, and plenty of both. The Lodge of the *Bruderschaft der Förster* was not for her.

"Then we must think of a way for you to have some money," Joachim had said firmly. And although they did not think of it then, they did hit upon it fairly soon.

Although not all Air Masters were expert marksmen, all Air Masters *could* be—in a way. The flight of an arrow or a bullet to its target was easily influenced by movements of the air, and that, after all, was what an Air Master was in control of. With sufficient cooperation from one's Air Elemental allies, even a poor natural marksman could hit marks that experts would have difficulty with.

And a good one, as Giselle was—well, she could be unbeatable. And so far this month, that was exactly what she was.

Joachim had opined that if she was careful, and never worked the same festivals at the same towns without at least a year between, she could continue to carry off the crowns and the prizes. He cautioned her that, at the largest contests, she must take care never to take first

prize too often—and the largest contests provided very, very generous prizes for second and third place. And she had two opportunities
a year to do so: Maifest and Oktoberfest. For Oktoberfest she might
even venture into one of the big cities and take the shooting prizes
there; they were substantial, and second or third place would more
than suffice.

Right now, though, well, the crowds in their colorful festival
clothing—the loden green wool of hunting costume, the bright
dirndls and embroidered aprons, the lederhosen and embroidered
bracers, and Sunday best suits—were making her uncomfortable
and claustrophobic. If she hadn't been constrained by custom, she
probably would have gone straight to the inn, claimed her horse and
ridden off. But she couldn't do that. No, part of the prize for winning
the shooting contest was a full barrel of Maibock. And the winner
was expected to share it with all of the other contestants.

So Giselle was making her way to the open field where all the tables and benches had been set up for eating and drinking, heading for
the section near the beer stall of the barrel's donor. The Maypole was
in the center of the field; a group of children were unbraiding the
ribbons so they could have a dance, and there was a little brass band
tuning up to provide the music for it. There were appetizing aromas
coming from all over the field, and once again, she reminded herself
that she needed to keep as much of her prize money in her pocket as
possible. *After all, beer is food, right? It's made from grains . . .*

As Giselle approached, her fellow contestants got up and greeted
her with congratulations and backslaps. They were a mix of all sorts,
about two dozen all told, from young men in their late teens to griz-
zled old fellows with ancient, tarnished hunting badges on their
wool hats. She accepted both congratulations and backslaps with
modest thanks and veiled relief; although it hadn't happened *yet,*
there was always the potential for someone who took losing badly.
She took her place on a stool placed at one end of a trestle table, the
rough equivalent of a "high seat," and nodded to the tender of the
beer stall, who made a great ceremony out of knocking in the spigot
on the special keg on the counter and starting to pour the brew.

She was rather pleased that she hadn't needed the help of her Elementals all that much, which made the victory feel thoroughly earned. It had been a bit grueling; she'd needed every bit of her concentration.

She actually didn't remember anything much except the shots that she had taken; when she was participating in a shooting contest, she concentrated on her targets to the exclusion of pretty much everything else. This had been one of those contests with clay plates strung up on a framework and an allowance of a single bullet for each plate; that was a good bit easier than actual targets. She was the only one who had cleared her frame of every plate, every time. The last contest had been a sort of shooting gallery with an actual target pulled across the field by a clockwork mechanism. All of her shots had been grouped in the center; her opponent's had been in the first ring.

She settled down at the table with six of the other marksmen, who had watched eagerly while the keg was tapped and the enormous steins filled and handed round. She knew better than to just sip at hers; no man would ever take anything but hearty gulps, and she needed to make sure every one of her mannerisms was masculine. So she feigned to drink twice as often as she actually swallowed, and no one noticed because they were too busy enjoying themselves.

She turned to a polite tap on her shoulder. "Gunther, lad! It was a damn good thing for you that each round was twenty shots!" said an older man in a well-worn hunter's gear, with a badge of a boar's head and a tuft of pheasant feathers on his hat. The grin on his face said that he really wasn't being serious, which was fortunate; other marksmen bested by "Gunther" had muttered darkly about pacts and haunted clearings.

Giselle chuckled. "What, did you think I was a *Freischutz?*" she asked, referring to the old legend of the hunter who makes a deal with a devil to cast seven magic bullets—the first six would hit whatever the hunter wanted, but the seventh was under the devil's control. . . . "Well, at my eighth plate, I proved you wrong, eh?"

"So you did!" The old man lifted his stein in a toast. "Well, aside from having an eagle's eyes and the steadiest hand I ever saw, how *did* you become such a good shot so young?"

Giselle thought about the hours and hours she had spent, not only practicing her marksmanship combined with her Air Magic, but learning to defend herself with knife, staff, club, and far more exotic weapons. Mother had insisted on that, and as it turned out, there were many Earth Elementals more than willing to serve as trainers. Satyrs in particular thought everything but pistol and rifle practice were great fun, and were expert archers, staff-fighters, and just as skilled with sword or club. And they were not in the least inclined to treat her gently on account of her sex.

But obviously she couldn't mention any of this. So instead, she just shrugged. "I am poor, and have been all my life," she pointed out. "If I miss, I don't eat." And certainly, the worn condition of her own clothing testified to that poverty. Her gear was actually second-hand, passed down from one of the younger fellows of the Bruder-schaft. It certainly lent credence to her story of poverty.

"Ah, well then, I am glad to have lost to a fellow who is in need of the prize," the older hunter replied, clapped his hand on her shoulder and went to get himself a refill.

As the sun went down, the dancing began in earnest, as did the eating and drinking. Fortunately for her growling stomach, which was *not* convinced that beer was food, some of her fellow hunters were inclined to beer-induced generosity. A pretty serving girl brought an enormous platter of grilled sausages, fresh bread, mustard and sauerkraut that had been ordered by one of the others at the table. He magnanimously paid for it all and invited them all to share in it. Giselle picked up a fork, stabbed what looked like a fine specimen of knockwurst and got a generous slice of rye bread before it all vanished. She was very, very hungry at this point, and feeling the beer, and very much wanted something to soak it up before it really got to her head.

As darkness finally fell and the great bonfire near the Maypole was lit, she began thinking about getting to her horse. And that was when she felt a heavy hand fall on her shoulder, and all the chattering in the vicinity suddenly stopped. She froze, her insides growing cold. This . . . was not a well-wisher. The eyes of her fellow feasters told her that much.

"Gunther von Weber?" rumbled a deep voice from behind her.

She turned in her seat, and saw that the person who had seized her shoulder was dressed in an army officer's uniform. She didn't know enough about such things to judge what his rank was, but there was a great deal of gold braid on his shoulder, and several medals on his chest. A man of considerable girth, with a shaven head and a square, red-flushed face that looked altogether too much like a boar's, he looked as if his spike-topped helmet was too tight for his head. With him were four more soldiers. She blinked at him in confusion. What could they possibly want with Gunther?

"Sir, I am, and might I ask what your business is with me?" she said, cautiously.

"I will be asking the questions!" the man snapped. "What is your age? Where are you from?"

"Twenty—" she replied without thinking. "The nearest village to me is Leinsdorf—"

"Ha!" the officer barked, as if he had caught her in something. "Well? Is he in the Leinsdorf rolls?"

A fifth fellow moved into the light from the torch nearby and leafed through a large leather-bound book. "No, Captain."

The hand clamped down harder on her shoulder, and the captain shook her, rattling her teeth. "So, boy, why aren't you on the rolls?"

Startled, too startled to think first, she blurted the first thing that came into her mind. "What rolls?"

The captain's eyes narrowed, and he gritted his teeth. "The military service rolls! The ones you were supposed to sign when you became sixteen!" The captain actually sounded offended that she didn't know—or—no—he sounded as if he didn't believe that she didn't know, and was angry. His next words confirmed that. "Don't pretend you don't know!"

Well, of *course* she didn't know . . . but he clearly wasn't going to believe her. Not only that, but before she could say anything else he had hauled her up out of her seat and propelled her into the custody of his four men. Before she knew it she was being frog-marched into a building, hands bound behind her in irons, and directly into a small room with a desk with a lamp on it and an iron-framed bed just visible behind a folding screen. Two of the soldiers shoved her against the wall opposite the desk and left, closing the door behind them. The captain sat himself down behind the desk and opened another book, taking a pen out of an inkpot, as the soldiers closed the door.

Well, this is a fine fix. She was more irritated than angry at the moment. It wasn't as if she didn't have a perfectly good way to get out of this mess. It would just mean she'd never be able to come back here as Gunther and take part in shooting contests. That was annoying. She'd probably have to find an entirely new district and make up a new name, perhaps even dye her hair.

"Captain—" she began.

"Quiet!" the captain barked. "You're being enrolled in the Army, boy, and from this moment you'll only speak when questioned! Now. Full name."

Giselle sighed theatrically, and he looked up at her sharply, anger written all over his face at her presumed insolence. "My name is Giselle Schnittel," she replied flatly. "And you are going to find a difficult time explaining why you inducted a woman into the Army."

At first, his mouth dropped open and his piggy eyes bulged in shock. Then his face reddened with even deeper anger. "What do you take me for, boy?" he shouted. "Do I look like a fool to you?"

She allowed her voice to drift up into a girlish lilt. "And do I sound like a boy to you?" she retorted. "I'm poor. I need money. Shooting contests are an honorable way to get it, but they would never let a girl enter. So I became 'Gunther,' and I won them fairly and rightfully."

His eyes narrowed, and . . . something in his expression made her blood run cold. This was not going as she had thought it would . . .

But she was not fourteen anymore, and she was not defenseless anymore either. She felt steel settle into her spine. She was not going to be a victim this time; she concentrated a moment on summoning her allies of Air.

Within moments she had a half a dozen, all what she called "night-sylphs"—creatures that looked much like her childhood friends but were . . . more capricious. Not openly malicious, but their humor was darker, and a little cruel, and they were far more curious than the sylphs that came by day. They circled around the room a moment, then settled on the rafters. They were semitransparent, though of course they were completely invisible to anyone not an Elemental Magician; all had batwings and long, thick, dark hair, long enough that it dangled far past their feet and they were virtually clothed in it. Like her hair, when she didn't cut it frequently. They stared down at the Captain and Giselle, waiting, with a look of keen expectation on their faces. Unlike the sylphs of the day, the night-sylphs thrived on high emotion, and there was plenty of that here.

"Well," the Captain said, his voice boiling over with menace. "We'll just see how much of a woman you are. And if you are lying to me, the first thing I'll do when you're inducted is to have you beaten within an inch of your life."

He doesn't care which I am now, because either way he's going to get something he wants . . . he thinks.

He got up, moving far more quickly than she had expected for such a fat man, and straight-armed her into the wall, knocking the breath out of her.

And she knew what was coming next. He'd yank open her coat and vest, and tear open her shirt, expecting to prove she wasn't a woman. And as soon as he saw she was—well, there she was, a woman in man's clothing, who presumably had no men to protect her, and all alone with him. And what proper woman would be cavorting about in men's clothing anyway? Only loose ones, like that notorious writer, George Sand! Even people who were illiterate knew about women like that!

The devil take you, she snarled in her mind. *I need no man to protect me!*

"Take his breath!" she shouted to the night-sylphs above her. There was a flash of puzzlement in his eyes—well, this was not the reaction he expected. But there was no time for him to do more than have that instant of puzzlement. Because the night-sylphs reacted immediately to her order.

Quicker than the tick of a clock, they dove down on the captain and enveloped his head before he even had a chance to respond to what must have seemed to him like the cry of a mad person, wrapping their long hair about his face and neck. He couldn't *see* them, of course, but he could most certainly *feel* what they were doing. They could not do *much* in the physical world, but they most certainly could make air move, and they made it all move out of his lungs.

She could see his head *through* them. He clawed at his throat, trying to gasp, and unable to. His eyes bulged, and he staggered backward, tripped, and fell behind his desk. The padded carpet meant he didn't make much of a noise, and it seemed he wasn't thrashing. But then again, his ramming her into the wall hadn't brought his men running into the office to see what the matter was, so perhaps they were used to violent sounds coming from within.

Sadistic bastard. She felt her mouth forming a silent snarl. Well, he had just taken on an opponent that was going to give him a taste of his own back.

But she didn't want to kill him, after all, so she added, quickly, "Once he is unconscious, give him his breath back," and turned her attention to getting herself out of those irons.

She closed her eyes and concentrated all her attention on her hands and wrists. The irons had been made for a man's bigger hands and thicker wrists and were very loose on her. Loose enough that she was certain she could get them off. She might lose some skin doing so, but she was sure she could get them off.

It was all going to depend on relaxing her hands while at the same time trying to squeeze them into the smallest possible shape . . . which was not the easiest thing to do, when you were crushing them *and* scraping the skin off. . . .

Painfully. And soon they were damp with blood.

At least the bleeding is making them more slippery.

She ruthlessly closed herself off from any distractions, the better to concentrate, and finally sensed the manacle on her left hand moving past the first knuckle of her thumb. By this time she was sweating freely, and unashamedly crying a little in pain, since by this time it felt more as if she was degloving the skin of her entire hand, not just scraping a little off.

And then, after agonizing moments—her left hand popped free! Now able to bring her hands in front of her, she managed to keep herself from tearing at her right wrist by an act of pure will, and slowly forced the other manacle off as well. Her wrists were definitely scraped and bleeding, but to her relief the damage wasn't as terrible as it had felt. Now she looked for her sylphs—and the captain.

"Where are you?" she called softly, when silence and an apparently empty room met her searching gaze.

"Master . . ." came a small voice from the other side of the desk. *"The man fell down and we let him go, but he is not moving."*

An ice-cold chill went down her spine at that. Surely not—

But her luck was well and truly out, because as she hurried around the desk, it was obvious that the captain was quite dead. He was completely still, his face set in an expression of horror, and his eyes—

Her first reaction was acute nausea, followed by terrible guilt, as the half-dozen sylphs looked up at her with solemn eyes. They might be a *little* malicious, but they never deliberately went past frightening their victims a bit. This was neither expected, nor welcome, to them either. What could have gone wrong? She had only intended for him to fall unconscious, long enough for her to escape! She hadn't wanted to *kill* him!

Too late for that . . . he was stone dead. And there was no bringing him back.

Her mind went black for a moment, then restarted like a balky horse and galloped off at a manic pace. *I was the last person with him.*

They'll blame Gunther no matter what. She had to get out of there, and . . .

And first she needed to lock the door. With luck, no one would try it for a long time, and when they did, they might think that the captain wanted privacy. That should buy her a few hours. Moving as quietly as she could, she flipped the lock, then went back to the corpse on the floor as the night-sylphs watched her, waiting for her next request.

Part of her was appalled that she was thinking so clearly and quickly with a man lying dead near her. Part of her remembered the ugly look in his eyes, so like the man who had tried to rape her, and was not sorry at all for what had happened. And the third part of her ignored the guilty part and the part that was insisting he got what he deserved, and that was the part that was in charge.

She tore her handkerchief in half and wrapped her wrists with the two pieces. She took back the purse of prize money that he had confiscated, but stole nothing else, although there was a powerful temptation to go through his pockets. . . .

But if I am caught and I rob him now, they will say I killed him to rob him. But if I leave him untouched, there is a bare chance that someone will believe me if I say he became so angry with me that he dropped dead of apoplexy.

"Go ahead of me and warn me of anyone in my path," she whispered to the sylphs, who seemed just as eager to leave that room of death as she was. As they whisked through the little cracks in the walls around the window, she, who could do nothing like that, eased the window open and looked cautiously out of it. There was no one in sight, and the Maifest was still in full and joyous cry, judging by the light and the lively music in the direction of where the field would be. So she eased herself over the sill, made sure she had left nothing of herself or her property behind with a last glance around the room, and closed the window behind her.

Then she bent over and ran for the inn's stable, where her horse and all her belongings were. Ordinarily that would be a bad place to leave property, but Giselle's wicked little mare was trained to let no one into her stall but Giselle herself. She was as good or better than a guard dog.

Where did I leave my hat? She wondered irrelevantly, as she moved from one shadow to another, listening for the sounds of footsteps under the faraway music of the Maifest. It hadn't been with her in the captain's office. *I must have left it at the beer stall.* . . . If this had been a situation where she was likely to be tracked by another magician, that would have been a catastrophe, but there hadn't been the least sign of another Elemental Master, not even an Elemental Magician, in the entire town. The hat could safely be left behind. She *certainly* wasn't going to go back after it now.

She was out of breath when she reached the stables and paused just outside. Her sylphs gathered around her, no longer mischievous. "Is there anyone in there but horses?" she murmured, pressed up against the wall, trying to squeeze every bit of herself into a particularly dark shadow.

"*No, Master,*" said one. "*We made the drunk have bad dreams and he went somewhere else to sleep.*"

She looked up at them, hovering above her head. "Well done. I'm going to get my horse and get out of here. Keep watch while I do, and scout ahead of me on the road." She intended to lead the horse to the edge of town by the quietest ways before mounting him. A man leading his horse calmly would not attract any attention, but someone galloping as if the devil was after him certainly *would*. And the latter would be remembered, which was not something she wanted.

Lebkuchen—her mare—greeted her with a whicker, but tossed her head with displeasure when it became apparent that Giselle intended to saddle her and ride in the darkness. No horse liked being ridden in the dark; it was too easy for them to make a misstep and break a leg. But Giselle didn't have any choice.

Everything was still there, and it was not long before Giselle was leading the mare, laden down with packs and her hunting rifle and supplies, down a street she knew let out directly onto the road northward. She had chosen the direction deliberately, to lead away from the abbey and her tower, despite every instinct she had screaming at her to head straight for that shelter. Instinct might tell her to run for her den, but reason told her that was the last place she should go. Just in case . . . in case someone had recognized a landmark or a village in some story "Gunther" had told, and thought to look in that direction. There were such things as telegraphs in the world, and every police station had one. Word of a fugitive could travel far faster than she could, and she might find herself riding into an ambush.

Every nerve was screaming with stress by the time she got across the bridge and onto the highway, where she could mount. Lebkuchen seemed to have picked up on her nerves. Despite her profound distaste for traveling at night, she transitioned almost directly into a trot, her hooves thudding briskly into the dust of the highway.

Finally on the move, Giselle hunched over in the saddle, her insides knotted with fear and guilt, her mind awash with so many emotions she couldn't keep track of them. *What have I done?* was uppermost, most of the time. Odious as that captain was, and sadistic, she had never meant to kill him—she hadn't really meant to *harm* him. All she had wanted to do was incapacitate him long enough for her to escape. In her mind, she'd planned on making him unconscious until she got out of the irons, then she would lock the door, tie him up, gag him, and leave him in his bed. Probably the humiliation of being left that way by a *girl* would have kept him quiet. She tried to remember the things that Pieter and Joachim had taught her, had said to her, about situations like this, but she couldn't recall a single word.

I killed a man. Not directly, and not on purpose, but a man was dead, and she had been the cause. What possible justification was there for that? That he had intended to harm her? *That doesn't make it right. . . .*

Her thoughts were interrupted by one of the sylphs coming to fly beside her. *"Master, there is no one on the road. Where do you wish to go?"*

She passed her hand over her sweat-damp face. "Find me another Master to shelter with," she said, finally, because she would rather trust her judgment and punishment to one of her own than to those with no magic. And she *would* have to give herself up to *that* sort of judgment, of that she was certain. She had used magic to kill, and anyone who did that and did not give herself up *would* find herself hunted down by the Bruderschaft in short order. That was, at least in part, what they did.

As Lebkuchen sped on through the night—a night lit by a bright, full moon—and she continued to wrestle with her guilt, she scarcely paid any attention to where they were going. She only knew it was well past midnight by the moon when the sylphs chivvied her off the highway and down a narrow little path through what looked—at least in the darkness—like near-virgin forest. Lebkuchen slowed to a hesitant walk immediately; deciding that her mare's safety was of more importance than her own comfort, Giselle dismounted and followed the sylphs, leading the mare carefully around the worst of obstacles, doing her best to clear the path of things like fallen branches that could trip her up.

At least concentrating on *that* left her unable to think about anything else but relief when she finally saw a dim, warm light shining through the trunks of the trees ahead.

But it wasn't until she saw the old woman waiting with a lantern held over her head to guide Giselle to what looked like a hermit's cottage that Giselle suddenly felt the full effect of the evening hit her with a hammer-blow of exhaustion. As she came in through the open gate of a little yard, Lebkuchen whickering eagerly at the sight of a little shed with three goats tethered in it, Giselle stumbled and might have fallen if the old woman hadn't been there in a trice, with a steadying hand on her elbow.

"Not a word, Liebchen," the old woman said in a firm voice that brooked absolutely no argument. "Your sylphs have told me everything. What you need now is a safe place to rest, and old Tante Gretchen is here to give it to you."

"But—" Giselle began, her tongue feeling oddly thick with fatigue.

"But me no buts," Tante Gretchen said, and took Lebkuchen's

reins from her nerveless fingers. "You go in that door and take the cot by the fire. I'll see to your mare."

Giselle did not even bother to argue. She stumbled across the threshold into a warm cottage, sweet with the scent of woodsmoke and herbs, spotted a cot at the hearthside and all but fell into it. She didn't even bother to take off her boots, and was dreamlessly asleep before she had even pulled the blanket over herself.

3

GISELLE woke to the smell of sizzling bacon, and her empty stomach reminded her that she hadn't had anything but beer and a sausage and bread the entire previous day. Tante Gretchen was sitting at a stool on the hearth, turning over strips of bacon with a fork on a flat griddle atop some coals. She looked over at Giselle and smiled. "There's sausages and flatcakes already done. Go help yourself while I finish these."

Giselle's stomach growled loudly, and she pushed off the blanket to get up—

And discovered that she also had to quickly comb her fingers through her hair and shove it back over her shoulders—because, as it always did when she was under stress, her hair had grown.

Tante Gretchen blinked a little at that. "Does it always do that?" she asked, with keen interest. "Your hair, that is."

Giselle made a face. "When things are not going well, it can grow as much as a foot in a day. I don't know why. Mother said she had never heard of anything like it, and the only thing she could think of was that the sylphs like to play in my hair, and when they do, they leave magic energy behind. So she thought that perhaps my hair grew fast when I was under stress to make sure I had extra power."

Tante Gretchen nodded. "That seems a reasonable explanation to me. Go get a plate of breakfast, Liebchen, and we can talk about your problems."

The thought of her problems—and the terrible thing she had done—almost killed her appetite. It probably would have succeeded if she hadn't been nearly starving.

The cottage was tiny. There was a loft, but it looked as if it wasn't used for anything, which made perfect sense for someone Tante Gretchen's age; she wouldn't be wanting to scramble up and down ladders. Beneath the loft was a cupboard bed where Tante Gretchen obviously slept. There was a table with four chairs under a little window framed with white, starched curtains, two cupboards and a wardrobe against the walls, a counter with a porcelain bowl for a sink, the stool that Tante Gretchen was using and the cot Giselle had slept it. The floor was old, worn wood, and the walls were whitewashed plaster that had some small, dark pictures hanging on them. It was very pretty, if a bit claustrophobic for Giselle.

There was a covered plate and an uncovered plate on the table, and another pair of plates stacked beside them. Since she was still dressed, Giselle just took the few steps to the table where she found that the plate covered by an immaculate towel held the flatcakes; a little bowl she hadn't noticed at first had butter in it, a pot held honey, and the uncovered plate held the sausages. In no time, Giselle had a plate full of food, including the bacon her hostess lifted directly to her plate from the griddle and a cup of chamomile tea. Tante Gretchen quickly made up her own breakfast from the rest, and they settled down at the table to eat.

The old woman did not permit her to say anything until they were both finished and the plates were cleaned and put away. Then she poured them both another cup of tea, and said, "Now. Tell me everything that happened, and leave nothing out."

Taking her at her word, Giselle began a lengthy recitation, starting from the shooting contest and how she had won it with the help of her Elementals. Tante Gretchen nodded when she described the abrupt arrival of the captain.

"Hauptmann Erich Von Eisenhertz," she said, sourly. "He was a bully as a little boy, and being in the Army did not change him for the better. Now he is a bully and a sadist. He has his men put on punishment detail, forces them to run until their feet bleed, or has them beaten on the smallest of causes, and people hereabouts have wondered how long it would be before one of them snapped and murdered him. But go on."

Giselle blinked a little. This, she had not expected. She went on, ending with her escape from the village. "The rest, you know," she said, unhappily. "And I am to blame for the Hauptmann's death—"

"Nothing of the sort." Tante Gretchen shook her spoon at Giselle's nose. "I am the nearest thing to a doctor hereabouts, and I can tell you that it was his own apoplexy that killed him, not you."

"But—"

"Which of us is the Earth Master?" she demanded. "Between all the food he stuffed into himself and his temper, it was only a matter of time—and probably a race between his heart and his brain as to which would kill him faster. All your sylphs did was accidentally frighten him enough that a vessel in his head burst—a vessel that was just waiting for *something* to make it rupture." Tante Gretchen snorted. "I am the nearest Master, and one of the oldest around here. So, it is my judgment that you are not guilty of murder-by-magic. At worst, it would be 'misadventure.' Frankly, I'd call it 'a stupid accident that befell someone who well deserved it.' And I won't brook any arguments."

Giselle slowly let her breath out in a sigh. "But, I'll still be hunted. I was the last person with him."

"I can tell you he was so little regarded that I rather doubt *any* of his men were bothering about looking in on him last night. More likely he wasn't discovered until his orderly found the door was locked this morning." The old woman drank her tea thoughtfully. "But you are right. You will be hunted. Or rather, *Gunther* will be hunted. No one will be looking for *Giselle.*" She put down her empty cup with a decisive gesture. "You will stay with me until your hair grows out more. While you are staying here, we will think about what you are to do next."

"But . . . I don't have anything to wear but men's clothing!" she protested weakly.

Tante Gretchen rolled her eyes. "That is scarcely a problem." She got up, and went to a clothes press under the mattress of her cupboard bed. She brought out hunting gear, but this was of much finer make than what Giselle was wearing, and it had clearly been tailored for a woman, with fine, subtle embroidery around each of the four pocket slits in the jacket. And instead of breeches, there was a divided skirt, which some women wore to ride astride. "That was mine as a girl your age, and I'll never fit into it again, so there is no point in my keeping it," the old Master said, laying the jacket, vest, and skirt out on the cot and stroking the wool once with a reminiscent hand. "No, you shall have it. And you are welcome to it."

Giselle hardly knew what to say. She was still feeling exhausted, and more than a bit befuddled, and she *certainly* did not like the feeling that she was being hunted—and this, clearly, was a safe haven. She stammered her thanks, but the old woman waved them off, going to the cupboard again and pulling out an old nightdress of the same size, yellowed with age, but still fine. "First, your wrists need proper bandaging. Then you can move the cot and bedding up to the loft so I have my hearth back. I am not risking a fall at my age, not to mention I don't think I could get the bedding up there myself, much less the cot! Then you can get out of that clothing and into this. And last, you can go back to bed. Then we'll talk about what you can do to repay me."

"What she could do" to repay the old woman at the moment seemed to consist of doing chores and reading books to her. Giselle didn't mind—it wasn't as if her savior was lounging about while Giselle worked, it was more as if Tante Gretchen was taking advantage of the situation by getting twice as much work done than she could manage alone. And Tante Gretchen liked to sit by the fire and knit of an evening while Giselle read. They had very similar tastes—and Giselle had discovered to her joy that the Earth Master had Karl May books *she* had not yet read. No matter what else was going on, or how her feelings of guilt and worry sometimes overwhelmed her, there was always that to look forward to: the warm fire, the old woman's cheerful companionship, and getting lost in a tale of the Wild West.

She wouldn't hear of Giselle moving on for right now. "Let's see what happens in the next few days," was all she said, and although Giselle was impatient to get back to earning some money, she also was not at all eager to find herself arrested for murder.

So Tante Gretchen was kneading dough for bread in the cottage while Giselle was sitting on the doorstep, shelling new peas into a bowl in her lap, when the soldiers came. There were four of them, all mounted on some of the most ordinary-looking horses she had ever seen, and they rode up the path to Tante Gretchen's cottage as if they knew it well. They weren't even trying to be quiet, so by the time they dismounted at the gate and tied their horses to the fence, the old woman had left the bread dough she was kneading and had come out to stand beside Giselle, wiping her hands on her apron.

They opened the gate and trudged halfway up the path through the yard, and stopped. "Good morning, Frau Wildern," said one who stood further along the path than the others. The sun was shining fully down on them, and Giselle wondered if they were getting warm in their wool uniforms.

"And what brings you boys here this morning?" she called, shading her eyes with her hand and peering at them. "You're the only one I know, Hans Pedermann. What are you soldiers doing out here in the forest?"

All four of them reflexively pulled their caps from their heads and stood there holding their headgear against their chests, for all the world like schoolboys in the presence of the headmaster. Three of the four stared at the fourth one, as if they expected *him* to do all the talking. After a moment, he did.

"Don't mean to disturb you, Frau Wildern, but we've come to ask if you've seen a stranger about in your forest," the young man said, his cheeks reddening with the effort of speaking to the formidable old woman. "He'd be a hunter, with a rifle."

"There are many hunters with rifles in my woods, and some of them are strangers—but not this season," she said, one eyebrow raised. "This is not the season for hunting. Nor have I heard any shots fired since last winter. Why do you ask?"

"There was a fellow calling himself Gunther von Weber who won the Maifest shooting contest. The Hauptmann didn't like the look of him, so he looked the fellow up in the conscription rolls, and he wasn't there. So he decided to conscript him on the spot." The young man twisted his hat in his hands as Tante Gretchen gave him a hard look.

"Is that legal?" she demanded, as Giselle sat silently, watching and listening. "He could have been an only son. He could have had a club foot. He might have been foreign-born—there are many reasons why he wouldn't be on the rolls!" She began tapping her foot impatiently, and the young man flushed.

"I'm sorry, ma'am but—" he made a little, helpless gesture with one hand. "—but it was the Hauptmann, you know? It didn't matter if it was legal or not, if the Hauptmann wanted something done."

There was a long silence, made deeper by the fact that the air was still and not even leaves were rustling. Tante Gretchen stood there, hands on her hips, giving all four of the soldiers the sort of look that would make any young man squirm as if he had been found stealing a pie. Finally the silence was interrupted by a rook calling in the distance and two of Tante Gretchen's hens who came clucking around the corner of the cottage.

Tante Gretchen snorted. "So, go on. Did the fellow desert?"

"In a manner of speaking. The Hauptmann took him into the office and locked the door." Now the soldier paled a little. "We all knew what that meant, and we all knew what would happen to *us* if we interrupted, so we just . . . went about our business. In the morning, the orderly found the door still locked, and nobody answered at his knock, so he brought men to break the door down. The hunter was gone, and the Hauptmann was dead without a mark on him."

Tante Gretchen rolled her eyes. "Now boy, don't you *dare* tell me you all think it was witchcraft and you want me to hunt out the man-witch for you! You know I don't hold with such superstitious nonsense! I am a good woman! I go to Mass whenever I can! I have a shrine to the Virgin right here in my front garden! And just because I'm an old woman that lives in a cottage in the woods by herself, that doesn't mean I'm possessed of magic powers and riding a broom to the Horned Mountain on Walpurgisnacht!"

Giselle had to hide her face by concentrating very hard on her peas. It was clear that her role in this was to observe. She might have observed that all four of the young men were rather good looking—but that encounter with "Johann" when she was fourteen had put her off good-looking young men, and after her sorties into Maifests, strangers were no novelty to her.

"No, no!" The scolding made the poor boy grow paler. "No, but the chief of police said we at least needed to find this von Weber fellow and bring him in for questioning, because he was the last man to see the Hauptmann alive! So we've all gone out as far as we think he might have gotten, and your woods would be a good place for a hunter to hide!"

"Did he have a horse?" the old woman asked shrewdly. "Because if he didn't, I doubt very much he got this far."

Now the four soldiers exchanged baffled looks, and one shrugged.

"We don't know, I guess," Hans admitted.

"Giselle, you went mushroom hunting yesterday," Tante Gretchen said, turning to Giselle. "Did you see a hunter, a horse, or signs of a camp?"

"No signs of a camp, and the only horse here is mine, Tante Gretchen," Giselle replied, truthfully. "And surely, if anyone had been hunting for food, we would have heard the shots."

"And surely, if someone had been afoot and on the run, and had come across this cottage, he would have *stolen* Giselle's horse," the old woman concluded. "I think you've been chasing a wild goose, at least in this direction." She surveyed them all. By now, they really were starting to wilt—both from the hot sun they'd been standing in and Tante Gretchen's forbidding expression. Giselle wondered what she would do next—after all, now she and the Earth Master had all the information they needed . . .

Tante Gretchen, however, had other things in mind. She sighed dramatically, and threw up her hands. "But I can't let you boys go all the way back empty. How about some beer and sausages? That should keep you filled up all the way back to Mittelsdorf."

All four of them brightened considerably at that. "Yes, please," said Hans, and so bits of wood were set up in the yard for them to sit on, and Tante Gretchen brought them wooden cups of beer from a cask that held a brew of her own making. Giselle brought them fried sausages, and they flirted clumsily with her. At least, she thought it was flirtation. They called her a "pretty maid," and thanked her far more than was necessary for being given a couple of sausages and a bread roll, and were careful not to do so when Tante Gretchen was within earshot. She feigned shyness, but it was mostly to hide the fact that she was so relieved that none of them recognized her, or even considered she might have been "Gunther," that she felt a little giddy. And while they ate, they dropped plenty more information. How the chief of police was determined to blame *someone* for the Hauptmann's death, for instance. How they suspected he was under pressure from *his* superiors to do so. How no one in the small garrison was at all unhappy that the Hauptmann had died, since their new officer was a vast improvement—"I'd give the man a medal, if it were up to me!"—but it wasn't up to them, and they felt that "Gunther" was going to hang, guilty or not.

"It's not right," Hans said, after enough beer to loosen his tongue. "But the authorities want someone to answer for it, and they won't take our word for it that the old b—I mean, that the Hauptmann probably died because he got worked up over the idea of another public lashing and broke a vein in his brain. And if it had been me that had been locked in there with him, I'd have run, too." The other three all nodded solemnly, though Giselle had felt chilled by their revelations.

When they were done eating, they bade a very respectful farewell to Tante Gretchen, a seemingly regretful one to Giselle, and mounted up and rode back down the way they had come.

"Peas," said Tante Gretchen, as Giselle stood in the yard, peering after them, to make sure they were really going, and not, say, sneaking back to spy on them. Because at this point she was rattled enough to suspect almost anyone of anything.

"Oh! Of course!" she said, starting a little, and went back to her interrupted chore, although she could not see how shelling peas was going to help *her* situation in the least.

"Well," the old woman said, going back to her dough as calmly as if they'd never been interrupted at all. "Now we know quite a bit. We know no one will recognize you now that you're wearing skirts, we know they don't even know you *had* a horse, much less that it looked like Lebkuchen, and we know that they have no idea what direction you traveled in. These are all good things."

"Yes, but . . ." Giselle didn't want to seem at all ungrateful to Tante Gretchen, but this only worsened her situation. "We also know that the chief of police ordered I be found, which means he has probably telegraphed to every town and village that *has* a telegraph about me. Every single stranger that turns up in hunting gear to join the shooting contests will be stopped and questioned. So what am I to do now? I *must* earn some money, somehow, if I am to live!" Perhaps that was an exaggeration, but not a great one. Yes, she could hunt, but gunpowder was not free, nor the lead to cast bullets. Mother had been the one that did most of the preserving of vegetables and fruit, and she was not at all certain of her ability to imitate her. Nor could she count on the brownies and the faun to keep serving her; in fact, she had taken the considerable risk that when she returned, the chickens, goats and garden would still *be* there and in good order, because she expected to have enough money to replace at least the chickens if she had to.

"Shell the peas," Tante Gretchen said. "If nothing else, you can go to the Bruderschaft. They might not have dwarf-hordes of gold lying about, but they can probably spare enough supplies for one slender girl to live on until October. Then everyone will have forgotten, you can dye your hair and take a new name, and go in a different direction and earn money for winter supplies."

She bit her lip. She didn't *want* to go to the Bruderschaft, hat in hand, but what choice did she have? And in good conscience, she was going to have to report to them anyway on the misadventure she had gotten herself into.

As if reading her mind, Tante Gretchen added "I've already sent word to them through the Forest Elementals about your situation; you needn't worry that you're in trouble, but you should go tell them in person eventually."

Giselle swallowed. "Well then, when do you think I should leave?" she asked.

Tante Gretchen left the bread dough to rest, and came to the doorway to peer up at the sky. "What do your sylphs tell you about the weather?"

As usual, there was one hanging about, this time asleep on a branch in one of the trees nearby; there always was at least one, still, although she had greatly feared they might desert her after the night-sylphs had accidentally caused the Hauptmann's death on her orders. *But how could I have done any different?* she asked herself, as she always did. *What he would have done to me . . .*

She shook off the dark thoughts, and woke up the drowsy sylph with a thought. *"Tante Gretchen would like to know what the weather will be for a while, please,"* she asked, silently.

The sylph yawned, and blinked sleepily. *"Rain tomorrow and the next day, fine again for at least three."*

"Thank you," Giselle said, and the sylph yawned again and went back to sleeping on her sunny branch.

"Well, you may as well stay until the rain is over," Tante Gretchen said, logically enough, when Giselle reported what the sylph had said. "I can use the help. And I'd like you to finish our book before you go."

"And I will happily give it, and even more happily finish the book," Giselle replied. Though as she finished shelling the peas, she tried not to think about the situation. She really did *not* want to be in the debt of the Bruderschaft—she was trying so hard to be independent, like Mother, and it felt like failure to have to come to them, proverbial cap in hand, in the very first year.

With rain pouring down as hard as Giselle had ever seen it, there was not much they could do but things that could be done indoors. Since the cottage was so small, and Tante Gretchen was meticulous about keeping it clean, it was less than two hours' work to have everything scoured. Obviously you could not wash clothing when it was raining, nor bake, so that left handwork. Tante Gretchen pulled her favorite chair up to the fire, piled her mending in one basket on her left and had her knitting in a second basket on her right, while Giselle had a lantern over her shoulder and the Karl May book about Winnetou she had promised to finish in her hands.

She did her best to immerse herself in the story, because to tell the truth, she was having a hard time with her emotions. Anger, one minute, at the Hauptmann for spoiling her carefully made plans. Fear that she might still be caught . . . or that when she finally reached the Bruderschaft Lodge, *they* would have quite a different view of the situation from Tante Gretchen. Something rather like anger at the idea that even if they felt the same as the Earth Master, she would be in debt to them—because obviously Mother had wanted no such thing, or why else would she have made their home in the old abbey? Guilt, of course, because no matter how many times Tante Gretchen told her that it hadn't been her fault, well, there was still a man dead, and it had been because of something she had done. Then anger again, because she knew very well what he would have done to *her* if he'd gotten the chance.

It was much better, all the way around, to try and lose herself in the story. And in speculation: she already knew, for Mother had told her, that Elementals often differed greatly in form from one country to the next, so what form would the Elementals of the Apache take? Karl May gave no hint.

Well, he was a writer, not an Elemental Magician, so he probably didn't know, and the Indians he had met that *were* would not likely have told him anything. Elemental Magicians kept their abilities secret, after all. If you weren't around others of your kind, and hadn't been taught, you might even think you were going mad when you saw all the strange creatures populating the world and no one saw them but you. She was very glad that Mother had taken her away from her blood family for that reason alone!

What would Mother think of the situation she was in now? Would Mother also have told her to throw herself on the mercies of the Bruderschaft?

But what else could she do?

"You're getting hoarse, Liebchen," the old woman said, putting aside the last bit of mending. "Time for a nice cup of tea and a cake, I think. I'm glad there's no need to go out in that tempest; listen to that thunder!"

"I like storms," Giselle replied, setting the book aside.

"Well, you would, your magic being Air and all." Tante Gretchen carefully took the iron kettle off the hook over the fire and went to the little table where the teapot stood ready. "You must be careful of that, you know. Your Mother surely told you."

Giselle went to the cupboard and took out the honey for the tea, and the plate of cakes. "That's why she had me living away from everyone, with her, at the abbey. Until I understood my magic and how to keep it under control and all."

"And are you doing that now?" Tante Gretchen asked, shrewdly. "Because this storm is stronger than I expected, and I can tell you're all of a pother inside, even if you are trying not to show it."

Inwardly, she cursed herself for not thinking of that, and hastily read the currents of magic around her.

"Yes, everything is fine," she was able to report, with relief. "*I might be all of a pother, but at least it's not getting out.*"

"Well then, in that case, I shan't worry." Tante Gretchen took her at her word, which did a little to soothe her anger at having to go a-begging to the Bruderschaft. It still *rankled,* that was the right word for it. It was more . . . her pride was being rubbed raw that she couldn't even manage a single year alone without having to go begging for help. She could just imagine the Foresters treating her like . . . like a child, when Mother had been treating her as an adult for years and years now. It wasn't *her* fault she didn't know about the military service rolls, or she'd have found some way to avoid towns with army garrisons in them! Why hadn't someone warned her about this, when they advised her to go to shooting contests?

Or worse . . . Joachim and Pieter had given her the respect that Mother gave her, but what about the rest of the Bruderschaft? What if all they wanted her to do was womanly things? All very well for Mother and Tante Gretchen to be adept at cooking and baking and tending gardens and all of that—but she wasn't them! She was an Air Master, not an Earth Master. She could do those things, certainly, but she didn't much like them and she wasn't all that good at them.

Just get your mind back in the book, she advised herself. *What's done is done. You can't pour the broken eggs back into the shell. Best to just concentrate on salvaging what you can.*

All very good advice, of course. Now if only she could bring herself to take it. . . .

With saddlebags packed with her new wardrobe, her rifle in a saddle holster, and Lebkuchen clearly impatient to be on the road, Giselle stood at her stirrup, waiting for Tante Gretchen to come out of her cottage. It was a beautiful day, and under any other circumstance, she'd have been overjoyed for the chance to ride out under cloudless skies, with balmy spring breezes lilting through the trees.

But given that she was figuratively crawling to the Bruderschaft to beg for their help and *hope* she was forgiven for her part in killing a man . . . well . . . part of her wanted to stay hidden with Tante Gretchen, pretending to be her niece.

That was impossible, of course. The cottage was cozy and pleasant while the two of them were getting along and while it was always possible to get away by tending the garden or hunting for mushrooms in the forest. But in winter . . . or if for some reason they had a quarrel . . . well, it wouldn't be cozy, it would be claustrophobic. Even with all the space in the abbey and her tower, sometimes *that* had been claustrophobic in winter when she and Mother were at odds.

Tante Gretchen finally came out with another, smaller bag she could fasten over the top of one of her bigger saddlebags. "Food for the journey, so you won't have to waste as much money buying things to eat," the old woman said, handing it to her. "Don't fret. Something will turn up, I feel it in my bones."

"I hope so," she replied, with less confidence. Earth Masters could be quite powerful, but they weren't known for their predictive talents. Impulsively, she hugged the old woman. "I think you have literally saved my life, Tante Gretchen. I don't know what I would have done without your help."

The Earth Master returned her embrace. "You would have managed. I have every confidence in you, even if you don't have nearly as much in yourself," she said firmly. "Now, just keep your eyes and ears open for opportunity, and if something turns up *before* you reach the Lodge, seize it! The Good God will put something in your path, but you have to be alert for the signs he is giving you something!"

Again, Giselle was nothing like as sanguine as Tante Gretchen was, but, well, who knew? And anyway, that sounded like something Mother would have said. So she gave the old woman another hug, then mounted Lebkuchen and turned the mare's head down the path leading to the cottage, as the Earth Master waved goodbye. In a few moments, the thick underbrush and the winding of the path had hidden her and her home from view.

When the path came out on the road, there was no one in sight, which partially quieted Giselle's fears that soldiers had been set to ambush her. It was a very silly fear, of course—the four who had been sent directly to Tante Gretchen to look for Gunther had not even considered that she might be the young man in disguise—but that didn't keep it from being a very real fear.

The first village she encountered made her tense up all over, but nobody paid any attention to her, except for the handful of women who looked startled and offended at the sight of a woman *riding astride* even though she was probably less prone to showing ankles, or even (gasp!) *calves* than someone riding sidesaddle.

By the third village she felt as relaxed as she was ever likely to get, and then she could think. Lebkuchen was being very well behaved; she wondered if Tante Gretchen had had a "word" with her. It was Earth Magicians who were good with animals, and Earth Masters the best of all. Giselle had always found Lebkuchen a handful, but maybe that had been because the mare had belonged to Mother, not her. Perhaps Tante Gretchen had "explained" the situation to her in a way she understood.

I have food for a few days, she considered, as Lebkuchen ambled along the quiet, narrow road. *Water I can get from the rivers and streams. It's probably not wise for a woman alone to take a room in an inn. So my biggest problem between here and there is where am I going to sleep? I can't ride day and night; Lebkuchen needs the rest even if by some miracle I don't.*

The easiest thing to do would be to make rough camps in the forest. It wouldn't be hard; Joachim had taught her how to camp ages ago. But if she could find a farm that still had haystacks in the fields, that would be preferable. She had a distinct advantage over most travelers and gypsies and tramps; she could ask an Air Elemental to stand guard for her and wake her before sunrise so she could get out and away before the farmer could catch her.

For that matter, she could ask her Elemental allies to scout ahead and *find* a field with haystacks. Then she could wait until dark, slip in before the moon rose, and have herself a cozy little roost without anyone the wiser.

I'll do it, she decided, and felt a good bit better. Lebkuchen would be taken care of too; the amount of hay the mare would eat overnight would be negligible to the farmer, but it would cost more than Giselle liked at a stable.

She whistled the odd little spell-tune she used to summon the friendliest of Air Elementals—those were usually, though not always, sylphs. This time she got one that *wasn't*; an odd little creature with the face of a girl and the everything else of a scarlet-feathered bird. She'd gotten Elementals like this one before, and they were a welcome sight when she needed a helper that was steady and not flighty. The bird-creature flew along beside her and listened as she explained what she needed: a farm near the road with haystacks still in the field, somewhere near where she and the horse would be at around sunset.

The bird-girl listened intently and whistled her agreement when Giselle was finished. Off she flitted, leaving Giselle only concerned as to whether or not such a thing actually existed. *Well, if it doesn't, I'll camp in the woods,* she reminded herself. It wouldn't be as nice a bed as a haystack . . .

But it's preferable to a gaol.

By the third day she had finally relaxed some of her vigilance and begun to enjoy the journey. Even sleeping in haystacks wasn't so bad; Mother had taught her how to chase away insects so she was able to burrow in and sleep peacefully until a sylph or a sprite awoke her.

And since she was, quite literally, seeing more people than she had ever seen in her entire life, even the most mundane things were entertaining. Sometimes it was all she could do to keep a straight face at some of the goings-on. Were the village beauties *really* so unaware of how absurd they looked, mincing about the way they did? Were the handsome lads not the least conscious that they acted just as absurdly? The prosperous also put on ridiculous airs, men and women both, when in fact they themselves might have done *nothing* to earn their prosperity, and had merely inherited it. Her sylphs were only too happy to flit about her, whispering tales of village life like the little gossips they were—and oh how chagrined those proud creatures would have been if they had known that the huntress riding through their town knew some of their embarrassing secrets!

This was altogether a new development, at least as far as Giselle was concerned. Then again, the nearest village to the abbey was miles away, and probably the sylphs that hung about the abbey had little to no interest in its inhabitants. The sylphs that were turning up on her journey were all local, and sylphs went where the air went. They saw and heard everything.

They probably would have told her a lot more, if she encouraged them. As it was, it was like reading a gossipy book every time she passed through a town or village.

Today, she was about to pass through her first *large* town, or rather, city, and she was definitely looking forward to it. There were things in a large town that she had never seen, only read about. Theaters, coffeehouses, street players . . . ladies in the sort of fashions she only saw in magazines . . .

Sadly, of course, things like theaters and coffeehouses cost money she was loath to spend. But street players were free, and so was watching fashionable ladies. And there were other things, like great cathedrals, and perhaps museums. . . .

Also, in a big town, she would no longer be an object of scorn or curiosity with her split skirt and riding astride. People saw much more scandalous things every day in a large enough town, and took them for granted.

It was easy enough to see her goal, the town of Schopfheim, as she rounded a curve in the road and a valley stretched out before her. Too many red-roofed houses to count, and she took a swift intake of breath at the mere thought of all those people. But it was exciting rather than daunting.

Lebkuchen's ears pricked up, as if she had sensed Giselle's excitement. Then again, she had come through big towns with Mother, and perhaps she was anticipating a nice inn, comfortable stable, and perhaps, apples.

Not this time, I'm afraid, she thought a little ruefully, as Lebkuchen picked up her feet and moved into a faster pace. *It's going to be another hayfield for us, I fear.*

4

WHAT Giselle had *not* expected was that just outside of town, there would be a great deal of commotion, with tents and some sort of display going on. Not the Maifest she had expected, but something else entirely.

Just on the outskirts of most towns and cities, and even some villages, there was a generally a sort of common field which had any number of uses, but which was always used to hold the Maifests and Oktoberfests. As it happened, her approach to Schopfheim brought her by this field. This was no collection of little beer tents and vendors, there were no games going on, and no Maypole. Whatever this was, it was completely enclosed in a wall of canvas. The wall was painted with huge banner-like scrolls with something written inside and equally huge pictures. Since the road was fairly clear, she urged Lebkuchen into a trot to get her there faster. She was nearly on fire with curiosity when she was able to get close enough to read one of the banners.

And then . . . then she was nearly on fire with pure desire. For the banner read, *Captain Cody's Wild West Show.*

A Wild West Show! Her heart raced as she craned her neck hoping for a glimpse of . . . something, anything! Alas, it was all hidden behind those canvas curtains that fenced off the area. There was not so much as a feather or a spur to be seen, nothing but the painted banners displaying the wonders to be seen within. Indian attacks! Bandits! The stampede! Captain Cody, the famous sharpshooter! Texas Tom, the trick-roper! Buffalo! All things she had read about in Karl May's books, and tried to imagine, and they were here, and . . .

And the reality of the situation brought her spirits crashing to the ground, even as the people of Schopfheim streamed toward the entrance in the center of that canvas wall. *She* couldn't afford a ticket. Not if she expected to get to the Bruderschaft Lodge without resorting to theft. It was dismaying, how much things *cost* when you couldn't make them for yourself. Food, for instance. Her prize money was slowly trickling through her fingers, and what had seemed like bounty as she collected it didn't seem like so much when you found out just how much an innkeeper was prepared to charge you for food you could have cooked yourself at a quarter of the cost.

Lebkuchen's head came up as she scented other horses behind those canvas walls, and she whickered, her ears pointed forward. With a sigh, Giselle turned her away from the tempting venue. *I can't. I've run out of Tante Gretchen's food. Things are more expensive in towns. I can't keep counting on finding hayfields to sleep in. Lebkuchen would need stabling too, while I went in there, and I can't possibly afford—*

"*Do you want to see the wild people?*"

That voice, as much inside her head as out of it, told her that one of her Elementals was nearby. She looked up. One of the sylphs— this one with white and silver butterfly wings—had just swooped in to hover above Giselle's head, eyes sparkling with excitement. She didn't know this one, but as always, the sylphs seemed to recognize her and what she was immediately. "*It is wonderful! You will like it so very much!*"

Giselle took a quick look around to be certain no one was near enough to hear her talking to thin air. Traffic on the road was nonexistent for the moment; it was all one-way, heading for those enticing tents. Narrow strips of meadow bordered the road here, with trees beyond. "I don't have the money," she said, sadly. "I'd need to pay for a ticket, and pay for a place to put my horse while I watched the show. You know that humans need money for—"

"*Wait!*" The sylph dashed off. Blinking with confusion, Giselle moved her mare over to the side of the road, under a lovely green beech tree, and waited as she had been asked. What on earth could the sylph be—

"*Here!*" The sylph was back, waving two scraps of paper, one in each hand, as she sped toward Giselle. For anyone else, it would just look like two bits of paper, swirling about on the wind. "*Here!*" The sylph dropped them, and hovered expectantly, as Giselle snatched them out of the air.

To her astonishment, they were tickets. One was for stabling on the show grounds, and the other—admission to all attractions and the show itself!

"But—how—" She gaped up at the sylph.

"*Oh, people lose things, drop things, and are very careless.*" The sylph danced about in glee. "*It was easy! Let's go!*"

She flew off, heading for the entrance, and it was obvious that she expected Giselle to follow. Not that Giselle had *any* hesitation about doing so! And Lebkuchen seemed eager enough to be with her own kind, too. Once they were within about a hundred feet of the entrance, Giselle dismounted and led her horse into the loosely packed crowd that was slowly making its way toward the entrance. There was a lot of excited chatter. She seemed to be among several family groups that knew each other and were rhapsodizing about how lucky they were for a Wild West Show to be here, at little Schopfheim. "I wouldn't care if the Maifest was put off until June!" one teenage boy proclaimed. "Think of it! Think of what we'll see!" He could hardly contain his excitement, and Giselle knew exactly how he felt.

She presented herself and her tickets to the ticket-taker at the front entrance, who, to her disappointment, was not an Indian or cowboy or frontiersman like Old Shatterhand, but was dressed in a

perfectly normal suit. Well, normal for a townsman, anyway; so far
on her journey, men were far more likely to wear the dress of their
villages than a town-suit. He directed her to a tent immediately inside, where she surrendered Lebkuchen to a young boy in exchange
for a tin tag with a number on it. Horses were tethered inside to posts
with identical numbers; each post had a pile of hay and a bucket of
water at it, so it looked as if Lebkuchen was going to be in good
hands. She got into her saddlebags and changed out Lebkuchen's
bridle for her halter so she could eat comfortably, then put her in the
boy's confident hands. There were only three horses besides Lebkuchen; it appeared most people had walked here. The boy was a
local lad and told her to hurry along to the main tent, as the show
was just about to start.

This was . . . well, entirely new territory, so far as the size of the
crowd was concerned. Villages, she was used to; she had gone with
Mother on occasion to the nearest one, once Mother had deemed her
powers safely in check. A town, well, that was just a very big village,
and she had steeled herself to deal with them as they came along.
But this . . . nothing in her experience prepared her for this.

She let the crowd carry her along the side of the biggest tent to the
entrance. To her right was the canvas of the tent, to her left was a row
of . . . canvas booths, she thought. They looked a little like the vendor
booths she had seen at the Maifest. She smelled food, some aromas
familiar, some not. She definitely heard men calling out to the crowd,
though she couldn't see what they were hawking, as she was a great
deal shorter than most of the people between her and the booths. But
in any event, now was not the time to be distracted by minor diver-
sions when what she really wanted was to get a good seat inside.

The side flaps of the entrance were drawn wide apart and held in
place by big canvas straps; a ticket-taker eyed her ticket, but did not
take it from her, as he did with some others. It smelled of animals—
not strongly, but definitely the scent was there. It smelled of dust,
and trampled grass. And some faint whiffs of perfume and tobacco
from the crowd. She wondered why the ticket-taker had not asked
her to surrender hers.

Perhaps not every ticket gives you the right to roam about the grounds?

She found herself facing an open space ringed with tiered seats. The sylph flitted by, caught her eye, and waved her to follow. A moment later she was glad she had; the sylph led her past the crowds that were jockeying for the seats nearest the entrance and to a tier of seats, still mostly empty, on the opposite side of the arena space. She climbed up the steps, glad of her divided skirt and feeling a great deal of pity for the townswomen in fashionable garb. Even those wearing humble dirndls were managing better than women encumbered by yards of skirt and tight corsets, much to the amusement of some naughty boys.

She sat where the sylph pointed: about halfway up the tier, with some children on the seats immediately below her, so her view was not going to be obstructed. Just as she settled in, a brass band at the head of the arena struck up a jaunty tune. She didn't recognize it, but then, most tunes she wouldn't anyway. Mother wasn't much for music, and Joachim and Pieter mostly knew hymns and drinking songs.

The band continued to play as people found their seats. There were vendors of food scattered about the arena, but fortunately they were mostly hawking fruit, candy, and nuts. None of those things had any aroma to them, so Giselle was able to put her hunger out of her mind and concentrate on her surroundings. The grass in the arena had been trampled flat but not yet pounded into dust. There was a low wooden barrier between the stands and the arena. The band was very colorful, dressed in bright red uniforms with a great deal of gold braid. Next to them was an entrance closed off by red curtains that presumably cloaked an opening in the wall around the arena. This, Giselle guessed, was where the performers would come from. Finally, when it appeared that no one else was going to want in, the tent flaps closed, and the band finished with a flourish.

Then there was a fanfare, a lot of strange shouting, the red curtains parted, and a man on a white horse, dressed in a white suit with a great deal of brass buttons and fringe on it and a white hat of a sort she had never seen before, galloped into the center of the arena and made his horse rear up while taking off his hat to the crowd.

"Ladies! Gentlemen!" a man next to the brass band called through a cone-shaped object. *"Welcome to Captain Cody's Wild West!"*

Captain Cody—since that was undoubtedly who this was—made his horse gallop at a furious pace around the ring, while the Captain was making whooping noises and firing his pistols in the air as the band played. He made one circuit of the arena seated—and then to Giselle's wide-eyed astonishment, somehow got to his feet, and while standing on the saddle made a second circuit as perfectly erect just as if he was standing on unmoving ground and not a galloping horse, while taking off his hat to the crowd. As he came around the second time, Giselle got a good look at him, and he would probably have been quite ordinary looking if it had not been for his costume, his long, flowing hair and his bushy moustache.

The band concluded their tune as Captain Cody somehow dropped back into the saddle and rode out through the red curtains at the far end of the tent that she could now see were held open by a couple of men. But the audience was not given a chance to catch their collective breath, as the announcer called out, *"And now, the Grand Parade March!"*

Now, oh *now,* she got to see everything she had been longing to see!

The first riders through the curtains were going four abreast, at a canter. The two in the middle were wearing tan leather outfits with long fringes on the sleeves and the seams of the trousers. One wore a hat like Captain Cody's, only brown, the other wore—oh! It was a hat made from an animal—a *coonskin hat* exactly like the one Old Shatterhand wore in the illustrations! The one on the right carried the flag of the United States. The one on the left carried the flag of the German Empire.

But then, bliss upon bliss, the two outermost riders were *Indians!* They, too, were clad in leather, with fringes and some sort of decorations, and had scarlet sashes about their waists and bandoliers of bullets across their chests. They wore feathers in their hair, and instead of flags, one carried a kind of curved pole with fur wrapped around it and feathers flying from it, and the other carried a wicked-looking lance with long cloth streamers tied to it just below the lance-head.

They rode straight down the middle of the arena then split at the end, with one pair going right, the other, left.

Then came what Giselle recognized from the illustrations in Karl May's books as a *covered wagon,* the conveyance favored by settlers, pulled by a team of horses. It went right. Behind it was a small herd of the most extraordinary cattle Giselle had ever seen—their horns were enormous, stretched out to either side of their heads by two feet or more! They were kept in check by four men in checkered or tan shirts, vests, bluish trousers with leather leggings over them and round bowler hats, who herded them to the left, right past Giselle.

After that came another conveyance Giselle also recognized, a *stagecoach.* It was pulled by four horses, whose driver handled them expertly. That went to the right, so she didn't get a closer look at it.

But then, in the next moment, she was fiercely glad of the pattern, because next to enter the arena were—*a whole tribe of Indians!* Men mostly, with three women and two little boys. The men were in a motley assortment of costumes: several were bare-chested, one wore a red cloth shirt with a vest, and one wore a blue uniform coat with leather leggings. Two of them had a sort of crest on their heads, like a Roman soldier's helmet crest, made of some stiff red-dyed hair. All of them had feathers in their black hair, which had a peculiar sort of fat ridge along the tops of their heads, and all had leather leggings and soft leather moccasins. The women were not nearly as colorful; they all wore simple cloth tunics and skirts with brightly colored hems, sashes, and had shawls wrapped about themselves. The boys were dressed like their elders.

She feasted her eyes on them as they went past, their own gazes unwavering and straight ahead, as if they rode their own plains unobserved, not a dusty arena ogled by an avid audience.

Behind them came four bison, carefully led by halters manned by walking handlers. They split into two groups, so both sides of the

arena could get a good look at them. Giselle gazed her fill at the odd
creatures, which played so huge a part in Karl May's tales. She could
scarcely imagine how they kept their huge heads up, and they didn't
look dangerous at all. . . .

Well, a bull doesn't look dangerous either, she reminded herself.
*Nor does a dancing bear. But either of them could tear you apart if they
were minded to.*

Then came more cowboys and frontiersmen, including some fellows in embroidered shirts and enormous hats, and lastly, when all
of the performers were arrayed around the edge of the arena, in galloped Captain Cody again on his beautiful white steed, which he
stopped in the middle of the area. He made it rear on its hind legs
again then bow in four directions to the four quarters of the arena
before galloping back out again, and the rest of the company rode
back through the red curtains, leaving the arena empty once again.

And then the real show began.

Certainly everyone who (unlike Giselle) had *bought* their tickets
must have felt they got their money's worth, because by the time it
was over, she realized that at least four hours had passed. There
were trick-riders, of which Captain Cody was the chief. The antics he
performed on what must have been the most patient horse in the
world left the audience gasping. There was a cattle stampede, an
Indian raid on the settlers, bandits ambushing the stagecoach, and
Captain Cody did an exhibition of sharpshooting that won her unal-
loyed admiration, because *he* did his tricks without benefit of helpful
sylphs. Texas Tom did things with a rope she half-thought were
magic tricks. There was a "grand quadrille," which was a dance done
on horseback, with four couples in bright satin gowns and suits. Captain Cody's "Wonder Horse, Lightning," showed off a battery of
tricks. And there was even more than that. By the time it was over
even Giselle felt sated with all the sights and sounds.

At the end of the show, the announcer told the crowd that those
with the same sort of ticket that she held were invited to leave through
the entrance on the side of the tent where she was sitting—a much,
much smaller entrance. There, he proclaimed, they would be allowed

to see the stagecoach, the covered wagon, the bison, and the long-horn cattle all up close, and speak with the performers and tour the Cowboy Camp, the Army Camp, the Settler Camp and the Indian Village.

Well, how could she possibly resist that?

She left her seat and joined the other audience members who had the special tickets and were passing through the designated entrance. Only as she filed out with the rest did a second ticket-taker examine and take her ticket.

"He dropped one and didn't notice. That was the one I stole!" said a silvery, laughing voice. Giselle looked up—trying not to look as if she was looking up—and saw the white-winged sylph hovering overhead.

Thank you, she thought, hard, knowing the sylph would hear and understand her, then she followed the crowd down a passage left for them to walk through.

By this time, the white-winged one had been joined by two more, all three of them chattering among themselves and looking back from time to time to make sure she was following.

"Ladies and gentlemen!" called the man who had been doing all the announcing. "I am conducting a tour of the camp! If you will please gather around me, yes, like that, the first object here for your pleasure and examination is the Wells Fargo Stagecoach!"

Well, the stagecoach did not hold a great deal of interest for Giselle, and anyway, the white-winged sylph was beckoning her onward, with her two companions fluttering on ahead. So she edged past the crowd and followed, and soon found herself wandering past wagons and tents that looked quite ordinary, like the farm-cart that Mother had used, except bigger, and people—mostly men—who were going to and fro and evidently had specific things they needed to do in a hurry. They ignored her quite as if they didn't see her—which was a good thing, as she was trying very hard not to be seen. There was a smell of cooking food: stew, she thought, but some other things she didn't quite recognize. And the bruised smell of trampled grass, a distant hint of a large animal that was not horse. The bison?

She came around a corner of a tent and found herself, suddenly, at the edge of the Indian Camp. You could tell it was the Indian Camp, since it was a circle of cone-shaped tents of painted canvas that *must* be teepees, arranged around a central fire. And standing not twenty feet away, just behind one of these tents, were Captain Cody himself, one of the Indians, and a fellow in a suit. They seemed to be discussing things, not urgently, but she could tell from their manner that whatever they were talking about was certainly important. She wished she could understand them. But at least she could try and remain unnoticed and get a much closer look at two of the show's stars.

This close, Captain Cody actually looked a little bit handsomer, and he was shorter than she had thought. The Indian, by contrast, was quite tall. He didn't speak much, only a word or two now and again, but whatever he said was listened to with great attention. Something about the way he held himself made her think he might be quite important—perhaps he was the chief? And there was something more about him that she couldn't quite put her finger on—

Just as she thought that, he happened to glance in her direction. And suddenly, his gaze sharpened and he stared hard at her. She shrank back a little—and then, as she watched his eyes flicker from her to what *should* have been empty air for him—she realized that *he could see her sylphs!*

Before she could move, or say anything, all three sylphs zoomed over to him, and as he turned, she could see that there was a bird, a small owl, perched on his shoulder. . . .

Except that it wasn't a bird. Or rather, it wasn't an *ordinary* bird. It shimmered with the same inherent power that her sylphs did, and she realized with a sense of shock that it was some sort of Air Elemental.

Her sylphs were talking to it—and it had its eyes fixed on the Indian's. He interrupted the conversation that was still going on between Captain Cody and the other man, and said a few sharp, excited words. And pointed.

At her.

Before she could back away and run, all three of them were striding toward her with purpose in every step. They literally surrounded
her so she couldn't move, with Captain Cody and the man in the suit
talking excitedly and gesturing at her.

Their German was . . . terrible.

She shook her head, trying to convey that she didn't understand.
All that accomplished was to make them repeat themselves, only
louder this time, as if by volume alone they could *make* her understand. She looked from Cody's face to the other man's and back, only
getting more bewildered and starting to feel more than a bit desperate.

Then the Indian interrupted them with an abrupt gesture and a
single word. They fell silent, and waited, expectantly.

The Indian pointed at her, then mimed something. After a moment, she understood what it was—he was carefully aiming, and
shooting, a rifle!

He pointed at her again. Was he asking if she could shoot? The
way he spread his hands afterward seemed to indicate that was just
what he was doing, so she nodded, and mimed shooting her rifle.

That got the two men even *more* excited, if that was possible.
They started babbling at her until the Indian snorted in disgust, and
that seemed to remind them that she couldn't understand a single
word they were saying. But Captain Cody seized her by the wrist and
pulled gently. The Indian made shooing motions in the direction he
was trying to take her.

"Go with them!" all three sylphs urged. *"Go with them! They want
to see what we can do!"*

She might have been frightened, and indeed, perhaps she *should*
have been frightened, except that it was clear to her, and more importantly, to her sylphs, that these men meant her no harm. If there
was one thing that an Elemental Master came to trust, it was the
instincts of her Elementals, for they saw deeper than any mere
human could. *Maybe if I had been paying more attention to them, I
would have left before the Hauptmann found me. . . .*

Captain Cody's grip on her wrist was not so tight that she couldn't
have pulled away if she wanted to, but with her own Elementals

telling her to do what these men wanted—well it would have been foolish not to do what they said. She didn't know *why* the sylphs wanted her to shoot for them, but perhaps . . . perhaps she could get a meal out of it if she impressed them, and maybe a bed in one of the tents for the night. That was certainly worth a few shots at a target, given the shrinking of her finances. So she let Cody lead her to a part of the camp where a target range had been set up, with the other two men following behind. There was a backstop of logs, against which there was a row of paper targets. There were stationary targets, and also a crate of clay targets meant to be tossed in the air. Behind the backstop was the canvas wall; it occurred to her that these people must be very sure of their own aim to know that any misfires would go into the logs and not to either side, through the canvas and then . . . hitting who *knew* what!

She didn't have her own rifle with her, but the Captain motioned for her to wait and went off to a nearby tent. He returned with a rifle, a carbine of some sort. It was somewhat more sophisticated than her own piece, and much newer, but after several moments of looking it over and miming to Cody he should demonstrate its action, she was satisfied she could handle it creditably once she got it sighted in on the stationary targets. She raised it to her shoulder for her first shot and glanced at the Indian.

He gave a slight tilt of his head in the direction of the three sylphs, and the sketchiest of nods. So, he intended that she "cheat?" Very well, then.

You may help me, she thought hard at them. *The bullet must—*

"*We know!*" crowed the white-winged one. "*This will be* tremendous *fun!*"

This gun was lighter than hers, so she braced herself for a bigger "kick." Kickback on any gun was dependent on two things: the power of the ammunition and the weight of the frame of the gun itself, as Joachim had carefully explained to her. And the first shot she took did, indeed, kick the butt of the rifle back hard into her shoulder. But since she was prepared for it, the muzzle rose only a fraction, and she was sighting in on the target again.

Within moments, Giselle was completely in love with this rifle. Her first shot would have been in the second ring from the center, if the sylphs hadn't interfered. She had it properly sighted in within five shots, and needed very little assistance on the stationary targets from the sylphs, perhaps a nudge on one shot in six or seven. Soon the center of the target had no more paper in it, and had taken on the dull sheen of lead as bullet after bullet flattened on each other. She lost track of everything except the gun in her hands, the target in front of her, and what the air around her was doing. Even the kick of the rifle into her shoulder no longer registered with her, at least not consciously.

She needed no assistance at all when Captain Cody began tossing clay plates into the air.

Plate after plate went up and shattered as she shot, pausing only long enough to reload. Her hands worked of themselves, she really didn't think about them. She could hardly have been unaware of the men's growing excitement, since the Captain whooped with joy every time she hit her mark, but she kept her concentration on her targets. If the sylphs thought she needed to impress these men, then impress them she would! She swung the muzzle of the carbine, tracking each plate and snapping off a shot as soon as she was *sure* everything was perfect, her brows creased slightly. She was vaguely aware she'd probably have a bit of a bruise on her shoulder when she was done, but that was offset by the fact that this lovely carbine was so much lighter than her own piece.

The Captain paused in throwing up clay targets; perhaps his arm was getting tired. But there was still plenty of ammunition in the bucket they had brought her, and she decided that she was not through trying to impress them.

Although on the whole neither Joachim nor Pieter approved of what they would have called "boasting shots," they still taught her several when she begged them. She looked at the Captain, fished in her pocket, and pulled out a pfennig. Inwardly, she winced at the waste of even one small coin, but then she reminded herself that if she could get supper out of these people, it would certainly be worth more than a pfennig. She mimed tossing it in the air and handed it to him. His eyes widened, but he nodded, pulled back his fist and flung it as hard as he could.

Of course, she was taking no chances; the sylphs assisted the trajectory of the pfennig as well as that of her bullet.

The Indian had sharper eyes than the rest of them, and strolled over to where it fell. He brought it back and the Captain let out a long, low whistle, when he saw she had punched a hole in it, slightly off of center.

If only I had a mirror, she thought, just a little smugly. *I'd make their eyes bulge!*

And as if the Indian had actually heard her thoughts, he reached into a bag he had slung over one shoulder and handed her a little ladies' mirror.

If she had not read Karl May's books, she would probably have been taken aback that he had such a thing—but she knew that Indians often used mirrors they got in trade for signaling each other at great distances. She took it with a smile and a little nod she hoped he recognized as thanks and turned her back on the target.

The trickiest thing about shooting backward, using a mirror, was setting the shot up and keeping the rifle steady once you had it sighted. When she had shot for Joachim and Pieter she had been scrupulous about not cheating using the sylphs. Now, however, she had no such compunctions.

With the hand holding the mirror firmly on the butt of the stock, and the other on top of the stock with her thumb on the trigger, she set the shot up, and gently squeezed . . .

The butt kicked back into her hand, jarring the mirror and ruining her view of the target. But this time the Captain threw his hat in the air, he was so excited.

I think we made the shot, she thought wryly. With another bow she handed the mirror back to the Indian, who took it with the faintest of smiles.

The Captain all but snatched the carbine out of her hands, and once again, seized her by the wrist. This time he dragged her back to

the big tent, intercepting a man who was clearly on his way somewhere else just before they reached it.

The Captain dropped her hand, and went into a rapid-fire speech,
gesticulating wildly. The other man listened closely, his brows
creased with concentration. Finally he made a placating gesture with
his hands and got the Captain to calm down and stop talking. He
turned to Giselle and, to her relief, he spoke in perfectly understandable tones, even if his accent was not one she was used to.

"If I understand my good compatriot, the Captain, you, *fraulein*,
are something of an extraordinary shot with a rifle?" he asked. That
was when she recognized his voice; this was the man who had provided all the announcements during the show.

She sensed that this was no time to be modest. "Yes," she said,
drawing herself up as tall as she could, and setting her chin. "I am."

"Forgive me for asking this, because it is, after all, a rather personal question, but—do you live in this town? Is your family here?"
He looked extremely uncomfortable at this point, and indeed, this
was *not* something that a stranger should be asking a young woman
whose name he didn't even know.

"*Tell him everything! Tell him!*" The sylphs had followed along,
and now they were fluttering overhead, dancing in midair with excitement. Giselle didn't look up at them, of course, but it was clear
that this was something other than idle interest.

"I come from a small village quite some distance away," she said,
ignoring the complete impropriety, and with growing excitement.
Could it possibly be—no, she wouldn't dare hope. *But . . . I'm a girl.
What if they want me to disguise myself as a young man?* Would those
who were looking for Gunther possibly seek him in the middle of a
Wild West Show? No, she would not dare hope. Maybe they wanted
her to teach one of the others. "My only relative was my Mother, who
died a year ago. I was going to seek employment with some family
friends when I came upon your show—" she shrugged a little "—I am
a great admirer of Karl May's books, you see—and I could not resist."

"Ah! Karl May! Of course!" He nodded wisely. "I haven't read any
myself, but I am not much of a reader of fiction. Well! In that case . . .

I shall come straight to the point. Captain Cody wishes to offer you employment here, with our show. Provided, of course, you have no objection to taking on the guise of a frontierswoman."

"As a—" She felt stunned, and couldn't finish the sentence.

"A young lady trick-shooter is considered to be a necessity to a Wild West Show," the announcer hurried on, perhaps fearing she would object. "Buffalo Bill has Fraulein Annie Oakley. Pawnee Bill has Fraulein May Lillie. The 101 Ranch Show has Princess Winona. But Captain Cody—well, you saw." He made a helpless little gesture. "Some audience members in our previous two towns have expressed disappointment that we do not have such a star attraction. We can offer you a wagon of your own for traveling and living, already furnished, or a tent, if you prefer. We can supply the wardrobe and the arms. You will have all meals that you care to take with the Company. And we can offer you a salary." And when he named the price it was all she could do not to show her shock and delight and jump up and accept right there. Because it was fully as much as she had expected, in her wildest and most optimistic estimates, to make from every shooting contest she entered put together. And that was just for a single month! This would be a similar income, *every month!*

"How long do you expect to tour?" she asked, pretending only mild interest.

"At least until November, and the rest is a long and complicated story, that I must, in all honesty, tell you before you accept." Captain Cody interrupted the man then, and they exchanged some words—a bit of worry on both their parts, although the Indian nodded confidently at her, as if he fully expected what her answer was going to be. "Would you come sit down with us, so we can give you a fuller explanation?"

"My horse is in your stabling tent. Would you have her and my belongings taken somewhere less public?" she asked. For answer, the man signaled a passing cowboy with a sharp whistle, she handed over the tag representing Lebkuchen, and the cowboy trotted off. She had the opportunity to look him over carefully while this exchange was taking place, and . . . well, aside from his fancy scarlet uniform, he looked quite ordinary. He had a very square face, short, pale hair, and nice, mild blue eyes behind wire-rimmed spectacles. Truth be told, he looked like a clerk or a merchant.

With Lebkuchen taken care of, the trio conducted her to a spacious tent in what appeared to be the Army Camp. This, evidently, belonged to Captain Cody, and looked as if it consisted of two canvas-walled rooms. Access to the back one was closed off, but the front was equipped with a table and comfortable chairs, lanterns, a small desk, chests, some comforts such as a rug on the canvas floor and a pile of cushions in a corner, and a barrel of beer. The Captain made himself the host and pulled glasses for all of them.

Meanwhile, the sylphs were flying mad aerobatics above her head, urging her to take the offer. She *wanted* to, naturally, and fully intended to—but it seemed to her she should not be too eager. *Best I find out everything I can before I agree.*

She accepted the metal stein of beer with a nod of thanks—beer was food of a sort, after all—and waited for them to explain just what had led to this extraordinary offer.

"So, let me first introduce myself," said the announcer. "I am Heinrich Kellermann."

She smiled. He was so formal! And she remembered then that they did not know who *she* was. "Greetings, Herr Kellermann, Herr Cody." She made a little bow. "My name is Giselle Schnittel."

Kellermann gave her a little bow from the waist. But Cody flamboyantly captured her hand, and with a roguish look, kissed it. She snatched it back, but couldn't help but smile at him. He winked.

Kellermann cleared his throat, and she politely turned her attention back to him. "I was working as the assistant manager and under-concierge of the Hotel Splendido, in Bagni di Rabbi, a spa town in Italy near the Austrian border, when this show came into our town. As it happened, the show was managed by a complete scoundrel, who, the day before the show was to leave and cross the border into Austria, ran off with every bit of money he could get his hands on. Cody and some of the other stars of the show were staying at my hotel, and since I speak English and Italian as well as our native tongue, and because I had come, in that brief time of acquaintance, to consider him a friend, I took on the task of explaining the situation to the authorities and everyone else."

Cody said something at length to Heinrich, once again gesturing broadly. Heinrich nodded, then turned back to her when Cody paused for a pull at his beer.

"I have to say that my confidence in my American friends was not misplaced. The show remained to pay their debts. Despite sometimes lackluster ticket sales, the Captain and his company did not leave until all debts were paid." He seemed as proud of that as if he himself had accomplished it.

"That's more than honorable!" she exclaimed, as the sylphs continued to dance about over her head. The owl on the Indian's shoulder watched them with bemusement, but of course, no one else could see them.

"Indeed. But once that happened, the company split up, to an extent. Word of their misfortune had spread, and several recruiters arrived with offers. About half the troupe left for other shows or smaller exhibitions, taking only their personal baggage. This left the rest with no money to return home and no good prospects except to somehow continue on. And with that, the Captain offered me the opportunity to manage what was left of the show." He shrugged. "Foolish of me, perhaps, to give up my position, which was secure."

"If your position was secure—" she raised an eyebrow.

"It was a boring little Alpine hotel," he replied. "And it was unlikely I would succeed to the position of manager or concierge until I was sprouting gray hairs. I had always wanted to be in the theater, and here was my chance! I knew that my own countrymen were keen on the American frontier, so I made certain of the original bookings, then made some more arrangements through the trade papers and friends, and here we are."

"Do you really think you can make enough money for all of these people to return home?" she asked, concerned. It was one thing for the sylphs to be agitating for her to join this show . . . but they had offered her what seemed to be a ridiculously huge sum of money, when they had only just extricated themselves from large debts.

"Absolutely," he replied with confidence. "It will take time, but we will. You understand, it is not enough merely to earn the money to return home for these good people. That would be a failure. They must return home with something substantial to show as well. If not a fortune, certainly enough to live on comfortably for some time, perhaps to purchase ranches or businesses of their own."

The Captain got them all another beer, and Kellermann paused to speak to him in English for some time. Cody's brows creased and he said something anxiously, then turned to her and repeated it, even though he surely knew she didn't understand a word he was saying.

"The Captain is most anxious to learn whether or not you will join us, *fraulein*—" Kellermann began—when he was interrupted by the Indian. That worthy gentleman spoke only a few words, in comparison with the Captain, but Kellermann's eyes widened and he glanced from one side to the other before leaning over the table toward her.

"Chief Leading Fox says you are not just a sure-shot, you are a magician . . ." he whispered. "Like him."

She sat up as straight as if an electric current from a nearby thunderbolt had passed through her. In fact, it felt rather as if one *had*. "He said—" She glanced up at her sylphs. They were all nodding, eagerly. She looked back down. "You know about magicians?" she demanded.

Slowly, Kellermann nodded. "I was not blessed—or cursed—with that myself. But I have relatives among the *Bruderschaft der Förster.*"

And it was Cody who now leaned over the table, and added, in a confidential tone, something she (of course) could not understand.

"The Captain says to tell you that although he is not a great magician like Chief Leading Fox, he has some small abilities with fire himself." Kellermann's face showed no sign that he was trying to fool her—but still—this seemed altogether too convenient.

Could they all be trying to trick her, just to get her to join the show? Did they need her that badly?

Then she went cold all over, as she remembered another man who had seemed kind and amusing, and had only wanted to trick her into giving him access to her tower—and her—

But before she could move or speak or—well, anything, really—the Captain was peeling off his long, fawn-colored, fringed leather gauntlet from his right hand. He closed it into a fist, briefly, then opened it.

In the center of his palm, a little flame danced.

The Indian made a little sound of approval as she stared, mesmerized, at the flame. Which was not just a "flame" at all, really, for it was easy for her to see that in the heart of it, there was a little fairy-like creature, nude but for her long hair, performing a little dance of her own.

The Captain closed his hand, gently, and when he opened it, the Fire Elemental was gone. He put his glove back on, and gave her a long and solemn wink.

"So," said Kellermann, after a very, very long pause. He regarded her, as she tried to get her head around the fact that not just the Indian but apparently *several* of these people knew about magic. "Now will you join us?"

She licked lips gone dry, but from excitement now, not fear. "I would be very glad to do so. It seems I have stumbled on a place where I am a perfect match in all things."

It seemed the Captain did not need Kellermann's translation. As soon as she finished, he whooped, pulled off his hat, and slapped his leg with it in glee.

5

CAPTAIN Cody was, as they said in the Karl May books, a "man of action." As soon as he had her agreement, he jumped up and opened the front of the tent, barking orders to someone outside. A moment later, two sturdy, dark-complexioned men appeared. One was still in his fringed leather from the show, the other in dark, worn trousers and a faded plaid shirt.

"Would you prefer a tent, or a wagon?" Kellermann asked her. "The wagon will be better in bad weather and afford more privacy, the tent will be more spacious."

"Wagon, please," she said, and Cody issued unintelligible orders to the men, who nodded and ambled off. "Well, now we must get your signature on a contract, and then go to our surplus wardrobe and get you outfitted." He stood up, and so did she. "Then we will go to the mess tent and introduce you to the company and get you fed, and by then your wagon will be ready and you can settle into it." He rubbed his hands together with immense satisfaction.

"But—I don't understand English—" she protested, the main problem facing her suddenly occurring to her. "How am I to feign being a frontierswoman when I cannot understand English?"

Never mind all the problems of trying to join an ongoing production!

Kellermann smacked himself in the middle of his forehead, and turned to Cody. But he had not gotten more than a few words out when Cody and the Indian both broke up with laughter.

Kellermann looked baffled. He looked even more baffled when Cody gave him *some* sort of explanation. "He says—and *fraulein,* I have no idea how this is to be done, but I have seen amazing things and I have no reason to doubt—that Chief Leading Fox will teach you English and Pawnee tonight."

English? *And* Pawnee? She turned to look at the Indian, who chuckled slightly, and nodded, then said a few words himself.

Kellermann just shook his head. "And he says that somehow, *you* will be teaching him and the Captain German. I look forward to seeing the results of this miracle."

And so am I. . . .

But she was given no time to think. Kellermann, trailed by the Captain and the Chief, took her to the wagon that served as his office and translated the simple little contract for her before she signed it. Then they all made their way to a spot in the Army Camp where a wagon and another, larger tent were presided over by a trio of black-haired women, who listened to Cody, then took charge of her. They took her into the tent and pantomimed that she was to undress. She stripped to her underthings, which seemed to satisfy them. They measured her all over by means of strings, then two of them disappeared and reappeared with armloads of costumes.

She had thought that Tante Gretchen's hunting suit was practical, but now she saw garments that were, if possible, even *more* comfortable and practical. Well, that did make sense. Women could not do all the things they had to do on the frontier if they were burdened with corsets and lace and ribbons and bustles and overskirts and . . . well, *things.* She quickly realized, as she was fitted not only with fringed skirts that only came to her knee, leggings, and fringed and embroidered shirtwaists, but with what looked like the same sort of costume that the Indian women had been wearing in the parade, and one of the voluminous satin skirts and blouses of the Quadrille, that she must be doing double and triple roles. *Well, I'd rather be doing something than sitting about,* she decided.

Once the costumes were fitted to the three ladies' satisfaction, they more or less helped her dress and shoved her out the tent flap into the hands of the three men who were waiting patiently for her.

By now, she was ravenous. It had been a very long time since the bit of bread and cheese that had served as her luncheon.

As if he could read her mind (or, perhaps, hear her growling stomach), Cody checked his pocket watch and gabbled something. Kellerman translated that simply enough. "We're going to eat now, and we must eat quickly to be ready in time for the evening performance."

They led her to a big tent full of benches and trestle tables, not unlike a *Festzelt,* or beer tent at a big Oktoberfest celebration. The venues for eating and drinking at a Maifest tended to be smaller than the big beer tents at Oktoberfest, so this was the first time she had ever seen a place where people ate that was so very large. At least sixty people could be seated here at once! This was where the aroma of stew had been coming from.

At one end of the tent were men in aprons ladling tin bowls full of stew and handing them over to the performers and workers. Cody led her to the queue, and she got a bowl full of stew that smelled so rich and good her stomach began complaining that she wasn't eating it *right then,* plus a huge chunk of bread and butter and a wedge of pie on a second tin plate and an empty tin mug. She got settled at a table, her tin cup poured full of coffee, and then Cody stood up and whistled shrilly, bringing all conversation to a halt.

He gestured grandly at her and launched into a speech. She recognized her name in it and that was about all. Then there was a pause, and Cody made a little beckoning motion with his hand, so she stood up and gave a little bow, feeling suddenly very shy. *I had better get over that, and quickly!* she told herself. *I am going to be a performer, I cannot be shy!*

That elicited a round of enthusiastic, but brief, applause. It looked to her as if many people were glad to hear what Cody had to say, but also were in a hurry to get their suppers. She was glad the applause was brief; she wanted to *eat*.

The stew was delicious, just as good as anything Mother had made, and that was high praise indeed. The bread, she thought, was probably local, since it would be difficult to transport bread ovens. The coffee was very strong and bitter, but after her first taste—and wry face—Kellerman went over to the end of the table and brought back a tin full of sugar lumps, which made it quite good. Mother had never made coffee, but she decided that she quite liked it. The pie was nothing like anything Mother made, but it was excellent, nevertheless. On the whole, when she finished her meal and brought the dishes to the front to go in a dry washing tub with the rest, she was more than content.

But her day was not yet complete, it seemed. Cody said something and bowed a little, and then left, taking Leading Fox with him. Kellerman took her elbow and she allowed him to guide her out of the mess tent. As she paused, confronted by the mass of tents of differing kinds, their sides moving slightly in the evening breeze, he let go of her and gestured toward a sort of path between the tents.

"As you heard, we have an evening performance that I must get to, but first I will show you to your new wagon," he told her. "We've had all your personal belongings brought there, and by now I am sure at least some, if not all, of your costumes are there as well. Cody also left orders that some spare American garb be altered and given to you. Some of us—Leading Fox at least, and I—will be back after the show."

"This is more than kind," she said, and would have added more, but he would hear none of it.

"You are one of us, now, *fraulein*," he said, with one of his courteous little bows. "We are a family, now more than ever, and you are doing us a great favor by joining us."

They threaded their way across the camp to an area set aside for wagons. It appeared that the members of the show, on the whole, preferred a tent to a wagon, for there were only half a dozen living wagons lined up in a neat row. Kellerman took her to a small bow-topped wagon of a uniform brown color, quite plain, unlike the beautifully painted and carved Romany *vardos* that had camped beside the abbey several times (with Mother's blessing). It was also a bit smaller than the *vardos,* which were, after all, intended to serve an entire family. There was a green door with a glass window in it at the front, and a glass bow window at the rear. It, like the others, had been parked so that the evening light fell upon the blank side, and not through either window. Kellerman opened the door for her with a flourish, and she went up the steps to survey her new home.

Well, it was small. But although clearly second- or thirdhand, it was stoutly built; the roof seemed to be tin over a wooden frame, and the rest was made of golden-brown wood the same color as the crust of a loaf of bread. There was a curtained platform bed under the window, with a storage cupboard underneath. Just inside the door was a tiny cast-iron stove—she wouldn't be using that much in the summer, but if the show was, indeed, planning on continuing to perform into November, she certainly would need it then. On the right wall was a chest of drawers, and a little bit of a bench seat with a cushion on it and more storage beneath. On the left wall was a bit of fold-down table with shelves above, and a stool, and a bit of storage beneath. And that was fundamentally all there was room for.

But really, what more did she need?

"I believe your belongings are on the bed," said Kellerman from the door. "There should be linens, a washbasin and pitcher, and assorted bits and pieces from the last person who had it in the cupboard under the bed. That would have been Fraulein Ado Ellie, who was our former lady trick-shooter. A most amiable lady, but nothing near as good a shot as you." She turned to see him smiling in the doorway. "However, she was, if I may say so, both stunningly beautiful and sweet-natured, so much was forgiven of her."

"She seems to have been a good housekeeper," Giselle replied, opening the cupboard beneath the bed and surveying with relief the neatly folded linens and a number of things that would make life very comfortable in this wagon.

"She was, and I hope this pleases you." Kellerman looked a little anxious at that. "We had been using it for costume storage, and occasionally as a place for some of the troupe to sleep in extremely bad weather."

"This will be most satisfactory, thank you," she replied.

He beamed as if it had been his hands that had constructed the wagon. "In that case I shall leave you to settle in and await Fox, and possibly the Captain."

He left the door open, and she climbed over the mattress to open the window over the bed to allow air through. With the curtains pulled, and the door open, and a little teasing of the air, there was soon a gentle breeze wafting through, smelling of hay, trampled grass, and faintly of food. The mattress was satisfactory; the linens she got out to make it up were, like the wagon, old but very clean, and there were some sturdy woolen blankets in there that were a welcome sight, and a great many cushions and pillows. There was even a fine spirit lamp that she could heat water over, and a kettle for making tea. Turning to her own belongings, she discovered that the previous owner had had proper gun racks installed above the bench seat, so her old rifle went up there, although she was hoping she would be given that sweet carbine to use. The music from the show rang out over the encampment, and though the wagon section of the campground was empty except for her, it didn't feel lonely.

Darkness fell and she lit the lamp she had found in the cupboard, giving a cheerful glow to her new home. Bit by bit she settled her possessions and her new costumes into places that suited her, taking care and thought about it. When the show was on the move, anything that might fall would have to be stowed carefully, so she needed to leave places for those things to go.

When at last she had everything put away, she checked around the outside of the wagon. There wasn't much there, but *someone* had left a small water barrel up by the front axle. *Good, that means I won't have to go hunting for water,* she thought with relief. She fetched and filled a pitcher and a small covered bucket, and brought both back into the wagon. Someone was going around the camp, lighting lanterns and torches; when he—for it was a *he,* a weathered, bowlegged fellow in canvas trousers and a checkered shirt—came by and lit a lantern at the front of her wagon, they nodded agreeably to each other. Then he touched two fingers to the brim of his battered bowler hat and moved on.

And then, having nothing else to do, she went back inside, pulled off her boots, moved the lantern to a hook just over the bed, and took out one of her two precious books. A Karl May Winnetou book, of course. Within moments she was lost in its pages, coming out only now and again to marvel that here she was, in the midst of the very people she was reading about.

She was in the middle of a descriptive passage of a herd of buffalo when a tap on the frame of the open door made her look up, as she realized that the music from the show was no longer sounding from the big tent. Kellerman and Leading Fox stood at the doorway, waiting politely for an invitation to come in.

"Please," she said, swinging her feet and legs over the side of the bed. "Come in!" Although technically she was "entertaining" in her "bedroom," somehow she did not feel shy or self-conscious about the situation. Perhaps that was due to the demeanor of Leading Fox, who was so solemn and dignified she could not imagine him even *thinking* anything improper.

"I won't be staying," Kellerman said, as Leading Fox entered the wagon and carefully took a seat on the bench. "Unless you would prefer me to. Leading Fox told me that you and he will be able to converse by means of your familiar spirits."

Well, that was less than accurate, but she let it pass. "I believe that we can," she replied, "And I am perfectly comfortable in the presence of Leading Fox, if you have work you need to do."

"Alas, yes, I do," Kellerman replied, with regret. "A bugle will wake the camp, and a second bugle call will announce when breakfast is ready in the mess tent. It will not be much like the breakfasts that you and I are used to, but it is quite good. You will meet with the Captain then and go to rehearsal, and he will integrate you into the show."

Well, how he was to do that without any shared language she had no idea. Still, wasn't that supposed to be what Leading Fox was going to address?

She thanked him, and Kellerman hurried away, vanishing immediately into the night and the camp, which had gone suddenly very quiet. These people went to bed at country hours, it seemed, no lingering at bedtime over a book or a beer. . . .

She turned to the Indian, who nodded, and whistled—not shrilly as Cody had, but softly. It sounded like a bird call, but it was answered by two winged creatures, flying in the open door. One was the Indian's little owl, the other a night-sylph. The owl flew to the Indian's shoulder, while the sylph balanced atop the cold stove. Her wings were a pale blue, very moth-like, and folded down her back as soon as she had landed, like a stiff cloak.

"You speak to me," the sylph, an imperious little black-haired beauty said. *"I will speak to the owl, who will tell his man what you said. And the other way around."*

Giselle nodded, and folded her hands in her lap. "Well . . . obviously Herr Leading Fox is an Elemental Master of Air?"

The sylph inclined her head to the owl, and silently conveyed what Giselle had said. The owl turned to the Indian and the same silent colloquy passed between them. It all happened in mere moments of course, in much less time than it had taken her to speak the words, and then the sylph had the reply.

"Leading Fox says that yes, he is very like that, and he is going to make it possible for you to learn English and Pawnee, as he promised."

She was going to ask how that could be possible, but evidently the sylph already had the answer. *"His owl spirit is to spend the night here, and if you command it, I am to spend the night in his teepee, and the owl will put English and Pawnee into your mind while you sleep, while I do the same for Leading Fox and our tongue."*

She blinked. "And all I have to do is tell—I mean, ask you to do this?"

The sylph lost a little of her imperious demeanor. *"You—would ask me, rather than order me?"* she said in astonishment.

Giselle blinked again. "Well, of course. It is always better to be friends, is it not? The only time I might give an order to one of you is if there is no time to be polite about it. And then I would apologize for being so rude afterward."

Now the sylph unbent entirely. *"You are much nicer than the one who was here before. He was rude, always ordering us about, and threatening if we did not obey immediately! You are as nice as the Bruderschaft are said to be! Thank you!"* She beamed at Giselle, who smiled back. Out of the corner of her eye she noticed that Leading Fox was smiling ever so slightly.

"Well, if you don't mind, would you please remain with Leading Fox and teach him German?" she said, with punctilious politeness. "I would very much appreciate it."

"I would be happy to!" the sylph crowed, standing on one foot in glee.

"But—" She frowned for a moment. "Couldn't Leading Fox have asked for himself?"

"He did not wish to offend us, since he is from so far away, and his Elementals are so unlike us," the sylph replied, and shrugged. *"Humans. I do not understand the rules you make for yourselves."*

"Sometimes, neither do I," Giselle sighed, and through the sylph, offered the Indian a cup of tea, but he declined politely and got up to leave. The owl spirit lofted over to a shelf running along the very top of the left-hand wall and made itself at home; the night-sylph flitted out the door, following Leading Fox. The Indian walked as softly as Winnetou did in the books; she could not hear a single footfall as he vanished into the night.

Giselle considered the little owl, who blinked at her. *I should feed it. Or at least offer it something . . .*

She could spin little orbs of the magic of the Air, and her sylph friends would devour them with glee, as if they were sugared fruits. Would the owl like them too? Well, it was an Air Elemental, chances were it would like the same thing the sylphs did.

She cupped her left hand, palm up, concentrated on seeing the currents of magic around her, twirled her finger in her palm, as Mother had taught her to gather some of that magic, and started to

spin up a little orb. The wisps of magic followed the twirling motion
of her finger, sparkling in the semidarkness of the wagon. The faster
she twirled, the more the magic took on the shape of an orb about
the size of a pebble, and the brighter the orb got. When it began to
illuminate her palm, she held it up for the owl to see. The owl's eyes
widened and his beak parted a little; she blew on it and sent it glid-
ing toward him, and he snapped at it and gulped it down eagerly, and
looked to her for more.

Well, if he was going to be giving her not one, but *two* languages,
the least she could do was to feed him generously. She continued to
spin up orbs and send them wafting to the little owl, who snapped
them up with glee. When he seemed to have had enough, he flitted
to another shelf just over the head of her bed, fluffed up his feathers,
and settled down, eyelids drooping. Giselle took that as a sign she
should be sleeping.

She closed the window above the bed and pulled the curtains
shut, then jumped down out of the bed and closed the door of the
wagon and pulled the curtains on the window of the door. A few
moments later she was in a night shift; a moment after that and she
had blown out the lantern and was trying to get comfortable in a
strange bed. It was not as soft as her featherbed at home, nor were
the sounds of the encampment anything she was used to. Somewhere out there, someone was playing a harmonica, or trying to.
There were murmurs of voices from the nearer two wagons. Still, it
was a great deal more comfortable than sleeping in a haystack,
though it wasn't as nice as the bed in Tante Gretchen's cottage . . .

Her dreams were strange, colorful, scenes of Indians, including
Leading Fox, out in some vast landscape that somehow looked *nothing* like what Karl May described. The sky was *enormous,* that was
the only way to describe it. The scenes were all very disjointed, and
didn't form any sort of coherent story. Unlike her usual dreams,
where she was an active participant, she was a passive observer here.
It was as if someone was opening a picture book at random places
while she watched. There were scenes of hunting, of village life, of
Indians with what she assumed to be American Cavalry, of dancing

and feasting, and of . . . well, virtually anything that people *could* do. These people did not live in the teepees she had expected, nor the pueblos that Karl May had described Winnetou's tribe as inhabiting—they lived in homes made of earth and wood, round mounds with a square tunnel for an entrance. This was . . . unexpected. In fact, as she flitted from scene to scene, there was a great deal that was unexpected. Finally she just stopped expecting things altogether and merely drank in the scenes as they were presented to her. Once she did that . . . she noticed there was a sort of voice murmuring in the wind, too soft for her to hear properly, but always present.

Then she drifted off into true sleep, but still with that voice murmuring in the back of her mind.

She woke up as she always did, at dawn, and the camp was already stirring. As she lay in her bed, listening to the unfamiliar voices and sounds, she smiled to herself. She thought she was going to get along well with these people. They all sounded amazingly friendly for so early in the morning.

"Clem! Didja make sure the water barrel's full fer that new liddle gal? The sharpshooter?" a female voice—an older female, Giselle thought—called.

"Right an' tight, Maisy!" called a nearer, male voice. "Topped her off a liddle bit ago."

And that was when her sleepy satisfaction turned to astonishment and wide-awakeness. *She could understand them!*

Quickly, she looked above her, to the shelf where the owl spirit had perched last night, but it was gone. As she continued to listen to the early voices around her, she held her breath, almost unable to believe that what Leading Fox had promised last night had come true!

Then a trumpet or bugle call sounded over the camp, and the sounds of the camp *truly* coming to life began. It sounded amazingly cheerful. People shouted questions about animals, about costumes or properties, teased each other about being lazy, swore they were going to douse them in cold water to wake them up—

She pulled the bed-curtains aside and hopped down onto the floor of the wagon. Last night she had filled her bucket, kettle and pitcher for the washbasin with the water from the barrel at the tongue of the wagon. Now she put the kettle on the spirit lamp to heat while she considered her clothing. There was her own hunting outfit that she had taken off, brushed out, and set aside last night . . .

But I am supposed to be one of these people, she thought, picking up the skirt and frowning at it. *I should start looking like them.*

So instead, she selected a skirt that appeared to be made of a gold-colored canvas, a lighter-weight fringed shirt to go with it, and leggings to go under that. The skirt was, by her standards, scandalously short, but she supposed the leggings made it more modest, and like the skirt of her hunting suit, it had been split for riding astride. Both the shirt and the skirt were much softer than she had expected canvas to be, and showed signs of having been altered. She poured some of her heated water into the washbasin, added cold, and gave herself a quick scrub, then put on the new clothing. It was . . . well, surprisingly comfortable.

Dressed, she unbraided her hair, combed it out, and braided it up again. It didn't seem to be growing as fast. And . . . now that she was *here* . . . she certainly didn't feel as tense as she had been since her encounter with the Hauptmann.

And the moment she remembered that, she had to put one hand on the table and the other on her stomach, feeling a little . . . sick. And guilty again. No matter what Tante Gretchen had said, a man was dead, and she was responsible for him being dead. Nothing was going to change that.

But nothing is going to bring him back, either, she reminded herself.

So when the sick feeling passed, she took a deep breath, stood a little straighter and went out to find the mess tent.

The sun had just barely cleared the horizon, the air was fresh and crisp, and the sounds of people and animals echoed from every part of the camp. The camp was now altogether awake, with people heading in the same direction that she was, men washing, shaving, bustling about half-dressed. There was no sign of the women, but she suspected they were either clearing up their tents or wagons, or dressing in more privacy than the men seemed to need.

She made a turn that she remembered and found herself not only at the edge of the Indian encampment, but nearly face-to-face with Leading Fox.

"*Rawah, Kiwaku Rahiraskaawarii,*" she said without thinking. Then her hand flew to her mouth as she realized that she had greeted him in Pawnee!

And she also understood in that moment that the *real* translation of his name was more complicated than "Leading Fox." "Fox Roaming the World In The Lead" or "As The Leader." Given how far he was from home . . . well that seemed almost supernaturally apt.

"*Guten Morgen, Fraulein Giselle,*" Leading Fox replied, with an almost imperceptible smile and in faultless German. "I told you we would have each others' tongues in the morning."

"But why could you not have done this with Herr Kellerman?" she asked. And then snapped her fingers. "Of course. Because he is not a—" she sought in her new language for the right word for "Elemental Master" "—a Medicine Chief."

"Even so." Leading Fox nodded. "Now that I have mastery of your tongue, however, I shall use a similar, but longer means to give it to the Captain. Even though I trust Herr Kellerman, there should be more than one of our company that speaks both German and English."

"And Pawnee?" she asked. Leading Fox smiled a very little.

"Captain Cody is the genuine article, a working Scout," Fox replied, this time in English. "He speaks tolerable Pawnee of both dialects, Apache in Chirakawa and Mescalaro, and Lakota Sioux. I believe he has a few words in several other languages."

"Enough to get by. Mornin' Fox, Miz Giselle." The Captain himself strolled around the side of a tent in the "cowboy" section and tipped his hat to her. "Looks like your witchery worked."

"Tolerably, old friend. Tolerably. Shall we escort our new sharpshooter to breakfast before the plague of locusts devours everything in sight?" Leading Fox replied with a faintly raised eyebrow. With a laugh, Cody pulled off his hat and waved them ahead of him.

As soon as she entered the mess tent, Giselle realized that Leading Fox's wry comment about "the plague of locusts" was not altogether out of line. Unlike last night, when people had been eating methodically, but not ravenously, the members of the show seemed to be frantically gulping down food as fast as they could. Bracketed between Fox and Cody, she was at least able to get her tin dish full of fried eggs, bread, and bacon without being trampled, although she was unable to reach the pancakes being served, and there were already piles of tin mugs and pots of coffee waiting at the table where Cody guided her. She took her place at the end, next to a dark-complexioned woman with a great mass of blue-black hair who greeted her with a cheerful *"Buenos dias, senorita,"* and went back to eating eggs with some sort of flat, thin, pancake-like bread.

"Right, now that we can palaver, I can tell you where you'll be fittin' inter the show," Cody said, after pouring his cup, Fox's, and hers full of black, steaming coffee. "Sugar?"

"Please—" she said, and dumped two lumps into the ebony liquid.

"You'll come in with the Grand Parade, of course. We'll gussy up your mare to look like ours. Then there's the cattle drive, the campfire and songs, then the Injuns attack and stampede the cattle. You'll come on after that for some straight-up target-shootin'. Then we'll have the Injun war dance. You'll be a squaw—we got black wigs you can wear, if you can stuff your hair under one. We ain't got any real Injun gals—" here he glanced over at Fox, who nodded.

"Only our men were willing to travel so far from home," Leading Fox said, quietly. "There are few enough Pawnee as it is. The Mexican ladies have been standing in for Pawnee women."

"I figgered since you kin speak Pawnee now, you wouldn't mind bein' a Injun in the show," Cody added. "Anyway, after the war dance, the camp packs up an' the settler wagon comes on, an' the Injuns attack the settlers. The cowpokes drive 'em off, everybody leaves th' arena, an' then you do a trick-shot turn, finishin' up with the mirror shot. Then we got the bandits attackin' the stage, then the cowpokes an' Injuns do trick-ridin', then the Mexicans do the Grand Quadrille on horseback, an' you're part of that."

"But . . ." she began to object. "My horse doesn't—"

"Don' worry yer head 'bout that," Cody said, breezily. "You'll use the Quadrille hoss. The hoss already knows the routine, the old cayuse could do it in his sleep. All you need t'do is sit on him an' look purdy. You'll be takin' the place of young Ned, an' I reckon he'll be right grateful that he ain't got to wear a dress no more."

She couldn't help but laugh at that, because she could well imagine the sort of mockery this Ned fellow must be getting from his fellow "cowpokes."

"Then I'll do trick-shootin', we get trick-ropin' from Texas Tom, we have us a little rodeo with the cowpokes, the broncs, and the bulls, then you come do mounted trick-shots against me, an' we finish up with another Grand Parade. Two shows, one afternoon, and one evenin'."

That was going to be a lot of work . . . but they were paying her a lot of money. "When do I actually join the show?" she asked.

"Soon's you catch on. You'll be in the Grand Parades, the Quadrille an' the war dance at least today, but the rest'll be whenever yer up to it. We have a run-through in the morning right after breakfast, then lunch, then open up soon as lunch's done." Cody eyed her outfit. "That'll do fer rehearsal, but you'll need costume changes inter fancier duds fer each turn."

"Turn?" she said blankly.

"A 'turn' is when you come into the arena," Fox explained, before Cody could. "That is why you have all of those costumes. The women will fashion you more, as needed. Two sharpshooter costumes, one of the buckskin or cloth dresses when you are a Pawnee, and the dress for the Grand Quadrille should serve you well enough for now."

Cody finished all but inhaling his breakfast, and stood up from the table. "We'll start the run-through in a half hour or so," he said. "Foller me, I'll show you where we stable the hosses, your gal'll be there."

Well, she knew from Karl May's books that Americans were *brisk,* but she'd had no notion what that meant until now! She left her breakfast dishes in the washtub and hurried after Cody. Sure enough, Lebkuchen was snugly stabled up with the other show horses in a spacious tent and seemed quite content with her lot in life. Following Cody's example, she got Lebkuchen saddled and bridled, but led, rather than rode, her to the big show tent.

There was an entirely separate entrance, concealed from the public, as she had expected. Things were nothing like as regimented and organized as they had been for the show. Only about half the band was in the stands, and instead of being closed, the "stage curtains" at the entrance to the arena were pulled wide open and tied in place. Without an audience in it, the tent seemed bigger and emptier than she had remembered it being.

"Since you're our other big attraction, you'll start off the Grand Parade right after the color-guard," Cody said, as the other show folk arrived and arranged themselves outside the tent for the run-through. On first glance it looked utterly chaotic, but as she watched, the chaos sorted itself out and no one seemed to get in anyone else's way. "We'll do the same plain target-shootin' that ya did when you showed us what you could do, an' end with fillin' the bull's-eye of the last target. That'll be your first solo turn. Then the trick-shot turn'll be clay targets, shootin' the center out of a coin, an' finish with the mirror shot. Anythin' else you kin think of, talk ter Ned. Yer other shootin' turn'll be on yer mare. We'll have knockdown targets set up at the band-end of the arena. You kin shoot a pistol, right?"

"I don't have as much exper—" she began, but Cody waved that away breezily.

"'Tween yer Elementals an' yer own good aim, shouldn't be a problem. We'll make three passes each. You ain't a trick-rider, so we'll settle fer goin' at the gallop. Later on I'll teach you some trick-ridin' an' that'll make it more innerestin'." She must have looked alarmed at that, because he laughed. "Don' worry. It's mostly a matter'f not fallin' off."

And with that not-very-comforting "encouragement," the run-through began.

It was nothing like the show. People were half-costumed, sometimes even half-clothed, and they laughed and talked, and even ate
and drank while they waited for their turn to perform. Only one buffalo and one longhorn cow stood in for the entire herds. No one galloped, or even trotted. Only when actual tricks were rehearsed did
anyone seem serious about what they were doing. Fox led her out for
the "Indian war dance," positioned her at a drum, and told her to
follow the other drummers. Dutifully, she did, discovering that the
other two "squaws" were both of the Mexican ladies who had altered
her costumes for her. All the real Pawnee but one danced, plus four
Mexican men; the drummers were all whites or Mexicans.

*It is a good thing my hair is not anything like as long as it was before
I set off on this journey,* she thought, contemplating the impossibility
of cramming four braids, each as long as she was tall, under a wig. *I
shall have to procure a pair of scissors and keep it trimmed every night!*

It turned out not to be at all hard to follow the somewhat monot-
onous drumming of the only Pawnee who did not dance. The singing
was something else entirely, and although the Mexican women sang
along with the drummer and dancers, she kept her mouth shut and
just listened.

The first thing she knew at once—because she understood
Pawnee—was that this was no war song. The words were simple,
interspersed with sounds that she understood served the same purpose of carrying the song as the meaningless melodic syllables of
European songs. The words were very simple, repeated several
times, interspersed with the "hey-yo" sounds that comprised most of
the tune. "Father is good. He gave me a pipe. He is good." The giving
of a pipe, she knew from Karl May, and also from those dream frag-
ments, was a matter of great honor and occasion, so this was something of an important song. Of course, she wondered *why* the Indians
were dancing to this, and not to a real war song, but she resolved to
ask this of Leading Fox when they were somewhere more private. It
was astonishing how so few voices managed to fill the entire empty
show tent with their haunting cries.

The "squaws packed up the camp"—which consisted of a couple

of props and the drums—and the Indians took their horses and rode around the arena three times, making no attempt at the bloodcurdling war cries they had done for the show. Then they exited, and the settlers and the stagecoach entered to circle the arena, camp, be attacked by the Indians and be rescued.

And now it was time for her first trick-shot performance.

Directed by Cody, she rode Lebkuchen into the center of the ring where someone had set up a portable gun stand with three identical rifles on it. Above her was the great expanse of the tent roof. The arena was empty except for herself, her helper, her horse, the gun stand and the targets at the band-end of the tent. To her great pleasure, the rifles were all the same as that carbine she had used to prove herself. There was a man in an outfit of fringed buckskin and an animal-skin hat waiting beside the stand. He took Lebkuchen's reins once she had dismounted and handed her the first rifle.

"Mornin' missy," he said, with a grin that showed he was lacking a tooth in front. "I'm Ned Toller. I'm more or less the stage manager. These here are Winchester repeating rifles. They hold fifteen shots each. Now what yer gonna do here, is take a shot at each one of those five targets. Then we'll move back, you'll take another five shots, and move back a third time, and you'll take another five. Each time, we'll take off the targets and five folks'll ride around the ring displayin' 'em. Then we'll pull the rabbit across the end an' yer gonna shoot it fifteen times. We'll just call out how many times ya hit it. Then we'll move all the way back, and yer gonna shoot one target fifteen times, an' we'll ride it around so people kin see how ya did."

Now by this point, the entire company had gathered at the target end of the arena—at a more-than-safe distance from the targets themselves, in her estimation, but certainly near enough to see whether or not she hit. She suppressed a smile. None of them, other than Kellermann, Fox and Cody, had any idea of how good she was. And Kellermann had told her that she was much better than her predecessor. She knew she was about to impress them, thanks to the sylphs. As she waited for Kellermann to finish introducing her, a thought occurred to her. It would be a very good thing if she could firm her own concentration over the forces of the Air enough that she could do without the sylphs—just in case.

By this time, the upper reaches of the tent were full of sylphs, drawn by all the excitement. She sent a brief thought toward them— *If you please, your assistance in this matter?*—and the white-winged one she recognized from yesterday gathered up three of her sisters and wafted down to the firing line.

Then she settled the lovely rifle to her shoulder, sighted in on the target, and went to work. Five shots—and five bull's-eyes—later, she and her helper moved back about ten paces. By the time she had emptied the first rifle, there were cheers and great excitement after every shot. By the time she finished perforating the poor paperboard rabbit, her audience could scarcely contain itself. And when she finished by rapidly filling the bull's-eye of the last target with lead, there were hats in the air, and the company was racing across the flattened, dusty grass to congratulate her. This time, of course—as she resolved to do at every actual show—she had taken no chances. She was not altogether certain how *much* the sylphs had assisted her, but until she could figure out how to do what they did, she had no intention of doing without their help.

And while she had shot, she had been thinking of trick-shots she could make for her second "turn."

She had more time to think about that while the other acts ran through their paces; she watched from the vantage point of the parted tent flaps until it was time for her horseback "dance." The horse was gentle and regarded her placidly as she mounted, and took its place in the line of the rest to parade in without any prompting on her part. And as Cody had promised, she had to do exactly nothing for the Grand Quadrille except not fall off the horse. In fact, the one time she had actually moved the reins a little the horse had turned his head to look at her with such an outraged expression that she and the others had all laughed.

So when everyone took a break for drinks of water, and Ned

Toller turned up to ask her just what tricks she was doing besides shooting tossed clay targets and the mirror trick, she had an answer for him.

The bandsmen had come down out of the bandstand, and she was standing beside Lebkuchen, watching as Texas Tom worked with his rope until he was satisfied with it. Ned strolled across the arena from where he had been consulting with someone and pulled the brim of his hat at her.

"Figgered what yer trick-shots are gonna be?" he asked. "Clay bustin', and finish with the mirror, but what's in between?"

"I would like to shoot the pips out of a playing card," she said. "If someone will hold a cigarette, I shall shoot it in half. I shall also shoot a coin, although I cannot guarantee to make a hole in it every time, I can certainly hit it."

"Kin ya light a match?" Ned asked. She thought about it, and nodded.

"Kin ya split a bullet on a axe blade?" His eyes glittered. She wondered if he was trying to trick her.

"I would like to practice that before I tried it in public," she replied, honestly.

"Kin ya split a playin' card edge-on?" She stared at him; that sounded impossible. He smirked. "Annie Oakley kin. Every time."

Well, if the famed sharpshooter could do it without the aid of sylphs, surely *she* could manage it with magical help! "I will try that too—in practice," she promised. He laughed.

"We kin work in whatever ye manage t'get up, jest let me know when ye wanta change yer act. Cap'n wants ta know what ya wanna call yerself. He says it cain't have no more letters'n Ado Ellie," Ned continued. "We're repaintin' her sign fer ya."

She stroked Lebkuchen's neck while she mulled that over. "Ellie" was not all that far from "Giselle," so it would make sense to keep that part of the name. She considered the names she knew from Karl May's books. "What about *Rio Ellie?*" she asked.

"That'll do!" Ned crowed, and scuttled off, his bowlegs making his gait very comical.

By the time she had finished her trick-shot routine, she was feeling as if she had all this business of being on display well in hand.

But then came Captain Cody's idea—target-shooting at the gallop with handguns. Initially, she hadn't objected; she'd seen how easily Cody and the other men handled their revolvers when they were firing blank cartridges during the battles with the Indians and the bandits.

But now that she was faced with the task, she was liking the idea less and less. She mounted Lebkuchen, Ned handed her the weapon, and that decided her. The only "pistol" she had ever shot wasn't hers, and it wasn't anything like the Colt "Peacemaker" revolvers. They were extremely heavy. And the moment she took one in her hand, she knew that even with the sylph's help, if she tried to shoot one from the back of a galloping horse, she'd probably injure or even kill someone.

"No," she said, firmly, handing the revolver back to Ned and getting off Lebkuchen.

Cody looked down at her from atop Lightning. "No?" he echoed, his moustache drooping with sudden disappointment.

"Not merely *no*," she repeated. *"Absolutely* not. Lebkuchen is not accustomed to having me shoot from her back. *I* have never shot from a walking horse, much less a galloping one. I've never shot a revolver in my life, and if I try this insanity, someone will end up with a bullet in him—or her. I do not think that bleeding customers will encourage more ticket sales."

Cody sighed theatrically. "Ado Ellie did—" he began, and was interrupted by someone from the company.

"You been eatin' loco-weed!" called a little bantam of a man in a cowboy's outfit. "Ado Ellie never did no such thing, an' yer a consarned liar, Cody Lee!" This was followed by jeers and a great many rude noises from some of the others in the crowd. Little Fred pushed himself to the front and stood just under Lightning's nose, shaking his finger at the star of the show.

"Jest because you got your name plastered all over this here show, don't you think you kin push this liddle gal inter somethin' she thinks she cain't do jest cause ye wanta prove you're better'n her with a Colt!" The Captain's moustache drooped further. Giselle sensed that Fred had hit on the *real* reason why Captain Cody had tried to get her to do something that would likely prove dangerous. His masculine pride had been touched, because she *was* better than he with a rifle. He wanted to prove he was as good a shot or better with the revolvers.

Well, he could *have* his victory!

"I wasn't born in the saddle, and I'll not risk anyone's safety on my aim with a revolver," she repeated firmly. "Besides, as Fred pointed out, it is your face and name that are the basis of this show; your expertise should be the last turn the audience sees before the closing number." And with that, she led Lebkuchen out of the arena, leaving Cody with no alternative but to run through his mounted trick-shots.

It wasn't as if he actually *needed* her as part of this turn! He combined his trick-riding with extremely accurate target shots, shooting while hanging from positions all over his poor horse. "I don't know how he gets Lightning to put up with that," she remarked to Lebkuchen, as he hung off the patient horse's neck while shooting. "He truly *is* a 'Wonder Horse.' It's a wonder he doesn't throw the Captain right off!"

Lebkuchen snorted, as if in total agreement, then it was time for her to mount up for the concluding Grand Parade. As she passed through the tent flaps and turned aside, Ned seized Lebkuchen's reins. "We all reckon yer fit fer the show," he said, flatly. "I'm a gonna send Carmelita t'help ye sort out yer costumes an' get 'em set up here fer changin'." He cackled. "Time t'start earnin' yer keep!"

Her heart was pounding and her mouth was as dry as the desert sands as she lined up with the others for the Grand Parade. She didn't feel *anything* like ready! It was one thing to perform in front of people who—truth be told—had not expected more of her than of their previous girl sharpshooter. It was *quite* something else to perform in front of a potentially critical audience, who were expecting . . . well . . . were expecting something like a Karl May hero!

But she had no choice. Although Ned had spoken as if in jest, she could read behind his words that he was quite serious. She was getting quite a fine bit of money, and it was his estimation that she'd better start earning it *now*.

The outfit she was wearing for the Grand Parade and her first turn was rather like the female version of Ned's own buckskin suit: fringed gold-colored leather ornamented with round silver buckles. Lebkuchen was wearing a different sort of saddle than the one that both of them were used to; it had a very high pommel, with something called a "saddle horn" that the cowboys used during their roping exercises, and was much larger and stiffer than the little riding saddle she used. Lebkuchen had laid her ears back on being presented with this thing, and had snorted at the additional weight, but seemed to have adjusted to it.

Somehow, Karl May had never mentioned these saddles in his books, even though they were wildly unlike a German saddle, and as much as he liked to describe things in prose, one would think he would have at least mentioned them! She was beginning to wonder if he had *ever* set foot in the West at all!

But all that went quite out of her head as the music began on the other side of the canvas. This was the music she remembered from watching the show, the brazen, bellowing, exciting stuff that made a thrill run down her back, not the lazy tootling of the rehearsal.

Ahead of her, Captain Cody's horse Lightning pranced in place and tossed his head, impatient for his gallop into the arena. Cody sat straighter in his saddle and seemed to somehow grow taller and more impressive than he had been a moment before. And then one of the curtains was pulled aside just enough for a single rider, and Lightning leapt through the opening.

Then the curtain was pulled aside again, and the color guard— the quartet of Indians and cowboys that carried in the flags—surged across the magic threshold.

And then, it was her turn.

She sat frozen as the curtain was pulled aside, suddenly too terrified to move—

She heard a *slap* behind her, and Lebkuchen bolted under the
raised curtain, propelling both of them out into the arena. And she
heard Kellermann call out through his megaphone. *"Ladies and gentlemen, the most beautiful sharpshooter on the prairie, the lovely, and
deadly, Rio Ellie!"*

Somehow she managed to bring Lebkuchen to a halt exactly
where she was supposed to, in the middle of the arena. Somehow
she managed to bow gravely to either side of her. And somehow she
managed to get Lebkuchen moving again, to the end of the arena,
and then around to the left, lifting her hand to wave at the audience
on that side, as Texas Tom rode out to the tumult of his own applause. Her chest felt tight, her face felt flushed, and the tent seemed
utterly airless—and yet, as the assembled company rode back out
again, she couldn't *wait* for her turn to ride back in again.

6

"AND there are no mountains in Texas?"

Determined to reconcile what she knew of Indians and frontiersmen from Karl May's books with what she had seen in her dreams the night that Leading Fox and she exchanged languages, Giselle had cornered Captain Cody.

They were about to pull up the tents and move on tomorrow, having, in Kellermann's opinion, extracted all the money from the local economy that they were likely to. Their next engagement was for next week; they would have plenty of time to travel the three-days' journey and practice on the way.

Giselle went out of her way to find Cody after the second show to cross-examine him. He invited her to a glass of beer in the outer room of his spacious tent, which served as a species of drawing room.

This close questioning was under the guise of being able to adequately counterfeit being a girl who could properly be called "Rio Ellie," but the fact was, she already knew it didn't matter what she told Austrians and Germans. If what she told them matched Karl May, they would go away happy.

No, this was purely for herself, because she was determined to know the truth.

The Captain had supplied her with beer, drawn from the little barrel of it he kept in this "drawing room," and made sure the tent flaps were tied open for the evening breeze. And there *was* an evening breeze, not too cold, not too damp, supplied thanks to Giselle's powers. An oil lantern fastened at the peak of the roof provided decent illumination, and out in the camp, the sounds of people packing up their belongings for the move tomorrow made an undercurrent to their conversation.

As they sat side by side in tolerably comfortable folding chairs of clever design, Cody scratched his head and settled back against the canvas of his chair. "Mountains in Texas? Not the sorta thing y'all call a mountain, no," he admitted. "They're all rock an' brush, there ain't no forest on 'em. Like if you scoured yer mountains here bare, down to the valley, an' jest scattered bushes over 'em. It's mostly desert where the mountains is."

If it had not been for those hectic visions, she would not have had an idea of what he was talking about. But she did. Even as he described those mountains, they rose, hazy, sunbaked, in her memory. She did not have to ask him about the lush forests so picturesquely described by May; she already knew they were a lie. She thought *kahuraaru* in Pawnee and what rose in her mind was not the deep greens, mosses, tender plants and towering trees of her own Black Forest, but trees scarcely taller than a good, two-story German cottage, deciduous trees of a green-brown or yellow-brown color with sparse foliage and small leaves, or evergreens of some sort that were no taller. And this was not the emerald lushness of *her* forest, These trees were widely separated, with parched and rocky ground covered with thin, dry grasses in between.

"And pueblos?" she demanded, for Winnetou's Apache people lived in a pueblo, very distinctly described to the point where, if she had had the talent, she could have painted it; a stone city of several stories, built against and part of a cliff. "Are there tall stone pueblos, cliff-dwellings, four and five stories tall in Texas?"

Cody looked at her as if he thought she had gone mad. Even his moustache conveyed his doubt. "Ain't *nothin'* like that in Texas," he averred. "Ye cain't build against a cliff, it's all clay an' sandstone an' shale, an' it'll crumble—"

And in her mind's eye, she could see that, of course, as those hazy mountains became clearer in her mind. The slopes of rock and gravel beneath any vertical surfaces only showed that those surfaces were unstable, and anyone building against them would be insane.

"Th'only pueblos I know of in Texas are made of mudbrick," Cody continued. "They ain't but one floor tall. Be crazy to build 'em any taller. I heerd there's stone ones off t'the West, but I ain't seen 'em. Why're you askin' me this hokum, anyway?"

"Because . . . because of a book-writer," she admitted, finally, and clumsily tried to explain the "Old Shatterhand and Winnetou" books to Cody, and how virtually everything that *most* people in Austria and Germany knew of the West and Indians and the frontier came from those books, and those about "Old Surehand" and "Old Fire-hand." She had to give Captain Cody a great deal of credit. He didn't laugh. And he didn't interrupt her. Although several times it looked to her as if he wanted to explode. His moustache fairly took on a life of its own.

When she finished, he let out a long, exasperated sigh. "Well," he said, finally, "Bein' as I ain't read these-here books meself, all I kin say is that Mister May of your'n ain't set foot west of the Mississippi for sure, and I'd lay good money he ain't never been in the United States a'tall. Seems t'me like he got hisself a buncha books by fellers that *had,* an' he studied 'em good and hard, but there was a buncha stuff they either left out or figgered people already knowed, an' that there is where he falls all over hisself makin' mistakes. Like, I kin tell you from personal experience, Apaches of whatever stripe ain't never been farmers and ain't never gonna be, they ain't never lived in pueblos, an' they ain't real fond of the *Dineh,* which is to say the Navaho, and the Navaho ain't real fond of them. In fact, there ain't no tribe whatsoever that's fond of the Apache, 'cept another Apache, bein' as they live by huntin' an' raidin'. The ideer an *Apache chief'*d be any kinda peacemaker 'mongst t'other tribes is enough t'make a cat laugh. An' sure, there's what y'all'd call a real forest or two in Texas, but they ain't a day or two's ride away from the mountains, it's more like weeks, an' they're over toward Loosiana. And there ain't never been no carbine ever shot 25 bullets without reloadin'. Only thing close is the Henry Rifle, an' thet's sixteen iff'n you got one in the chamber. But—" he continued, holding up his hand to keep her from speaking "—here's the thing. We ain't sellin' the gold. We're sellin' the treasure-map."

She knitted her brows in consternation. "I have no idea what you're talking about," she said, hesitantly.

"We ain't here t'edumacate nobody," he explained. "Back home, you bet we gotta be careful. There's plenty of people that'd call us phonies in the papers if we got it wrong. Here, well, what you jest tol' me is thet what people *know* is what they read in this May feller's books. It ain't our place t'tell 'em they're wrong. We don' need t'sell 'em gen-u-wine gold, we jest sell 'em a treasure map they ain't never gonna foller, an' it don't matter if thet map's a Lost Dutchman. So, I reckon you an' Kellermann kin go right on tellin' 'em what they wanta hear, an' that'll be all right. An' I'll pass word on thet if any of us tell 'em somethin' thet don't agree with what they think they know, not to argue 'bout it, jest say somethin' like, 'Oh, well, thet's 'cause we're from *Wyomin',* or *Colorado,* an' thet's what it's like *there.*' You jest pick me out a couple'a places this May feller never wrote 'bout, an' thet'll do."

She must have looked crestfallen—and she certainly felt somewhat crushed to have discovered that this idolized writer had betrayed her faith in his words. Here, all these years, she had been dreaming about Old Shatterhand and Winnetou, and those sweeping landscapes through which they traveled, and now to discover it was all a lie—she could scarcely bring herself to answer Cody.

And he looked sharply at her, then reached for her hand. "See here, *liebchen,*" he said, squeezing her hand comfortingly. "Don't go thinkin' just 'cause he made it all up, thet means them stories ain't no good! Hellfire, people been makin' stories up fer as long as they been people t'hear 'em! It ain't whether th' *stories* is true, doncha see?"

"No," she said, choking back a sudden sob, "I *don't* see!"

He patted her hand, his moustache drooping with distress.

"Stories ain't about the feller what wrote 'em, even if he pertends they are. They don' even hev t'be true to be right! Stories are 'bout what they make *you* feel. If'n they make *you* feel good, an' make y'all wanta be brave, an' good, an' do what's right, *thet's* the important thing!" He suddenly seemed to realize he was holding her hand, and let it go with a laugh. "Think 'bout that there *Odyssey!* Hunnerds an' hunnerds of years, people been listenin' to it, an' readin' it, an dreamin' bout it, people make up their minds what a hero is, 'cause of it! An' there ain't a word of truth in it! Pshaw! You think there ever was them one-eyed giants, or men thet was part horse, or big brass stachoos what fight? 'Course not! It's all made up! But thet don't matter, not one particle! So what if'n this May feller made it all up? Ain't that what storytellers is supposed t' do? He jest made up a liddle more'n y'all thought he did, makin' out like *he* did all thet stuff. Thet's all right. Reckon ol' Homer made out like he was right there an' heerd it all firsthand too."

She nodded, slowly.

"Give him this fer bein' honest. He tried t'find out stuff best as he could. An' it weren't like he were makin' all thet up for a guidebook, where he *could* git people in trouble with what he wrote." Cody leaned back, evidently seeing that he was convincing her, and took a long pull on his beer. "There you go. Jest go right on readin' an' likin' the books. You wanta look at a fine *man* what's a Injun, you don't haveta look no further'n Fox an' his boys. An you was disposed t'like 'im on account of that there Winnetou. So ain't no shame in still likin' them books. I'm mighty partial t'Mister Verne an' Mister Twain, an' there ain't a *word* of truth in thet, neither, an Mister Twain right often makes out like he was there!"

She sighed. What Cody said made a great deal of sense. The stories were still *good* stories; the characters were fine people, people she wished she knew! They just weren't . . . true.

And Cody was right. They didn't have to be true to be good.

But that brought up something else. "I overheard you saying

something to Kellermann . . ." she ventured. "About not understanding why there were so few people who came to the show a second time."

Cody blinked at her, and pushed his hat back on his head. "Huh. Well, ayup. Thet's got me puzzled. We got good crowds first couple'a days, then arter thet, it jest peters out. Thet didn' happen in England, nor in Italy, same people'd turn up two, three times. We got outa France purdy quick, seems they jest didn't cotton t'Wild West shows, an' it ain't jest us, Buffalo Bill had th' same problem."

"Well . . . I think it is because of Karl May," she said, hesitantly. "It is because in Karl May's books, the Indians are heroes. They are noble people, who only fight because their land is being taken. And in your show, they are savage bandits. You just told me not to contradict what people think because of Karl May, but that is what the show itself is doing."

Cody stared at her. He opened his mouth, closed it, opened it again, closed it again, and stared at her some more. His moustache bristled with alarm before it settled down again.

"All right," he said, finally. "Our job ain't t'edumacate people, like I said. Our job's t'make money. So . . ." Now it was his turn to furrow his brow and sit in silence, thinking. "I reckon . . ." he said, slowly, sounding as if he was thinking out loud. "I reckon we gotta change th' show. Like, 'stead of th' Injuns attackin' th' settlers . . . the bandits could."

He cocked an eyebrow at her, inviting her comment.

"The Indians could rescue them," she offered. "And instead of starting that off with the war dance, perhaps they could all become friends and have some other sort of dance?"

He shook his head. "No, we need th' war dance, but th' war dance kin be 'cause they're chasin' the bandits off. An' the settlers kin be goin' t' Californy, steada Texas."

"So they could have a peace pipe ceremony?" she suggested. "Karl May thinks pipe ceremonies are very important. I think everyone will want to see one."

"'E got thet right, at least," Cody mumbled. He drank the rest of his beer. "Lessee . . . I wish't we had more buffalo. We could hev a buffalo hunt. But them critters is hard 'nuff to control as 'tis, an' I wouldn' wanta risk runnin' 'em on account of they might take a notion t'go through the barreecade inter th' stands, an' anyway, there ain't 'nuff of them t'make a good show. The ones we got was trained from calves, an' they're still no picnic t'handle, but at least they kin be controlled pretty reliable."

He was rambling. She did her best to get him back on the subject. "Well, Leading Fox is an Air Master, why don't he and I have a shooting contest?" she suggested. "Or . . . you know . . ."

It was an audacious idea. And if she had not trusted Fox and his control of *his* Elementals, she would not have suggested it.

". . . he could do knife and perhaps tomahawk tricks with me as his target." She began to warm to this idea, as Cody's eyes widened in alarm and his moustache practically stood up by itself. "He could make my outline in arrows or knives. He could split an apple on the top of my head with an arrow or a tomahawk! I could hold things for him to shoot! He could shoot a cigarette out of my mouth!"

Cody stared at her in utter disbelief. "You . . . you'd let him do thet?" he gaped.

"He is an Air Master. He cannot miss as long as his Elementals *and* mine are making sure all is well," she pointed out. She grew even more enthusiastic. "We could say we are blood brothers! That is very important in the Winnetou books, and in fact, we are, in a way. We could say that I trust his aim because of that!"

"An . . . you think people'd go fer thet?" He shook his head. "If'n this was back home, people'd hev my hide fer riskin' your'n that way, with a Injun."

"It would make people come back again and again," she said, firmly, sure of her own ground. "But . . . we must ask Fox first. If he is against this, then we won't do it. But you need to find a way to make the Indians heroes all through the show if you wish to make more money."

"I'll think on it." He shook his head. "It's a furrin' way t' think."

"You're *in* a 'furrin' country," she pointed out.

All he could do was shrug, thank her, and wish her goodnight.

There were a good three days of travel by horse between Schopfheim and their next destination of Silberbrucke. Since no inn could possibly hold all of them, they had already planned on camping, making a more abbreviated camp than they did for the shows. They also planned on making the trip leisurely, to spare the buffalo, and to allow them to camp early enough to get in some practice sessions. Giselle drove her little wagon-home, sitting in the front door to do so, very grateful that all she would have to do would be to unharness and feed the horses and tether them to the wagon overnight. She did not envy those who had tents. Their quarters might be more spacious than hers, but it came at a cost of inconvenience—though they all did seem to be able to pull up camp quickly, so probably they could make camp just as quickly. Or perhaps they did not intend to pitch the tents at all. According to Karl May, frontiersmen often just laid down on a horse blanket with a saddle for a pillow and—

And perhaps she needed to *stop* thinking about what Karl May said about Americans, and just keep her eyes open to what they actually did.

Lebkuchen was harnessed in a team with a Grand Quadrille horse, whose name was Polly. Lebkuchen had been in harness before, of course, but never beside another. She didn't like it, but Polly was not inclined to take her nonsense, and before they had gone many miles, Lebkuchen had settled into grudging acceptance of the situation.

The entire company settled into a steady pace down the narrow country road—a pace, she suspected, that was far more pleasant for them, here, beneath the towering trees of the Black Forest, than it would have been back home. And this time, instead of referring to Karl May, she was comparing the road they were traveling with those glimpses of the West she had gotten from Fox's language lessons.

Here there was cooling shade, there—there was none. The road had seen enough rain that it was not dusty, but neither was it muddy—there, dust would have risen beneath the hooves of the foremost in the party to choke all of those who came behind. And the sun would have scorched down on them, punishing them from daybreak to sundown.

Plus, she could encourage light breezes all along the road, just enough to keep the flies off the beasts and freshen the travelers. Without an Air Master in attendance, they would have had no such comfort. Perhaps that was why everyone seemed so cheerful.

As they moved along, whenever they passed a farm, children and sometimes all the adults would drop whatever they were doing and run to the roadside to gape at them. Cody encouraged the entire troupe to smile and wave, and he would have Lightning do a few simple tricks, or Texas Tom would rope a fencepost or twirl his lariat above his head. Then Kellermann would hand the father, or at least the oldest boy, one of their handbills. "Y'never kin tell," Cody said, when she asked him about this. "They might decide t' pack up an' come t'the town to see th' show."

About midmorning, Leading Fox, who had been traveling at the front with the Captain, came trotting back along the line of wagons and beasts. He turned his handsome spotted horse when he came to her *vardo,* and rode along beside her.

"Cody tells me you have given him revelations that cause him some concern, and make him think he will need to change the show, somewhat." The Indian's tone was more amused than anything else, so she nodded to him.

"I would like to hear these revelations for myself." He waited, clearly prepared to wait for as long as it took for her to tell him. So, once again, she found herself explaining the difference in how *her* people viewed the American frontier and especially its Indians, and how all this was due to the overarching influence of a writer who probably hadn't *ever* been as near to a single real Indian as she was now, much less been the actual hero of the Western escapades he had written about so voluminously, and with such apparent authority.

When she finished, Leading Fox rode beside her in silence for a long while. She didn't dare say anything. All those things Karl May had said about Indians . . . what if he was angry? What if he was insulted? What if—

Beneath the well-worn leather of his buckskin shirt, his shoulders were shaking. After a moment, she realized he was laughing, silently. Finally he spoke.

"Apache . . . living in a pueblo! The Mescaleros friends with the *Dineh!* Apache *farming!"* His shoulders continued to shake. "And this is all only in the first book, you say! And there are many more such . . . *books* . . ." He finally calmed himself, but it was clear he was greatly amused. "Well, that does explain why your countrymen seemed to regard me as an object almost of veneration—and without ever realizing I am a Medicine Chief. I should like to meet this Karl May of yours one day. Although I fear he would not like to meet me. It would not be pleasant for him to have his illusions exploded."

She opened her mouth to object, but Leading Fox raised his hand.

"No, I completely agree with the Captain that we should not explode these illusions. We should work within them. My tribesmen and I came over the great water in order to make a great deal of the white man's money. The best way that we can do this in your land is to give your people what they *wish* to see. Cody is using our time between stops to think this over, and how he can change the show to match these expectations without changing what we actually perform all that much." Fox smiled slightly as she heaved a sigh of relief. "I will tell you, it will improve *our* spirits, my tribesmen and I, to be transformed into heroes, and I do not think the others will care once Cody puts it to them that we stand to make much more money."

"I . . . I thought Indians didn't care about money . . ." she said, hesitantly. "I don't mean to . . ."

Fox's raised eyebrow caused her to stop before she said anything else. "Under most circumstances you would be correct. But my people, my little tribe, have been studying you whites for some time, working for you and among you. The Pawnee have been Scouts for the Union Army for many years now, partly because the Union Army fought the Cheyenne, the Arapaho and the Sioux, who were our enemies. Our reservation lands are poor. We have observed that time and time again, when something that a white man wants is found on our reservation lands, we are pushed to poorer lands yet. The only thing that the white man respects is a deed of land bought with money." Leading Fox shrugged, slightly. "So, now in Cody we have a white friend who will buy land for us, and my tribe, at least, will never be pushed out again. If a white man tries to take it from us, we will go to the white man's court, and show our paper, and he will go away unsatisfied. We may not have the breadth of land that we once were able to roam across freely, but we will have good land, land we can farm, land that will feed us. We will have to give over hunting the buffalo in favor of keeping cattle, yet that is a small price to pay for being free. But for that—"

"You need money!" she exclaimed.

"Even so," he replied, with a nod. "In the Scouts, we learned to fight with the white man's weapons. So we shall do so again, and the weapon is money. My tribe, at least. Perhaps, in time, we will seem to vanish into the white man's landscape, as we vanished into our own, and he will take no heed of us, and we will go about our living in peace."

It seemed horribly unfair that Leading Fox and his people were being forced to work so far from home in order to buy back what *should* have been theirs by right. But as Giselle was sadly aware, there were many, many things that were horribly unfair. At least Fox and his tribe had a plan, and as far as she could tell, it was one that had a good chance of success, as long as they could all make this show prosper.

"Now, Cody thinks, and I think, that some, indeed, many, of your ideas have merit. But they are scattered and unconnected as leaves before the wind," Fox went on. "So we will take your ideas and give them substance and form. Cody is good at this. He would not have been able to save what is left of the show if he were not. He intends to hold a meeting tonight when we are camped, to explain what he has thought out. Once he makes the others understand why this

must be, he will wait to see if they have an idea or two. He will probably call upon you to explain this writer to the others. But do not be
surprised or unhappy if he claims your ideas as his own. You are new
to the company; he has their confidence. You are a girl, he is a man,
who has commanded. What comes from your mouth might be objected to. What comes from his will be heeded." Again Fox shrugged.
"It is what it is."

Well . . . she *was* surprised, and a little hurt, and rather disappointed to hear that. It made her feel a bit cheated.

But she swallowed her disappointment, and nodded, because Fox
was also right, and not just because she was new to the company, but
because, as he had pointed out, she was a girl. She didn't *like* it, not
a bit . . . but it was what it was.

Kellermann, riding ahead, had found a farmer who was willing to let
the show camp in his pasture for the privilege of having his family
come and gawk. The stolid little family certainly got enough to make
their eyes go very round, as Cody had ordered that as many of the
company as were inclined should get some practice in before sunset.
The extensive family marveled at the bison from a safe distance, exclaimed over the longhorn cattle, watched her as she began trying to
cut a playing card in half with a single shot, admired Texas Tom's rope
tricks, fed Lightning the Wonder Horse carrots until he was likely to
become flatulent, and nearly went out of their minds with excitement
over Leading Fox and his small band. Eavesdropping on them, it became clear that the entire family was composed of Karl May readers.
Their cup of joy overflowed when Fox spoke to them in slow, extremely dignified German, answering their questions selectively.

Quite selectively, Giselle noticed. Fox carefully avoided mentioning anything that would contradict what *she* had told him about Karl
May's writing. She wondered very much why it never occurred to
them to question that an Indian spoke perfect German, but then
again, given that Winnetou apparently spoke perfect German in the

books, perhaps it never occurred to them that Indians normally did not. . . .

Finally, just after sunset, Captain Cody shooed them gently off and gathered everyone under the mess tent for dinner and the meeting. Word had been spread of this meeting, and it was clear people were curious, and perhaps a little apprehensive.

Perhaps because the *last* such meeting he'd called had been to announce that their manager had absconded with all the money.

Lanterns on every table gave plenty of light, and it took remarkably little time for the company to sort themselves out and get seated. Once everyone was served, Cody stood up, and got instant silence. He looked around, his demeanor relaxed, and smiled. "First off, lemme tell y'all this ain't bad news."

A wave of relief spread across the tent. Spoons and forks that had been held in tense hands now clicked against tin plates. If Cody was going to talk, that was all well and good, but so far as his troupe was concerned, it was no reason to refrain from eating, when you could listen and eat at the same time.

"So, here's what I done figgered out. Now, you all know Miz Ellie's from these here parts, and I was askin' her 'bout how folks felt 'bout our show an' all, an' she commenced to tellin' me 'bout a writer feller in Germany who, well, from ever'thin' she an' Kellermann says, he's just about Twain, Dickens, Mister Alger, an' Shakespeare all rolled up inter one. An' he mostly writes 'bout our parts back home."

Now she saw he clearly had the attention of everyone in the tent. They didn't stop eating, but their eyes were fixed on him, intrigued.

"Seems like 'bout everybody buys his books and reads 'em. Herr Bauer an' his herd, on this here farm? Yeah, ev' one of them, iff'n ye can reckon that! Shoot that's like—like our boy Johnny Dermot *an'* alla his family back home gettin' thesselves every consarn one of Twain's books soon as one comes out an' settin' down ev' night t'read one over supper!"

They all laughed at that as Johnny blushed, but grinned, since it was common knowledge that the cowhand could barely write his name. Still she could tell that made an impression on them all.

"So that's why folks hereabouts are likin' us way better'n the Frenchies did," Cody went on. "But there's jest one problem. This Mister May feller, the one that wrote all them books . . . he ain't never been to the West. Hellfire, he ain't never been to 'Merica. So he . . . kinda got a lotta stuff wrong." Now Cody nodded at her. "So, tell 'em 'bout these books, Ellie."

She stood up, all eyes on her, and licked dry lips. "The books that people like best are about a German, who is supposed to be May himself, and an Apache chief named Winnetou," she began. And choosing her words carefully, she began telling them the narratives of the books that she had read.

Her audience began with raised eyebrows.

The explanation ended with howls of laughter on the part of the others, and with herself a bright scarlet. Cody motioned for her to sit down, and she did so in mingled embarrassment and anger. *If I'd thought he was going to make a laughingstock out of me—*

Her anger smoldered as Cody waited patiently for the laughter to die away. At that moment, if it had not been for Fox putting a restraining hand on her shoulder, she would have gotten up and stalked out of the tent . . . possibly even out of the show altogether.

"All right, settle down," Cody said as the last of the laughter faded, casting her a slightly apologetic look. "I might could remind some of y'all 'bout the times *you* stuck yer feet in it right up to the knee, when we got over t'England now . . . like when you got drunk an' shot up that pub in Manchester, Tom, an' we had t'bail y'all out . . . or when Jem mistook that fancy anteeky Chinee pot fer a spittoon." Cody's eyes were scanning the entire tent, and there were several people who tried to avoid his gaze, wearing expressions of chagrin. "Right then. Iffen y'all was actually *listenin'* t'what Miz Ellie was sayin', 'steada laughin', y'all mighta noticed somethin'. Seems like when the folks hereabouts read them stories, there's one thing that stands right out. Injuns is the *heroes.*"

Stunned silence fell, a silence so absolute that the lowing of a cow from the next field over sounded so unnaturally loud that Giselle winced. Glancing around her, she could see her fellow showmen in various levels of shock and disbelief. And it looked as if some of them were about to open their mouths and—say *something*.

But Cody did not give them that chance.

"And *that* is why almost nobody comes back a second time to our show!" Cody said, with authority. "It'd be like us goin' t'the meller-drama, an' instead of the hero winnin', it's the villain what gets the girl, the gold, an' ever'thin'! We wouldn't be comin' back a second time if that happened, right?"

That stopped those who'd been about to speak up dead in their tracks. Giselle actually saw it happen. First, the sudden jolt. Then, the mouths opening, then closing again as they digested what Cody had just said.

Cody began walking back and forth across the little space in front of the tables, his voice turning persuasive. "So I said t'myself . . . Cody Lee, jest what *are* we over here fer? T'make money, that's what! An' what d'we do t'make money? Well, it's purty damn clear we *ain't* gonna make money by showin' 'em somethin' they don't cotton to!" He paused to let that sink in. Eventually, he got nods. Some more reluctant than others, but nods all the same.

"So, this's what we're gonna have t'do. Same turns, but mebbe in a different order, an' this time, the Injuns gotta be heroes." He stopped pacing and crossed his arms over his chest, setting his weight back on his heels. "Ain't like that's completely outa the question. Pawnee like Fox been Scouts wit' the Cavalry forever, seems like. So, I figgered I'd set my ideers up, an' y'all tell me iffin it ain't gonna work, an' how we kin make it work." He nodded sagely. "An' I thought a good place ter start would be with the attack on th' settlers."

Giselle kept her eyes on her food, and as the attention of the rest of the troupe left her, and the heat in her face began to fade, but the formerly savory stew tasted of chagrin now. "They could do with learning manners," Leading Fox said quietly in Pawnee. "But they mean no harm."

She shrugged a little, and thought about some of the comments she'd overheard her countrymen making about the "barbaric fron-tiersmen."

"They were not laughing at me," she admitted. "They were laughing at what the writer said."

"Which is absurd," Leading Fox pointed out.

". . . well . . . yes," she admitted. She ate a few more bites, then listened to what the Captain was saying with more than half an ear.

And she had to admit that he had given all of this a great deal of thought. *Then again, he does know these people very well.*

They certainly were a *contentious* lot, however. Every single one of them seemed to have an opinion, every single one of them wanted to voice that opinion, and every single one of them thought his opinion, however unconsidered, was *worthy* of being heard. She got tired of it all long before it was over, but not before Leading Fox had silently gotten up and left. When it became clear that far too many of the troupe found arguing to be entertaining, she gave up as well. If some of her fellow players wanted to waste time when they could be sleeping in favor of listening to their own voices, well . . . that was one Americanism she was not inclined to emulate!

7

SILBERBRUCKE was a handsome town, a little bigger than Schopfheim. The narrow river that gave it its name neatly bisected the
place, with three handsome stone bridges crossing it. They camped
beside the river and set up the show in the river meadow on the opposite side of town from where they had entered. Kellermann had
ridden ahead and plastered the place with handbills, and by the time
the cavalcade had reached it, there were people lined up on both
sides of the road to see them enter.

Anticipating this, Cody had ordered that they all don show costumes that day, so Giselle was in her fringed leather leggings, skirt
and shirt, with a red neckerchief and a broad-brimmed leather hat.
Someone else was driving her wagon, which had been pulled to the
campsite ahead by two of the Quadrille horses, while she rode Lebkuchen. Her mare was sporting that odd American saddle with rifle
sheathes at either knee, complete with rifles.

Cody had assembled them in a particular riding order as well. He
led, of course, but per the plan to make the Indians as prominent as
any of the white men, directly after him came Leading Fox and
Giselle riding side by side, followed by the rest of the Pawnee. An

abbreviated version of the band marched behind them, playing a song she now knew to be "The Yellow Rose of Texas." It certainly was lively, and the people of the Schwarzwald loved brass bands. As they passed between the lines of eager spectators, horses seemingly nodding their heads in time to the music, the townsfolk cheered and clapped along.

Fox stared stoically ahead, which matched what the readers of Karl May expected out of an Indian, but Giselle smiled and nodded and waved to either side of her, all the way to their camping grounds. The advance crew had already performed the duty of setting up the canvas "wall" around what would be the show grounds, keeping those who had not paid out. The show parade trooped in through the entrance, passed by the ticket booth, and made their way around the right side of the show tent to where the camps had been set up.

This meadow was not as big as the one at Schopfheim, so the canvas wall had been set up to enclose some of the trees. Giselle found her wagon set up and waiting underneath a fine old oak, with a little chair and table set out at the base of it. By this, she gathered that she was now to be part of the "tour of the camps," and would be expected to be sitting there, willing to make conversation and doing something appropriate to her role.

Well, I can certainly clean my guns.

She had left Lebkuchen at the stabling tent for the show horses; now she went to see if Cody was at his own tent. The camps had been set up exactly the same way they had been at Schopfheim, with slight adjustments for the trees, so she had no trouble whatsoever finding him.

He was answering questions and directing some of the others, and she gathered as she listened to him that there *would* be an afternoon and evening show, she should stay in her show costume, and that a cold lunch was already waiting in the mess tent. Since that answered every question she had, she trotted to the mess tent to get her hands on food; breakfast had been at the crack of dawn, and she was starving.

Luncheon apparently consisted of slapping cold cuts of smoked or cooked meat between slices of bread and the ubiquitous coffee, which it appeared Americans lived on. The local butchers who must have supplied this meat had helpfully included pots of horseradish, pickles, and sauerkraut. The Americans did not appear to know what to do with these things—other than the pickles, which they were devouring with great relish. She was perfectly happy to heap sauerkraut on her sliced roast pork. Perhaps the others would learn from her example.

It was . . . strange . . . still strange . . . to think where she had been a mere month ago, and where she was now. If anyone had predicted this, she would have laughed first, then wondered if such hallucinations were dangerous.

People were not actually hurrying over their meal, so she took her cue from them, taking her time to enjoy something that actually tasted like the food she was used to.

She was not the earliest in the lineup for the Grand Parade; Captain Cody was already in place when she arrived, as were all the Pawnee and pseudo-Pawnee. For the first time since she had joined the show, the Pawnee were . . . smiling.

She didn't blame them. In her opinion, they finally had something to smile about. She was feeling as nervous as the day of her first performance; what if she had been wrong about all this? Oh, of course, the show could go back to the old way—but Captain Cody would never completely trust anything she had to say again.

Maybe it's not such a bad thing after all, having the Captain take credit for all of my ideas. If this fails, he'll be the one taking the blame for the failure, and not me . . .

The rest lined up; the formation of the Grand Parade was the same, the music was the same, and yet, there was a sense of a bit of nervousness. This wasn't the same show. This was a new show, and in the opinion of some who still were not convinced by either her explanation or the Captain's, a very risky show.

But there was no time for second thoughts. The band began Captain Cody's entrance music, the curtains parted, and the Captain galloped in. He did his salute to the crowd, came out again, and the Parade began.

And it was *not* her imagination: although the color-guard maintained their fierce and solemn expressions—properly, really, since after all they were carrying the two national flags and the sacred standards with the eagle feathers on them—the rest of the Pawnee, instead of looking straight ahead, waved and nodded soberly to the crowd. And the spectators nearly went insane at being acknowledged by the Indians. Some of the boys in the audience even dared to attempt what they thought were war whoops. By the time they all left the arena, she was feeling more confident.

Captain Cody was the first turn, of course. She was the second, doing her non-trick shooting, and waited patiently for him to ride back out. She forced herself to concentrate on her targets; she really, really needed to be able to do this with her own skills and powers, because the sylphs, while well-meaning, were not reliable. The newer rifles helped immensely, of course, as did the fact that she was shooting inside a great tent, so there was very little windage to speak of. She finished the last of her targets, mounted Lebkuchen, and made a circuit of the arena, accepting the applause with smiles and waves.

Once outside, she dismounted and drank thirstily from the barrel and dipper left at the entrance. She felt drained, more drained than after her first performance!

"Nervous?" She looked behind her. Cody was sitting at ease in Lightning's saddle.

"I am," she admitted.

"Don' be," he advised. "You was dead right. I heerd how them folks shined right up t'the Injuns. Jes' wait'll they come on as heroes." He nodded. "Now you better run'n' get inter yer next costume."

Cody was right; now came the Cowboy Camp and the "cattle stampede," during which the cowboys got to show their riding, roping and "bulldogging" expertise. Then the Grand Quadrille, and she really needed to be in her dress and on her horse well before time for that. So far, there was nothing changed in the show except the order of the turns, but that was going to change.

The new arrangements meant that she had to wear her Indian dress *under* the Quadrille dress, which took some . . . arrangement.

And she had to wear her black Indian wig as well, with the wig braids hastily pinned up. She was in place before the cowboys had finished their "round-up" of the cattle, joining the other riders, who were all Mexican. They grinned at her; she grinned back, and they all rode in to perform what was probably her most relaxed turn in the show.

But next, Kellermann announced the "Pageant of the Plains." Cody had rearranged some of the turns into a kind of pantomime play. There was some music to set the mood as Kellermann made a little speech setting the scene and stalling for the time needed for the new costume change. And she had to scramble with the help of one of the Mexican ladies to wiggle out of the satin blouse and skirt, get the braids of her wig taken down, then turn to help Juanita make the same change. It made the men grin to see them "disrobing" right out in the open, but they didn't say a word, perhaps because they knew Juanita was as handy with a knife as Giselle was with a rifle. She wasn't the only one; the four Mexican men really *did* have to jump right out of their satin trousers and shirts and into buckskin leggings, and they didn't seem to worry very much about modesty!

She was barely ready to join the procession into the arena for the Indian war dance.

Then she and the Indians, and "Indians," left to great applause, and the "settlers" drove their "wagon train" into the arena and made camp. She ran off to the little changing tent changed into her embroidered skirt, shirt, boots and vest, and ran back. There were a few songs and a "square dance," then came the change. It was *bandits,* not Indians, who attacked the wagons.

The bandits seemed to enjoy their role very much.

And then, it wasn't the cavalry that ran off the bandits, it was the Indians! And *how* the spectators cheered when they did! As for the Indians, they *certainly* enjoyed themselves; their war cries were positively bloodcurdling, and they certainly used up their entire allotment of blank cartridges in the process of defeating the bandits. Giselle was in the wings, waiting for her next turn and peeking around the side of the curtain, and was deeply gratified to see the audience reaction.

Half the "Indians" pursued the bandits. The real Indians all stayed behind to see to the settlers. The cavalry (with Cody in the lead) turned up with the horses and the cattle, and the Pawnee pantomimed an elaborate peace pipe ceremony with both Captain Cody and the chief of the settlers. Then the entire group rode off out of the arena together, with cavalry and Indians riding point and rearguard for the settlers. *Exactly* as the readers of a Karl May book would have liked. And the cheers were deafening. Certainly much more enthusiastic than Giselle remembered hearing before.

Then came bull riding, which was quite wild and exciting, and after that, Texas Tom. But *then* it was the turn of the Indians to target-shoot from the backs of their galloping horses. Neither she nor Leading Fox participated in this. For the sake of impressing the audience, all the targets were clay plates in holders; the explosion of shattering pottery was very dramatic, and the plates disintegrated in a most gratifying manner whether they were hit in the center or nearer the edge.

This was a new "turn," and Cody had included it with a little reluctance at Leading Fox's and Giselle's urging. Considering the wild applause it got, she hoped his reluctance had turned to the realization that they had been right.

Then it was time for her trick-shots. She still hadn't mastered the trick of reliably cutting a playing card in half, even with the help of the sylphs, but all the rest were consistent. The gasps and "ahs" that marked each successful shot were gratifying in every possible way. The only thing that clouded her satisfaction was the knowledge that this one trick eluded her. All she could think, as she took her bows, was *If Annie Oakley can do it every time* without *magic, why can't I?*

Captain Cody came on again and did his trick-riding and shooting, which marked the end of the marksmanship section. It was time for another little pageant.

And now her nerves were on fire. This was the riskiest thing she had suggested trying. Cody was still dubious about it. Did she really know her people well enough?

She and Fox rode into the arena side by side, as Kellermann described the great friendship that was between them—in vague
terms. There was silence from the audience, and she bit her lip a
little, wondering if it was the silence of appreciation or disapproval.
They had gotten halfway around, when the wicked bandits returned,
pounding up on their horses. The audience gasped.

She and Fox were quickly surrounded, forced to dismount, and as
Kellermann narrated the story, and the bandits pantomimed it, they
threatened to murder both of them.

Her nerves dissolved as the audience reacted by whistling their
disapproval of the bandits. Even though they really were dreadful,
even in pantomime. They kept laughing, and even when they managed to stay in character, it was so exaggerated it was all that Giselle
could do to keep up *her* appearance of being terrified.

She kept her ear tuned to the audience, and as they called out
advice to her and Fox, shouting at the bandits to "Let them go, black-
guards!" she knew that she had them.

Then their leader pantomimed that he had come up with an idea.

The "idea," of course, as Kellermann narrated, was for Fox to perform knife-throwing tricks with Giselle as the target—

Well, everyone here knew the story of Wilhelm Tell and the apple.
She could hear the collective intake of breath as the bandit leader
dragged her, kicking and screaming, to be tied to a . . .

. . . rather large piece of wall that had been set up as the bandits
emoted. That just happened to have convenient wrist and ankle
straps built in. Just loops, really, she could pull free any time she
cared to, which was completely on purpose.

"Kick me iff'n I hurt ya, missy," the "bandit leader" whispered as
he slipped the loops around her wrists. Then he bent and held the
ankle loops for her to slip her foot into, far too polite to actually *touch*
her leg.

Well, no one in the audience minded that the "ties" were only
loops. They were all very excited, anticipating what was about to
happen. Bad acting notwithstanding.

But, of course, the first thing that happened was that Fox made an outline of her body with thrown knives. *Both* of them were using their power over air to make sure the knives missed, so she was never in the slightest bit of danger, but every time Fox drew back his arm to throw, there was a collective intake of breath, and when the knife hit in the "safe" zone, there was a sigh of relief and a cheer.

Not trusting the sylphs to keep their minds on the task, Giselle was creating strong eddies between her body and the spot where each knife was *supposed* to hit. She knew from experience that these eddies would provide a cushion that would force the knife away from her body if Fox somehow lost his concentration. To the part of her that actually saw magic, each of these eddies was a little whirligig of white sparks that pushed outward rather than drawing inward. She was so intent on creating them and keeping them going that she actually didn't see much of what Fox was doing. They had practiced this at every opportunity when the troupe stopped to camp for the night, using every minute of daylight.

It wasn't that Captain Cody was worried about her safety . . . it was that he had been worried about audience perception. Evidently, back in America, he would have been drawn and quartered if he had dared to put the safety of a white girl in the hands of an Indian.

Well, that wasn't the case here. The German audience *loved* this, that much was clear from the time the first knife thudded into the board.

And when he had finished with his outline, the audience screamed its approval.

Now was going to come the fun part.

All the while this had been going on, Fox's fellow Pawnee had been "creeping up" on the bandits. The audience could see them, of course, and if the bandits had bothered to turn around, they would have seen the Pawnee too—but of course, they didn't turn around. Now Giselle had to fight to hide her smile. Of course the audience didn't *expect* them to turn around—that would have spoiled everything!

Fox turned to make a threatening gesture at the bandit chief, and Two Crows waved a hand at him. There was an expectant murmur from the audience, who knew this meant that rescue was at hand.

But what they did *not* expect was that Fox would pull four more knives at once, and send them sailing in rapid succession at Giselle— *so* rapid that the first was hitting its target as the last left his hand. With four loud *thuds,* the knives cut the straps binding her to the target! And as the Pawnee swooped in on the bandits, she bent and retrieved a small handgun from the top of each boot and shot the bandit chief, who "died" with a bloodcurdling scream.

The audience roared its approval.

Had one of the knives failed to cut its target—unlikely—she still could have pulled her hand or foot free without the audience realizing the knife had missed.

The bandit camp erupted in gunfire, every man firing at once, just as a string of the Pawnee horses were driven into the arena. Each of the Pawnee performed jaw-dropping running mounts on his horse, including Fox.

She wasn't capable of that, of course, but she was light and small enough that Fox could stop his horse beside her and pull her up behind easily. They had practiced this as well, and she managed the trick not *too* ungracefully. Then they were off, leaving the cursing bandits behind, including the miraculously resurrected bandit chief. The bandits ran in futile pursuit. As the last of them vanished out through the curtains, the audience went wild.

That was the last of her official turns. Captain Cody performed his trick riding and shooting. There was wild-horse riding—"bucking broncos," they were called, and the goal was to stay on as long as one could. All the rest of the remaining acts from the original show were fitted into this final third of the new show, then there was the repeat of the Grand Parade and the show was over.

But her work wasn't over yet. Like everyone else, she had to rush to her part of the "camps"—in this case a little tent set between the Indian encampment and the cowboys. There she sat down in a camp chair not unlike Captain Cody's, and prepared to meet the audience.

Or at least as many of them as were prepared to pay the extra for the "special" ticket.

Kellermann was conducting the "official tour," of course, which meant that only those who were independently minded approached her on their own. There were not that many of those; most people, however excited they had been by the show, seemed to prefer standing behind the guide. When they asked her questions, they did so diffidently, and with immense politeness.

Well, except for the children and young adolescents.

"How did you meet Chief Leading Fox?" blurted one lanky boy at the front of the group, looking as if he was likely to burst.

"Oh, that is a long story, would you like to hear it?" she replied, amused that not one of the group seemed to question the fact that she spoke perfect German although she was allegedly an American.

Then again, it probably never occurred to any of them that she wouldn't, even though Kellermann had to translate for the others in the show. *But perhaps they haven't asked questions of anyone else.*

"Yes, please, Fraulein Ellie!" the lad said eagerly. The adults, just as eager to hear but thinking themselves too dignified to show it, still leaned forward a little.

"Well, my father died when I was only seven. I was the oldest child, and we needed food, so I took his old gun and went out to try and shoot something. I was very lucky that I ran into Chief Leading Fox in the forest before I hurt myself. He did *not* tell me to go home, as a white man might have. Instead, he asked me why I was all alone in the forest with a rifle that was as tall as I was."

She paused, and the boy immediately asked "What did you say?"

"I told him the truth, of course. That my father was dead and if I didn't hunt, we would all starve, because my mother could not leave the babies." She smiled as the youngster nodded solemnly. "So he said, 'Then perhaps you will allow me to come along.' He didn't say that he would help me, although that was what he did. From then on, until I was as good a sharpshooter as I am now, he met me every day to hunt together. He became like the father I had lost."

She knew that Kellermann was committing all of this to memory, and would probably use it in the show. She made a note to tell it to Fox so that they had the same story—although his version would probably be better than hers.

A few more people began to ask questions—if the Indians were Apache, or Navaho, or any of the other tribes they had read about. What her home had been like, and had she hunted grizzly bears or buffalo. Did she know Annie Oakley, Buffalo Bill, or Sitting Bull?

When they finally moved on—urged by Kellermann, since he needed to move them through in a timely manner—she thought she had satisfied them. And she took the chance when no one was crowding around her to go over into the Indian Village to tell Fox the story she had concocted. He invited her to sit beside his fire with a nod, and she sat cross-legged on the grass and related her story.

I do like this clothing, she thought, and not for the first time. The Western clothing was so much easier to sit on the ground in, and so sturdy she didn't need to think about grass or dirt-stains.

He was amused when she had finished, and chuckled, his eyes crinkling up at the corners. He had a fine, strong face: older than the way she had imagined Winnetou, more like Winnetou's father. "It is a good tale," he told her. "And what happened to this mother and your siblings in this tale?"

"My mother remarried a shopkeeper and took the family to St. Louis, because she did not wish to try to keep the farm going," she decided on the spur of the moment. "Everyone who has read those books is familiar with that city. I remained with the old cabin, now that I was able to hunt and fish and supply what I needed for myself. Then I joined the show." She shrugged. "We don't need to get any more elaborate than that."

"It is best if we do not," he agreed. "Although you have never told us much of your past, you know."

"Oh!" she realized he was right. "Well, there is not a lot to tell. My real parents traded me to Mother for food. Mother was an Earth Master; her name was Annaliese Bundchen, and she wanted me because she knew I would grow into magic."

Fox looked startled at that—the first time Giselle had ever seen him look unpleasantly surprised. It was an odd expression on his generally stoic face. "Your parents . . . did what?" He shook his head. "I have difficulty with this."

"It's not common, but it's not uncommon either; more often an unwanted child is left on a doorstep, or at a convent," she said, a little bitterly. "But sometimes, if a childless couple sees a pretty baby they like . . . it can happen. But most often, instead of being outright sold or *traded,* a child is sent off into servitude at a very young age, as young as five or six. Too many children, not enough food, and there are many laws about hunting and fishing, but few about what you may do with your children."

". . . and you say *we* are the barbarians." Fox looked as if he had bitten into something nasty. She didn't blame him.

"On the other hand, I was one more mouth to feed when my father could not feed the children he had, and by that, I mean they were literally starving, in the dead of winter." It was her turn to make a sour face. "I likely would have died anyway, and possibly my mother and more of my siblings with me."

Fox shook his head. "We would never permit a child to starve. The parents, perhaps, if they were too lazy to hunt, fish, or grow food, but never a child."

Giselle sighed. "Yes, but you live in very small tribes, when you compare your tribe to a whole city. You've seen what cities are like. People often do not even know one another, and they have few bonds. There is no place to grow food, even if there were no laws about hunting, there is nothing to hunt. If one wants food, one must earn it with labor. But there are more unskilled hands than there are jobs to be done. My father was one of those sets of unskilled hands."

Fox frowned. "Surely, there must have been somewhere he could have gone if his children were starving."

She thought about telling him about workhouses—and that you could starve there, too—but decided that was getting too complicated.

"Well, really, although he didn't know it, my father did me a great favor," she pointed out. "And . . . instead of dying of hunger, I was taken by someone who, I think, loved me more than either of my parents ever would or could have, given that they had eight other children." Her voice softened at that last. "I called her Mother until the day she died. She truly was my mother in every possible way."

Fox was silent for a while. "Then, perhaps it was for the best, after all." He sat there, deep in thought, while Kellermann brought another group by and she answered questions.

"Well," he said when they were gone, "I think your story of how you and I met is a good one. It is very much the sort of thing I would have done, I believe. How *did* you learn to shoot so well?"

She felt her stomach clench up, even after all these years. Too much to want to tell Fox anything about the attack by that horrible young man. "To explain that, I will have to begin with something else. The Bruderschaft, which I should tell you about anyway, since we are in their lands and one or more of them might turn up here."

By the time she got done explaining about the Brotherhood of the Foresters, and how two of their number had taught her to shoot and fight, they had been interrupted several times by more people touring the camps, had made a mad dash to get their supper eaten, and it was time for the second performance.

If anything, the second performance went better than the first. People were confident now that the changes were going to meet with audience approval, so they threw themselves into their parts with great enthusiasm. Almost *too* much, but after all, this wasn't on a stage, it was in an arena, so perhaps at that distance "too much" was just about enough.

There were so many people wanting to make the "tour of the camps" that it was not until well after dark that the last of them were escorted out.

Feeling more than a little drained, Giselle sat by her little campfire after the last of them were gone and the camps settled down, not doing anything, not even thinking, really, just enjoying the sounds and letting her mind empty. It was a lovely night, balmy, and there was a nightingale singing somewhere in the distance. People were talking quietly; someone was playing a banjo, though not in an irritating fashion, just tinkling out a little melody. *I didn't realize how tired I was,* she thought. Now that she wasn't explaining things to Leading Fox, answering questions, or doing her turns, her energy had just run out. She was just about to get up and head for her wagon when a voice, a female voice, addressed her in German, out of the darkness.

"That was quite an impressive show, Fraulein Giselle."

She stiffened.

The speaker stepped into the light from her campfire; it was a young woman perhaps a year or two older than Giselle, blond and dressed in a red cape and a loden-green hunting jacket and divided skirt, exactly like the one that was packed away in Giselle's wagon.

Giselle knew the moment she laid eyes on the stranger that this was an Earth Master. The Earth Energy, golden and vital, was strong enough around her to practically taste. That and the hunting gear could only mean one thing: this was a Hunt Master of the Bruderschaft. And since this young woman knew her by her real name, and not as "Rio Ellie," she also must know . . . everything. Giselle scrambled to her feet, a cold thread of fear running down her spine.

But the young woman laughed. "Oh don't look at me as if you think I am about to eat you! Tante Gretchen already sent us a full report on your . . . unfortunate accident. The Brotherhood tentatively concurs with what she told us. I'm just here to hear it from you, directly."

Giselle didn't bother to ask *how* this young woman knew that Giselle and Rio Ellie were one and the same person. Tante Gretchen would have reported her direction, and after that, it was only a matter of asking the Elementals if there was a strong female Air Master about that they did not already know. It wasn't as if she had been trying to conceal her presence.

Giselle licked lips gone dry. "I would rather it . . . wasn't out in the open. Most people don't know about . . ." She gestured vaguely. "Well, only a handful of the people in the show even know about magic in the first place."

"Of course, and I can understand you not wanting them to know about your misadventure. It could have a negative effect on your new companions. Have you a more private place to talk?" the woman asked. "I'm Hunt Master Rosamund, by the way." She held out her hand, and Giselle shook it, gingerly.

"My wagon," Giselle replied, took the time to put out the campfire, and led the way. She had left a lantern burning on a hook beside the door as she always did and brought it inside for light, carefully closing the door, the window over the bed, and the curtains to indicate she wanted privacy.

Rosamund looked around curiously and took the little stool, leaving the chair for Giselle. "This is very nice," she remarked. "I spent some time traveling in a wagon, but this is much more comfortable. Quite cozy and homelike, and it should be snug in the winter as well. I think I'll ask the Graf if he can find me a gypsy *vardo* after this. It would be more convenient than taking rooms in inns, *much* more private, and given the arsenal I often travel with, it would be much easier than having several trunks to haul about."

"The Graf?" Giselle asked, putting the kettle on over the spirit lamp to heat for tea.

"Hmm. Yes, the Master of the Munich Lodge, Graf von Stahldorf. I work more with him than with the Bruderschaft, but I was visiting my guardian in the Schwarzwald, and he asked me to come have the needful chat with you." Rosamund settled herself on the stool, putting back her hood, but not removing her handsome red cloak. "He thought that it needed a bit of a woman's touch, I think. So. Tell me what happened. From the very beginning. Assume that I know nothing. Why were you in disguise as a young man in the first place, and what did you do to catch the Hauptmann's attention?"

Giselle sat on the chair, her hands knotted tensely in her lap, and once again forced herself to recite, as clearly as she could, the entire story. She didn't spare herself, either; she made it very clear that she blamed herself for setting the night-sylphs on the Hauptmann and causing his death.

The stranger's handsome face remained absolutely unreadable throughout the entire story. And when Giselle was done, she sipped her cup of now-lukewarm tea thoughtfully. The light from the lantern fell softly over her face. She looked—like a lady of good birth, an aristocrat of some sort. Without that aura of magic power, Giselle would never have taken her for an Earth Master.

"Well," she said, finally, "Tante Gretchen was right. You should have strangled that bastard with your own two hands and robbed him before you left. I would have."

Giselle felt her jaw dropping and stared at her, not quite able to believe what she had just heard.

"Mind," Rosamund continued, casually, after finishing the tea, "That certainly would have gotten you in trouble. It would probably have involved a trial, at least by the Bruderschaft, to prove it had been self-defense. So it is probably just as well that you didn't."

"I—ah—" Giselle stammered.

"As a Hunt Master of the Bruderschaft, *and* an Earth Master, I assure you that it is my opinion that this was, at worst, death by misadventure, and that the wretch had probably been a heartbeat away from death by apoplexy for years," Rosamund concluded. "You certainly may go right on feeling as guilty as you like, but I'm telling you it's not necessary." She held up her cup. "Now, if you would be so kind, might I have a little more of this truly *excellent* tea while you tell me about the other Air Master here?"

8

ROSAMUND declined to allow Giselle to send a sylph for Leading Fox. "I would not be in the least surprised if you were exhausted," she said. "Just give me a little bit of information about him, and the others here who know about magic, so I will know whom I can speak freely in front of."

"There is not a great deal to tell, in that case," Giselle admitted, and quickly summed up the two others, Captain Cody with his Fire Magic, and Fox with his strange Air Mastery. "The others who know about magic are Herr Kellermann, the announcer and also the business manager of the show, and the true Pawnee. Some of the people playing Pawnee are Mexicans; they know nothing of magic, so far as I am aware."

"Good, much simpler that way." Rosamund stood up. "I'm going to wish to speak with Captain Cody, Kellermann and Leading Fox at some length. You are in the territory governed and protected by the Brotherhood. We really do have a right to know what's walking about in our house, after all."

She raised an elegant eyebrow, as if she expected Giselle to dispute with her, but frankly, Giselle felt simply too intimidated. It was very clear that although Rosamund was only a couple of years older, she was vastly Giselle's senior in experience. Worldly and magical!

"I could go—" she began, but Rosamund shook her head.

"Please, don't bother them now. Let them know over breakfast. Send a message to me at the Golden Sheep Inn. I am at my leisure right now, you folks have a show to run." She smiled; it quite lit up her face, and Giselle felt herself relaxing a little. "Shall I let myself out?" the Earth Master continued. "It seems silly for you to try and squeeze past me just to open the door in such a small space."

"Please do," she said, trying not to sound as intimidated as she felt.

Rosamund chuckled a little, and bade her a good night and good rest.

Giselle sat back down again and poured herself a second cup of tea, feeling even more exhausted than before. Rosamund had to be the most *forceful* personality she had met since Mother died! And it wasn't as if she had tried to be intimidating, either, she merely exuded sublime self-confidence and an aura of *being in charge*.

I doubt anyone has ever dismissed her *as being "just a girl,"* she thought, with more admiration than resentment. *If she had been in my shoes, Cody wouldn't have tried to pass her ideas off as his own.* He wouldn't have needed to. She had no doubt at all that when Rosamund spoke, people *listened*.

Was that an aspect of Earth Magic? It might be. Certainly Tante Gretchen had commanded the respect of all those young army lads.

At any rate, after dealing with such a formidable personality, on top of the exhausting day she'd had already, she felt a bit limp. She had a quick wash, and crawled, rather than jumped, into bed.

In the morning, it might have seemed like a dream, if it had not been for the two unwashed teacups on her little table. No matter *how* tired she had been, there was no chance she would have been so addled as to pour herself *two* cups of tea.

She closed her eyes and called a sylph. One flitted in through the window over the bed almost immediately; this was a tiny little thing, with brown wings with orange spots. It hovered expectantly, orange hair floating about its naked little body.

"Would you be so kind," she said aloud, "As to tell Chief Leading Fox that I will need to speak with him urgently over breakfast? And if you can get Captain Cody's attention, tell him the same?"

"*Yes!*" the little thing said gleefully, and darted out the window again.

Goodness. That was a lot of enthusiasm . . .

She got another washup—it was getting warm enough now in the mornings that the tepid water in her pitcher was quite warm enough—and got into her canvas skirt, shirt, and soft Indian boots. After the exertions and surprises of yesterday, she was famished.

Before she had gone three steps, the sylph was back. *"They will meet you at the back table!"* the little thing said, and sped off, without even asking for a treat of magical energy.

The "back table" was the one farthest from the tables where the food was dished out. It was generally the last to be filled, which made it a good place to have a semiprivate conversation.

She hurried off to the mess tent, only to find the other three already waiting there with solemn expressions on their faces. She got her food and joined them, and before she even sat down, Cody spoke.

"So, we intrudin' on somebody's claim, or what?" he asked, looking concerned.

"I tried to explain, but I have an insufficient knowledge of how these things work in the Black Forest," added Kellermann.

She blinked several times, as she tried to sort out just what Cody was asking. Finally a possible definition for the word "claim"—related to gold and silver prospecting—surfaced in her memory.

"The Brotherhood of the Foresters is something like sheriffs and deputies," she said, slowly. "It is not that they have staked a claim to an area, it is that they have taken the job of protecting ordinary folk from the bad magic and bad magicians within that part of the country. This is usually done by groups known as Hunting Lodges. The Brotherhood of the Foresters is somewhat unusual in that their area extends to the entire Schwarzwald, not merely one city or town within it."

"So—like Texas Rangers." Cody relaxed. "So a gunslinger comes t'town, sheriff comes t'make sure he ain't gonna make trouble, that it?"

"That's close enough," she decided aloud. *They certainly don't need to know about my . . . misadventure.* "My Mother was known to the Brotherhood, and it was two of their number that taught me to shoot. When she died, I found myself without income to support myself. I was advised to come ask the Brotherhood for their advice, and possibly help." *True enough, although that came afterward . . .* "I was on the way to one of the Lodges when I encountered the show, and the rest, you already know."

"So, what's this feller got t'say about you—an' us?" Cody wanted to know.

"First of all, *he* is a *she.* Her name is Rosamund von Schwarzwald and she is . . . very highly placed," she warned. "She is a Hunt Master, someone who decides when a threat is dangerous enough to warrant sending an entire Hunting Party instead of a single member of the Brotherhood, and the person who would lead that Hunting Party. Other than that, I believe she merely wishes to meet with you and assess you."

Cody's face registered extreme surprise, Kellermann's only a bit less. Only Leading Fox seemed unperturbed. *"She!"* Cody exclaimed. "You folks let wimmen . . ." He cut off whatever he was going to say. "Huh. Ah guess. When's she wanta meet up?"

"As soon as you have the time. She told me herself that as *we* are the ones with a show to put on, and *she* is at her leisure, you should be the ones to choose the time." It was both gratifying and a little amusing to see Cody at a loss for once. After having him take credit for her ideas, having to deal with a female who outranked him took the sting out of her wounded pride.

"She's where?"

"The Golden Sheep Inn, in the town," Giselle told them. "I believe that she can speak with my sylphs; I can easily send her a message."

Cody rubbed the side of his head, pushing up his hat slightly.

"Well. Best deal with this right quick, I guess. After the second show an' tours, we'll come t'her. Figger just after sundown." He looked to the other two, who nodded agreement. "Don' want t'put 'er off and make 'er think we got no manners."

"That is probably wise," Kellermann agreed. "The Brotherhood's word is law where magic in the Schwarzwald is concerned. And to send a Hunt Master . . . you do not wish to insult her."

Cody took a long breath. "Right. Well, we got a show to put on. Better get to't."

The four of them made their way from the show enclosure into the town, following the guidance of one of Giselle's sylphs. They attracted curious glances from the townsfolk, since all four of them were wearing their best. Cody was resplendent in his white, fringed doeskin outfit, with a matching hat. Leading Fox was equally resplendent in a costume Giselle had never seen him in before: a beaded buckskin version of Cody's costume, with a colorful blanket, his hair adorned with eagle feathers. Kellermann looked plain by comparison in his sober best suit.

And she—well, she had been torn. Whether to keep up the illusion that she was the American Rio Ellie, or wear the loden-green hunting costume that Tante Gretchen had given her. . . .

In the end, she decided that the illusion was more important as far as the townsfolk were concerned. And as for Rosamund herself, well, wearing her Western gear would make it clear where Giselle's alliances lay.

The sylph that guided them was a night-sylph, an odd one, actually, since this one was fully clothed. She had midnight-blue wings like lacework, a long, flowing midnight-blue gown, and raven hair that streamed behind her as she flew, looking back over her shoulder to be certain they were following. Only she and Fox could see her, of course.

The townspeople did not pretend that they were not startled and pleased to see the quartet, although Kellermann was largely ignored. There was no effort at being polite, either; there *was* a great deal of pointing and whispering.

Leading Fox ignored it, striding after the sylph, full of dignity. Cody, however, went into his arena persona: smiling broadly, waving, even pulling off his hat and bowing deeply to particularly pretty women.

The particularly pretty women generally blushed, smiled back, and giggled. The men with them were not nearly so amused, though they took some pains to hide their displeasure.

Fortunately, Cody didn't follow through on any of his flirtatious bows, just kept moving.

The sylph brought them down cobblestoned streets of black-beamed, white-plastered houses and shops. Giselle tried not to look longingly at the shops . . . now that she actually had a little money to spend . . .

No, I must be good. I must save for winter.

They turned a corner, and there, about halfway down the street, was a hanging sign with a yellow sheep painted on it. And painted on the white plaster of the walls were garlands and flowers, and pictures of people eating and drinking.

The sylph flew up and away, no longer needed. Captain Cody eyed the sign, then regarded the painted drinkers with approval. "I think I'm likin' our choice pretty well," he drawled, smiling.

"Just remember," Kellermann cautioned. "You'll probably have to pay for what you drink."

"Killjoy," Cody muttered, as Kellermann waved at her to go inside first.

Inside, Giselle sniffed the air, then took a deeper breath with approval. She had seen rather too many . . . poorly kept inns. This one, however, would have met with even Mother's approval.

The common room was spacious and clean, with wooden floors, wooden ceilings, and plastered walls with more paintings of happy people on them. The paintings looked old, much older than the ones outside; they were much more stylized, more like the illuminated letters in old manuscripts. Or actually . . . now that she came to think about it, the decorations were almost exactly the sort of thing you saw on elaborate beer steins! Then again, the ones outside were subject to the wind and weather, and presumably every so often had to be repainted. These probably dated from when the inn became an inn. There was a huge fireplace in one wall, which probably held enormous fires in the winter. And there was a counter across the back, with big ornamental steins on it and three barrels beneath it.

The furnishings were simple: wooden benches and wooden tables with candles stuck in their own wax in the middle. Many were already occupied with people smoking, eating and drinking. Two pretty young women, both blond and looking like sisters in their black dirndls, white blouses, and red aprons, bustled among the tables laden with heavy wooden trays holding food and drink.

As they stood in the doorway, one of the girls unloaded her tray at a table and turned toward them. "You're expected!" she said cheerfully. "Come this way!"

She moved off as Captain Cody eyed her swaying hips with approval. Then he seemed to come to himself and started off after her. Giselle rolled her eyes and followed, the others trailing after her.

The girl brought them to a private room, just off the main one; the door to this room was standing wide open. Like the main room, the walls were decorated with paintings of scrollwork and hunters and their game. It was just big enough to hold a table and benches, and Rosamund was waiting there for them, seated at the end of the table, with food and drink in front of her.

So were four more beer steins, two pitchers of beer, four place settings, and big platters of steaming sausages, potatoes, bread, butter, cheese, and kraut. The aromas made Giselle's mouth water; they'd had to leave without eating, and she had been hoping that since they were meeting at the inn, she might be able to get a sausage or two.

"I supposed you might have to hurry off without getting any dinner, so I took the liberty of ordering you some," Rosamund said. She gestured at the food and drink. "Close the door behind you, sit, and eat. We have plenty of time for talk."

Captain Cody did not hesitate for a moment, and as Kellermann closed the door he moved right along the table. He sat down at Rosamund's right hand as Giselle sat at her left, took a fork, and stabbed some bratwurst, transferring them to his plate. The other two sat down, and Giselle got sausage, potatoes, kraut and rye bread, unspeakably happy to be partaking of a meal that was homey and familiar.

"So," Rosamund said, and suddenly switched to English. "First of all, let's conduct our discussion in *your* language. Just in case someone is listening. It would be very unlikely for anyone else in this inn to know it."

"That is a wise precaution," Giselle replied in the same tongue. She did not ask *how* Rosamund knew English; that was fairly self-explanatory. Unlike Leading Fox, Rosamund would have had no qualms whatsoever about getting one of her Elementals to extract a new tongue from Giselle, Fox, or even Captain Cody.

After all, she was a Hunt Master. . . .

"And while you are eating, you can tell me about yourselves," she continued. And her eyes glinted. "Everything, if you please."

But Captain Cody only laughed. "Sure thing, sheriff," he said genially. He looked around the table, cut off a big bite of sausage and ate it, then took a pull from his beer. "Reckon I'll go first."

"No, I will, I have less to tell," said Kellermann. "You all eat, please."

Well, that completely suited Giselle, who contentedly dug into the sausage and kraut and spicy mustard to her heart's content.

"I am liking this food and drink," Fox said to her quietly in Pawnee. "This beer seems stronger. Should I be wary of the drink?"

"Somewhat," Giselle cautioned, remembering from Karl May books that Indians had problems with alcohol. Evidently that part was true. "It is not as strong as . . ." She searched for the word. ". . . the water that tastes bitter and burns. But enough will act upon a man like loco weed upon a horse."

"I shall take care, then." He nodded, and had more sausage. "But this is most excellent, as are the sour strings. They are like the white man's *pickles*. Very good."

"Sauerkraut," she said, and turned her attention to Rosamund.

The Hunt Master did not betray anything as she listened to the others give their stories and summarize their abilities. Well . . . all but Fox, who went last.

The Indian sighed with content, and put down his knife and fork before taking up the narrative. "I am a Medicine Chief. I believe that is the same as your *Elemental Master*. However, my spirit creatures are not the same as yours. Mine are *nahurac* of the Air, but they are Spirit Animals like unto the natural ones." He paused a moment. "I have had power of all of the *nahurac,* but the ones that speak most to me, and grant me the greatest power, are those of the Air, the birds and the insects."

"Huh," Rosamund said, surprised. "I don't believe I have ever seen that. Well, go on."

"Some I can still summon in this land of yours. Some I cannot. Some I have not tried. Otherwise, I seem to be able to control the forces of the Air itself, as if I was at home." He shrugged. "And that is all I can say."

"It's enough, thank you, Leading Fox." Rosamund took time for a drink of her beer. "Well, you all understand that you are entering an area that is under the protection of the Brotherhood of the Foresters. What you do *not* understand, I suspect, is why it is under our protection."

"Well, 'cause you're the sheriff," Cody said, as if that was obvious. "You're the law in these parts."

"No," Rosamund said sternly. "It is because this part of the world has seen four thousand years of continuous magic use . . . and I would say that at least half of that was magic in use by bad people. There are things living here. Bad things. Old things that were once gods, and half of those were gods of evil. There are pockets of bad magic. Elementals that, themselves, are evil. This is an ancient forest, it holds many things, and it is easy for them to hide here. Just by *being* here, you might attract them. Just by doing the wrong thing in the wrong place, you can awaken things that are sleeping. There are thousands of years of blood magic in this land. At least half of that was done purely for the purposes of raising power to harm and destroy, and I do not believe I need to tell you what that means . . .”

Giselle swallowed. Mother had warned her about such things. The forest around the abbey was full of dangerous creatures, made more dangerous by the practice of evil and blood magic in the distant past. Mother had speculated that this might have been why the abbey had been established there in the first place, as a bastion of light against the darkness.

The others, Kellermann and Cody, at least, nodded. Fox looked thoughtful. She wondered what he was thinking. Kellermann sat back in his chair and fired up a pipe; Cody poured himself another beer.

The serving girl came in then, and asked if they needed anything else. Rosamund paid for their feast and waited while she cleared things away, leaving behind only the beer.

“So, here is the situation I find myself in,” Rosamund continued, when she had gone. “I’m satisfied that your intentions are good, but intentions are just not enough to safeguard you or anyone else in the Schwarzwald. The problem that I have is, can I let you go on, deeper into the Schwarzwald without supervision, when you have no idea what you are likely to encounter? Or, more importantly, stir up?”

They all looked at each other, nonplussed. “We haven’t had any trouble so far,” Cody finally pointed out. “None of us have done much magic, other than that odd bit of Air stuff that Fox and Ellie do, an’ that’s only in the shows.”

Hmm, that’s a lie, Cody, and it’s not a good idea to lie when you are a magician, Giselle thought, her brows creasing. *You know very well that all of us use our magic all the time. What’s more, she’s a Master, so she knows it too.*

“Anyways, I don’ see any reason why anybody needs t’fret ’bout us,” Cody continued. “We’ll jest go on our tour, an’ take care not t’rile anything up, an’ that’ll be fine.”

Rosamund frowned at him. “Just from my point of view, I don’t think that is a good idea. I have only your word for it that what you do will have no effect on what’s already here.” She gave Cody a stern look, and to Giselle's feeling of satisfaction, she saw Cody cringe just a little. "Moreover, *you* have no way of predicting what might decide to come at you, regardless of how careful you are. So I have a plan. I am coming with you."

Giselle blinked. *Well, that's certainly . . . unexpected.* The Captain stared. Kellermann shook his head, and Fox chuckled under his breath.

She wasn't at all displeased by this demand. She already liked Rosamund, and she missed the company of another female who was also her countryman *and* a magician. And Rosamund might be able to teach her more about her own powers than Mother had been able to.

"This is a joke, right?" Cody said, after a moment.

"I have never been more serious," the Hunt Master replied. "You might encounter nothing. But given how luck plays out . . . it is not that I am averse to having your rotting bodies discovered some time next spring. It is that I am averse to finding myself forced to call a Hunting Party together to clean up what you awoke. I greatly dislike having to clean up other people's disasters." The look on her face should have warned Cody that she was not joking.

Evidently it did. ". . . oh," Cody said, weakly. "Well . . . all right, I guess."

"So you don't object?" Rosamund smiled. "Good. Because I wasn't going to give you any choice. Now . . . what choice of housing do you have?"

They all looked at Kellermann, who put his head in his hands and sighed. "Would you prefer a tent?" he asked. "Or a *vardo?*"

Rosamund smiled broadly. "A *vardo* would be perfect, thank you."

Rosamund turned up in the morning with two horses and cart. The handsome bay horse tied to the tail of the cart was hers; the other and the cart were borrowed. And the cart itself was laden with three heavy trunks.

Kellermann had a *vardo* cleaned out and waiting for her, parked next to Giselle's. It was not as nice as the one they had given Giselle, since this one had been stripped of the comforts that had made Giselle's *vardo* such a pleasure to move into, but it was clean and it had all the basic requirements of bed and storage built in. Cody had asked Giselle to help the Hunt Master move in.

"I dunno how she'll take t'this, seein' as this here is pretty bare," he said, for the first time in Giselle's knowledge showing some signs of nervousness. "But it's about all we got, an' a tent wouldn' be much better."

But the Hunt Master seemed pleased enough with what she found. "As soon as my gear is stowed, I'll go back into town and get whatever else I need," she said, and winked at Giselle. "I have a Graf for a patron. I can afford a cushion or two and some sheets."

Giselle bit back a surge of envy. On the one hand, if *she'd* had such an exalted and wealthy person to rely on, she'd still be snug at the abbey! *A Count. A Count for a patron. I wish I had such a thing . . .*

On the other hand, she had the suspicion that, whatever good things Rosamund was getting from this patron, she was *earning* every bit of it. And perhaps . . . *from the little she said last night, I do not believe Fraulein Rosamund has much spare time. And her work sounds . . . rather dangerous.* "Well, you get yourself settled," she replied. "The rest of us have two shows to put on."

Rosamund waved Kellermann off, accepted her help, and began taking items out of the trunks, examining them, and putting them back to stow them in the under-bed compartment of her new *vardo*. After a glimpse into the wide variety of weaponry that was *in* that first trunk, Giselle no longer had any doubt that Rosamund had more than earned her position as a Hunt Master . . . and that this position was probably a *lot* more dangerous than she could guess.

And she made up her mind that the next time she sat down and talked seriously to Rosamund, *she* was going to be asking a great many questions.

"Do you . . . really need all of this?" she asked, surveying what looked like a full suit of leather armor, a pair of swords, several daggers, a hand-crossbow, a coach gun, a pair of pistols, an axe, a mace, a morning star, and many boxes of ammunition.

"All at once?" Rosamund asked, picking up, counting, and replacing a box of quarrels for the crossbow. "Not generally. But you never know what you might need, and we are rather too far from a Brotherhood Lodge for me to be comfortable without having *everything* I might need with me." She looked a little sideways at Giselle. "Something you should keep in mind is this: when you are fighting against something or someone that is powerful in magic, and they know that you, too, are a magician, more often than not they completely forget to guard themselves against a purely physical attack. That has saved my life, and more than once."

The second trunk, to Giselle's relief, contained nothing more lethal than clothing. That all went straight into the under-bed storage, still in the trunk, after just a cursory look.

The third trunk held . . . well, some interesting things. Some of the sort of equipment that Giselle remembered Mother using for various bits of minor magic. Books, quite a few of them. Some items that were clearly personal. Something not unlike a mirror, except it seemed to be made of black glass. Some of that stayed in the trunk, and some got stowed in various drawers and on shelves about the *vardo*.

"Well now," Rosamund said cheerfully, when she had finished. "Linens and curtains, a featherbed and a few nice comforts, I think. I'll be back—"

A tap on the side of the *vardo* interrupted them. They both turned to see Captain Cody standing there. "If yer goin' to come along with us, you might as well be of some use in the show," he said, sounding just a little bit cross. "Poor Ellie hasta move like a cat with her tail on fire t'change after th' Quadrille. You kin take her place as a Injun gal. Ellie, give her yer costume an' show her." He started to move off, then came back. "An' I ain't payin' ye," he added, then truly left.

"Well," Rosamund said, both eyebrows shooting toward her hairline. "Is he always that . . ."

Giselle shrugged. "It is *his* show," she pointed out. "And you *did* just attach yourself to it without asking leave."

"So I did." Rosamund gazed at the empty doorway. "Well. I'll do it. But only after I make myself perfectly comfortable."

She leapt down out of the front of the *vardo* where the door was, tied her horse to the side of the wagon, and climbed up into the cart, chirping to the horse and slapping the reins on his back.

Giselle smiled to herself. Things were beginning to look . . . very interesting. In Hunt Master Rosamund von Schwarzwald, Captain Cody might just have met his match.

9

"**W**ELCOME to my new home," said Rosamund, as Giselle settled onto a fat cushion on the floor and accepted a cup of tea. "What do you think?"

"I really like it," Giselle confessed. Rosamund had opted to get someone to come attach fold-down seats to the inside of her *vardo,* with permanently attached cushions. For the rest, she had added curtains in the expected earthy colors, and a lot of leather straps to hold things into their shelves. Even the bedding was in earthy colors. It didn't look like the sort of décor most people would think of as "feminine," but it certainly seemed to suit Rosamund.

"Fewer things to tip over. I am not an expert at driving," Rosamund confessed. "But that is not why I invited you here. I expect there is a lot you want to ask me about."

Giselle was silent for a moment. "What exactly do you *do?*" she asked, deciding that this pretty much summed up all of her questions. "Mother was not in the Brotherhood as such, and the visitors we got never told me very much about it."

"Ah . . . now that . . . is a good question." Rosamund settled back on her cushion, as a light breeze stirred the curtains covering the open door and the curtains closing off her bed from the rest of the wagon. "The Brotherhood mostly kills things, quite simply," she said, without any hesitation at all. "Bad things, of course. I've disposed of *vampir,* werewolves—and a werebear. A witch or two. Several Elemental Magicians that had gone to the bad. I've sent many sorts of spirits on their way, which I suppose is not technically killing things, since they were already dead."

"What are *vampir?*" Giselle asked. "Mother never mentioned them."

"She likely wouldn't have encountered any, they prefer to lurk in ruins. They live on the blood of living creatures. I have been *told* that there are some who do not kill their victims, and who actually live on the blood of animals rather than humans but . . ." Rosamund shrugged. "I have never seen any. All the *vampir* I killed were murderers, and the only things 'living' that they left behind were unfortunates who they turned into others of their kind." She gestured at the shelves. "I have a book, I'll loan it to you."

"That . . . would be useful," Giselle replied. "Have you dispatched more things than that?"

"Some bad trolls. Other things that one might think were only in fairy stories. I've done so alone, and with help. I know how to recognize most Elemental creatures on sight, and how to combat them if need be. Yes, I am an Earth Master, and yes, most Earth Masters are healers, like Tante Gretchen, but I am not." She shrugged. "All things considered, it's just as well. Most of the active warriors of the Brotherhood are Fire Masters, actually, although my guardian Gunther is also an Earth Master."

"How did you . . . come to be this thing?" Giselle asked.

"Oh . . . that is a very *short* story. I showed my magic quite young, and was being taught by another Earth Master whom I called my Grandmother, although we were not related. A werewolf attacked us both. I was rescued by the man who came to be my guardian, with others of the Brotherhood. Everyone decided it would be safer for me *and* my father and mother if I were to live at the Lodge." But Rosamund's expression had darkened a great deal, and Giselle knew

immediately that there was more to the story than just that. "I literally grew up training to be one of the Brotherhood, especially after
they all realized that hurting, and not healing, was my forte." She
sipped her tea. "I have the advantage of you. I know, more or less,
your story. Gunther passed it to me when he sent me to intercept you
and this . . . lot."

Giselle giggled; in part with relief that she would not need to tell
over her tale, and in part because of the expression Rosamund had
on her face when she said "this . . . lot."

Rosamund sighed. "Amateurs," she elaborated, a little sourly. "I
can only assume that because the distances are so great in the New
World, and because the native Elementals do not respond signifi-
cantly to white Elemental Masters, they are accustomed to vast, barren spaces in which their actions have few, if any, consequences."

"Well," Giselle suggested, "Perhaps you should compare the Black
Forest to territory crawling with hostile troops, troops who have
often left traps behind them."

"It's accurate," Rosamund agreed. "Perhaps not *crawling with hostile troops,* but certainly the part about traps being left behind." She
took a hearty drink of her tea then smiled over the teacup. "I do believe we are going to be excellent friends, you and I."

Giselle started a little in surprise, which turned to pleasure. "I
haven't had many friends," she confessed. "Three, really. Mother's
friends from the Brotherhood and Tante Gretchen."

"Ah! Pieter Meinhoff and Joachim Beretz." Rosamund nodded,
and offered Giselle more tea. "Joachim taught me to shoot. Most of
my friends as a child were adults, too. Introducing me to other children didn't . . . work out very well."

"How so?" Giselle asked, curiously.

"Well, it generally began with me quizzing them on what sorts of
lethal skills they had—I knew better than to talk about magic, of
course, but it seemed to me asking about their ability to shoot, or
stab, or bash in heads was just making sure we were all able to defend ourselves if something dangerous came at us. And then they'd
ask me *why,* and I'd tell them, and they'd run away screaming and

have nightmares for months." Rosamund smiled as Giselle gave her an odd look, not sure whether or not to believe her. "It's quite true. You can ask Gunther if you ever meet him. Or Joachim."

"I'm beginning to get the notion that those of us born to magic are not easy children to raise," she said, finally.

"Oh we aren't. It's just as well it generally runs in families. And to change the subject entirely . . . am I going slightly mad, or is your hair longer tonight than it was this morning?" Rosamund looked at her with her head to the side, quizzically.

Giselle realized that the braids wrapped around her head had begun to sag and put her hand to them. "Oh bother. Yes it is. It grows ridiculously fast, but it grows faster when I am perturbed. Mother said it had to do with the fact that the sylphs like it, but she never told me anything more than that."

"Probably because she didn't know, herself. If I were you, I'd ask another Air Master if you ever meet one. None in the Brotherhood, I'm afraid. Mostly Fire, then Earth, and a few Water. But I can ask the Graf if he knows one." Rosamund nodded, and poured the last of the tea for herself, as Giselle put her cup aside. "It's a good thing that I'm taking your place as an Indian maiden, then. If your hair grows that fast, you'd soon have a hard time stuffing it under that wig."

"I've been cutting it," she replied.

Rosamund shook her head. "Don't. I mean, stop cutting it, unless it actually gets so long it gets in your way."

"Oh?" That was interesting. Mother had always insisted she keep her hair as long as possible. "Why?"

"Two reasons. The first is showmanship. A pretty lady sharp-shooter with long golden hair is just *too* perfect. The second is . . . I think the sylphs might be using your hair as a place to store Air Magic." Rosamund held up a cautionary hand. "It's just a theory! I have nothing to base that theory on!"

"My hair . . . as a place to store Air Magic." Giselle giggled. "That's a very silly theory. But I do think your notion of showmanship is a good one."

There was a tap on the doorframe, on the other side of the curtains. "It is Leading Fox, who wishes to speak with Miss Schwarz-wald."

"It is Rosamund, and it will be a little crowded but you are welcome to join us," Rosamund called back.

Fox held the curtain aside to mount the steps and enter the wagon. This time the bird on his shoulder was a magpie. "Kellermann said that you wished to speak with me?" the Indian said gravely. His very presence made the *vardo* feel much smaller.

"Since I'm to be part of your tribe, I wondered if you would mind teaching me Pawnee?" Rosamund asked, with an ingratiating smile. "You know, the usual way *we* do it."

"I do indeed, and it was in anticipation of that that I brought my friend." The magpie lofted from Fox's shoulder at his nod and somehow passed through the bed-curtains hiding Rosamund's bed from the room. "If you could play the Pawnee woman during the tours of the camp as well, it would free Rosalita, which would be agreeable to both herself and Pablo."

Rosamund laughed. "I think I can do that. It seems only fair."

Fox smiled slightly. "Thank you. Now that you have the teacher, I shall depart." And with no further words, he pulled aside the curtain again and left.

"And I shall, as well," Giselle said. "The morning begins extremely early with this show."

"Oh do trust me on this: it begins even earlier with the Brotherhood," Rosamund laughed. "I shall find sleeping until dawn to be an unexpected luxury!"

The only reason that the show left three days later was because there was another date to be met, and they would never have managed to get to Reichenbach on time if they stayed any longer. People were still paying to see the show. More people than ever before were paying the extra to take the "tour of the camps." To say that the changes were successful would have been grossly understating matters.

And despite some initial reservations, it seemed that adding Rosamund to the group had been an excellent idea. She was outstanding with the horses *and* the cattle and buffalo; no surprise to Giselle, who knew how easy it had been for Mother to handle any animal of any sort, but quite the shock to the original trainers of the hairy beasts. She was able to lead all four of them in the Grand Procession all by herself, which she did in her Pawnee costume. She suggested that, given a little more time, she might be able to get them to do a controlled stampede as well, and that, all by itself, won her Captain Cody's heart. Giselle no longer had to half-kill herself getting out of her Quadrille costume and into the war dance piece. Rosamund pleased the other Pawnee by not only drumming correctly, but joining in their song correctly. It appeared that the magpie had given her much more than the Pawnee tongue.

Giselle was a *little* jealous of that, but only a little. She had never had a female friend of her own age before, and she found herself enjoying Rosamund's company quite out of all expectation.

When they set off down the road to their next destination, the town of Reichenbach, Giselle was looking forward to the trip. She would have much more free time in the evenings with Fox and Rosamund, and Rosamund had promised to do what she could to enhance Giselle's Mastery of Air Magic.

"I cannot do *much*," Rosamund had cautioned. "But I know from what Gunter and Joachim told me that there are certain things Annaliese had not gotten around to coaching you through, and what she had planned *is* something I can do. We just need to find the right place for it."

"Place?" Giselle had said, quizzically.

"You'll understand when you see it," was all Rosamund would say.

The journey started off without a single hitch. There was none of the fuss there had been before getting the buffalo into their two carts. Rosamund turned up, and the huge beasts walked right up the ramps and into the carts with no trouble.

So now the caravan was making its way down another road that wound among the great dark trees of the Schwarzwald. This was very thickly forested territory; the trees grew right up to the edge of the road, and canopy overhung it, blotting out the sky. They traveled in a dim, green light, the very hoofbeats muffled by decades, if not centuries, of fallen leaves.

Giselle found it . . . a little unsettling. And a little stifling. It wasn't *hot* beneath these branches, the opposite, in fact. It was chill and damp, and there was the scent of wet earth and moss and old leaves. But she had to keep reminding herself that she *could* breathe, and that the trees were not somehow closing in. *Rosamund probably loves this,* she thought, wondering how close it was to noon, when they would all stop for lunch and to water and feed the cattle and horses. The buffalo, precious cargo that they were, had buckets of water and mangers of hay in their carts, but both would probably need refilling by that time. Of course Rosamund would love this, she was an Earth Master, and this deep, dense forest was the perfect home for her. Giselle wanted sky, and lots of it.

This forest felt haunted as well. The only time she glimpsed Air Elementals, they were furtive and shy, and darted off the moment she spied them. And she didn't know why, because they weren't staying to tell her.

Finally Leading Fox, who had been somewhere behind her, rode his horse up the verge of the path to pace beside her. "This is a very little like the Pawnee's real home," he said, wistfully. "This is not unlike land we will buy, when we return with white man's money."

"Really?" she said.

He nodded. "The trees are not so tall, but they are old. There are more meadows among them. But my people are lovers of river and forest, and we do not love the dry land we have been sent to." He had the magpie on his shoulder again, instead of the owl, and it cheered her a little to see at least *one* Air Elemental that was not fleeing. "We have spoken of this, before I left. We will buy many acres, we will maybe cut our hair and wear white man's clothing, and build homes like the white men, farm like the white men. If people ask if we are Indian, I think that we will lie. The Pawnee are used to disguising themselves as others. We will be white on the outside, and Pawnee in our hearts. In our homes, in our hearts, we will keep the traditions. Our children will not be taken from us, to be sent away to school to learn to be white all the way through."

She blinked at him, shocked. "Is that what is happening?"

He nodded. "It is why we decided to do this. We have heard of it happening to many tribes. When the white man comes to take the children of my clan, we will not be there. We will be gone, into the wind, and the white man will not find us."

"Say you are Italian," she suggested, after a long pause.

"Eh?" Fox turned, finally, to look at her.

"Say that you're Italian. You can get the language from Kellermann, he speaks it. Or, for all I know, Rosamund speaks it. I expect no one in the middle of where you are going has ever seen an Italian. If you say that's what you are, and you speak something they don't recognize, they'll probably believe you." She watched as Fox considered that, and slowly nodded.

"Italians do have black hair," he agreed. "I will speak to the others. This has great merit." He rode along in silence for a mile or more; she was used to long silences from him by now.

"Rosamund has said these forests are dangerous," he said, finally.

"They feel dangerous to me," she admitted. "Not like back where we were camped. It feels like there are things out there that don't like being disturbed."

"Even so," he agreed. "My little friend does not wish to fly in there." He looked over at her again. "I hope that there is a meadow to camp in ahead."

I hope so too. But the animals didn't seem at all uneasy, and it seemed to her that their instincts could be trusted. Her horses and Fox's just plodded along with apparent contentment, and if the buffalo, which were extremely skittish creatures, had not liked the surroundings, they would certainly have made their unease known long ago.

Just as she was beginning to wonder if there was going to be any end to these woods, she saw golden sunlight beaming down on the road ahead, literally like light at the end of a tunnel, and the nearer they got to it, the more there was to see. There *was* a big meadow ahead, and once she and Fox actually reached it, she saw it was a water meadow with a stream cutting along one side of it. Some of the animals were already being watered there, and their handlers were holding others. Her horses smelled the water and it took no urging to get them off the road and into the long grass, even though it was rough going for them. She pulled up beside Rosamund's *vardo*, hopped down off the front of her *vardo*, where she drove from the open door, and slipped their bridles off so they could drink and crop grass for a while. Fox led his own brown-and-white horse to drink.

"I have food!" Rosamund said, waving from the door of her *vardo*. "I have enough for the three of us."

"Good, thank you," Giselle replied. The cooks were distributing food to everyone from the back of what the Americans called the "chuck wagon," and Giselle presumed Rosamund had gotten it there.

It wasn't fancy: bread and butter, cold beef and spicy mustard, but Giselle was famished suddenly, perhaps because the open sky of the meadow had relieved some of that feeling of being closed in too tightly. She raised her eyebrow at the spicy mustard, however; she'd never seen that on the tables of the Americans so far.

Rosamund smirked. "I realized I was going to have to supply a few things for myself if I wanted them," she said, as Fox took his portion with thanks. "I've got a nice crock of sauerkraut, another of pickles, and pots of mustard. They don't take up much room."

"I should have thought of that," Giselle told her with chagrin.

"*You* are not used to traveling," Rosamund pointed out. "Now, I want to talk with you two. I don't much care for the spot we're supposed to camp in tonight, but it's just about the only option. But I want you both to be alert. We might even want to think about keeping a watch."

"What are we watching for?" Giselle asked, stopping before she bit into her bread and meat.

"I don't know," Rosamund admitted. "But it's an abandoned mill and a little village, and there are four Elemental Magicians among us. That could attract . . . things. Things we'd rather not attract."

Fox nodded. Today, for the sake of traveling, he was not in his finery. He wore faded canvas trousers and an old shirt, like the rest of the men wore, and his hair was braided tightly going down his back. Giselle was in her split canvas skirt and a soft shirt, and she had rebraided her hair this morning and wound it around her head. Rosamund was in her hunting gear.

"There are too many of us to attract bears or wolves, even if they are tempted by the cattle," Rosamund continued. "But . . . I don't know why this village was abandoned, nor how long ago. It might have been plague. It might have been that the people just died off or left. Or it might have been something . . . else." She shrugged. "The worst that happens is that each of us loses a couple of hours of sleep."

"Are you going to warn Captain Cody?" Giselle asked. Rosamund nodded, but her mouth twisted up into a wry expression. "Not that I expect him to pay any attention to me. He's too used to America, where the hazards are purely physical."

"But this is the Schwarzwald," Giselle agreed, somberly.

"I am not sure we need lose sleep," Fox said thoughtfully. "I know that my spirit creatures will stand watch. Will yours?"

Giselle and Rosamund exchanged a look. "Maybe," Giselle said. "The ones around here seem shy."

"Possibly. Probably. We can try. It's a good idea though, and I have more than enough cream to bribe mine." She smiled.

Giselle laughed. "I remember Mother doing just that! Cream and anything baked. . . ."

"The domestic ones like brownies can bake for themselves, but the wild ones are mad for the taste of anything baked, butter, cream and honey," Rosamund told Fox, who was looking at both of them as if he suspected they had lost their minds. "You'll see, when I call them. Cheese too, they are mad for cheese." She cocked her head at Giselle. "Do you think you can convince something to come out of hiding and stand watch?"

"I can try," Giselle said. "I don't like to coerce them."

"Neither do I. That's a slippery slope to go down." Rosamund gazed at her with approval, which made her feel better about not ever forcing one of her sylphs to do anything. "All right then, when we camp for the night, we'll do a little walking about, see what we are dealing with, then see about getting our Elementals to take a night watch for us. Captain Cody, too. And I might be overreacting. Just because we're feeling that something is watching us doesn't mean it might not lose interest and go away before we camp."

"Oh, I am *so* glad to hear that I am not the only one feeling that!" Giselle blurted with relief.

"You are not," Rosamund and Fox said at almost the same time. They looked at each other. Rosamund laughed, and Fox smiled a little.

"Even the trees have the potential to be . . . alive in more than the usual sense, here," Rosamund said, and turned to Giselle. "That reminds me. The book. Or more accurately, it's a sort of guidebook to the Schwarzwald that everyone in the Brotherhood gets. I'll give you my copy, I can get another." She finished her lunch, hopped up into her *vardo,* and came back out with a book bound in soft brown leather, like a handmade journal. "Here you are," she said, handing it to Giselle. "I'd be careful about reading it before you sleep. It can make for nightmares."

"I'll keep that in mind," Giselle replied, untying the thongs that held it closed, and leafing through it, gingerly. It looked to be handwritten, with many, many illustrations. She closed it when she came to *Vampir,* with a little shiver. But she didn't give it back. "I can probably read it while I drive. Or look at it, at least."

At just that moment, one of the "trail bosses," riders that had been assigned to get and keep the wagons, riders and herds organized and moving, rode up. "Time to bridle back up and mosey along to the road, ladies, Fox," he said, with a pull on the front of his hat. "We got us a good campground 'bout four-five hours off. Thet'll give us a couple hours t'set up and get water afore dark."

"No rehearsal or practice tonight?" Giselle asked in surprise.

"Not 'nuff room." Without another word he rode off, to pass the word. Giselle interrupted Lebkuchen and Polly, the Quadrille horse, and coaxed them back into their bridles. They snorted, but they'd been happily cropping the lush grass and clover of the meadow for some time, so they didn't object too very much.

Once everyone was back in line, and the trek continued, Giselle reached into the capacious pocket of her skirt for the book and began perusing it in earnest.

Rosamund is right. This is the stuff of nightmares.

She didn't stop reading, however. This wasn't just going to apply to this trip through the Schwarzwald with the show. This was going to apply to the land around the abbey as well. Mother had managed to protect her from what lay out beyond the safe area around the abbey, but Mother wasn't here anymore, and she was going to have to learn how to deal with these things herself.

She read very slowly, and carefully—rereading passages often, to make sure she had the information set in her mind. There was no actual organization to the book, it was, more or less, just a catalogue of the creatures of the Schwarzwald, listed randomly, perhaps as they had been discovered by the Brotherhood. There was no particular differentiation between things that were just plain monsters and things that could be Elementals gone to the bad, except notes saying that "some are good, but when they are bad, this is how they behave." Some, she was already familiar with. Kobolds, for instance, which were purely bad Earth Elementals; she'd actually run some of those off when they tried to invade the abbey cellars. Then there was the *neck*, the brook-horse, a purely bad Water Elemental, which appeared as a handsome white horse that would try to coax you onto its back and once it had you, carry you into the nearest body of water to drown. There was one of those near the abbey, and she knew to carry a horseshoe nail with her to throw at it so that it would run away.

But others, well, she only knew from stories, or had never heard of. Dwarves . . . they could be both good and evil, and the evil ones, it seemed, were *very* evil indeed. She had heard of the Water Elementals, the *nixe*, but had not known they could be female *and* male, nor that they could appear as handsome humans, gray horses (like the *neck*) or as wizened little green-skinned creatures. And the *Weisse Frau*—dressed all in white, she posed as a washerwoman. If you were lost, she would help you find your way. If you were a child, she would protect you, and her kiss would make you almost indestructible. But if you had ever harmed a child . . . she would lure you near, then grab you and drag you into the water to drown. The *Hay-frau*, however, was entirely evil, as evil as she was beautiful. The book said that the lorelei was one of these creatures who loved to sit on dangerous rocks in rivers and lakes and on the ocean and lure the unwary to their doom.

Each of the creatures described came with at least one, and sometimes several, drawings, and a detailed depiction of its habits and how, at need, to combat it. The writing was beautiful, quite clear and easy to read. The drawings, well, she was no expert, but they looked as if they had been done by quite a fine artist. And Rosamund had mentioned getting another copy! How on earth could one person make so many duplicates?

But then she got a notion, and leafed further in. And the writing, and the style of the drawings changed, subtly. So it hadn't been made by one person, but probably many people over a long time. And if all of the copies were the same . . . someone was duplicating them. And that was when she realized how copies were made: by magic, of course. She had watched Mother make copies of old books that way, so that she could give some in her library to Joachim. You touched the book to the blank book, you set the spell in motion, you supplied the ink, and the pages of the original would be duplicated onto the blank. *That* was why the book looked handmade. It was! It would have to be handmade in order to set it up for the spell. Possibly even the paper was handmade!

A lot of work, but how else to keep the lore of the Brotherhood up to date? Likely there were blank pages at the end . . .

She leafed to the end, and sure enough, there were. So if someone from the Brotherhood encountered a new creature, he would detail it all on one or more of the blank pages, and every member of the Brotherhood he met after that would duplicate the new pages into his own book by the same method. When you ran out of blank pages, you sewed in a new set, and the cycle continued.

"Oh, *clever,*" she said aloud, and Lebkuchen flicked an ear back at her. "I need to learn that spell."

It was evident from the thickness of the book that she had a great deal to study. The creatures of the Air she knew, from the malevolent *Rubezahl* to the Four Winds . . . but of the other Elements, or the things that were *not* Elemental creatures, not so much. And it was becoming increasingly clear that as long as she and the show were traversing the Schwarzwald, she was going to need to be able to recognize hazards when she saw them.

So she kept her nose in the book and one eye on the road, until midafternoon, when she could see ahead that the others were turning off the road and up onto the verge and beyond. And that there was a break in the trees up there, though how much of a break it wasn't possible to say from where she was. But the line had slowed from a brisk walk to a halting plod, so evidently there wasn't an easy way to reach where they were overnighting.

When her *vardo* got closer, it was possible to see exactly what was going on. This was a cleared space forming a half circle in front of a ruin that the forest had encroached on. Had it been a village? There was more than one building. But it had been in ruins for a very long time. The roofs were long gone, the walls were breaking down, and the ruins themselves were overgrown. There was going to be just enough room for them to all camp overnight, and it would be very tight quarters indeed. Kellermann was directing people where to put their wagons, and the buffalo and the cattle had already been penned inside one of the ruined buildings. "No tents!" he was saying. "If you aren't sleeping in a wagon, sleep under it! Set your brakes or use wheel-blocks! Tether your horses to the forest side of the wagon! We'll bring fodder and water along for them!" He waved her along and pointed where she was to go: right alongside Rosamund's *vardo*. Rosamund already had her horses unhitched, the harness draped over the wheels to dry, the horses tethered to the shaft, which was pointing to the forest. Giselle pulled up alongside as closely as she could and still allow movement between the wagons, and one of the tent wagons pulled up beside her *vardo*. She jumped down and got her horses unharnessed, rubbed down, and tethered and went around to the back of the *vardo* to see what Rosamund was doing.

Rosamund was staring at the ruins with a slight frown on her face.

"What's the matter?" Giselle asked.

"That's not a village," Rosamund said, shortly. "I need to go look at those ruins."

She started off for the ruins. Giselle scrambled after her. "Why?" she asked, when she had caught up.

"Because ruins are not always empty."

Together they threaded their way through the wagons and the show folk setting themselves up for an overnight stay. Those who normally camped in tents had extracted blankets and canvas to bed down under the shelter of the wagons, and were setting up several central fire pits against the fall of night. It looked as if they had done this before, since no one seemed in the least put out by the change in camping arrangements. No one paid any attention to the two young women who were making their way toward the decrepit remains of what must have been some imposing . . . and unfriendly . . . buildings. Unfriendly, because the windows in those battered walls were *very* small, and there weren't a lot of them. It must have been dark and gloomy inside those places, when they had still been standing.

Rosamund clambered her way into the largest. There were huge chunks of masonry and fallen pillars scattered about the interior, which was probably why the buffalo and cattle had not been penned here. It would be a disaster if one of them was to step into a hole and break a leg in a panic. Giselle waited at what had been the doorway as Rosamund poked around inside.

Finally Rosamund came out, and her frown had deepened.

"What did you find?" Giselle asked, as the Earth Master began a determined trudge back to the encampment.

"It was a convent. Not just any convent. A Magdalene convent. And that . . . could be bad. I need to talk to Cody and Fox at once." They both spotted the former seeing to his own comfort under the bandwagon, and Rosamund picked up her pace.

"Why?" Giselle asked. "Mother and I lived in the abbey and it was fine. Very peaceful, in fact."

"Because Magdalene convents were where girls who got themselves into trouble were often essentially imprisoned," Rosamund
explained. "There are generally unhappy ghosts. There are sometimes angry and dangerous ghosts." She bit off what she was saying
as they reached Cody. "Captain! A word!"

"Anytime, Miz Rosamund," Cody drawled, straightening up from
where he had been kneeling in the grass. "But iffen it's a complaint
'bout the accommodations, I'm a-feared I can't help y'all."

"Not . . . exactly." Rosamund crossed her arms over her chest and
took a stance that suggested that she was not to be trifled with or
cajoled. "You need to issue orders that no one is to go wandering in
those ruins after dark. And if you have some sort of Elemental that
can guard you as you sleep, I cannot stress enough that you should
do so."

"Already did the first—took a look-see, and I don' need nobody
breakin' a leg in there." He gave her a quizzical look. "I ain't no Master though; jest got a liddle Fire Magic. What's got your tail all
bushed?"

"That's what's left of a Magdalene Convent, and there could be
dangerous spirits about once the sun sets—" Rosamund began, and
was interrupted by Cody chuckling.

"Missy, I dunno what spooks you Germans, but us Americans ain't
a-feared of no ghosties. Specially not ghosts of *nuns,* of all damn
things." At the sight of Rosamund's fuming face, he just laughed a
little more. "Iffen y'all had said there was some sorta old god, or
other nasty critter in there, it'd be one thing. But ghosts cain't hurt
nobody, all they kin do is skeer ya. An' I ain't a-feared of ghosts, an'
anyway, y'all don't even know *if* there's any in there."

Rosamund looked as if she was ready to explode . . . and then she
just turned on her heel and left Cody chuckling behind her. Giselle ran
to catch up with her. She was fuming under her breath as she headed
for where the Pawnee were encamped. Giselle couldn't make out what
she was saying, but she really didn't need to.

"He's trying to assert himself, you know," she pointed out. "His
pride was hurt because you invoked your authority as one of the

Brotherhood and attached yourself to the show without so much as a *by-your-leave,* and he sees this as a way to get some of his own back."

"That doesn't make him any less of an *idiot!"* she snarled. "He has no idea!"

By this point they were at the fire pit the Pawnee had set up, and she made a visible effort to get her temper under control before she spoke to them.

"Medicine Chief Fox-Who-Leads," she said, formally, in careful Pawnee. "I wish to speak with you and your warriors about the dangers that may be dwelling in yonder stone houses."

Seeing that this was a serious matter, Leading Fox stood up, and the rest of the Pawnee turned and gave her their complete attention. "We have spoken of the need to stand a watch, Medicine Woman," Fox replied. "Have you learned something more?"

"I have learned that this is a place that may be full of angry ghosts," she told them all, her lips thinning a little. "Captain Cody does not believe that ghosts can harm him."

"Captain Cody is my friend, but sometimes a fool." All of the Pawnee nodded at this, and Rosamund relaxed a little, looking a bit mollified by their reaction. "The wise man knows that angry ghosts have many ways of causing harm. Do you know the exact sort of angry ghost that may be harbored there?"

She shook her head. "There are many possibilities. If I tell you to look for one, and another, different sort comes, you may be caught off guard. I ask you only to set your spirit animals to watch and warn."

"It shall be so." Leading Fox quickly agreed. "We will take great care, and should something alert us, we will come to you."

"My thanks," Rosamund told them, and she and Giselle went to find the "chuck wagon," queued up to get their bread and stew, and ate it in silence. No one else seemed to notice, however, since just about everyone else was grumbling good-naturedly about the "unnatural" abundance of trees that was making a decent camp so hard to put together.

They left their dishes to be cleaned up, went back to their *vardos*, and sat in the front doors, facing the forest as the sun began to set. "Do you think you can coax out some Air Elementals to stand watch?" Rosamund said after a long silence.

"I can try," Giselle replied, and spun up tenuous little tendrils of Air Magic, sending them wafting out into the woods—*away* from the direction of the ruins—bearing the message that she would like, please, for something friendly to do her a favor in return for another. Meanwhile Rosamund had gotten down on the ground and had placed one hand on the earth, presumably doing some "calling" of her own.

Giselle actually had not expected to get any response, since she had seen absolutely no sign of Air Elementals lurking anywhere since they had entered the deeper forest, but it was she who was answered first.

Not a night-sylph, but three of the smaller, shyer creatures she knew as "wisps." Not the more dangerous sort, that lured the unwary into marshes to drown, but the ones that could only be seen faintly, at night, at a distance, and vanished if they sensed they were being watched.

Up close, they were tiny, thin, sexless creatures floating in the middle of barely visible orbs of light. They approached her cautiously, and hovered just in front of her face.

?

Not an actual sentence or even a thought, just a general sense of inquiry.

"My friend, the Earth Master, fears there may be dangerous things sleeping in the human ruins," she breathed, being very careful not to startle them.

Again, the reply she got was not in words. It was more the feeling of, *"Of course there are dangerous things. And?"*

"Would you stand watch and wake us if one of our humans is in danger from them?" she asked. "I can offer this—" and she spun up a ball of Air Magic for them.

!

They gathered around it, yearning for it, not daring to touch it, glancing from it to her and back again.

And the feeling she got from them was, *"Is that all you want? In return for this?"*

"Yes, this is all I want. Watch the night through. If any of the humans here are endangered by anything in the ruins, wake me."

The three little things turned toward her and nodded emphatically. She released the ball of Air Magic to them, and they gathered around it, for all the world like three little moths drinking from a drop of nectar. The ball contracted, then vanished, and all three of them were glowing visibly brighter. They hovered in front of her again, all three bowed at the waist, and then flitted to the top of the *vardo,* where they took up a posture of watchfulness.

When she turned to look at Rosamund, she found her friend surrounded by at least twenty odd little creatures that looked as if they were made of bits of forest detritus. Very peculiar little things they were too, no two alike, covered in odd garments of moss and leaves, spiderwebs and pine needles, flowers and woven grasses. She was apportioning bread and sugar cubes out to them with all the gravity of a paymaster giving out wages. When the last of them had taken up his or her burden and vanished into the long grasses, she straightened. "Well, my lot is a little braver than yours. Then again, Earth Elementals are very difficult to hurt, and I very much doubt that a ghost will even take notice of them. I think we can go to bed. But . . ."

"But?" Giselle asked.

"Sleep in your clothing," Rosamund replied. "And sleep lightly."

10

GISELLE was certain she would never be able to sleep, but the moment she put her head down on the pillow, it was as if sleep suddenly smothered her. Just like that, instantly, she was asleep and aware of absolutely nothing. She lay utterly insensible until the moment a sharp pain lanced her nose.

It *hurt!* And it jolted her from her nose to her toes.

She came awake at once, only to hear a *snap*, see a spark arc from one of the wisps to her nose, and feel the same sharp, jagged pain again, although this time it was confined to her face. That didn't mean it didn't hurt any the less! "Ow!" she cried, sitting up and clapping both hands to the offended appendage. "Why!" Then it dawned on her. This must have been the only way the wisps could wake her up! *I have never, ever, been that thoroughly asleep.* "Oh! Thank you!"

She scrambled out of her bed, glad she had followed Rosamund's instructions to lie down fully clothed. Her feet hit the floor with a thud—she'd worn her boots as well—and she called up a glow on her own hand, making it shine as the wisps did. It was far safer to do that than to fumble for matches and a lantern in her half-befuddled state. She felt almost as if she had been drugged as she shook her head to clear it, but she knew that the only things she had had to eat and drink were those that Rosamund shared. Rosamund would not have drugged her. There was no reason for anyone else to drug her.

Therefore, that left magic. Magic which, by the utter silence of the entire camp, was intended to keep everyone in his or her bed. No wonder the wisps had had a hard time waking her. She knuckled her eyes and took deep breaths of the chill, damp air, and forced her mind to clear.

!!!! said the wisps, dancing urgently and madly. And they flashed an image of . . . someone, someone male by the outline, walking into the ruins. Well, *that* certainly woke her up! It looked as if all of Rosamund's fears were justified. But who could be the idiot stupid enough to go strolling into the ruins in the middle of the night? And why was *he* awake, and not the rest of the camp?

Now fired with urgency of her own, she unbolted and opened her door and jumped down into the grass next to the horses, who themselves were so deeply asleep they didn't even snort. And that was even more alarming. If even the horses had been sunk into sleep . . .

A mere heartbeat later, she heard Rosamund snatching open the door of her *vardo* and held up her glowing hand to give her fellow Master light to see by. Rosamund nodded her thanks and swung herself down out of her wagon, dropping down beside Giselle, a coach gun in one hand.

Giselle shivered in the chill, damp air. The scent of old, dead leaves and pine needles hung heavily around them. "Do you know who—" she began not even bothering to whisper, because clearly you could fire off a cannon through the camp and not wake anyone.

"Captain Cody," Rosamund bit off, her face full of annoyance and anger. "Damnation! I *warned* him—"

"I believe he was singled out," said Leading Fox, coming around from the side of Giselle's *vardo,* walking so silently neither of them had heard him. "I do not think your warning made any difference. He has just enough magic to be susceptible, and not enough to protect him. We should have thought of that and taken steps. I blame myself. I could at least have left an owl with him." Fox had an owl on each shoulder, and three more hovering above his head.

Rosamund bit off another curse, and thrust the coach gun at Fox. She reached into the *vardo* and brought out a pair of hand-crossbows. "Can you summon more than just those little things?" she asked Giselle. "They won't be of much help, but if we are up against ghosts, Air is the best power to use against them."

Well, if they are not afraid to come. . . . Giselle shut her eyes and gathered Air Magic around herself, calling it down out of the sky, envisioning it collecting around her like an ever-thickening cloud. Then she tried to summon any Air Elemental that might be within reach, thinking how much they needed help right now. If this was a case of spirits or ghosts, Rosamund's Earth Elementals would not be of much use, but Rosamund was right, Air would be. She felt the summons whirling out of her impelled by the Power of Air, and hoped there was something nearby besides her three wisps that might be brave enough to reply.

Something . . . several somethings at least . . . answered word-lessly. She continued to call.

When she opened her eyes, she felt a little faint with relief to see a good dozen sober-faced night-sylphs, at least as many pixies, and several dozen of the tinier Air Elementals, all of them—well, all the ones near enough for her to see—looking determined. The night-sylphs, all of them, were armed with what looked like swords of glass. The pixies and the tiny ones were armed too, if not with knives and miniature swords, then with their own long claws. The pixies were creatures the size of dolls, but with strange attenuated bodies and long limbs, mostly clothed in colorful rags, and with dragonfly wings. Their joints were knobby, and their faces more than a little animalistic. The smaller ones—Mother had never called them any-thing but *alfar*—were also winged, but looked half-human and half-insect, with touches of bat and bird.

She glanced at Rosamund, to see if *she* could see the little army. Evidently she could, for she nodded with satisfaction and hoisted one of her crossbows. "Now we need to run," the Earth Master said, "or at least as close as we can without breaking our necks—I don't—"

But as if to answer her, the wisps zoomed in front of them and began glowing with all their might, until their combined light at least equaled that of a very good lamp. That gave the three of them enough light to see by that they could scramble, if not precisely run, through the camp and into the ruins. *Thank the good God that we always lay out an orderly camp,* Giselle thought, as she jumped over wagon tongues and skirted the edges of glowing fire pits. Then they reached the edge of the ruins and the going got slower, as they had to avoid fallen stones or risk breaking a leg. The wisps seemed to know which way Cody had gone, from the direct path they were taking. *Bless you little ones!* she thought at them, and in answer they glowed just a little brighter.

They fled through the ruins and then into the woods beyond them. The vast number of fallen branches and yet more stones made the going slower—and here, as opposed to the opposite side of the ruins where they had camped, there was a lot of undergrowth that even the wisps were having a hard time pushing through. They all slowed to a crawl. And now . . . now Giselle thought she could hear . . . music? *Dancing* music?

Rosamund cursed, and hung her crossbows on her belt as she shoved her way past some bushes. "Give me the gun!" she shouted to Fox, who tossed it smoothly to her. She caught it and sped up, the wisps increasing *their* speed to keep ahead of her.

What does she know?

And then, they burst into a clearing.

No.

A graveyard.

Nothing grew here but moss, as the entire graveyard was heavily overhung with trees that must have kept the spot gloomy and dim even at noontide. The headstones were old, old and small, and many of them had toppled over. But that was not what made Giselle stumble to a halt.

It was the sight of Cody Lee being whirled around in a dance in the center of the graveyard, *clearly* against his will, by nine ghosts.

At least, Giselle assumed they were ghosts.

They were all female, and all wore something like a nightdress made of some tattered material. They all glowed, and were as transparent as any sylph; in fact the entire graveyard glowed with a strange, blue, unearthly light. But they had no wings, their hair had been shorn, and they all wore expressions of fierce glee as they concentrated on passing Cody from one to another in the wild dance. There was music coming from all around, but it didn't sound modern, it didn't even sound like the dance music played for the Maifests. It was frenetic, and Giselle couldn't even recognize what sort of instruments it might be being played on. If there were instruments at all. It wasn't exactly *faint,* and yet it sounded as if it was coming from a great distance.

There was a faint, foul stench of rot here, of things that were long dead. And it was *freezing* cold, Giselle's breath puffing out in clouds.

Cody looked terrified, as well he should, as he passed from partner to whirling partner. He also looked exhausted, and these spirits did not look as if they intended to let him rest, not even for a moment. *Can you force someone to dance long enough that he dies of exhaustion?*

For one moment, Cody was on the very edge of the group, about to be tossed back into the middle. That was when the coach gun roared, shattering the music, as Rosamund fired into the midst of the spirits, literally shattering them as well, for a moment at least. Cody managed to stumble free, to stagger to Fox's feet and fall, panting. But the spirits gathered themselves back together again, and *now* they were fully aware of the interlopers. They bared their teeth in ferocious snarls, and began to flow toward them, and a wave of paralyzing fear preceded them.

But with a cry that was more like a squeak than a battle trumpet, Giselle raised her hands—and her winds. And behind the winds came her army of Air Elementals and Fox's owls.

Shrieking and screaming, the Elementals dove at the spirits, weapons flashing in their hands—swords and knives of glass, ice, silver and bronze, and their own claws if they had such things. The owls lashed out with wicked talons, slashing their way through the horde. Where they cut at the spirits, ribbons of . . . whatever it was they were made of . . . separated from the whole.

And Giselle's whirlwinds tore those ribbons of ethereal substance away and dissipated them.

The spirits shrieked their own outrage, and tried frantically to snatch back the bits of themselves that the Elementals were tearing away. They howled, and fought back. But they couldn't catch either the Elementals or the owls, and as more and more pieces of them were torn away, they grew dimmer and more transparent.

"Keep them busy, Giselle!" Rosamund ordered. "Fox, help me carry Cody out of here! Giselle, follow as soon as you can, they won't go much past the graveyard!"

How does she know that? Giselle wondered, as Rosamund and Fox each picked up one of Cody's arms, hauled him to his feet, and stumbled off into the darkness with him. One of the Wisps detached itself from the attacking mob and sped off to give them light, while the rest continued the fight.

When Giselle figured they had enough of a head start—and it looked as if her impromptu army was beginning to tire—she retreated, step by step, backward, hoping she wouldn't fall over something. When she got just past the bounds of the graveyard she called out loud "Retreat!" which seemed like a reasonable enough command, and turned and ran for it herself. The other two wisps passed her and lit the ground ahead for her.

She caught up with the others just as they reached the campgrounds. Only then did she look back over her shoulder to see that, as Rosamund had promised, the spirits had not followed. She slowed to a walk, hand at her aching side, and caught up with the others.

Captain Cody was utterly spent. Evidently the spirits had managed to lure him out before he had gotten ready for bed, since he was still in his trousers, bracers and a shirt. But his hair and shirt were soaked with sweat, and his boots were scratched and scuffed.

The other three had reached a fire pit, where they had dropped Cody. There was enough light from the dying fire to see very well by. He was on his hands and knees where Fox and Rosamund had let him go, still panting. "What . . . th' blazes . . . was those things?" he managed, the words rasping from a throat that sounded raw.

"I warned you," Rosamund said—evidently not able to resist an *I told you so!* "I told you this place was haunted, and to keep clear of it."

"I . . . did!" he protested. "I . . . was gettin' . . . ready . . . t'bed down. An' next thing . . . I know . . . I'm . . ." He shook his head, unable to continue.

"Those were *Vilis,* the restless, angry spirits of young women who have died betrayed by the men they loved," Rosamund said, looking back, and biting off each word. "They take revenge on any man they can lure into their graveyard by stealing his life-energy as they dance him to death." She turned a look of disfavor on him. "Men who have also betrayed or left women who loved them are the most susceptible to their spell."

She left those words hanging in the air. Cody swallowed. "I . . . ain't never done that . . . that I know about," he said, weakly.

"Antonia in Naples?" Fox prompted. "Isabella and Elizabetta in Florence? Those three sisters in Vicenza? Flor—"

"Hey!" Cody interrupted. "I didn' ask for none of that! An' I never oncet wrote back to 'em, or invited 'em t' the' camp or—anythin'! Ast Kellermann! He'll tell ya!"

Giselle looked askance at Fox. Fox chuckled. "Young ladies who came to every performance, sent presents and notes to the Captain, and threw flowers at him and his horse from the audience."

"Ah." Giselle glanced over at Rosamund, who shrugged. "If they have been without a victim for a very long time, I suspect any excuse would do," she admitted. She offered her hand to Cody; Fox did the same on the other side. Both hauled him to his feet.

"But . . . all right, how in Hades did man-hatin' ghosts end up in a *convent?*" Cody asked in bewilderment. "I thought nuns was supposed t' be all holy an forgivin'!"

"It was a convent of the Sisters of Mary Magdalene," Rosamund replied. "Let's go to my *vardo*. You need food and something to drink, and I can explain better when I am sitting down."

Once at the *vardos,* they all sat down next to the nearest firepit. The warmth of the coals was very welcome after nearly freezing in the graveyard. Rosamund supplied Cody with a splash of brandy in a small glass and some buttered bread, and Giselle brought him water in a pitcher. He drank about half of it, then poured the rest over his head.

"The Sisters of the Magdalene are rather less a convent of nuns and rather more a set of jailors," Rosamund said dryly. "I am not one to disparage the clergy . . . but their order is a cruel one. Girls who have had children out of wedlock, or who have dared to love the 'wrong' young man, or sometimes even those who have done nothing at all but perform actions their parents deem 'disobedient,' are sent to them. They are *not* taken as novices, they are *not* permitted to become part of the sisterhood. Instead, they are held as prisoners, forced to labor from dawn to dusk, and presumably repent of their ways, for the rest of their lives, kept out of the sight of everyone but their captors."

Fox uttered some words in Pawnee that did not bear translating. Cody stared at her.

"As you might assume, the lives of some of these young women are not very long," Rosamund continued. "Their children, *if* they live, are sent away. If they do not, they are discarded like so much refuse. This is so that their mothers do not have the temptation of a grave to mourn over, as they are supposed to be fixing all of their attention on their own sins. And at any rate, according to the Magdalenes, an unbaptized child is one destined for hell, so why give it a grave?" She looked over in the direction of the ruins. "You most likely encountered some of the ones who did not survive the births of their children. And as you can imagine, they have a great deal to blame men for."

Cody appeared speechless. Fox crossed his arms over his chest, his face stormy.

"I think," the Pawnee said, finally, "That it is a very good thing this place is in ruins. Or I would be tempted to take scalps."

"I would be tempted to let you," Rosamund agreed. "But by the look of things, whatever happened to end this place was over two hundred years ago, perhaps even more than that. Whatever punishment was due to those who kept the Magdalenes in such misery has long since been meted out." She paused. "And we cannot have a place of such danger where anyone can wander into it. I shall send a report to the Brotherhood when we reach Reichenbach. They will come here and lay the spirits to rest."

"Speakin' of . . . I need some rest of my own, only not so permanent," Cody said. "Only—am I like to get called out there again?"

"Not tonight, and we'll be gone in the morning," Rosamund assured him. "It has been a long night for all of us," she added, giving a pointed glance to Fox, who took her meaning—and Cody's elbow—and led him off.

"I should reward my 'army' . . ." Giselle said, looking back in the direction of the graveyard. But there was no sign of her Elementals, and the night was silent once more.

But Rosamund shook her head, and motioned with her hand, suggesting that they both go to their wagons. "As you diminished those spirits, the Elementals took in their energy," she said, as Giselle followed her. "Which in turn, was life-energy they stole from the Captain. They have been well rewarded, and by the same person they rescued, which is why they are not here begging from you."

"Just as well. I think that all I could manage right now would be poor fare for them." Giselle mounted the steps into her *vardo* and paused. "What was in the coach gun? It was momentarily effective."

"Blessed salt. It disperses spirits, at least temporarily. I had brought my crossbows because their wooden arrows are good against *vampir,* and I was not sure which we would encounter until I heard the music." Rosamund reached for the door of her *vardo* to close it. "Good night to you, Giselle. You did very well in your first engagement."

Giselle retreated into her own *vardo,* shutting and latching the door securely. Once again, she thought that she would likely not be able to sleep at all, but once again, she was mistaken. The next thing she knew, the sun was streaming in through the window above her bed, and the camp was awake.

And only then did it occur to her to wonder why Rosamund might have expected *vampir* in the ruins of a convent. . . .

The engagement at Reichenbach was a resounding success. When she wasn't performing, practicing, or trying to master the card-splitting shot, Giselle studied the book that Rosamund had given her.

And at night, when it was too hard to study the tiny words on the densely packed pages, Giselle would pepper Rosamund with questions about the creatures she had encountered. Fox would often join them, listening without saying very much, and about half the time Cody would join the impromptu sessions as well.

"One thing I cain't figger," he said on the fifth evening of their two-week-long engagement, as they relaxed in the outer "room" of his tent. There was cider instead of the usual beer, which was always refreshing on a warm night, and the Captain's clever canvas chairs were remarkably comfortable. "Why is't that y'all cain't allus tell when a critter is gonna be good or bad? I ain't never run inta that back in America."

"And how many Elemental creatures have you run into until now?" Rosamund asked, passing around some pastries she had picked up at a bakery in the town that morning. Kellermann was exceedingly pleased with Rosamund, who had contacts that got her the best quality supplies at the best price here in Reichenbach. Even the quality of the food in the mess tent had improved.

Light came from a couple of lamps hanging from the top of the tent. Cody scratched his head, his brows creasing. "Well," he admitted. "Not many. Seems like most of 'em are either Injun spirit critters, and don't have no truck with a white man, or they're jest—" he gestured with his hands. "Big. Way, way bigger'n I'd wanta wrangle, even iffen I could, which I cain't."

"And you are likely to see or encounter only Fire creatures, and only those that wish you to see them," Rosamund pointed out, as Giselle bit into a slice of *apfelkuchen*. "In a country where the population is sparse, and there are many opportunities to avoid men, and in which Elemental Magicians are few on the ground. Whereas here . . . well, we have thousands of years of history. Generation after generation of Elemental Magicians, from the earliest who were little more than shamans, to now. We have a dense population, and a great deal of human meddling with magic, for good or ill. We also have the remains of old gods, and the spirits that the pagans worshipped. It is a wonder that you went as long as you did here on this continent *without* encountering Elementals."

"All right," Cody said after a moment. "But y'all didn't answer my question. How do y'all tell what's good an what ain't?"

"Ah. Sometimes they could be either. That's because, of themselves, many Elementals are neither good nor evil. They just *are*. And left to themselves, they are indifferent to humans. But Elemental Magicians and Masters can and do command them, and those Magicians and Masters have put those they command to tasks both good and evil. As the tree is bent, so it grows," Rosamund concluded. "An evil Master will make evil out of any neutral Elemental he can coerce."

"And there are evil Elementals, too, of course," Giselle pointed out, dusting the crumbs from her fingers. "Things that naturally just like to do harm, because they get some benefit from fear or killing. Things like, oh the *Eiswurm,* or the *Nekke,* or . . . well, lots of things. Rosamund gave me a book."

Cody's eyebrows rose, and he looked at her with a certain amount of accusation. "There's a book? We're trottin' through the middle of this crazy territory, an' there's a *book,* an' y'all didn't give me a copy?"

"I only had one copy," Rosamund replied, evenly. "And it's a book that is *supposed* to be only in the hands of the Brotherhood." She heaved an enormous sigh. "But I knew at some point you were going to find out about it, and I *knew* you were going to want one, so I took the precaution of getting some supplies yesterday in the town. I'll make you a copy, and me a spare. It's never a good thing, really, to have only one copy of something important."

"Right, an' that'll take *how*—" He stopped at the amused expression on Rosamund's face, and shook his head. "I ain't never gonna get over how easy a Master kin jest do stuff—y'all are gonna make them copies with magic, ain't ya?"

Rosamund smirked. Giselle giggled a little, but she also felt a little sorry for Cody Lee. Ever since Rosamund joined them, she'd been . . . not exactly acting *superior,* but never allowing him to forget which of them was the Master.

"Yes, I am. It is much faster than copying by hand, and unlike *most* such things, doing the copying by magic is also less effort than doing so by hand." Rosamund spread her hands wide. "As you probably know, most times, it is far easier to just *do* something than it is to do it with magic."

"But—the book—" Cody persisted.

"This book is something that the Brotherhood has been making and sharing for hundreds of years," Rosamund said, "And it's supposed to be only in the hands of a member of the Brotherhood because if the general public ever saw it . . . well, things could go badly."

"I don't follow." Cody frowned. "I mean, it ain't likely anybody's gonna ask about magic, but—"

"It was not that long ago that the Brotherhood had to remain secret in order to keep from being burned as witches," Rosamund pointed out. "Weren't they still hanging witches in *your* country two hundred years ago?"

"Huh." Cody scratched his head again.

"And these days, while that isn't a problem anymore, we prefer not to frighten the folk we are supposed to be protecting." She sucked on her lower lip, thoughtfully. "When you see the book, you will understand. And of course it is always possible that one day we will have to keep this book out of the hands of ordinary folk because anyone who reads it will think we are mad and try to lock us up. That is a problem that Elemental Magicians in the great cities have now."

Cody's cheek twitched a little. "Uh, ayah. I might could've run into that little problem myself, a time or two back home."

"I'll get the book," Giselle offered. "You're going to need it back to copy it anyway." It wasn't far to the *vardos,* and she knew where to put her hands on it in the dark. It was a very lovely night, warm and balmy, and the camp had settled into the cheerful sounds of people just about ready to look for their beds. She took her time sauntering back, in part because she hoped that the Captain's temper would have cooled by the time she returned.

By the time she came back with the book in her hands, Cody's feelings indeed seemed to have been soothed. She started to hand the book to Rosamund, but the Hunt Master shook her head. "Let him see it first," she said. "He deserves it, after his interaction with the *Vilis.*"

"Actually, let me find their page!" Giselle replied. "I was just looking at it."

She had left a stem of grass to mark the place, intending to ask Rosamund about them once there was time. She'd also left a stem of grass marking the *vampir,* but that was much earlier in the book. "Here," she said, finding the page and opening it, before handing the book over to Captain Cody.

"Huh," he said, looking from the book, to her, and back again. "How come I kin read German now?"

It was Leading Fox who answered that. "Because that is what I asked for when my spirit birds and Giselle's Elementals exchanged languages," he told Cody. "And when I used my own magic to grant you Giselle's language, I made certain it included both spoken and written."

"Huh," Cody said again. "I didn' know you could read."

But he said it with a sly expression, and Fox aimed a buffet at his ear, which he ducked. "One day," Fox threatened, "You shall awaken without your scalp."

Cody laughed, and turned his attention back to the book. "How come not all of these ghost-women are made out t'be as bad as the ones we run into?" he asked, his eyes still on the page, his fingers tracing the lines of a sketch illustrating the *Vili.*

"Most likely because the members of the Brotherhood that wrote those passages did not, for whatever reason, incur their wrath," Rosamund responded. "Perhaps the *Vili* that the others encountered were sated. Perhaps they were not subjected to the terrible things the Sisters of Saint Magdalene inflicted on the poor young women in their care. I was not there, I do not know, and there could have been any one of a number of reasons. But it is generally wise to assume that a creature is at least as dangerous as the worst report in the book, and proceed from there."

"Point," said Cody, and continued to peruse the volume. Then his eyes got big. "Sweet Jesus!" he said, pointing at a page. "Y'all say them things is *real?*"

Both Rosamund and Giselle got up and stood on either side of him to see what he was pointing at. It was the page that Giselle had marked on the *vampir.* "Oh yes," Rosamund said, matter-of-factly. "I killed one last year in Hungary."

"Sweet Baby Jesus. I hope they *never* get to America," Cody said fervently. "Read that thing 'bout Varney the Vampire as a kid an' I didn't sleep fer a week. . . ."

Rosamund reached across the distance between them and put her hand on the top of the book. "Are you sure you want a copy of this now?" she said, warningly. "It is definitely nightmare fodder."

"I druther not be able t'sleep an' at least know what's out there," Cody replied.

Rosamund allowed a tiny little smile to cross her lips. "Very well, then. I'll copy the book tonight, and you'll have your own version in the morning."

"I think that's 'bout all I wanta look at tonight, thenkee," Cody said, giving the book to her. "An' I'm thinkin' a strong drink afore bed's in order." He stood up, and so did they.

"In that case, think about another successful pair of shows tomorrow, because that should chase away the shivers and the nightmares," Rosamund said cheerfully. "And we'll be on our way."

She strolled off, heading for the *vardos,* and Giselle caught up with her. "Why do you plague him?" she asked, quietly.

Rosamund did not pretend that she didn't understand. "I'm test-ing him," Rosamund replied. "I want to know what he is made of. You, I know. I know who you are, I know who your blood parents are, I know all about your Mother. I know *nothing* about Captain Cody."

Giselle started to say something, then paused. "It is true that all I know of him directly is that my Elementals told me to trust him, and that he promised me, and pays me, a very handsome wage. Keller-mann gives it to me in full at the end of every week. Everything else I know is what he told me."

Rosamund paused at the door to her *vardo*. "I am not saying not to trust him. Our Elementals are very good at reading people. But I *am* saying that he might not be as simple as he appears, and that is why I am testing him. I am a Hunt Master of the Brotherhood, and he is in my house. I would be foolish not to test him."

"Yes," Giselle agreed. "So you would. And he would be very wise to admit what he does *not* know, and to understand that he cannot take command of situations in which he is ignorant, no matter what his sex or what he used to do back in his homeland. But . . ."

"But?" Rosamund prompted.

"But if you were . . . if you had any notion of . . . a romantical attachment . . ." Giselle felt herself blushing. "This is not . . ."

Rosamund threw back her head and laughed aloud. "With Cody Lee? Oh, that's absurd! He suffers from that ridiculous masculine notion that as *the man* he is always to be deferred to, in all things. That he is the toughest, strongest creature in *any* battle. That it is *his place* to defend us, and *our place* to defer to that. He dares not at-tempt that attitude openly with *you* because he is in too much need of your skills and talent. And he is too much the businessman to take the risk that extending things outside of the show—such as a romance—might ruin things altogether. I have a suspicion that he might have done so with your predecessor, and the need to put some distance between them prompted her departure."

"That, and the precarious financial state of the show when she left," Giselle mused.

"Taken together, a shrewd woman would have left before her

would-be paramour tried to persuade her to do without a salary, 'for his sake,' especially if she was not too attached and she had far better prospects elsewhere," Rosamund replied with a nod. "But no. I have no interest in that direction. Once the show is gone from the Schwarz-wald, neither will the Brotherhood care where he goes, or what he does. He will become some other Hunt Master's responsibility."

Giselle sat for a moment on the wagon tongue. "I have no intention of leaving with it," she offered. "The show, I mean. I am only trying to make enough money to take care of the supplies I need to go live in the abbey."

"Well, both the Graf and Hunt Master Gunther wish me to remain with the show for now, to help with your training and make sure nothing gets stirred up that cannot be put down again," Rosamund told her, which relieved her. "If there is a dreadful emergency that requires my services, I might leave for a time, but I will return." She patted the side of the *vardo*. "I think, however, I shall keep this. Small enough compensation for saving the Captain from those rapacious *Vili*, don't you think?"

Giselle laughed. "I think he would be a very stupid man not to give it to you with a smile when you ask for it. And if there is one thing I know about Captain Cody Lee, he might be, on occasion, a little reckless, and he might have a somewhat inflated notion of his own importance, but he is definitely not stupid."

"And that is good to hear. So, good night to you, my friend. I have an hour or two of magic ahead of me, and morning comes *far* too early with this show!" Rosamund laughed, and swung herself up into her wagon. After a moment sitting there chuckling, Giselle did the same.

Because Rosamund was right, again. Morning came far, far too early with the show.

*T*HIS . . . *is perfect.*

The show had moved to Bad Schoensee, where they had set up in a beautiful Alpine meadow. It was a very welcome change from the gloomy, depressing, deep forest they *had* been moving through, and everyone in the company felt the better for the change. The moment they had come into the wide, open valley, it had felt as if a great weight had come off of Giselle's shoulders, and she had stopped feeling as if *things* were watching her. The animals were basking in the sun, especially the buffalo, who had seemed particularly oppressed by the forest gloom.

And now Giselle knew what Rosamund had meant when she had said "You'll know it when you see it," in regards to where she was going to undertake her next phase of training in her Air Mastery. She had known where they would be going as soon as she had set her eyes on the mountains above Bad Schoensee. And now she was currently standing on the top of one of those mountains, surrounded by no vegetation taller than her knees, with nothing between her and the sky but a few clouds. Below her was Bad Schoensee, a tidy little village of white-walled, red-roofed houses, Gasthauses, and a lovely

Kirche. And she, Rosa and Fox were fundamentally alone up here, which made it perfect for working magic in the daylight. Right now the only person any nearer to her than Rosamund and Leading Fox was a shepherd halfway down the mountain with his flock of goats.

They planned to be here in Bad Schoensee for two weeks. It was a spa town on the Schoensee, and as such, they could expect to fill the tent every day for that long thanks to the changeover of visitors. So Captain Cody had decided that the company should have the Sunday in the middle off.

That gave Rosa and Giselle a full day *and* the perfect setting for Rosa's plan. Giselle had known from the moment she arrived here and looked up at these mountains that a spot up here would be ideal for any sort of Air Magic, especially summoning. Her only concern had been that between the shows and everything else they simply might not have the time. Thanks to this Sunday off, they had the time.

It had not been a particularly difficult climb up here. In fact, Giselle could see most of the path that had brought them. And here was Rosamund's cunning; the path was too difficult for a casual hiker, or one of the ladies who might be here at the spa for the sake of her health, but it was nowhere near challenging enough for the athletic. The mountain had a pleasant view of the valley, but there were much better views from other peaks. There were goats grazing on it, which might give pause to the timid city dweller. They could expect to be left alone. There were much higher mountains around the lake and valley, some of which were barren rock, or nearly, but this was certainly tall enough for their purposes.

Although she gazed just behind her at those scoured rocks of a much higher peak a little wistfully. She had not realized until they had come out of the forest just how much she had craved height and free air. This mountain was good, but that one was so much better. The view from there would have been wonderful . . . even if the climb would have required ropes and rock picks.

Maybe someday. Rosa had told her of a wicked Air Master who had contrived a way to be carried where he willed by dual use of a hot-air balloon and his Elementals to push him where he wanted to go. She had thought about that quite a lot, after Rosa had told her the story. Of course in the story Rosa had told, the Master in question had been coercing his Elementals, and if she were to try that . . . well, first of all, she'd have to find a way to persuade the Elementals in question to help her without coercion, and secondly she'd have to have the help of much more powerful Elementals than mere sylphs. Until now, she hadn't dared even try to contact the sort that managed winds and whirlwinds.

Today, that would change.

"All right, remember what I told you," Rosa said calmly, from where she was seated on a round boulder nearby. "Make sure you are calm. Call in the magic of the Air to you. Bring in as much as you can—as much as you can hold, if there is enough here. Then tell me what you see."

She was calm, although she was also excited; it was a peculiar sort of excitement, not one that made her nervous, but one that gave her energy. Air Magic was all around her, and there was *more* than enough up here, in the heights, that she could fill herself with it to overflowing. It sparkled in the air, all the colors of blue that there were, swirling and dancing in the sunlight. Air Magic had been abundant back at the abbey, but here . . . here it was as thick as the scent hanging over a field of flowers.

She gathered it to her, *breathing* it in, watching it swirl slowly around her, absorbing it until she, at least, could literally see the glow of it just under her skin. She filled herself, *far* beyond the point where she had ever dared to before, until she fairly hummed with it and she was sure she could not take in one bit more.

And that was when she raised her eyes to the sky, and saw them, as she had seen them only a few times before.

The Winds. . . .

Not the traditional "Four Winds" of folklore, but the greater Elementals that moved the winds, and moved *with* the winds.

"What do you see?" Rosa asked calmly.

"The Elementals of the wind," she whispered, her eyes still on them. "I have seen them as a child, but far off up in the clouds. These are so close!"

"We're nearer to them," Fox pointed out.

Unlike the sylphs, these creatures had no one form. They shifted from a kind of stylized human, to a flowing birdlike shape, to just wavy shapes in the air, to something vaguely serpentine . . . well, they didn't stay the same from one moment to the next. Yet somehow she was able to tell individuals apart: tell that one might be shyer than the others, one friendlier, one cold, one very emotional. Personalities. She could tell what personalities they had, although she could not have said *how*. It was more something she knew, on the level of instinct.

"Do they see you now?" Rosa asked.

They were indeed looking at her, not steadily, but regularly glancing down at her as if they were curious about what she intended to do next. Giselle nodded.

"All right then. The Greater Elementals, you don't *call*. You *invite*." Rosamund's voice brooked no argument, not that Giselle disagreed with her! She was the Master here, after all.

"Exactly so," Leading Fox agreed, who was standing behind her. "Reach up to them, make yourself known to them and ask them if they would care to come meet you."

Silently, she "reached" for them as she did when she was trying to call sylphs, but the "feeling" was different. As if she was speaking in a higher pitched tone, or singing soprano instead of contralto. And she saw the effect immediately: those nearest her suddenly stilled, and she felt their attention riveted on her.

I am a new Air Master, she said in her mind, trying to keep her thoughts humble. *Would any of you care to meet with me?*

They took their attention off her and transferred it to each other. A knot of them swirled lazily up there, apart from the rest. There was a silent colloquy going on above her, and finally, they seemed to come to some decision. Then several of them—it was hard to tell how many, because of the way they swirled and twisted around each other—plunged down out of the heights and headed directly for her.

The wind picked up around the three humans as they arrived, sending their clothing flapping and billowing as the Elementals circled, examining her.

Finally, they stopped, all of them in a knot, facing her, and the winds died. She held her breath, waiting to see what they would do.

"Greetings." It was a chorus of many voices, breathtakingly beautiful, and like nothing so much as the wind passing over the strings of a perfectly tuned harp.

She bowed. *Greetings,* she thought. *Thank you for meeting with me.*

The reply was a chorus of pleased laughter. *"You are courteous, and careful; well done. You* are *an Air Master. We accept you as our friend. You may call us at need and we will answer."*

How? she asked, both elated and bewildered. *How do I call you?*

"Like this." And her mind filled with . . . a sound. It was like nothing she had ever heard before. She could not have described it if her life had depended on it. And yet, she knew she would be able to reproduce it perfectly if she needed to.

She also knew that doing so would require a tremendous amount of magic from her—rather as if she were to try and blow an *Alphorn.* In fact, that *sound* was something like an *Alphorn.* Or maybe, like an entire chorus of *Alphörner.* Hundreds of them, sounding a single chord in a great and noble harmony.

Thank you, she replied, and bowed again, feeling as if she ought to. She sensed their approval, and when she rose, it was to see something even more astonishing.

There was a bird flying toward the mountain, except that it was like no bird she had ever seen before. Eagle-like, except that the neck was too long, the tail was too long and forked, and there was a crest of feathers on its head. And as it drew nearer, and its shadow fell over the side of the mountain next to the one she was standing on, she suddenly realized *just how far away it still was,* and yet she could see every detail of it perfectly—the dark golden feathers, the golden eye, the way energy *crackled* along the shaft of every feather.

The Air Elementals moved aside for it and it glided in, then hovered just above them, as if it was hovering on the breast of a tremendous updraft that only it could feel. The sense of immense power and control so absolute it made her shiver fell over her.

"My brother," said Fox, putting his hand to his heart. "You do me great honor to have come so far."

She felt, rather than heard, the bird's answer, even though she knew the answer was not meant for her ears. She felt as if she could not breathe, and yet, did not need to. If this creature was not a god, then it was very near to being godlike, and if her knees had not been locked, she thought she might have fallen to the turf, overwhelmed by its presence. And then the bird tilted sideways, circled up, and vanished into the sun, followed by the native Elementals. Then they were all gone, leaving her feeling exhausted and exhilarated at the same time.

The walk down the mountain had taken place in silence, as if none of them wanted to spoil what they had experienced by talking about it. And in Giselle's mind, it was a very good thing that they had plenty of time to get themselves collected before they encountered their first people again. The walk was lovely; she was still *full* of Air energy, and every step felt buoyed by it. Fortunately the path they took down the mountain did not end in Bad Schoensee, but near a farmhouse, and from there, they could walk through the meadow grass to the camp without crossing so much as a beaten track.

By the time they got to camp, she felt almost normal, if a little breathless, a little giddy, and as if she held a wonderful, tremendous secret inside her.

And still, she had to act, and speak, as if nothing had happened, as if they had only taken a walk up the mountain and back down again for pleasure. But the rest of the company had matters of their own to think about; they were back from doing a little shopping or drinking in Bad Schoensee, from doing sightseeing on the Schoensee, or even from going to the Kirche. Or they had taken the opportunity offered by the rare day off to take care of things they had long put off. The camp was *full* of lines strung with washing, for instance, and people were mending harness and saddles and the garments they called "chaps." Some of the big canvas banners had been touched up, as were some of the pieces of the barriers. Wagons had been washed. Bedding was being aired out. And once they reached their *vardos,* she and Rosa followed that example, since there was still plenty of afternoon left to do it in. She was still so buoyed by her experience that none of it seemed like a chore, and she went about giving the *vardo* a complete cleaning in a cheerful sort of trance, humming the entire time.

As the sun began to wester and she put her *vardo* back to rights, the rest of the camp started to settle again too. Rosamund beckoned to her, and she followed her lead, joining everyone else in the mess tent for supper, letting the conversation just wash over her. She really didn't want to eat, and yet, she was ravenous. The food tasted odd, but not in a bad way, but as if she was discovering nuances to it that had not been there before. Captain Cody joined them at their table and kept looking over at Giselle while he talked to Fox and Rosa. He had known what they were going to do, of course; Rosa had told him when he'd decreed the day off. And she suspected he could tell that it had worked.

Finally, he confirmed that. "Damnitall, I envy ya," he said, shaking his head. "I wisht . . . well, if wishes was fishes ev'body would eat. But, hey, y'all wanta try somethin'? T'night, afore the sun goes down?"

"Like what?" Rosa asked, eyeing him curiously.

"All the shootin' tricks. I got a suspicion they're all a-gonna be better." He shrugged. "Iffen they ain't, no harm, an' y'all jest got a good practice in."

"I'd like to do that," Giselle agreed. "I think it might settle me. I'm still feeling—" *not giddy, not buoyant, not . . . merely happy . . .* she groped for the right word, and gave up. "I'd like to see if I can manage the card-splitting trick at last."

She discovered, as Fox and Cody set up targets for her, that there was indeed a difference now: her eyesight was slightly sharper, her awareness of every faintest breath of air keener, and once she began actually shooting, she discovered her reflexes were faster.

And she *knew* things. Like exactly how that coin was going to fall, and exactly when to shoot it so that she could hole it instead of sending it spinning. Like the precise motion of the "rabbit" target, so she could not just hit it, but hit it in a neat little daisy pattern.

Then Cody set up the edge-on playing card for Annie Oakley's famous trick. And suddenly, literally out of *nowhere,* she understood that if she created a kind of tunnel of air for the bullet to travel down, and leaned *infinitesimally* to the right, she could guide the bullet and . . .

. . . hit it.

Splitting it right down the middle.

Just like Annie Oakley could.

The roar of cheering that broke out behind her startled her so much she nearly dropped her rifle. She realized only at that moment that most of the company had gathered behind her to watch her "practice."

Then her rifle was snatched out of her hands, and she was engulfed by the crowd of her fellow showmen and friends, hoisted on their shoulders, and paraded around the camp like a conquering hero, with everyone cheering and singing *"For she's a jolly good fellow!"* until they ran out of breath. And only then did they carry her to the Army Camp and let her down in front of one of the fires, where Captain Cody was waiting with a glass and a particular bottle she recognized.

That was when she came very close to fleeing. Because that bottle . . . that bottle held the Captain's cherished whiskey from America, and it was something she had no desire to experience after sniffing its potent fumes. Beer was one thing, even schnapps, but this? She was absolutely certain that it would remove the skin from her tongue, throat and probably stomach.

But the gleam in Cody's eye, and the grins on the faces of everyone else, convinced her there was no escaping this particular "honor." *I'd better face it and get it over with,* she thought with mingled dread and resignation. So when Cody poured a glug of the gold-colored stuff into one glass and handed it to her, and did the same for himself, she accepted it.

Cody held the glass over his head, signaling he wanted silence, and got it. "Today," he proclaimed. "Our very own Ellie showed herself the equal, maybe even the better, of Miss Annie Oakley. There ain't nothin' Miss Annie kin do that Miss Ellie cain't. So! I call fer a toast! I give you the deadliest shot on this here continent! To Miss Ellie!"

"To Miss Ellie!" came back the reply as a roar of approval, as she solemnly clinked glasses with the Captain. And steeling herself, she threw down the entire shot in one gulp.

It didn't *quite* remove the skin from her tongue and throat, but it certainly felt as if she had gulped down a mouthful of fire, not liquid. Somehow she managed not to choke or gasp, although tears started up in her eyes as some of the cowboys pounded her back in congratulations. Fortunately, a moment later, Rosa thrust a stein of beer into her hands, and with gratitude she quelled the fires in her mouth and throat with its familiar bitterness.

It seemed that the rest of them felt that a celebration was in order. More glasses and steins appeared, and a tapped keg. A couple of the band members fetched their instruments and began some impromptu dance music. Dancing around the fire began, not at all hindered by the fact that there were very few females to partner with; it seemed that cowboys in a dancing mood would dance with each other, or with a broom or a coat, or with nothing at all. The beer flowed generously, the rejoicing became more general, and it wasn't long before Giselle was able to slip away from her well-wishers and go sit in the shadows outside her *vardo* to look up at the stars, and breathe, and think.

"That was the *Hu-Huk*," said Fox, strolling around the side of her *vardo*. "White men call him the Thunderbird. I never dreamed that he would come to me here, in this strange land."

She didn't need to ask him what he meant; he had probably been thinking about that giant birdlike Elemental all afternoon and evening, and just as probably had been waiting with customary patience for her to be free to talk about it. "The One with the Thunder in his wings and the lightning in his claws," she replied, with a nod, and then steadied herself as a wave of giddiness hit her. "He was . . . like nothing I have ever seen before, except . . . except maybe once, when I might have seen a storm dragon." She blinked a little. "I think I am a little drunk."

Fox sat on his heels next to her, and peered into her eyes without touching her. "Only a little, but I think it was wise of you to leave the celebration before that changed to 'falling down.' Wait a moment." He got up, went off, and came back with a bucket of drinking water and a dipper, set the former down next to her and handed her the latter. "Water will help. It was a very good day."

"It was a very, very good day," she agreed, following his advice and drinking three dippers-full of water, slowly. "I was always a little afraid to call the great ones, before. Mother warned me of the consequences if something went wrong."

"Hmm. The storms that angry great ones can bring are . . . dangerous," Fox agreed. "And the danger would be not only to you, but to anyone else unfortunate enough to be in the area. But you conducted yourself well, and you have pleased them. It is good."

"Oh yes," Rosa said, approaching from the direction of the party. "Oh yes, it is very good. I brought you some bread and cheese I got from the cook tent. You shouldn't go to sleep with nothing but beer, water and that *vile* drink the Captain loves so much in your stomach. You'll regret it in the morning otherwise."

"In fact, she should not go to bed until she no longer feels even the breath of the firewater in her head," Fox agreed.

"I don't think I could go to bed right now anyway," she admitted. "I feel like a spinning top! Only in a good way, not a dizzy way."

"I'm going to *guess,* because it doesn't work that way for an Earth Master, that this is the effect of conquering the final Air energies and taking them into yourself," Rosa told her. "Everything feels more alive, right?"

"And clearer, and sharper, and as if I am more in control," Giselle told her eagerly.

"Eat," Rosa scolded, before Giselle could launch into a longer description of how she was feeling. "From now on, you won't have to wonder if lesser Elementals will answer when you call, they always will. But don't take them for granted, ever, or you'll lose the respect of the greater ones, and your control and power will fade. Treat them well, they'll treat you well, just as always."

"Is that why the *Hu-Huk* came to you?" Giselle asked Fox.

"I think yes. And that He understood that it would do me much good to see Him again." Giselle could sense what Fox was not saying, that he missed *his* forests and plains, *his* land, and most of all *his* people and their spirit creatures.

"But now you know the *Hu-Huk* will come to you," she pointed out. "And that the distance is nothing to him."

"Even so," Fox agreed. "A very good day."

They talked without saying very much until Giselle finally felt completely sober, and said so. "Thank you, both of you, for today," she added, with all the feeling she could muster (which was quite a bit at this point).

"It was a pleasure. I'm just glad it went smoothly," Rosa replied, with a smile in her voice, and yawned. "And on that note, I am going to bed."

She went up the steps into her *vardo* and closed the door. But Fox lingered a moment.

"Do not be surprised if the spirits visit you in your dreams," he said, finally, as she waited to see what he would say. "This seldom happens for those whose spirits are of the earth. But for us . . . often. What happens during waking is often only half of what is to come."

She felt a thrill, and a little frisson of fear. *Only half? But . . .*

"They will test your courage," warned Fox. "And your mettle. Be prepared to hold nothing back from them."

"What will they do?" she asked, one hand on the doorframe to steady herself.

But Fox shook his head. "I cannot say. Every test is different."

And with that, leaving her without any answers at all, he turned and vanished into the darkness.

She was almost afraid to sleep, until she reasoned with herself that there was no point in trying to put this off. If the Elementals were determined to test her further in dreams, there was really nothing she could do to prevent that. She would have to sleep eventually, after all.

So she did everything she could think of to steady herself, climbed into her bed, and composed herself for sleep.

One moment she was lying in her bed. The next she was . . . somewhere else.

It was like swimming, or rather floating, but in the air rather than in water. There was no sign of the ground anywhere around, but it didn't feel as if she was falling, so she felt no fear at all.

There was no horizon, just an endless blue all around her. An empty, endless blue, with light everywhere, but no actual light source.

It was so quiet . . . so very, very quiet.

Then the universe shivered with a single, low note. As if someone had softly struck a gong the size of a mountain.

And then . . . it faded into her view.

It was huge, bigger than the Thunderbird had been. And she couldn't have said what, exactly, it was. It certainly wasn't human. But it was no animal, no bird, that she recognized. It had eyes, but everything else was constantly changing, as clouds changed even as you watched them. She couldn't read the eyes, either; they showed no emotion that she was able to recognize.

Wasn't the Greek God of the Air . . . Chaos?

Without any warning at all, she found herself—or her mind, anyway, being leafed through like a book. One moment, she was just hovering there, and in the next, it was as if something was calling up memory after memory at a dizzying pace. Memories of being tiny, and watching the sylphs play above her. Of being a little older, and watching the pixies, and ever so carefully, to keep from frightening them, trying to get their attention.

Of Mother teaching her the rudiments of magic. Of learning to shield, and to use it wisely. Of calling small storms to water the garden, of clearing clouds away so the wash would dry. Of making lights in the darkness, of feeding the sylphs bits of it. And then . . .

When that handsome, terrible man had tried to hurt her.

The moment froze. She froze, caught in the terror of the time, reliving it as if it was still happening.

She felt the Being examining the memory, the emotions, carefully. Weighing it. Measuring it.

And then, dismissing it and moving on. She watched herself learning to defend herself, and learning to shoot, and then the memories began passing through her too quickly for her to recognize them properly, until suddenly they froze again.

Froze on the moment that she had told the night-sylphs, "Take his breath!" and the Hauptmann had died.

Now the Being turned its attention, not on the memory, but on her. It asked her no questions, and yet . . . it questioned.

It examined *her,* in that moment. Examined every nuance of thought, every hint of feeling. Scoured the moment, looking . . . looking . . . for something.

The memory inched forward, to the next moment, when the sylphs had told her that the Hauptmann was not moving.

Once again, she felt everything about that memory being scoured, examined, taken apart, reexamined.

The memory inched forward, slowly, agonizingly, those all-seeing Eyes watching, watching for . . . what? She couldn't tell. She was inside the memory, and yet outside of it. Experiencing it again, able to feel and think everything she had felt and thought at the time, and yet somehow outside of it, as much a spectator as that Being was.

Then she was out the window, and her memories sped up again, flying past, so that she could only recognize a moment here, a moment there, and in that recognition they were gone again.

Then she got a glimpse of the mountaintop of this morning, of the Great Air Elementals, of the Thunderbird, and then . . .

Then it was over. And she was back to being herself and not a compendium of remembrances, hanging in front of those fathomless eyes.

"Would you have done what you did a second time?"

The Being didn't just mean inadvertently killing the Hauptmann. It meant *everything*.

"Without knowing what I know now, how would I have been able to change anything?" she asked, honestly. "I am absolutely responsible for the death of that man, no matter what Rosamund and Tante Gretchen say. But without having had some way to see the future, I don't know what else I could have done besides allow myself to be . . ." She choked on the word. She still couldn't bear to say it. "I can be responsible, regret it, and still know I would have had to act to save myself, all at the same time!" she said, at last. "And I *am* responsible, and I *do* regret it, and I wish there was a way to change it. But not at the cost of letting myself become someone's victim."

"Interesting."

"It is the truth," she said, meeting those Eyes squarely.

"It is." There was a very, very long silence.

"I will never, ever, ask an Elemental to harm someone again," she said into that silence. "If harm is to be done, I will do it myself. It is not fair to ask *them* to be used as a weapon. If I had the chance to do that over again, that is what I would do."

"Ahhhhhhhhh." Another long silence. *"And if they elect to provide . . . aid . . . on their own?"*

"I don't know." How to answer *that* question? "I suppose it would depend entirely on what was happening. I think I would try to prevent them from hurting another human but . . . I don't know." She felt absolutely helpless. What was the right answer? Was there a right answer? "Coercing them to keep them from harming someone is still coercion! I won't do that! I won't! They are free creatures and how can I enslave them even if I think it's for their own good? How is that right?"

"How, indeed."

"Friends are not slaves," she said, finally. "And no friend would make another a slave. That's all I know." She looked deeply into those Eyes. "I'm not very wise. I'm not very old. I'm often not right. But I . . . try my best to *do* what is right."

"You have been heard."

The *sound* came again, and the Being . . . dissolved away. And she dissolved into sleep.

12

IN the morning, she wasn't sure if she had passed or failed her tests. But Air Magic came to her just as easily, and there were pixies frisking about the inside of the *vardo* when she pulled back the bed-curtain, so she could only assume with that evidence that at least she had not failed.

The feeling of uncertainty passed, as the camp woke around her and everyone went back to the daily business of the shows. She incorporated the card-cutting trick into her act that very day, but the whole time, during her turns and in the breaks, she thought about what that Being had asked her. And what she had, more or less, promised.

That was when she decided that yes, there *was* something she could do that would keep her from ever having an Air Elemental in the position of having to decide to kill for her.

And that was, to make sure she had such control over her *own* powers that if any killing was to be done, she would be the one with the skills and the will to do it.

And that meant no more relying on the sylphs or the other Air Elementals to help her with things she could control herself. It was time to learn how to control every single aspect of Air, from snuffing a candle to calling a storm. After all, it was just a matter of control and practice, right? *And how do you become good at anything?* she reminded herself. *Practice, practice, practice.*

The entire run at Bad Schoensee was a success. And the two weeks in the sun and under clear skies did wonders for everyone. It was quite clear at this point that the folks who hailed from the American plains had very much missed the sun; everyone was more cheerful, from the cooks to the band. The buffalo fattened up on the lush meadow grasses, and became even more docile thanks to Rosa's intervention with them. The horses acquired glossy coats and a definite spring to their step, even the ones used for "bronco busting." By the time they were ready to pack up and leave for their next venue, they were all more rested and in better fettle than when they had arrived, despite the two weeks of two shows every day.

Their next destination was Todtnau, another alpine village. Between here and there . . . was more dense forest. But they headed out on their journey feeling more than ready to deal with the dark and gloom for a couple of days.

It helped that the forest they wound their way through on the first day was cut back from the road a bit, and there was none of that *uncanny* feeling about it. Every time Giselle looked up from her book to make sure her horses weren't lagging, she caught glimpses of sylphs, pixies, and zephyrs among the trees. Probably there was just as high a population of Earth Elementals, she just wasn't seeing them.

They found a sunlit meadow big enough to make a decent camp in halfway between Bad Schoensee and Todtnau. There was no water source in the meadow itself, but there was a spring not so far up the valley that it was *too* much effort to get the water barrels filled with the help of a wagon and horses. The more that they traveled, the more Giselle was glad she had chosen a *vardo* to live in, instead of a tent. While the *vardo* could get a little stuffy once the sun was beating down on it, and she certainly was a bit short on room, setting up at a campsite was merely a matter of parking where she was directed to go and unharnessing the horses to take them to the common area for tying up overnight.

Because she could set up so quickly, Giselle got in her practice before supper, and afterward had been planning on an extended read in Rosa's Bruderschaft book. But Rosa had other plans in mind, it seemed, for she rounded up not only Giselle but Captain Cody as soon as dinner was over.

Giselle followed her when she beckoned, and the two of them caught the Captain just before he left the mess tent. "I wanted you both to see something," Rosa said, looking mysterious. "Someone. Both, really. He lives not too far away from here."

"Someone who's also some*thing?*" Cody said quizzically, tilting his hat back on his head. "Now y'all got my attention."

Rosa grinned. Giselle reflected that there was a lot less verbal prodding going on between them, now, which made things much more pleasant all around. During their time in Bad Schoensee, it seemed she had gotten tired of "testing" him—or was satisfied with her results. "Come along, then, it will be worth your while," she said. "It's a nice walk, and I promise that there won't be any *Vilis* along the way."

The Captain mock-shuddered. "Iffen I never see another of them, it'll be too soon," he admitted. "But . . . walkin'? Couldn't we ride?"

She shook her head. "Not advisable. Where we're going is fine for walking, but if the poor horse shied or slipped, it would mean a dead horse."

He shook his head. "Hang if I know why you people like walkin' so much, but all right. I'm game."

Rosa led the way up the path that led to the spring, shouldering a rucksack that she picked up from her *vardo* on the way. Light tree cover began right at the edge of the clearing, but it looked as if people camped here regularly, so the path was well trodden and clear. The trees were in full leaf now; they were just into June and proper summer. There were flowers in the meadow, and even things like violets under the trees, and as an Air Master Giselle was acutely sensitive to their delicate perfumes.

The path itself was not beaten down to hard earth, just flattened grass, which was nice for the feet. Rosa was right, it was a very pleasant walk, and even better, it didn't get appreciably cooler or damper as the sun dropped behind the mountains. This valley evidently held the sun most of the day, which meant it kept some of the warmth well into the night.

The spring gurgled out of a cleft in the rock only about a foot off the ground and formed quite a respectable stream. Once they reached the spring, the path traveled alongside the swiftly flowing stream that it fed. The water looked very inviting, and Giselle stopped just long enough to scoop up a handful to drink. She expected it to be cold, but it was just pleasantly cool. The stream descended into a steep gorge, but the path continued along the edge, with the cliff to their left and the upward slope of the mountain to their right.

I can see why she said no horses. The path was quite narrow: perfectly safe for humans to walk on single-file, but one slip and a horse would have been over the edge of the gorge. Giselle caught glimpses of little Air Elementals flitting through the branches of the trees growing up the slope, watching her with avid curiosity, and to her surprise, also caught sight of small Earth Elementals in the underbrush. The latter paid no attention to her, of course, but she was rather surprised that she could see them at all, since they were trying to remain hidden. Perhaps this was another manifestation of her increased powers?

At any event, just as the sky overhead began to darken a little as a herald to sunset, they reached a gray stone bridge that spanned the gorge. It looked old, very old. She couldn't figure out what style it was, who could have built it, and almost as importantly, *why* they would have done so out here in the middle of nowhere. It was only wide enough for a single person, but it did have low curbs on either side. Ferns grew up all around it, and probably down the side of the gorge as well. Here Rosa halted them.

"Stand back, and don't do anything," she cautioned, and putting two fingers into her mouth gave a peculiar, shrill whistle.

The sound echoed down into the gorge. A few birds flew up out of it, startled by the noise, but for a moment nothing else happened.

Then . . . another sound altogether echoed up out of the depths of the gorge. It sounded like . . . rocks scraping together. Giselle cocked her head to one side and glanced over at Rosa. Rosa gazed at the gorge, not at all alarmed, but as if she had been expecting this very thing.

After a few moments of this, something came up over the edge. It looked like a huge rock . . .

. . . no, it looked like a huge *head* . . . and she nearly jumped out of her skin as she recognized it from tales and Rosa's book.

Holy Mother of God! It's a troll!

"Jumpin' Jesus . . . what the *hell?*" Cody said, but not terribly loudly, though he had one hand on the pistol he always wore, though what use a little lead slug would be against a *troll* Giselle could not imagine.

But Rosa was practically skipping *toward* the creature, a huge smile on her face.

Well obviously . . . this is what she wanted us to see.

"Pieter!" she cried, as the troll heaved the last of his bulk up over the edge of the gorge, and simply stood there, grinning at her. "Pieter, it has been too long!"

The troll looked like nothing more or less than a statue hewn roughly out of granite, with a little moss for hair. It had a huge bulbous nose, and when it smiled, even its teeth looked like two rows of rocks. It was clothed, more or less, in a shapeless garment that looked as if it had been made out of bark.

"*Greetings, Red Cloak,*" the creature rumbled. Its voice sounded like rocks tumbling down a hillside, and yet, somehow, Giselle could understand it. "*Pieter has been very, very good. Pieter has not frightened anyone, and Pieter has only eaten goats Pieter got from Pieter's own flock.*"

"You *have* been good!" Rosa exclaimed. "Pieter, these are my friends. This is Giselle," she continued, waving her hand at Giselle. "And this is Cody."

"Friends of Red Cloak? Hunters?" the troll asked. He raised his head a little, and stared at them, eyebrow slowly rising.

"No, not Hunters, but they have Power." Rosa gestured to the two of them to come closer to the troll. Trusting her friend completely, Giselle stepped right up, close enough to touch the creature. Cody was a little more wary, staying the length of the troll's arm away. From close up, the troll was . . . somehow less intimidating. She shouldn't have been able to make out an expression on his rocky face, and yet, she could. It was benign. She would have said, gentle, if she hadn't been standing underneath a towering form that was at least four times as tall as she was.

"Remember that I said that you couldn't always tell if an Elemental was good or bad? Pieter is a case in point. Most trolls are incredibly dangerous. Pieter, on the other hand, has been an ally of the Bruderschaft for centuries." Rosa patted Pieter's hand, which lay on the ground beside her and was nearly as big as she was. Pieter's arms were very much longer than his stubby legs, so as he stood there, his hands were palm-down on the ground.

"Pieter is old," Pieter agreed, nodding slowly. *"Pieter guards the bridge. Pieter keeps bad things from crossing."*

"Trolls are traditionally found around bridges, and usually demand a toll of something living to cross it," Rosa continued. "Pieter, on the other hand, has been a shepherd for as long as I am aware. The Brotherhood brings him goats, or sometimes he buys them when he needs to replenish his herd. When any of us gets into trouble around here, and we're being chased, we lead our pursuer here, to the bridge, and Pieter usually makes short work of them."

"Pieter guards the bridge," Pieter agreed.

"Can I touch you?" Giselle asked, fascinated.

Pieter nodded and made a vague noise; there were no words in it, but the general tenor was that he was fine with being touched. Giselle reached out and touched his hand. It felt exactly like sun-warmed rock. "Are you made of rock?" she asked, looking up into his craggy face. He had a nose like an elongated boulder, a split below it for a mouth, and two solid black orbs under overhanging moss-covered juts for eyes. His . . . skin, if you could call it that, was the texture of a water-worn boulder, a bit rough, but not unpleasantly so. Only his eyes were shiny, but despite the fact that they were as black as night, they somehow looked kindly.

"Yesss," Pieter said. *"All rock. Pieter is tough."*

"I personally have never seen anything that could take him on in a fight," said Rosa, and patted his hand again. "He's figured as a bit of a hero in our histories for a very long time now. I wish there were more like him! Pieter, you will know them again if you smell them, yes?"

By way of an answer, Pieter raised his head a little and inhaled. Well, "inhaled" was putting it mildly. He sucked in air so hard that her skirt flattened against the back of her legs and Cody's jacket flapped in the breeze he made.

Then Pieter stopped inhaling, and let out his breath in a long sigh. She had expected a fetid aroma, given what she had heard about the sanitary habits of trolls, but instead his breath smelled of nothing worse than a damp cave.

"Yesssss," he said, looking down at Rosa. *"Pieter will know them."*

"Thank you, Pieter," she said, and turned back to the two of them. "Now if you run into trouble anywhere near here, just run for Pieter's bridge. He'll protect you."

"Yesss," Pieter agreed, nodding. *"Pieter go back down now. Goats must go to bed. Then Pieter will listen to the rocks sing."*

"Thank you for coming up to see us, Pieter. Oh! And I brought you some honey from Bad Schoensee!" Rosa opened the rucksack she had carried all this way and brought out an enormous brown pot with a waxed stopper. "Here you are!" she said, giving it to the troll as Pieter reached carefully for it.

"Red Cloak good," Pieter said, somehow getting an expression of glee on his rocky face. *"Red Cloak never forgets what Pieter likes. Pieter thanks Red Cloak."*

"You deserve it, Pieter," Rosa replied warmly. "Good night!"

"Good night, Red Cloak, Yellow-hair, and Hat Man," said Pieter,

and then, carefully cradling the enormous jar of honey in one hand, he began climbing back down into the gorge. Within a few moments he was gone. From the bottom, they could hear . . . well, if rocks could hum, that would be the sound of it. Something like gravel falling, but somehow holding a tune in it.

"Hat Man?" said Cody, as they turned to go back to the encampment. *"Hat Man?"*

"I never know what he's going to decide to call people," Rosa chuckled. "I think he's never seen a hat like yours before." Cody was wearing his white, broad-brimmed hat as usual, so Giselle could understand why Pieter had taken that as the mark of his individuality. "The first time I ever saw him, I was wearing the red cloak that my mother made for me, so that became my name, so far as he was concerned. He calls Hunt Master Gunther 'Face-Moss,' so I think you got off lucky, Master Lee."

"Reckon I did, at that," Cody chuckled. "So . . . trolls is generally bad?"

"Almost always," said Giselle, before Rosa could answer. "There are all manner of children's stories about them, and they generally end with someone getting eaten." She glanced over at Rosa. "I thought that daylight turned them to actual stone, though."

"It does. Sunlight never falls in that gorge," Rosa pointed out. "Pieter knows every inch of it, and every place where it might be dangerous for him to venture. So if you are ever pursued by a troll, you should do your best to get somewhere that sunlight will fall."

"I'll keep thet in mind," Cody responded, "Though I've no intention of kickin' up a troll!"

"Stay out of caves, then," Rosa and Giselle said at the same time, looked at each other, and laughed.

"Trolls sometimes guard treasure," Rosa elaborated. "Pieter almost certainly has some. It's not that hard for a troll to get, even without ambushing travelers. People have accidents upstream and their bodies get washed downstream. When that happens, Pieter is not in the least squeamish about picking over the bodies." She shrugged. "At least he doesn't eat them. He's a troll, and it's remarkable enough that he considers any human beings at all as friends. You can't expect him to act as if the bodies of dead strangers mean anything to him."

"Well, I wouldn't," Giselle agreed, just as they reached the spring and the start of the broader trail that would lead back down to the encampment. "The only thing I am *not* surprised by is how long he has considered himself to be an ally of the Bruderschaft, since he seems to be a very good creature, and probably has been from the time he was . . . well however trolls are made. Trolls live a very long time, I believe."

"Very. Really, I have never heard of one dying of old age." Rosa looked back at the dark gorge behind them. "I've asked him *how* long he's been our friend, and how he came to *be* our friend, but he only looked confused. I don't think he understood the question, because I don't think he understands the passing of time in the way that we do."

It was deep twilight on the trail now, but Giselle did something she had only just learned how to do: she gathered Air Magic, made it visibly glow like a lantern, and set it to float above Rosa's head. She did the same for herself and Cody, and was rewarded by their nods of thanks. With the help of those lights, it was possible to see the trail quite clearly.

"Well, whatcha think happened?" Cody asked shrewdly. "Miz Rosa, I been around you long enough t'know there's likely one good notion, and prolly three or four buzzin' round that head of your'n."

Rosa laughed. "You are right, and I do have an idea," she said. "I think that when he was a very young troll, he must have encountered a proper Earth Master before he got a chance to learn to prey on people. I think that Earth Master found him this gorge, protected him, taught him how to be a shepherd, and got him his first flock. By treating him well, and respectfully, Pieter became a friend, which is how Giselle and I treat our Elementals."

"A'course, that there Earth Master got hisself some mighty fine protection thataway," Cody pointed out.

"Of course," Rosa agreed. "Nothing is ever one-sided. I think that long-ago Earth Master recognized what a good bargain it would be for both of them. But trolls do not generally understand the concept of *bargains,* so he made the arrangements without mentioning anything of the sort, and only when Pieter grew in understanding did he introduce such things to him. Now, of course, Pieter understands such things very well; he bargains with us for the few things that he needs, and considers himself well paid for his protection with what we bring him. He recognizes us at once, even if he doesn't quite grasp how time passes for the rest of us. He's shown great sorrow and some confusion when we've told him someone he knew long ago is dead."

"He understands death?" Giselle asked, then shook her head. "Of course he does, if he has a flock of goats and eats some, and sees dead bodies in the stream."

"He has quite a sophisticated concept of death," Rosa replied. "I have been down in that gorge, and near his cave he has . . . well I would call it a *memorial garden,* made with stones with the names of people he has learned are dead on them, all planted with ferns and mosses. Sometimes he just sits there and contemplates them."

"Really!" Giselle found herself touched. She would never, ever have expected that sort of behavior out of a troll, of all things.

The encampment was in sight now, and just as well, because twilight had truly fallen, and the lights and campfires were welcome sights ahead.

"One day, when I am not being run from pillar to post by my duties, I intend to come here and sit down with Pieter for several days and write down his history," Rosa continued. "He might not understand the passage of time, but there is nothing at all wrong with his memory. And he might not remember peoples' proper names, but he never forgets what he calls them. I think that by starting with me and going backward, I can figure out how long he has been there. And I can certainly get the tale of his earliest recollections out of him. After that I can at least match the rather descriptive names *he* calls people with the records of the Brotherhood."

"That'll make for a hell of a yarn," Cody agreed, as they reached the edge of the encampment. "Jest a damn shame nobody'll ever read it but yer Brotherhood."

"Yes," Rosa agreed wistfully. "It is."

Todtnau was a slightly smaller town than Bad Schoensee, and although it did have a lovely waterfall, it lacked the lake, and so it was not as much of a spa destination. Still, they were able to support a run of four days, and even better, because Kellermann had made sure the show was there over a market weekend, the cost of supplies was cheaper than it had been in Bad Schoensee. Kellermann had counted on this, and made some very shrewd bargains while they were there. The Americans did like their meat, and sausages and hams would keep in the warmer weather better than anything other than salt beef.

Kellermann called the foremost of the members of the show together after the last show in Bad Schoensee. He had a map spread out on the table. "I wanted to show you all this, so there would be no rumors that I was leading you around in circles," he said, looking at each of them in turn. "Look, there is Bad Schoensee," he said, pointing. "And here is Todtnau. Now, here was my problem. We could have gone this way, up to Freiburg, which is a city and we probably could stay for two weeks or more. But it is a long way, and only one village on the way, so there would be no way of earning much money on the road there. So I rejected that."

Everyone nodded, including Giselle.

"Or, I could see that we could backtrack a little bit, and take this route to Neustadt. It's longer, and circuitous, but there are seven towns on the way, and we can stop and do at least two days in each. It won't be a lot of money, but we also don't have to do the full show, just the main tent, so there won't be as much to set up. So that is what I arranged." His finger traced more of their route. "From there, we go to Donnau-Eschingen, then back this way to Freiburg with a great many shows on the way, and from *there* I can arrange things farther north, all the way up to Strasbourg and Baden-Baden. We can have at least three weeks in Freiburg, I think, which will give me plenty of time to arrange more bookings."

"That looks pretty fine to me, Kellermann," Cody said as they all contemplated the map.

"I'm not planning on taking us farther north than Baden-Baden, because Wild Bill's show is in the north." Kellermann shook his head. "You know what happened when you followed him in France. Half-filled tents. That was why you canceled the rest of the bookings and went down to Italy."

"It was worse'n half-filled, sometimes we didn' have no more'n a dozen customers," Cody told him, as the others nodded, agreeing with him. "I knew you was smarter than that thief that made the first set of bookin's!"

Kellermann relaxed, and smiled. "Well, I do know my country-men. And I do know that the people here in the Schwarzwald tend to be overlooked when it comes to traveling entertainments of our size. I'm glad you approve."

"Say, Kellermann," Texas Tom spoke up. "You reckon we'll be able to go home by November?"

"Go home?" Kellermann said. "Well . . . yes. You'll have more than enough to book passage for everyone home from, say, Amster-dam or one of the Italian ports. If you all plan to disband, you won't need to bring the tents, or any of the livestock except those you really want to, and I can certainly arrange for all of it to be sold. But you won't go home rich."

Faces fell all around the table.

"On the other hand," Kellermann continued, "If you were to stay another year here, as Buffalo Bill is planning on doing, your reputa-tion will have increased dramatically *and* you will benefit from the reputation of Buffalo Bill. I will be able to book you for a month or more at Heidelberg, Ulm, Stuttgart, Munich, *none* of which will have seen Buffalo Bill's show, since he is planning on returning to England next year. I can confidently predict that yes, if you remain until . . .

October after next, you *will* all go home rich. We only need to find a cheap place to spend the winter. Italy, perhaps. . . ."

Giselle did some quick mental calculations. "What about free?" she asked. "You'd only need to provide provisions for yourselves and the animals."

Now everyone was looking right at her in astonishment. "Where would we find some place to winter for free?" Kellermann asked cautiously.

"Where I came from," she told him, and quickly described the abbey. "It's in very good repair. It used to hold several hundred nuns. The only thing that is not in good repair is the old chapel, which we had deconsecrated. You could probably put the cattle and the buffalo in there, and some of the horses that wouldn't need stabling, if there are any that tough. It would be rough living, but"—she shrugged—"free. And more sheltered than winter camping."

"If'n we got there early enough, we might could snug it up a bit," Cody mused. "Most of us're good rough builders."

"Free . . ." said Texas Tom. "I'm a-likin' the sound of that."

"I am too." Cody looked to Kellermann. "Whadya think?"

"I think we have our winter quarters," Kellermann said. "Show me where, on the map."

"Here," she said, pointing.

He looked the map over carefully. "Yes, this is good. I can easily arrange for the last bookings to be within easy striking distance." He looked up at her and grinned. "My dear Giselle, the day you became our lady marksman was a good day for this show in more ways than I can count. Thank you for the offer of hospitality!"

She flushed. "The worst that will happen is if I miscalculated and some of you have to spend the winter in wagons."

"That is no hardship," Kellermann assured her. As she looked around at the others, she was relieved to see that they were nodding.

"For that matter," Fox spoke up for the first time. "We know ways to make good shelters with turf and some good long logs. Good enough to sleep warm in, at any rate."

"There's plenty of turf," she said, the remembrance of those strange earthen houses that the Pawnee called home flashing across her mind. "And it's the Schwarzwald. There's no end of logs."

"Well, there you go. We'll be fine." Cody chuckled a little. "Cain't imagine that anybody near to a city would have been too happy 'bout us diggin' up their purdy meadows t'make sod houses, no way. An' . . . be honest with y'all, I dunno how we'd git anyone t'put us up inside four walls for free."

"Hmm." Rosa had been listening all this time, and although she didn't say anything she gave Cody, Giselle, and Fox looks that suggested she had something to say that wasn't for general consumption.

"Well, that settles that, then!" Kellermann said cheerfully. "I will leave you all to settle in for the night, we complete loading in the morning and go back down the road we came."

The group broke up then and, responding to Rosa's silent signal, the four Elemental Magicians and Kellermann gathered together and began to walk slowly toward the wagons. The main show tent was already down and had been taken down after the show, as had the sideshow tents. "So what were you arching your eyebrows about, Rosa?" Giselle asked, as they got out of listening distance of the others.

"I can help with some of that, if you end up needing to make those earthen shelters," Rosa said. "I'm an Earth Master, and my Elemental allies could build those easily enough, so long as you have instructions or plans."

Cody snorted. "In that case, we ain't got nothin' to fret about. If there ain't enough shelter in this here abbey, we kin make 'nuff. I spent plenty winters in a sod house, an' they kin be right cozy."

"And it isn't as if anyone would have to spend the entire day there," Giselle pointed out. "It would just be a warm place to sleep. For that matter—" she looked at Rosa. "—if your Elemental allies would not *mind,* they could be at work rebuilding the chapel and adding onto the other buildings while we are still performing. Then no one would have to sleep in a dirt shelter."

Rosa snapped her fingers. "Now that is good thinking! Given that your Mother was an Earth Master, I am sure they all know where it is—and given that the abbey is far away from the nearest village, they could work openly. I'll just let them know how many people, and how much livestock to build for."

"And food storage!" Giselle reminded her. "It isn't likely that Talinsdorf or Marekdorf could supply food for as many people as we have all winter long! Whatever we need, we should plan on getting in a bigger town and bringing with us." She thought about that a moment. "Would Earth Elementals know how to harvest hay?"

"I can find out," Rosa promised.

"Then they should be able to get at least two harvests from the meadows around the abbey, and that should be enough for all winter long." Giselle was feeling extremely happy now, and it showed in her voice.

And the others noticed. "What're you so chipper 'bout, Ellie?" Cody asked, sounding amused.

"After all this time with all of you, I wasn't looking forward to the winter alone," she confessed, flushing. "I was perfectly happy when it was just me and Mother, and I thought I would be all right with her gone and just my sylphs, but . . . I find I like being with other people much more. And the idea of spending a whole winter by myself was not very appealing."

Cody patted her shoulder awkwardly. "'S'all right. I know how you feel. Hellfire, most've us thet've had t'spend a long winter 'lone know it ain't somethin' a human oughta do. I did thet once. I ain't never doin' it agin, if I kin help it."

"Well, now that we have all of that neatly settled, I will do some investigation and see if I can't persuade some dwarves in your part of the world to show off their skills." Rosa laughed. "I suspect I can, if I start now. And if I can't, Papa Gunther almost certainly can."

And what would happen the winter *after* next, when the entire company would presumably be gone?

Perhaps I can persuade the Bruderschaft to establish a new Lodge in the abbey! she suddenly thought. *I shall ask Rosa about that . . . later.*

"Do you think you'll be staying the winter too?" she asked Rosa instead.

"I can't promise anything," Rosa replied. "It will depend entirely on if the Graf wants and needs me for that season." Giselle felt her heart drop a little. But then Rosa added "It's as good a place to over-winter as the next, and the Graf does a great deal of the sort of entertaining in winter that I am not all that fond of." Her voice took on a wry cast. "I do like luxury, and I do like the fine food and the lovely clothing he supplies me with, but I don't much care for catering to the whims of a lot of inbred idiots whose pedigrees are as long as my arm, but who have more hair than brains. And last winter, persuading some of them that my favors were *not* part of the Graf's hospitality cost me a great deal of my temper, and they are fortunate I *have* an even temper, or three of them would be missing hands!"

"Well then, I hope the Graf does *not* need you," said Giselle, with a laugh.

"An' on that cheerful thought, I'm sayin' good night," said Cody, parting from them as they reached his tent.

"As am I," added Fox, heading across the campground to the Pawnee teepees.

Since Kellermann also was one of the few who had a *vardo,* he walked with the two of them to where the wagons were parked and paused at his. "I am grateful beyond words for all you have done for us, Giselle," he said. "But the offer of a wintering spot . . . makes me very happy indeed. I cannot think of anything that would suit me more than to be able to spend Christmas in your company."

With that, he took her hand, and squeezed it, and went to his wagon.

"Well!" said Rosa, after a moment. "I was going to give you a little warning about not getting attached to the Captain . . . but . . . I'm going to say *no* such thing about our friend Kellermann!"

"Oh don't be silly," Giselle replied, blushing, and glad it was too dark for Rosa to see it. "He's just being extremely polite."

"Hmm. I don't think so," Rosa opined. "But suit yourself. I'm going to bed!"

13

IT occurred to Giselle that a seasoned walker could probably go faster than the show train did. They were forced to keep their speed to what the cattle would do, and the cattle were not at all eager to move past an amble. That was why it was taking them so long to travel the winding roads of the Schwarzwald. On the other hand, the leisurely pace gave them all a bit of a rest between the nonstop, even frenetic pace of show days.

And when they found an absolutely *perfect* meadow to camp in overnight at the place where the road to Menzenschwand branched off from the one they were on, they even stopped early. The meadow was bordered on one side by another sparkling stream, which meant no one would have to carry water, and there was plenty of grass. The farmer who owned it was happy to share it with them, since he was going to get free entertainment as they practiced, and his children were nearly over the moon on seeing the Pawnee set up their tee-pees. Once again, Giselle got her practice in early and settled down after an equally early supper thinking she was going to get a good read in on the Bruderschaft book.

Which was, of course, when Rosa tapped on the door.

The sun was just going down, and Giselle repressed a sigh of exasperation. "What is it?" she asked, opening the door. "I hope there isn't something else you want me to meet."

"No . . . no, it's that . . . there's something not right about this place." Rosa cast a look over her shoulder. "Not like the ruined convent. And it's not *here,* specifically. But off that way." She waved vaguely in the direction of the north. "Somewhere between here and Pieter's bridge. Earth Elementals don't move very fast. So . . . I was wondering . . ."

Giselle rolled her eyes, but only a little. "All right, give me a moment. I'll get a sylph, they're the most articulate."

She waved Rosa inside and shut the door, then opened a bottle of lavender water and spun up a ball of magic. She'd learned since Todtnau that sylphs liked perfumes and incense almost as much as magic.

It seemed as ridiculously easy now to call a sylph as it had been when she was very little, and they just came. It was a night-sylph, this one with velvety batwings, who wafted in through the window over the bed, snatched the floating ball of magic and ate it, then hovered over the vial of lavender with a blissful expression.

"What do you need, Air Master?" she asked.

"My friend wants to know if there is anything amiss to the north—" Giselle only got as far as the direction, when the sylph's expression of bliss turned to one of terror.

"No! No! No! We do not go there! It is death! It is death!" she shrilled. And vanished.

Rosa and Giselle exchanged a look of alarm. Finally it was Giselle who cleared her throat and spoke first. "And I thought you were being overly nervous because nothing has happened for several weeks. . . ."

"Not nerves. Instincts," Rosa replied, her jaw set. "Once you've been in the Brotherhood a while, you get them, very keen, very accurate. The only question I have is if you are game to go with me to find out what this 'death' is."

Giselle bristled a little. "Of course I am. Should we get Cody or Fox?"

But Rosa shook her head. "Not just yet. We two are natives here, this has nothing to do with them. In any event, Cody doesn't have all that much in the way of power, and I don't know what Fox can actually *do* besides call on his own version of Elementals. At least I know how you've been trained."

"Well, my Elementals, at least the little ones, are clearly too terrified to be of any help." Giselle reached up to get her gunbelt and her newest acquisitions; since Bad Schoensee she had been learning to handle the revolvers that Cody Lee was so good with. She was a fair shot with them now, and was used to their weight and kick. She very much doubted that she'd be ever be as good as the Captain was unassisted, but with another month of practice she thought she might be able to do some trick-shooting with them.

Right now, though, if she and Rosa were going to go hiking through the forest in search of something dangerous, they presented a better option than a rifle, no matter *how* good she was with the rifle.

She buckled the belt on and settled the weight of the revolvers so they rode comfortably, and made sure she had enough cartridges. "Anything else I should take?" she asked.

Rosa considered. "Salt," she said. "Lots of things besides ghosts are discomfited by salt."

Giselle added a pouch of salt, procured from a box in the ammunition chest, to her belt.

Rosa got her crossbow, her coach gun, a pair of daggers and— somewhat to Rosa's surprise—an ax from her arsenal. She stared meditatively into the chest for a moment, staring at something that Rosa couldn't see. Then she shut it resolutely. "Not the silver armor," she said. "Your sylphs would not have been the least afraid of a werewolf or a *vampir,* and those are really the only two things that the silver armor is useful against."

Rosa came back down the stairs, holding out some leather straps. "Bind that split skirt close to your legs. More mobility." Giselle noted then that Rosa had done exactly that already, and followed her example. "I don't want anyone to stop us from leaving or try to go with us, so we're going to sneak out of camp."

"Probably best." Giselle made a face. "No matter how many times we prove otherwise, the men don't seem to believe we can take care of ourselves."

"Which is ridiculous," Rosa agreed, "Especially when you consider how many settler women over there on their frontier are doing just that." The wagons were always placed at the outside of the camp, so it was a simple matter for them to slip across the strip of meadow between them and the forest, then find a game trail into the trees. It was going west, not north, but once they were under cover, Giselle made a dim little light, just enough for them to pick their way among the trunks and start going in the right direction.

What was it that Rosa was feeling, anyway? If Rosa could sense something amiss, and the sylphs could, surely *she* could. As Rosa led the way, she extended her senses, or tried to. Earth Masters were typically very sensitive to the "health" of their Element. *That might be because their Element doesn't move about,* she considered, still unable to "pick up" whatever it was that was making Rosa so anxious. Had the sylph actually sensed the danger too, or had she reacted out of experience?

Probably experience, Giselle decided, as Rosa struck a game trail that was going in the right direction. Sylphs were not particularly known for anything but "living in the moment." As long as a danger stayed in one place, and it was a place they could avoid, they really didn't much care or think about it. It was only when you reminded them of it, or asked them to go there, that they reacted with distress.

"What do you think it is?" she asked, in a low voice, but not a whisper. The sense of the forest here was . . . not oppressive, but not welcoming either. *Wary,* that was the word she would have used. As if all the Elementals here were not quite sure of them or their intentions.

Then again, there was a farmer here. Elementals didn't care for farmers. Farmers tamed things, and although there *were* "domestic" Elementals, like brownies, they were rare. Most Elementals were creatures of the wild, and like creatures of the wild, they did not approve of anything that went about taming the wilderness.

Giselle didn't blame them, actually.

"Well," Rosa said, after a long pause, as they picked their way down into a little gravel-strewn valley and back up again, still following the game trail. "Whatever it is, it's affecting mostly the Earth. I gather you aren't feeling anything?"

"Nothing," Giselle replied.

"Well, that only leaves about a hundred things it *could* be. And if you eliminate the ones that wouldn't be 'death' to a sylph, that leaves about fifty. Which is why I have a coach gun, a crossbow, and an ax. Most things it could be are things we can deal with by simple material violence." Rosa held aside a branch so it wouldn't slap Giselle in the face.

There didn't seem to be anything more to say. *So watch where you step, and don't make any more noise than you can help. . . .*

"That?" Giselle whispered doubtfully, peering through the parted branches of the bush she and Rosa were hiding behind. They were looking at one of the most charming little woodland cottages she had ever seen. Its windows shone with warm, friendly light, its thatched roof looked practically new, it was clean and neat and all the plaster was freshly whitewashed. There were flowers in the yard, and yellow curtains at the windows. The only anomaly was that there was a big oven in the yard going full blast. You'd never be able to bake anything in an oven that hot, you'd have to wait until the roaring fire in there burned down to coals. Which did not look to be happening any time soon.

But it was hard to imagine that something that innocuous, even welcoming, could hold any sort of a menace.

"Really?" she said doubtfully. "That?"

"That," Rosa affirmed grimly, as if her teeth were clenched. "If you were an Earth Master, you'd be throwing up at this point, because despite its looks, that place is pure poison. It's a lair, a horrid, tainted, vile lair. It's supposed to look like a friendly cottage to lure victims in. And now I know what the problem is. It's a Blood Witch."

"I haven't gotten that far in your book . . ." Giselle said, uncertainly.

"It's . . . special," said Rosa, grimly. "When a witch who practices blood magic manages to find and mate with an Erlkoenig, and she has a child, the child is much, much worse than she is, and absolutely not human. If the offspring is male, it's another Erlkoenig. If it's female, it's a Blood Witch. They're rare. Thank God, they are rare, in part because an Erlkoenig is as likely to kill the witch as mate with her. But we have a Blood Witch here, and we are going to need help. The damned thing is as fast as a snake, as strong as a troll, and its hide is as tough as a crocodile's. My crossbow bolts will just bounce off, and I'm not too optimistic about your bullets."

She let go of the branches, and Giselle did the same. They both slid deeper back into the bushes and put their heads close together so they could talk. "What do we do?" Giselle asked.

"You try and get some Air Elemental to come close to this cottage and take a message for us. An Earth Elemental won't be fast enough." Rosa looked over her shoulder. "We need to get some distance between us and it. I don't want to take the chance on it sensing us before we can get that help."

They retreated into the dark forest and took shelter in the middle of a circle of juniper bushes. Nothing was going to be able to find them in there, not with the strong smell of juniper covering their scent. Giselle concentrated, as hard as she could, bringing in all the Air Magic she could hold to bolster her plea. She wasn't trying for a sylph this time; they were too timid, and given how the last one had reacted, probably would not come close. Anything smaller would never, ever take the risk if a sylph was too frightened. She was trying to reach something she had only ever encountered once.

She was trying for an aether.

"Aether" could refer to the Greek god of air and chaos, or a greater spirit of air sometimes identified with storms and tempests. But an aether was not, in fact, either of these. It was aloof, and powerful, and according to Mother was rarely seen, yet the one she had encountered as a child had regarded her in a kindly fashion and actually hovered outside her window and told her stories. It was certainly powerful enough not to be concerned with a Blood Witch, or so she hoped.

She concentrated on her plea, trying to make it as forceful yet as humble as she could, and holding the image of the aether she had seen in her mind. It had been as if there was a man before her entirely made of air, something she could only see vaguely, mostly by the way things behind it were slightly distorted. She might not have been able to see it, but she had *felt* it, and so had Mother when she had come back from a trip to one of the nearest villages. Mother had been extremely surprised to see it, and when it had gone, had warned her to always treat such creatures with great respect.

If this doesn't work . . . I'm going to have to hope that one of the sylphs will get up enough courage to . . .

The sharp tang of ozone made her eyes fly open. She couldn't see it . . . but once again, she could certainly *feel* it. And it *felt* just like the one she had met so many years ago.

Its first words confirmed that yes, it was. *"My little friend, the protector of the sylphs. It is good to see you grown into your power."*

The voice was quiet, barely above a whisper, but she could hear it clearly. And by Rosa's startled expression, so could *she!* Giselle got a little thrill down her back.

"What is it you ask of me?" the Aether continued. *"I will do what I can for you, but I fear I cannot help you with the evil that dwells behind you. I have no power over her kind."*

"No . . . sir," Rosa whispered. "But my friend Pieter, the troll to the north of here, does. Could you possibly take a message to him swiftly?"

"Ah! A simple, trivial request. So trivial, I gladly go out of friendship. What shall I tell him?"

"Come as quickly as he can!" Rosa begged.

"I shall carry your scent with me, and leave him a trail to follow. Farewell!"

The scent of ozone vanished. "Is he gone?" Rosa asked. "The last time I encountered something like that . . . well, it was the remnant of a god."

"Yes," Giselle told her. Rosa nodded, and they crept back to the bushes, parting them to look at the cottage.

Time crawled. She knew that the aether would probably get to Pieter within moments. How long was it going to take Pieter to get here? She didn't think the troll was all that *fast*. And would he understand the urgency? She had no idea how bright he was, but . . .

The door to the cottage opened, and a flood of light came from within, a light too strong to have come from something like candles or an oil lamp. A strange creature emerged from the door, and there was so much light Giselle could see it perfectly clearly. It looked vaguely human . . . but its arms and legs were too long, and too spindly; its torso was too short, and it seemed to have next to no neck, just a hunched-over back with a head jutting from the top of it, a head covered with an unruly shock of straw-like hair. The more Giselle looked at it, the more inhuman it looked, as if everything about it was wrong in some way. It didn't move right, the joints bent in unnatural places. It made her a little sick to look at, and her skin began to crawl.

It was dressed in black rags, and when it turned sideways for a moment, she saw it had a face that was like the caricature of an evil witch in a child's book, all nose and chin, with glowing green eyes. It was the eyes that made her feel truly horrid, although she could not have said why. The eyes were the least human thing about it. There was a malevolence there that she could not even begin to measure.

It reached into the cottage and pulled out something. No, it was not a something, it was a someone.

A child. A young girl, who was sniveling and shivering, all pulled in on herself as if she was doing her best to keep away from the creature. It was easy to see her in the light pouring from the doorway, too; she wore the typical smock and apron of a farm child, but both were dirty and tattered. Her hair was coming out of its braids, and she was barefoot. Her face was filthy, and tear-streaked, and had that blank, stunned look that only came with utter terror. She was carrying something in her arms, something bulky, like a bundle.

The Blood Witch shook her. "Go, my pretty, and feed the piggies." The voice that came from the thing sounded like creaking hinges. "One of them is surely fat enough by now. I'll follow you and test them, yes I will. I am ready for a feast!"

She shook the girl again, then shoved her forward, toward the far side of the cottage. The girl stumbled and recovered herself before she fell, careful not to drop what she was carrying. Then she shuffled around the side of the cottage with the creature no more than a couple of paces behind.

And that was when the screams and cries began, coming from the opposite side of the cottage. Giselle felt a fresh jolt of fear mixed with nausea. What in the name of all that was holy was going on here?

"Oh blessed Jesus, it's worse than I thought!" Rosa said. "She's got an entire pack of children back there, and she plans to cook and eat one right now. We can't wait for Pieter! Come on!"

And with that, before Giselle could object, she charged out of the bushes, heading for the cottage, already pulling her ax off her back.

Oh no—Giselle lurched to her feet to try and stop her, but it was too late.

Giselle followed, skin crawling with fear, both revolvers in her hands, although she couldn't remember pulling them from the holsters. Rosa might be used to fighting things like some sort of lady-Siegfried, but she *wasn't!* And she couldn't imagine what good her Air Magic could do here; she certainly couldn't call on any of the Lesser Elementals for help, and if she called, would a Greater One even answer?

But she couldn't leave Rosa to face that monster alone. So she ran as fast as she could, trying to catch up, hoping she wouldn't stumble over something in the yard and fall flat on her face. She was going hot and cold in turns, and she was very, very afraid.

The two of them charged around the side of the cottage, and the light from the windows on that side cheerfully illuminated the row of rusty iron cages there, six of them, each cage holding a child standing inside. The girl they had seen before was just now shoving a chunk of bread and cheese through the bars of the nearest as they came around the corner. Tears streamed down her poor little face. The children inside the cages, howling and weeping, had backed themselves as far away from the fronts of their prisons as they could, as the Blood Witch cackled and reached her long, skinny arm through the bars for the first one.

The girl didn't hear their feet thudding on the ground as she and Rosa raced toward them. But the Blood Witch did.

The creature whirled to face them, and Giselle was reminded of nothing so much as a poisonous, four-limbed spider with a witch's face. She nearly turned and fled at the sight of the thing; if she had been alone, she probably *would* have. She was absolutely frigid with terror now, but there was no way she was going to leave Rosa to face this monster by herself.

The Blood Witch shrieked at the sight of them, sounding like nothing so much as a cross between a steam whistle and an angry fishwife, and before Rosa could get in the line of fire, Giselle holstered her left-hand revolver, took careful aim and emptied her right-hand revolver at the creature, using a trick that Cody had shown her and fanning the hammer instead of pulling the trigger.

It shrieked again, and even though Giselle was fairly sure at least half of the bullets had struck it, it didn't act as if it had been wounded at all. Rosa closed with it, but it somehow leapt *over* her head and came down behind her, moving faster than anything Giselle had ever seen in her life. She grabbed and emptied the second gun into its back, with as little effect.

Giselle felt her throat closing up in panic. If bullets did nothing, how were they ever going to stop this thing, or even hold it off long enough for Pieter to reach them in time?

Rosa whirled just as the thing charged her; it had a knife as long as Giselle's arm in one of its skeletal hands, a cleaver in the other. Rosa parried the first with her ax, and dodged under the wild blow from the second, then danced backward out of reach.

Giselle pulled the bag of salt off her belt and threw it as hard as she could at the monster's head. The bag hit the side of the creature's head and split open, sending salt spilling all over the Blood Witch's head and shoulders.

That had some effect. The salt actually sizzled where it struck the monster's skin. The horrid thing screamed, and turned to see what had burned it. But turning sent the salt flying into its eyes and it screamed again, shaking its head in pain.

That gave Rosa the chance to charge it from behind, cutting through the air with her ax. The thing turned instantly, and stopped the cut only just in time, leaping backward in Giselle's direction.

She backpedalled as fast as she could, and spied another ax buried in a stump beside the woodpile. It didn't look like much, but it was better than two guns that had no effect at all! She dropped her revolvers, ran to the ax and wrenched it out, then turned to help Rosa, her heart pounding and her nerves on fire. Her breath burned in her lungs and somehow flooded her with electric energy. If only she knew what to *do* with it!

Rosa was fighting for her life. The Blood Witch hadn't marked her yet, but the thing's speed was incredible, and it was clear that it was all Rosa could do to keep the knife and the cleaver from connecting. It was concentrating on Rosa as the truly dangerous one, however, and didn't sense Giselle charging it from behind until Giselle struck it in the back with *her* ax. She managed to hit it at the top of the thing's humped back, between where the shoulder blades *should* have been.

The ax bit for a moment, and stuck, and the Blood Witch screamed. It was a sound so piercing, so painful, that Giselle fell helplessly to her knees, clapping both hands over her ears.

The Blood Witch whirled furiously to meet the new attack, only to have to turn back to face Rosa again as the Earth Master resumed her attack. Giselle staggered to her feet and looked for another weapon, as the Blood Witch redoubled her blows on Rosa, driving her back, and back and back—

Now she panicked. Rosa couldn't bear up under that punishment for much longer! *Something! Anything! I have to—*

"RED CLOAK!"

Before the Blood Witch could beat past Rosa's defenses, a deafening howl of rage and outrage shattered the night. The Blood Witch turned again, and Giselle felt herself shoved to one side as Pieter charged past her, his other hand outstretched to seize the monster.

The Blood Witch howled in response, and leapt to meet his charge, Giselle's ax falling off its back as the monster jumped.

She landed on Pieter's face, more like some kind of hideous insect than ever, and clung there, hacking away at his eyes with her cleaver. Pieter cried out. In anger? In pain?

Rosa threw her ax.

Giselle watched it fly, shining in the light from the cottage windows. It spun through the air, lazily turning over and over three times. And then it hit the Blood Witch squarely in the back, right in the same place that Giselle's woodcutting ax had cut it open. Giselle prayed it would at least slow the monster down.

But this weapon nearly split the Blood Witch in two when it hit.

The Blood Witch screamed again, and this time both of them, all the children in the cages, and the girl who had been feeding them, clapped their hands to their ears and dropped to the ground from the pain. It felt as if someone was driving red-hot needles into her brain!

Only Pieter stayed erect. And *he* pulled the Blood Witch from his face with both hands, threw her to the ground, and stomped on her. There was a terrible crunching sound. The screaming stopped abruptly. And in the silence that followed, Pieter rumbled something unintelligible. But it sounded very, very angry.

Giselle sat up, slowly. *Is Pieter all right? That thing was trying to dig out his eyes!*

Then Pieter allayed her fears as he spoke up. He peered anxiously at both of them, and shuffled toward Rosa. *"Is Red Cloak all right? Is Yellow-hair all right?"*

Rosa got up first and staggered toward him. He held out his massive hands, and she embraced him. "Oh Pieter!" she cried. "You did it, Pieter. You were wonderful! You got here just in time. You saved the life of at least one of these children. And very probably mine as well."

Both Pieter and Rosa were so engrossed in each other that neither of them was paying attention to what was left of the Blood Witch. But just as Giselle stood up and started toward them, she caught motion out of the corner of her eye.

The Blood Witch was pulling itself erect, broken limbs snapping back into place, split body pulling back together again.

Giselle shrieked at the top of her lungs and pointed, and Pieter whirled, faster than she would have ever believed possible for a creature of his bulk, and grabbed the reforming Blood Witch in both hands.

It screamed shrilly, and writhed in his grip, clawing at his massive hands, scrabbling for his face with its long arms.

"The oven!" Rosa cried. "Pieter, the oven!" She ran over to the oven, knocked the red-hot latch open with a piece of firewood, and the doors swung apart, showing the interior, so blindingly hot that Giselle winced and looked away. That was when she saw the bread-peel, like a flat-bladed shovel with an iron blade and a long wooden handle, leaning up against the brick wall that held the oven. She ran to it and snatched it up as Pieter marched toward the oven, holding the Blood Witch out at arm's length. The closer he got to the oven, the more she screamed. Giselle ran to his left side, as Rosa snatched up an ash-rake and converged on his right.

The heat from the fire was so intense it felt as if her skin was burning. Pieter shoved the screaming witch in through the oven doors, and as he pulled away, shaking his hands, Giselle and Rosa put their implements into the Blood Witch's chest and shoved her all the way inside. They jumped back, and Pieter slammed the iron doors closed again and dropped the latch in place.

"Pieter!" Rosa exclaimed, dropping the rake to grab at one of his hands. "Are you . . ."

But Pieter chuckled. *"Pieter not hurt. Pieter tough."* And sure enough, when Giselle examined his other hand, although there were scorch marks on it, he didn't seem to have taken any real damage. *Better than me . . .* the skin on her face and hands felt very tender. *On the other hand, we could be dead, so I think we got off easy.* She was very glad Cody hadn't been along. He probably would have tried something recklessly brave and gotten himself killed or badly wounded. *Probably killed. He would have gallantly thrown himself in front of Rosa to protect her and just as gallantly been hacked to bits.*

"Let's get those children free," Rosa said, patting his hand.

"Won't they be as terrified of Pieter as they were of the Blood Witch?" Giselle asked, anxiously. But then she turned around, and saw that all of the children were now pressed up against the bars of their cages—saying nothing, but reaching out with yearning hands. The one little girl that had been free was huddled against the bars of the middlemost cage, eyes as big and round as teacups.

Giselle ran to the first cage. "It's locked!" she said, rattling the door angrily. "And I'll bet that wretched Witch had all the keys on her!"

The little girl burst into tears, but Pieter just laughed. *"Pieter strong,"* he pointed out, and proved it by putting a hand on each of two of the iron bars and literally bending the bars apart until the boy inside could squeeze out. He did the same with all the other cages, and the boy in the middle one fell on the girl who had been free and the two of them hugged and cried with happiness. It was so moving that Giselle felt a lump in her own throat.

Meanwhile the other five children clustered around Pieter and Rosa and Giselle and clung to them, some laughing, some crying, some doing both at the same time. The poor things were so filthy, their clothing in rags, their hair in dirty mats, that it was impossible even to tell what sex they were.

"Where did they come from? How did they get here?" Giselle asked, trying to figure out how to comfort them.

"Mutti left me in the woods an' never came back," said one.

"Mama and Papa died," another said sadly. "I tried to find some-one to live with, but they all sent me away."

And so went the tragic stories. Three, the boy and the girl who still clung together, and the first one that had spoken, had been taken into the woods by a parent and left there. Three had been orphaned and had been searching for someone to give them a place to stay. And the last had run away from a father who beat him until his bones broke. All of them had found the cottage, been drawn to it, and had been taken in by what they *thought* was a kindly old woman, who fed them, and put them to bed—

—whereupon they woke up to find themselves in cages. Or, in the little girl's case, the Blood Witch's slave.

"She cooked an' ate us," the little girl said, shaking like a leaf in a windstorm. "Since Hans an' I got here, she ate Fritz, an' Dietrick, an' Franz, an' Josef."

"She likely ate a lot more than four," Rosa muttered to Giselle and Pieter, who nodded. "It has been a while since someone from the Bruderschaft who was also an Earth Magician has been through here."

Is the light . . . going away? Giselle realized it was getting difficult to see, and glanced over at the cottage. And her jaw dropped.

The light from the windows was fading, but more than that, the cottage itself seemed to be aging before her very eyes. Black mold was visibly growing over the walls, the plaster was forming cracks, and the thatch of the roof was rotting. Even as she looked, astonished, one of the shutters on the window nearest her started swinging by only one hinge. "What's happening to the cottage?" she gasped. Rosa cast a glance in the direction she was looking.

"The Blood Witch's magic is wearing off. Or rather, her illusions are. That's the way the cottage really looks," Rosa said flatly.

Any thoughts that Giselle might have had about the children staying here evaporated as the last of the light faded out of the windows and enormous holes appeared in the roof. Giselle spun up a ball of magic, set it alight, and put it to hover over their heads so they could all still see. Then she went and retrieved her revolvers from where she had dropped them, and reholstered them.

"What are we going to do with these children?" she asked Rosa, helplessly. "We can't take them back to the show! Even if there was a place for them in it, how would we ever explain where they came from? Or how we rescued them? Or *why* we went charging out into the night to do so?" It was one thing to speak openly of magic and monsters to the Captain, Leading Fox, and Kellermann. It was another entirely to do so to *anyone* else.

The children's heads all came up at once. But before they could start begging or crying, Pieter spoke up.

"Children come stay with Pieter." And it was very clear from the tone of his voice and the way he patted the backs of the two clinging to his legs that he meant it.

Now the children raised their voices to plead to be able to do just that. "Children," Rosa ordered, in a stern voice. "Hush a moment."

It was clear from the way that they quieted immediately that they were all too used to obeying without question. Instead, hopeful— and some tear-filled—eyes turned toward Pieter as the ultimate arbiter in this question.

"Pieter, are you sure you want to do this?" Rosa asked. "Are you sure you *can?* Children need more than food, they need clothing, they need warm beds, they need to be clean—"

Pieter chuckled. It sounded like rocks falling. *"Pieter's cave is warm. Pieter has goats. Pieter knows where many things grow. Pieter has human monies. And Pieter has Bruderschaft friends. Pieter even has books. Pieter can teach children books. Pieter can teach other things. Children will learn to tend goats, to build, to lay stones, all useful things."*

"I can spin and sew and knit and cook," said the little girl, rubbing her nose with the back of her hand.

"I can chop wood, and I can cook, too," said her brother. The others all volunteered things *they* could do, until Rosa held up her hands, laughing.

"All right, all right! I am convinced. You can all go and live with Pieter." She smiled as they clapped their hands and laughed. It looked as if it had been a very long time since any of them had worn a smile.

Rosa looked up at Pieter. "After you feed them and let them sleep the *first* thing you must do is get them clean, Pieter," she said, sternly.

Pieter looked down at all of them. *"Pieter must shear your heads like sheep,"* he said. *"You will have bugs in that hair. All except little girl. Little girl must keep pretty hair."*

Thankfully the children all thought that idea was hilarious, and the one that looked to be the eldest agreed, ruefully, that they *did* have bugs in their hair. Pieter nodded solemnly. *"We go home, Rosa,"* he said. *"Help children up."*

By this, he meant that Rosa and Giselle were to help the children to climb up on him, for he intended to *carry* all of them to their destination. The biggest one straddled his neck and clung to his head; he had one on either shoulder and more cradled in his each of his massive arms. So that he could see and would not stumble—or crush something—Giselle made a second light, and sent it to float above his head until he got to his cave.

"Good night, Yellow-hair, Red Cloak," Pieter rumbled, his mouth turned up in a curiously charming smile. *"Pieter was happy to help. Pieter is happy to have new friends. All is good again. Yes?"*

"Yes, Pieter," Rosa said warmly. "All is well that ends well. Time to get your new friends to their new home, and put them to bed."

Giselle nodded. Two of the children held in Pieter's arms were already nodding off. Pieter smiled, nodded instead of waving, and turned. The last they saw of him, he was lumbering—carefully—off into the distance, along the swath of destruction he had cut through the forest to get here.

Rosa looked at the cottage, which was now nothing but a ruin. She frowned, and turned to the oven. A few pieces of wood had fallen out when they pushed the Blood Witch inside and were lying on the ground, still smoldering. Rosa walked over and picked one up, blowing the end into flaming life again. Striding deliberately to the ruined cottage, she tossed it inside, where the old straw from the roof immediately caught and blazed up.

She and Giselle stood together and watched the cottage burn. It didn't take very long; the place must have been as dry as old paper.

"You were very lucky, you know," Rosa said, soberly. "An extra child, given away to someone who wanted and loved you. We of the

Brotherhood hear stories like the ones those children told far too often. Except that what we *see* is bones, or sometimes bodies, in sheltered places in the woods. Parents who can't feed themselves, much less their children, lead them out into the woods and leave them there. . . ."

Giselle shuddered. "How often does something like that happen?" she asked.

Rosa shrugged. "Once is too often. But what happens in cities can be worse."

"I'd rather not know," Giselle replied faintly. "At least not right now."

Rosa nodded. "Let's go home. I mean, back to—"

"I know what you mean," Giselle replied, "The camp feels like home, now. And . . . we saved those children and destroyed that horrid monster. I think we can sleep well tonight."

"What's left of it, anyway." But Rosa laughed quietly. "Yes, we did. We saved the children. They are not going to go work as near-slaves on someone's farm or in someone's inn. They are going to go have a good life with Pieter."

"I would say that is virtually guaranteed." The scent of ozone and a cool breath of air was the only warning either of them had that the aether was back. *"Well done, you. But let's err on the side of caution shall we? I can carry a message for you to the Bruderschaft der Förster, Rosamund. If you like."*

"That would be . . . unbelievably kind of you!" Rosa exclaimed, as Giselle beamed her thanks at the ripple in the air that was the aether. "Please tell Gunther what happened, and that someone needs to look in on Pieter and make sure he has everything he needs for those children. I have no idea how he thinks he's going to get clothing for them, for instance. It might be summer *now,* and they'll be fine in clean rags, but winter will be coming all too soon."

"Easily done. I can be there before Master Gunther goes to bed." There was a wild wind that tossed everything around for a moment, and then the aether was gone again.

"You must have impressed that aether," Rosa said thoughtfully, glancing over at Giselle. "I've never known one to volunteer to do that much before."

"You also don't know too many Air Masters," Giselle pointed out hastily. "And neither do I. I have no idea what's *normal*. For all I know, aethers are like Pieter, they like people and want to help if they can."

"Point," Rosa replied, and yawned hugely. "And since we are *not* aethers and will have to walk back, let's get started. I can't see my bed soon enough."

14

FREIBURG was the biggest city that Giselle had ever seen, and in many ways she was very, very glad that the show had been booked here for most of the month of October as part of Oktoberfest, because it meant she was *working,* and working hard, six days in the week, and didn't have much time to think about how very big and very intimidating the city was. She could not even begin to imagine the sheer size of cities like Hamburg and Salzburg and Vienna, when Freiburg made her head spin.

The way Kellermann chuckled over the receipts each night made her think that they were probably bringing in more money than the show had ever seen before. And certainly the show, *and* the tour of the camps, *and* the sideshows were all immensely popular. So much so that tickets had sold out for every show so far, even after Kellermann had arranged to expand the seating, and the stream of people coming through the "camps" on tour seemed endless. They really did not stop coming from the moment that the box office opened until the last of them was chased out at night. Kellermann had even been considering opening up the practice sessions to spectators! Paying ones, of course. Captain Cody persuaded him that this would be a bad idea, for which Giselle was quite grateful.

The show was so very successful that the show enclosure was completely surrounded by other vendors, other exhibitors, and tiny shows of dancers and freaks, jugglers and magic acts, acrobats and feats of accuracy and strength, all hoping to take advantage of those who were leaving disappointed because they could not get in.

The Pawnee were in great demand by photographers and journalists—none of which were surprised by the fact that Leading Fox was highly articulate in German. After all, wasn't Winnetou?

It was fortunate that in a slightly smaller city, Neustadt, back in July, the entire show had really come to understand how much the German public relied on Karl May's works to form their idea of what the American frontier and its denizens were like.

That had been at the point where their journey was scheduled to wend back westward, and the Captain had quickly decided after the first couple of days that he should be as much like Old Shatterhand as possible. He had quizzed Giselle long and in detail about the hero of those books, no longer treating them as a source of fun. The rest of the company had also picked up pretty much what Germans would expect of them—which really, aside from a few details, was what they had already been portraying. A bit more exaggeration of the eccentric, really; they'd added embellishments to their costumes in the form of leather pieces, animal teeth and skins, most of which were, ironically enough, bought in Germany to be added to their "rigs." A moth-eaten stuffed bear, for instance, gotten at a secondhand dealer for a pittance, had been turned into two dozen necklaces featuring teeth and claws, and ragged fur collars and hatbands. For the rest, Kellermann, now fully acquainted with the contents of the first three Winnetou books, at least, "translated" what the others said with a "frontier" flair.

Now the whole business ran as smoothly as a well-oiled machine, with everyone knowing exactly what the Germans most wanted to hear and see, and making certain to give it to them.

If Neustadt had been a kind of dress rehearsal, then Freiburg was the full production.

The show was but one part of the enormous Oktoberfest carnival, which covered an area that was itself the size of a small city. The Oktoberfest field played host to huge tented beer halls able to hold hundreds of people at a time, to vendors of every sort of food and goods, to amusement rides, and musical entertainments and exhibitions— well, anything that you *could* fit under a tent and make money doing, you would find here just past the two pillars that marked the entrance to the field. On their weekly day off—the Captain and Kellermann chose Tuesday, at the request of the other shows—the company really didn't have to leave the grounds to get pretty much anything they wanted. And more often than not, they didn't ever have to pay. If it wasn't for the vendors themselves giving them food and drink and entertainment just for the "draw" their presence made, it was random strangers thrusting drink and food and presents into their hands. Convinced that she and Rosa were Americans, the two girls had found themselves gifted with dirndls and blouses, shawls and embroidered stockings, and urged to "wear these when you go home and think of us." All the women in the show had been gifted with these garments, but most of them had been given to Rosa and Giselle because they were most often together outside the show environs, and people seemed to be under the impression that they were sisters. It was a reasonable assumption, being as they were both blond and rather typically Bavarian in looks.

Carefully putting the latest of these away into storage in the morning, Giselle wondered if she would need new gowns for the next twenty years—so long as she stayed the same size! *At this point, I think I have a dirndl in every color of the rainbow,* she thought, patting the latest, a blue one, a bit flatter. If the last two weeks were anything to go on, she'd be needing room for more.

Rosa found these gifts terribly amusing, which Giselle understood, knowing what Rosa *usually* wore, as well as the fact that *dirndls* would probably raise amused eyebrows when she spent time in the household of her patron, the *Graf*. Giselle could imagine . . . barely . . . the sort of outfits that Rosa probably wore. *Much* more stylish and fashionable than those of the good ladies of Freiburg.

But she suspected that the ladies who gifted the two of them with these dresses fondly assumed that, for them, this would be . . . fashionable. They'd never recognize Rosa if they ever saw her in one of *those* gowns.

It also would have left most of the kind ladies who pressed these garments on them fainting, had they seen what Rosa called her "armor"—a set of leather garments lined in cloth-of-silver, that were, well, tailored for her but identical to what her masculine counterparts wore.

"I'll never let our dear benefactors know," Rosa had said after the fourth such gift, "But mine are all going to find a home with some of the other ladies. We aren't that dissimilar in size, after all."

Rosa had already regifted most of her gowns to the other ladies and one each to the Pawnee men to take home to their wives. What the Pawnee women would make of them, Giselle had no idea . . . but then again, Leading Fox's idea was that they should make themselves look as much like the whites as possible once they got their land bought, so perhaps the dirndls would serve that purpose.

Certainly no one could have asked to be treated better than she and Rosa and the others were. Every gift was bestowed with real kindness and the sense that these folks were trying to offer the hospitality of their city.

As for the way the Pawnee with the show were treated when they ventured outside of the enclosure, well, all they had to do was look at something with interest, and generally *someone* would find a way to gift them with it. They all had at least two brand new hunting rifles each (Leading Fox had four *and* a shotgun), enough handsome shawls to fill three steamer trunks, and enough silver hunting badges to gladden the heart of any of them wanting to play the plains peacock.

The cooks had very little work to do, since any time one of the company wanted to eat, he could stroll out into the public areas outside the show, turn up at any of the food or drink tents, and be fed royally—either he would be treated to a meal by someone who wanted to pepper him with questions, or the stall or tent owner would give him a free meal as long as he sat there to be gazed at. This, too, was making Kellermann very happy; less spent on food meant more profit. He had, in fact, instituted a new rule, that if you intended to eat in the mess tent for a particular meal, you had to sign up on a sheet so the cooks would know how much to make. Most people attended breakfast, but when it came to luncheon and an after-show supper, well, why bother when you could get yourself stuffed at a beer hall?

It was partly a matter of the simple fact that late fall was slaughtering time. Anything that could not be preserved had to be eaten. For instance, hens too old to lay eggs anymore and all the roosters but the chief of the flock were often killed at this time. Roasted chicken had been an uncommon treat for the show folks back in America, since flocks of chickens were uncommon on the plains, and each one precious; chickens were common in Germany, and at Oktoberfest chicken was standard fare.

Then there were the sausages, using every scrap of every sort of meat available; without smokehouses, it was hard for the folk of the plains to make things like sausage, bacon and ham. For some of the cowboys, the many sorts and flavors of sausage had come as a revelation. And several of them had vowed to eat their way through every variety of sausage they could discover.

And then there was Schwarzwald ham. Ham was a rich man's meat, back in America, especially where these folks were from. Beef was everyday food for them, they were surrounded by cattle. Pig . . . no.

But especially during Oktoberfest, pork was common, not only domestic pig but wild boar, and Black Forest Ham was a readily available specialty. The cowboys were . . . well, very happy.

"Where are we going for supper?" Giselle asked Rosa, as she closed the cupboard under the bed on her latest gift. They had both returned to her *vardo* after breakfast. Rosa was perched on the little pull-down seat and tapped her lips with a finger thoughtfully.

"Hmm, good question. We haven't been to the *Alpingarten* yet, and the owners have come by several times asking me pointedly if you and I were going to visit." Rosa licked her lips. "I'm told the *spaetzel* is as fluffy as a plate of clouds."

"Oh, not a *biergarten* then?" Giselle grinned.

"Not one of the giant ones, no, a nice little tented version of their restaurant. I thought you might appreciate something other than sausages." Rosa raised an eyebrow. "And appreciate eating with all the utensils, not just a knife and fork."

"But I *like* sausages," Giselle retorted.

"*Sauerbraten mit spaetzel,*" tempted Rosa, a little smile on her face.

"Oh!" Giselle exclaimed, her mouth watering at the mere thought. "Yes, yes, yes!"

"I'll send word they can expect us then. You'll have your sausages at luncheon. Kellermann just made an arrangement this morning with Stuck's. They're going to supply our luncheon from now on, on condition they can say so outside their tent and at their *bierkeller* when Oktoberfest is over." Rosa laughed at Giselle's expression of surprise. "Yes, yes, Kellermann has us endorsing restaurants now. I suspect if the show were to stay here instead of returning home, he'd have you endorsing soap and corsets. Honestly, Kellermann has taken to this sort of promotion as if he was born to . . . what's the English word? Ah, *ballyhoo.*"

"He certainly takes good care of the company," Giselle said, standing up. She felt her head, frowned at the looseness of her hair, and began to unbraid her it. "Time to cut this again. Have I got coals in the stove?"

Rosa checked. "All set. Shall we get this over with as quickly as we can?"

It took nearly an hour to get Giselle's hair unbraided, cut and braided up again, and every scrap of it burned in the little stove that heated her *vardo.* Burning the hair in the stove was the only way to keep the entire wagon from stinking of burned hair, but the smell still wasn't pleasant until Rosa tossed a couple of pinecones on the coals to take the stench out. The oddest thing was, the sylphs and pixies and even the zephyrs that loved sweet smells would *flock* to the chimney and act like cats in catnip when she burned her hair. *There truly is no accounting for taste.*

Giselle felt very sorry for Kellermann each time she had to do this—when he'd realized how fast her hair grew, he'd gotten a wild idea to sell locks of it as souvenirs, and the poor man had been jumped on by herself, Rosa, *and* Fox. "Put the *hair* of an Elemental Master out there for anyone to get his hands on?" Rosa had said, horrified at the very idea. "Why not just put Giselle up on an auction block and be done with it?"

"Uh—would it be that risky?" Kellermann had gulped.

"Yes!" all three of them had said, together. Then Giselle had explained how having her hair in his possession could allow any magician—particularly those practicing dark or blood magic—to quite literally control her. "From the moment I left the abbey," she told him sternly. "I have made absolutely certain that every strand of my hair was accounted for and burned to ashes."

"Oh . . ." Kellermann said faintly. "But it is such a pity . . . are you sure?"

"Yes," they all three chorused, and that was that.

At least it wasn't growing quite as fast as it used to. *I wonder what Mother intended to do with all those long braids of it she had.* As far as she knew, they were all still locked up in a chest in Mother's room, back at the abbey. She hadn't been in there since Mother died.

She cast the thoughts aside, and finished putting her hair in order. Once her hair was properly braided and coiled up, she was ready for the first show. "Ready?"

"Lead on." Rosa gestured to the door.

The *vardos,* along with the living tents of those folks who were not amused by having their every move watched curiously by spectators, were behind a second wall of canvas just inside the first one. They hadn't needed that particular arrangement elsewhere, but here, those ticket-holders who were allowed to roam the camp seemed to take that as liberty to go *everywhere.* Having that canvas wall there had been working so far, at least. Giselle had a sort of three-sided tent with a campfire and a little arrangement of camping equipment in the Cowboy Camp that she was supposed to be in when she was not performing or practicing. She sometimes wondered if these people actually believed she lived like that. She was beginning to get a very good idea of what an animal in a zoo must feel like.

There were already people wandering through the camps as she took her place in "her" tent. She and Rosa exchanged a look, and Rosa shrugged. "I'll go to the mess tent and get luncheon for both of us," she offered.

"Then I'll start the coffee." Giselle had managed to learn the trick of brewing the bitter drink, which she had become quite fond of, as had Rosa. It lent an air of verisimilitude to her campsite, to have a coffee pot on a grate over the fire. By now the days were cool enough that both the fire and the hot coffee were welcome, and she was glad of the heavier buckskin garments in her costume wardrobe.

Rosa returned with a straw basket full of food. By this point, Giselle was surrounded by people asking questions about her presumed life in America, about her shooting, and so on. Giselle was about halfway into the narration she could have told in her sleep by this point, but interrupted it to put the sausages that Rosa had brought on the grate over the fire to rewarm while Rosa poured them both coffee and added sugar and cream. To facilitate eating while talking, Rosa wrapped a piece of dark rye bread around a bratwurst on a bed of sauerkraut, dabbed on some mustard, and handed it to her.

At that point, Rosa got included in the questioning. She had decided on her own story. No one recognized her as one of the Indians when she wasn't wearing the black wig, which was all to the good as far as she was concerned. So when she was out in the camp with Giselle, she had decided that she was a horse-tamer. As an Earth Master that had been simple enough to pull off, and Cody had even added a couple of places in the show where she could demonstrate that. One, where she and a brown and white "Medicine Hat Pony" called Pitalesharo ran through a number of clever tricks, and one where she "tamed a Wild Stallion" that was one of the bucking horses. Both routines could easily be dropped from the show when she'd had to go off on mysterious errands on behalf of the Brotherhood—which she had done at least six or seven times over the course of the summer. She never explained where she went, or why, and no one ever had the temerity to demand she tell them. According to her story, she had learned her trade from her father and she had tamed Lebkuchen for Giselle, which was how they had met. Captain Cody had taken her on to be in charge of the company's horses and buffalo.

Giselle had finished her luncheon and was deep in explaining to a group that was about three deep around her that no, she had never met Old Shatterhand, and no, she had never seen the mysterious gunsmith "Mr. Henry" who had supposedly made his amazing rifle when . . . she got the oddest, and most unpleasant sensation of being watched.

She couldn't exactly break off what she was doing to look around. And she couldn't summon one of the sylphs to see if her feeling was correct, either. All she could do was glance at Rosa to see if *she* was exhibiting similar unease. For all she could tell, all was well with Rosa, which did nothing to make *her* feel any better.

It made her skin crawl, actually. It was nothing like the feeling she got when someone was gazing at her with rather too much admiration. No, this was as if someone was measuring her, sizing her up, judging her. It was the feeling she would have associated with being weighed by a predator she couldn't see.

The feeling did not go away. In fact, if anything, it got slightly stronger, right up until the moment when the visitors were chased off so the first show of the day could begin.

And at last, as she and Rosa hurried toward the staging area, she got the chance to say something. "I had the most awful feeling that someone was *watching* me, and it wasn't friendly!" she said, as the two of them lined up for the Grand Entrance Parade. "Did you?"

"Not at all," Rosa replied, and frowned. "I know better than to ask another Master if that was just her imagination, so it must have been concentrated only on you. Do you have any idea why anyone would be spying on you from a distance? I assume it was at a distance."

"Not at all," Giselle said, mounting Lebkuchen. "I couldn't catch anyone nearby at it, and I felt as if I shouldn't give away the fact that I knew it was happening by looking around. But I don't like it, not one bit!"

"Try and give me a signal if it happens again," Rosa replied, bringing her pony up beside Giselle. "I'll try and slip off and see if it's being done magically. I might not be able to tell if it's Air Magic, though," she added warningly.

Giselle tried not to feel a little sick. "Ugh! It makes me feel unclean, or somehow naked. And if it's being done magically, there's no telling what whoever it is might try to see. I suppose if I don't want to be spied on in my *vardo* I'm going to have to ward it, but wards aren't going to do me any good at all when I'm outside. I mean, I can ward myself, but all that would do is make a blank me-shaped spot in the scrying bowl or whatever he's using, and that's not much better."

Rosa nodded, but they didn't get to say anything more. The entrance curtains opened, and the Grand Parade began.

Twice more that day, Giselle got that feeling of being watched, and each time, the sensation wasn't as if the distant voyeur was the friendly sort. The opposite, rather. The second time, she managed to signal Rosa, but as her friend had warned, the Earth Master wasn't able to detect anything. It happened a third time as they left the show enclosure to go to the *Alpingarten* for supper, but it appeared that once they were moving, the crush of the crowds made it harder for the watcher to find her, and he never managed to catch up with her again. So Giselle was able to relax and enjoy a rather delightful dinner, sitting at a huge table and entertaining an enraptured, and thankfully quiet, group with her manufactured tales of life on the frontier.

It was very dark by the time they finished and returned, and it seemed that the watcher had either given up for the night or wasn't able to find them. The grounds of the Oktoberfest were astonishing.

There were electric lights strung down the main thoroughfare—an innovation Giselle had never actually seen for herself until now—and the effect was quite startling to someone used to the light of candles, lamps and fires all her life. Of course, most of the grounds were still lit by lamps and even torches, but seeing those glass bulbs glowing steadily without so much as a flicker seemed more magical than the use of her own powers.

"Do you want me to help ward your *vardo?*" Rosa asked, as they entered the now-quiet grounds of the show. It looked as if the visitors had just been cleared out; people were relaxing at their tents, rather than being "on show," and people were eating various delectables they had gotten out in the grounds and brought back to share. Pastries and pretzels mostly; Giselle spotted a lot of decorated gingerbread and jelly-filled donuts being devoured, as well as both hard and soft pretzels.

"Yes, please," Giselle said gratefully. "And . . . I think I ought to start refusing presents of food. Or at least we should start testing it somehow. I didn't like the way that watching *felt,* if you know what I mean. It . . . it seemed cold, measuring. Not at all friendly."

"I completely agree, and it will be easy enough to for me to make sure anything you are given is safe to eat," Rosa replied, waiting to mount the stairs of the *vardo* behind Giselle. "Earth Magic is good for that sort of thing."

"I'm glad you don't think I'm being silly." Giselle lit a paper spill at the coals in her stove, and lit her two hanging lanterns with it.

Rosa snorted. "I've been stalked by werewolves, hunted by other Elemental Magicians *and* by a ghost, threatened by *vampir,* and . . . well, I am the last person to think you are being silly if you feel as if you are being watched by something or someone unfriendly. I don't know what enemies you could possibly have, but who knows what enemies your Mother collected! And for all *we* know, that wretched Blood Witch has an ally here, and that's what's watching you!"

"Or it might be an Elemental of some sort. I don't know enough about what's likely to be around a city," Giselle said doubtfully.

"Or it *might* be one of the Greater Air Elementals that has been coerced in the past and is *not* pleased to see an Air Master about that might think about coercing it again." Rosa set about gathering the few things she would need for her warding. Giselle didn't need anything more than a bit of incense, which she got out of a little box and started burning.

"I hadn't thought of that. I hope that is what it is," she said, sitting herself down at the table and composing herself so that she could concentrate on building her wards. "If it is, well, it will see I am no threat eventually, and go away."

Building the wards was one of the first things that Mother had taught her once they had *really* started in on her lessons, but Mother had warned her not to use them unless she actually needed to. "Merely putting up wards signals to other Air Masters and all Air Elementals that there is an Air Mage there," she had said. *"Not* putting them up is often safer than doing so, if you are not planning on working any magic. Doing nothing at all keeps you invisible unless something is looking for you."

Well, something had not only been looking for her, it had found her. *So, wards it is.* She breathed in the scent of the incense, and pulled in the energy of the Air and infused the incense with it, willing it to protect her from every sort of magical attack. Once the air was saturated with scent and magic, she gently compacted it all, "pushing" it away from herself and infusing it into the porous walls and floor and ceiling of the *vardo,* and creating invisible walls of scent and power over the windows and across the chimney vent. She left nothing to chance, and when she was absolutely sure she had every possible entrance blocked, she set it all in place with a final burst of power and opened her eyes.

Rosa had *her* eyes closed, and Giselle felt the pulsing of golden Earth Magic about her still. So she remained quiet, to keep from disturbing Rosa's concentration, until her friend exhaled and sent a final pulse of magic of her own radiating out into the *vardo* walls.

"Well!" Rosa said, opening her eyes with a smile. "That's that. If anything manages to see past what we've done, I will catch it and eat it."

Giselle chuckled. "And speaking of eating . . ." She reached over her head and brought out a box of marzipan formed and colored into the most delightful shapes of fruits. "Look what I have!"

"Oh . . . marzipan . . ." Rosa licked her lips. "I really think though, just to be sure, I should test it first. You know. Just to be safe."

"Of course!" Giselle chuckled. "Just to be safe. I'll make some tea while you test it. Just make sure you don't test it until there is none left for me."

15

WITH the visitors shooed out for the night, all of the chief members of the company had gathered around a table in the mess tent. There was just a little more than three weeks before they needed to be in winter quarters at the abbey, and plans to get there needed to be finalized. And it was not enough for just Kellermann to make those plans; anyone who might need to have a say needed to be here to speak up . . . just in case. There was a big map spread out over the table, and Kellermann had his ever-present notebook out.

"We have one more week of Oktoberfest, and then we move out," he said. "And now we need to start transitioning to our winter quarters, the abbey that Giselle has so graciously offered to let us use."

"I've heard from the builders I commissioned," Rosa said immediately, not mentioning that those builders had been Elementals—dwarves, mostly, she'd said, but with a handful of brownies to make sure things were going to be comfortable. Dwarves tended not to think of *comfort* when they built, but rather making something substantial, that would last. If dwarves had their way, everyone would be sitting on stone furniture, at least, according to Rosa. "All of the repairs and needed additions are complete. I have a crew in place to start actually getting everything ready for us."

A crew . . . that would be the brownies? Giselle wondered.

"They are headed up by a relative," Rosa continued smoothly. "So I know that we can trust that things will be safe there and there will be no pilferage."

That clarified things a little. *A relative. That will be a member of the Bruderschaft. Or an ally, but definitely human, and probably another Earth Magician. Excellent.*

"That was my next question. So if I were to start sending supplies, and possibly parts of the show ahead?" Kellermann asked.

"I'll make arrangements ahead of time from the nearest train depot. You can rest assured that everything will be safely stored in all the proper places by the time you arrive," Rosa promised. "I'm intending to leave the company at the end of this stint in Freiburg, in any event, and journey on ahead to make absolutely sure nothing goes amiss. I can travel much faster alone, and I intend to go by rail most of the way. Once I leave you, I can be at the abbey in no more than three days. I'm arranging to have a horse waiting for me when I arrive at the station in Meiersdorf."

"Ah!" Kellermann said. "That is excellent." Both Kellermann and Cody looked a little surprised and a little relieved at that.

"You sure you'll be all right alone?" Cody wondered aloud.

Rosa laughed. "I have made journeys across three countries alone and never had a bit of trouble. I'll be fine, I promise you. And if I do that, I'll actually be there ahead of the first lot of supplies. It will not be the first time I have been responsible for a task like this. Anyone who thinks to cheat me or steal from you is going to discover that I open every barrel, cask, box and sack and double-check the contents." She raised an eyebrow and patted the handle of the revolver that Cody had given her. She had proven to be a reasonably good shot with it and it was certainly easier to carry than her coach gun. "They will discover I am not a person to trifle with."

The Captain laughed. Kellermann just shook his head. "In that case, does anyone have anything to add or object to?" Kellermann looked around the group, but everyone seemed satisfied with the plans, and to have confidence in her competence. "Good. I think the entire scheme is a sound one. After Freiburg, we will run a smaller show. We'll break down everything we won't need for that show and ship it on ahead to the station at Meiersdorf."

Rosa nodded. "I'll arrange for pickup there and see it all gets brought to the abbey."

"I'll do as much purchasing of winter supplies as I can here, where the prices will probably be lower, and also send that on ahead," Kellermann continued, as the rest of the company's leaders listened and nodded approval. "The rest of our engagements are no more than three days each. I'd skip them altogether but they'll offset the expenses of travel. But as I see the opportunity to pick up more supplies, I will, and either send them on ahead or we'll bring them with us."

One of the men in charge of the cargo wagons spoke up. "If'n we pack tight for space, instead of fer how easy it'd be to unload and set up, if we pack up the Midway that way fer the year when we break down at the end of this here Oktober thing, we kin load a whole lotta supplies along the way on the Midway wagons."

Cody and Kellermann looked at each other. "I don't see us needing the Midway after Freiburg," said Kellermann. "It will be small towns. One show, two or three days running, for each."

"If that," warned Giselle. "Once the snow starts, no one will want to watch a show in a tent."

"Once the snow starts, I ain't a-gonna wanta *be* in a show in a tent!" protested the chief "wrangler."

"We'll take every show we get to do as a bonus," Kellermann promised. "And once the snow starts, *we* will not stop except to camp until we reach the abbey."

"Don't be fooled by light flurries," Giselle added, frowning a little. "There is no real road to the abbey, and the last part of the journey will be over rough land."

Kellermann looked over the heads of the others to where the chief carpenter of the show stood. "Can you have runners made for all the wagons in a week?" he asked.

The carpenter spit tobacco into the spittoon in the corner of the tent and nodded. "Skids is simple. Plenty of good wood hereabouts, and four skids for each wagon ain't gonna add much to the load. If'n this was gonna be for use all winter, I'd want iron skids, but wood ones'll git us there."

"Get it done," Kellermann said. "I'll leave that in your hands." He looked around. "Is there anything else?"

"There prolly will be, but we kin handle it when it happens," the chief wrangler said, laconically.

"All right then. Git t'yer beds. We have 'nother week of hard work ahead." Cody brought the meeting to a close. Rosa and Giselle left together.

"Any more of your watcher today?" Rosa asked, quietly, as they headed for their *vardos*. "He doesn't seem to have let up at all."

"Yes. It doesn't seem to be more, or more intense, but if I'm not outside the show grounds, it's off and on all day." By this point, Giselle was less fearful than angry. She had tried getting her sylphs to find whoever it was, but they said it was not someone using a sylph or any other Air Elemental to do his watching for him. Fox had tried some other way to find the watcher—some Pawnee magic, he wouldn't give her any details—and he didn't have any more luck.

"It has to be by scrying, then, and good luck with tracing it back if you don't *already* know who it is," Rosa decided. "That means the likeliest is a Fire or Water Magician, although . . . it could be Earth. There's a technique for scrying using a mirror made of obsidian or flint that works for some Earth Mages."

They had to pause for a moment as a couple of the cowboys walked past them, chewing tobacco and speaking about the horses.

"But don't you know who the magicians in Freiburg are?" Giselle asked when they were out of hearing range. "Can't you at least check to see if it is one of them?" She was getting rather desperate at this point, after two whole weeks of feeling those eyes on the back of her head. Every evening, Rosa would ask if the unseen watcher had given up yet, and every evening she would have to say no.

But Rosa shook her head as they reached their *vardos,* and paused beside Rosa's. "Most of the magicians in cities are not part of the Bruderschaft," she said. "It's different in a village or a small town, where there generally aren't more than one or two, and quite often there's none. So being part of the Bruderschaft is an advantage, even if you don't live at the Lodge, because if there is something going on that you cannot deal with yourself, you can call on the Bruderschaft."

Giselle nodded, and pulled her woolen shawl closer around herself. Over the course of their stay here it had gotten colder. Very soon she was going to need a coat or a cloak—or both, because if it got cold enough she could wear a cloak *over* a coat. "Now that I think about it, I believe Mother might have gone to help the Bruderschaft a time or two."

Rosa nodded, and leaned against the side of her *vardo*. "Most magicians in the country make a point of knowing at least a few others. But in the cities, well . . . there's no advantage at all to being in a Lodge if you are the sort that doesn't care for being dragged into other peoples' problems. Magicians are people; plenty of them want to be left alone, and there are always the ones that use their abilities selfishly. That's *not* against the law or even our customs, or anything like that, but . . ." she shrugged. "You can imagine how someone like that would feel about constantly being asked to do this or that for the common good."

"Like a rich man being asked to give to the poor," Giselle grumbled, already disliking these people, and she didn't even know who they were. "It isn't as if they couldn't spare a bit to keep someone from starving. But when you see them being approached, often as not from the way they react you'd think they were being asked to sacrifice a limb."

"Exactly. But if it's any comfort, magicians who only use their powers for selfish purposes don't get any help when *they* are in trouble." Rosa paused with one foot on the steps to her *vardo*. "But to get back to our wretch . . . whoever it is has to know now that not only are you a Master, there are two other Masters here who helped you ward your wagon. Yet whoever it is only seems interested in you. That makes me think it has to be someone you've had *some* sort of encounter with in the past."

Giselle shivered, and the shawl wasn't helping with the cold sensation of vague fear Rosa's statement made her feel. "Me too. But I can't think who it could be."

"Well, think of the bright side. It might not be anything sinister at all! It could just be you have a very shy admirer." Rosa laughed, but Giselle frowned. She didn't like that any better! If someone was an admirer . . . it might *sound* romantic to be gazed on from afar, but the reality was, it was extremely uncomfortable to know you were being watched but not know by whom!

"In a way, that seems worse," she complained. "Why would he sneak around like this when I'm out in public all the time? Why would he hide himself? I haven't been unkind to a single person who's approached me, even when they were horribly intrusive."

"Because *he* might not be a *he*. It might be a *she.*" Rosa's eyebrows arched, as Giselle's jaw dropped. "Yes, I am implying what you think I am implying. But I will come right out and say it. It might be a female who finds you attractive in the romantic sense."

"But . . . but . . . but . . ." Giselle sputtered, her brain coming to a complete halt. How was that even possible?

"It happens, in nature, and with humans, my dear friend," Rosa said, sounding more sympathetic than Giselle had expected. "Wolves, swans, geese, all of these sometimes mate with their own gender. Sometimes boys prefer boys, romantically, and girls prefer girls. Any priest would tell you that is an abomination, but in the Bruderschaft we are more . . . pragmatic. Frankly, we don't care. It harms no one, so why should one care who someone else loves? The only time it's been awkward for me was when I knew that another young lady had gotten a pash on me, and I am afraid my affections don't tend in that direction, no matter how 'mannish' I may act." She shook her head. "That may be the case here. You have a secret admirer, and she is afraid she will be rebuffed." She waited, watching Giselle, as someone over in the camp played a harmonica into the night.

Giselle finally got her brains to work again. "No," she said firmly. "No, I really do not think so. This does not feel at all as if someone is shy, nor does it feel as if whoever is doing this admires me in the least. This feels distinctly *unfriendly,* I'd even say hostile at times."

The harmonica player switched tunes to something livelier. "Then it has to be either someone you have encountered in the past that considers you unfriendly or even an enemy, or someone who thinks that you have somehow wronged him, or . . . it might be a magician hoping to steal your power." Rosa sucked on her lower lip.

"How likely is that?" Giselle asked. She frowned in consternation. "Mother never said anything about . . . something like that happening."

"About as likely as the other possibilities." Rosa thought for a moment, as the harmonica player gave up for the night. "In that case, your best defense is to never be out of the company of one of us. Don't answer any invitations that ask you to go somewhere alone. Once you're on the road again, never leave the compound. I think it's time to tell Kellermann and Cody about this."

"Tell Cody an' Kellermann 'bout what?" The very two people they were talking about strolled up at that moment on their way back to their tents; evidently they had remained behind to continue discussing the arrangements for the move into winter quarters.

Quickly, Giselle explained about the unseen "watcher" that had been plaguing her for the past two weeks. It was a great relief to her that neither of them treated her as if she was overdramatizing anything.

Or worse, making it up. Because if she hadn't been the subject of this intense and intrusive regard, *she* would have a little difficulty believing in it.

"If'n I was home, I'd'a say it was likely 'nother mage tryin' t'figger a way t'steal yer power," Cody said, finally. "My Ma—she's the Master in the fam'bly—she warned me 'bout that. Gen'rally fer a feller, it's a purdy straightforward ritual murder."

The way he paused made her mouth go dry. Rosa filled in what Cody had not said grimly. "And for a woman, it's violation," she said, mincing no words.

Giselle found herself clutching the side of her *vardo* as her mind flashed back across the years. In her mind's eye, she saw "Johann

Schmidt," if that had indeed been his name, as clearly as if it had been yesterday. She saw him kneeling over her, just before Mother burst through the door of her room and attacked him. The cruel expression on his face made her shudder even now. And now . . . now she wondered. Had he known what she was? Had stealing her power been his plan all along? She felt her knees going a little weak, and steadied herself.

"Giselle, are you all right?" Rosa asked in concern.

"Yes . . . yes, I am," she said, and shook the memory off. "Just, I never knew that before. And it might explain something that happened to me a long time ago. Please, don't concern yourself about it."

"How can I not?" Rosa demanded. "You are as white as snow!"

"Giselle," Cody said slowly, using her real name as he rarely did. "You kin tell us. Ain't we friends?"

We are . . . and I have trusted them with so much more. . . . Steeling herself she told them, briefly, what had happened. As briefly as she could manage. And it was still hard; she was shaking before she was done.

"Could . . . *that* person be the one who is stalking you now?" Rosa wondered. "Do you recognize anything about the sense you are getting? Magicians are known to hold grudges for a lifetime. If you thwarted him, or someone else did, he might never give up."

"Only if he could survive a four-story fall," Giselle said, trying to keep from clenching her teeth. *But when we looked for him, he was gone. He must not have been alone. Could whoever took his body away be . . . but how on earth would that person know who I was, or that I was the girl in the abbey tower?* It seemed ridiculous. She was supposed to be an American, not a native to the Black Forest. Her public persona and her public name were different. There was nothing, nothing at all, connecting "Rio Ellie" to Giselle of the abbey.

But what if that doesn't matter? What if all that matters is that I look enough like what he remembers to make him fixate on me?

"*Whoever* it is, we will make sure you are never left alone," said Kellermann, instantly. "Do you have the feeling you are being overlooked now?"

"No," she said instantly. "Not since we began the meeting. I think such things bore him, and he must have known I would come straight back to my *vardo* where he cannot see me. Fox, Rosa and I all warded it against any intruding eyes. Once I am in my *vardo,* I am invisible."

"So he does not know that *we* know, now. All the better." Kellermann nodded. "So long as you always remain within the show walls, I do not think anything can happen to you. But to be sure, do not accept packages or letters that one of us has not examined first. And do not trust *any* message that is given to you that purports to be from anyone in the show. Anything that must be told to you, I will tell you in person. Even if it is an emergency."

"That is an excellent plan," Giselle said, feeling extremely touched. Any other time, she might have been irritated—but she'd been watched for a fortnight, was no closer to knowing who was watching, and was beginning to feel more than a little paranoid. She was aware that these self-appointed tasks had the potential of adding yet more burdens to Kellermann's already too-busy day. He would not have insisted on this if *he* was not sure it needed to be done. "And I cannot thank you enough. I don't want to burden you more than you already are."

But Kellermann waved off her concern. "I see you often enough to pass on whatever needs to be said in the course of the day," he replied, then bowed. "Think nothing of it, and it is my pleasure to be able to assist you in something. And now, it is more than time for all of us to sleep. Perhaps more ideas will come to us then."

"Perhaps," she replied, and went into her *vardo.* She knew it well enough now that she didn't need to light a lamp to move about, and there wasn't much she needed to do. She'd wash in the morning. Right now, she just needed to add a little more wood to the stove, and then get rid of her clothing and bundle herself into bed. The wood was beside the stove, and the padded leather mitten she used to open the stove was on top of the wood. She blew on the coals to bring them to life, and carefully stocked the stove for the night. Her clothing went on the bench, folded, and her warm, heavy flannel nightdress was on the bed. Soon, she was in the bed, under a new eiderdown, staring up at the ceiling of the bed cubby.

But her last thought before sleep was troubling. For she and Mother had found no sign of "Johann Schmidt," all those years ago after his fall. He was not below the tower where he should have fallen, and Mother had not been able to find any trace of how he had gotten away. Nor had the two experienced Bruderschaft hunters.

In fact, except for the fact that she and Mother had *seen* him, fought him, and watched him fall, there was no evidence that he even existed.

So if he had survived the initial fall, which seemed wildly unlikely, where *had* he gone? He would have been seriously injured; Mother had thrust him out the window in such a way that he would have tumbled to the ground without any control. Who or what had rescued him? How had they gotten away without a trace and without Mother knowing? Where had they gone after their escape?

If he *had* been an Air Magician trying to steal her power, why hadn't she sensed that? Why hadn't her sylphs?

And was there any way that the watcher really *could* be him?

There were no answers. But her dreams were troubled.

The show had been packed up the night before, and the company moved out as soon as the first light of predawn lightened the sky. Kellermann had arranged with a local baker at a coffee house to have steaming rolls and coffee delivered in the darkness, and the cooks had precut slices of cold ham, beef, and cheese, and kept out bowls of butter, and they all ate a solid breakfast standing beside the cook wagons, with nothing for the cooks to pack up but the rinsed cups, and the sugar and cream. The cowboys grumbled that the coffee wasn't strong enough, but Giselle noticed that they drank the milk cans that the coffee had been brought in dry.

Hot rolls and butter, ham and cheese and plenty of coffee and cream were *her* idea of an ideal breakfast, so she began the day in a

good frame of mind. Evidently this was too early an hour for the
watcher, for as they drove down the road that paralleled the railway,
Giselle felt no eyes on her, to her intense relief. Lebkuchen and the
show horse Polly had worked out their differences and pulled alongside each other willingly. There was plenty of light thanks to street
lamps within the city, and by the time they were actually past the
point where the gaslights ended, the sun had crested the horizon.

Within an hour, they were well outside the city. Had the watcher
recognized what was going on last night, or had he concentrated on
Giselle, and missed the fact that the show tent was coming down, the
midway packed up, and the canvas walls packed away? She had
tried to stay away from all that activity, hoping to mislead him if all
he was watching was her.

She'd never felt his gaze this early; it always began around midmorning, as if he was a late riser. *With any luck,* she thought, as she
chirped to the horses, and got them past a pushcart they were eyeing
with suspicion, *by the time he wakes up, he won't be able to find us.*

It felt good to be on the road again.

They were by no means the first to leave the Oktoberfest, but also
not the last, merely the largest. The enormous beer tents were all put
up by local *bierkelleren,* and were coming down today; the pretty
girls that waited on the tables would go back to their regular lives, as
daughters and housewives. This was a yearly bounty of income that
many counted on to pay for Christmas.

Smaller shows had left earlier to get into winter quarters. Most of
the single-tent shows had stayed, getting the last pfennig they could
eke out before the lean season—or at least, before they could do
some business at the *Christkindlesmarkt* here or in another city.

But soon, they would all be gone, and there would be nothing
festive until it was time for the *Christkindlesmarkt*. That would not
be held in the great field, but in the city square and spill out into the
streets beyond it. Stalls would have everything that one could want
to prepare for Christmas: gifts, decorations, baked goods, foods from
the potatoes to the goose to be roasted. There would be food to eat
and hot things to drink, because shopping was a taxing business.

And since people needed to be entertained while they shopped, there would be that, too, although it would have to compete with groups singing carols and the local brass bands. Many of the people of Freiburg who had come to meet Giselle had asked if she and the company were staying for Christmas, and had described the *Christkindlesmarkt* in great detail.

She wished she could see it. As so many things, since she had spent all of her life alone in the abbey with Mother, she had never seen a *Christkindlesmarkt*. It sounded delightful, and a great deal less overwhelming than the Oktoberfest had been. It would have been even better, since she would not have been performing, but would have had leisure to see and do things herself.

Another year, perhaps. This time next year the show would be on its way home to America, hopefully with everyone's pockets stuffed full of money. And she could come to Freiburg, stay in a nice little hotel, shop, go to a play and concerts, see the university and the cathedral . . . and surely by then, the vexing problem of the unseen *watcher* would have been solved.

Meanwhile it was far more important to get this entire cavalcade back to the abbey and under stout shelter before the worst of the winter weather set in. Christmas would be great fun with all of them there. She wasn't sure how Americans celebrated it, but given the zest with which they met *any* occasion to celebrate, they surely had some delightful, if slightly mad, traditions themselves. There probably wasn't enough goose in the district to feed all of them, but there would be plenty of other things, and already Kellermann had sent wagonload after wagonload of supplies ahead. And this would be the first Christmas she had ever spent with so much company!

And finally, at long last, after four solid weeks, she could look forward to an entire day in which she could be *herself,* and not "Rio Ellie." Today would be an entire day in which she would not be performing—for sitting there in her "camp" and answering questions was performing, an even more intense sort of performance than being in front of the audience in the arena had been.

"I am so glad we are going!" One of the sylphs flitted up out of

nowhere, her pale-blue butterfly wings looking altogether out of place amid the falling leaves. *"There are too many people in that place. And too many stinks! Ugh!"*

"Are you coming with me all the way to the abbey, Flitter?" Giselle asked her. Flitter had been the only sylph to tag along from Neustadt. Giselle had no idea why she had followed the show across so many miles. Perhaps she was just so amused by the show she had decided it was worth the effort of coming along. Sometimes sylphs took on a notion and were actually able to hold onto it for months at a time.

"Yes. I want to meet your friends there. I think I might want to stay there. The meadow where I grew up is all under bricks now." The sylph alighted on the rump of Lebkuchen (who took no notice of her) and sat there. *"I want to see a beautiful meadow again. I would like it if there were not many humans about. I am tired of noise and I have not found anywhere else that I want to stay, yet."* Clearly she didn't feel the cold, since even though Giselle was bundled up in that fine loden wool winter cape she had been given, with mittens and the hood up and a knitted scarf wrapped around her neck, the sylph was still clothed in little more than a few gauzy ribbons and her long blond hair.

"Well, I shall enjoy having you along. And if you like, you can travel in the wagon. I'll part the wards for you. I don't want you to end up somewhere strange, too tired to fly on. Winter is a bad time for that." Giselle concentrated long enough to make a "door" in the wardings—one that she specified was *only* for the sylph—and let Flitter dart inside. Even though the sylphs didn't seem to mind the cold, they all loved heat, and Giselle was fairly sure she would spend the day curled up over the stove, drowsing.

It would be nice to have her company. Already Giselle missed Rosa.

Another day on the road brought them to their first show, in the small town of Bludbehren. Despite its name, it was a lovely little place, and the abbreviated show was well received. There was a telegram waiting for them there from Rosa, a simple "All well." Bludbehren was home to a rather impressive, modern flour mill, and Kellermann was able to procure enough bags of flour there to last them the whole winter at a very good cost, *and* grain for the horses. Meat, they were well supplied with; besides what he had sent ahead, he'd had the brilliant idea of going around to every one of the food vendors at the Oktoberfest before they left and buying up their surpluses. The vendors were happy to be rid of things that otherwise might have spoiled, and he was happy to have it. He arranged for what was fresh to be salted down in barrels and then packed up and sent over, and what was smoked or otherwise preserved to go straight into in the wagons.

As far as Kellermann was concerned, anything could be salted and preserved. Salt beef, salt fish, salt pork, even salted-down fowl; Giselle had the feeling he'd salt down anything that didn't run away fast enough.

They would be able to hunt once they got to the abbey, since the forest all around was full of game, most of it unmolested for as long as she and Mother had lived there. That was why "Johann Schmidt's" story had been so believable. It was entirely likely that a professional hunter would have investigated such a relatively virgin forest for hunting. But virtually everyone with the show could shoot, and fresh game would liven up the table as the winter went on.

The next town they stopped at, their show coincided with the weekly farmer's market, and again, Kellermann was able to find things at a good price. This time it was root vegetables. Burlap bags full of them were added to the wagons. Everyone was carrying foodstuffs now. She even had things that would not be harmed by the weather piled on the top of the *vardo* in order to make room for food inside other wagons, and shared some of her space with casks of spices he entrusted to her. He was completely in his element, and utterly happy, whenever he could make these bargains. It made Giselle smile to see him so happy.

But then, she had a great deal to smile about. It seemed that the unknown "watcher" had lost them when they left Freiburg, for she had not felt those eyes on her since.

The show finally arrived at Meiersdorf just as the first flurries of snow appeared in the now-overcast sky.

There would be no show at Meiersdorf, given that it had begun to snow and not even the inhabitants were eager to brave the cold in a tent, no matter how exotic the promised production was. They had planned to camp in the field normally used by the village for their little festivities, for it was a good long day's journey to the abbey under the best of circumstances. Giselle was not expecting to see Rosa until then, but to her great joy, her friend was waiting, bundled up in her gorgeous scarlet cloak and hood, mounted on a sturdy hunter, right at the entrance to the village.

Giselle did not actually see Rosa right away, as she was in the middle of the caravan. Rosa waved at her, but then turned her attention back to Kellermann and Cody. Giselle understood perfectly, and got her *vardo* maneuvered into the circle it belonged to in the meadow they were using to camp overnight. All of the wagons were circled up at night since they'd left Freiburg, rather than parked in rows. This was to provide a windbreak for people who were still forced to sleep in their tents. The horses were left tied at night to wagons outside each circle, each with his own blanket, bucket, and pile of hay and grain. The cattle were corralled inside a circle of the transport wagons. The buffalo went into the same space as the cattle. They didn't seem to mind.

The cooks came around to each circle with a big pot of stew and some sort of hard cracker—unless it was possible to buy bread where they were camping, which case everyone got a piece of a loaf instead. There was bread tonight. For the sake of making things easier on the cooks, each of them was responsible for his own plate, cup and utensils, and coffee was made on the central circle fire. Giselle lined up with the rest when the cooks arrived. That was when Rosa turned up, armed with plate and cup herself.

They got their food and quickly retreated to the relative warmth of the *vardo*. "Is your watcher still watching?" was the first thing

Rosa asked, once they were settled into seats on casks of pepper-corns and salt.

"No," she said shortly, and Rosa smiled with relief.

"Good. I was hoping once you were on the move, he'd lose track of you, or simply would not be able to scry you out at any real dis-tance." Rosa ate with a good appetite, and so did Giselle. It was lovely to have hot food after a long cold day of driving.

"I'm glad you came to meet us," Giselle said. "How are things at the abbey?"

"Very good." Rosa grinned with satisfaction and wiped her bowl absolutely clean with her bread. "We've a hard day of driving ahead of us, but when we get there, absolutely everything will be ready. There will be hot food waiting, we've even got sleeping arrange-ments in place, and everyone can just put the horses and cattle in their stable, eat, and go straight to bed, then deal with what needs to be unpacked in the morning."

Giselle gaped at her. "How on earth did you manage that?" she asked.

Rosa shrugged, but looked pleased with herself. "Dwarves and brownies, of course. I don't know what sort of arrangement your Mother had with them, but they didn't even *charge* me for any of it, they said they'd already gotten what they needed when the work was done! The chapel has been rebuilt into a stable for the animals with a hayloft over it. I got mowers to come and harvest the meadow twice for hay, there's enough to last all winter. What isn't in the hay-loft is in haystacks next to the stable. What used to be the east wing has a second floor now, and the dwarves made up beds and wooden partitions on both floors. The west wing has the kitchens on the first floor and storage above. Did you know there was a cellar under it?"

Giselle shook her head.

"Well, there is. With all you have with you, it will be stuffed. There's more storage above the kitchens, which we will need, with all the food we'll need to produce for all these people until spring. The north wing with your tower, I've had redone as quarters for the couples and families, the Pawnee, Kellermann and Cody. I moved a bed into the floor below your bedroom in the tower for me. If you don't mind?" Rosa's voice faltered a little as if she was afraid that Giselle would be annoyed at this intrusion on her privacy.

"Not even a little! It will be grand to have you there!" She reached out and impulsively hugged Rosa's shoulders. "It all sounds amazing."

"I'm not sure you'll recognize it. The dwarves took a lot of liberties with the design, but it's as perfect for the purpose as it can be." Rosa hugged back, and finished her stew before it got cold. "I can't wait for you to see what it's all turned into."

"Neither can I!" Giselle said, and meant it.

16

THE horses seemed to sense that this was the last leg of the journey, and although what they were hauling the wagons over barely qualified as a rough track, they actually got their pace up to a fast walk, rather than the plodding pace they usually took. Even the cattle seemed more willing to move.

But maybe that was Rosa. As an Earth Master, she could communicate wordlessly with animals and birds, and perhaps she had "told" them that a warm stable, good food, and rest were waiting for them at the end of the day.

When the abbey appeared in the distance, serene and oddly beautiful in the middle of its meadow valley, the animals *truly* put their backs into their work. They seemed to recognize that this was where they'd find shelter and food and hauled the wagons over the trackless, shorn meadow at a pace that rattled Giselle's bones.

Rosa was right: she barely recognized the place.

She doubted that the original inhabitants would, either. The rebuilding had been done in a purposeful, blocky manner more suggestive of a fortress than a place of retreat and worship. Windows had been reduced to the barest slits. The original roof had been tiles;

it was now slate, and looked as if it would last a thousand years. And the original buildings had *not* been connected; now they were, so that the abbey was now one single building with a protected central courtyard. It had been two single-story (with attic) and two double-story buildings, with Giselle's tower forming the corner of the building in the north. Now it was a uniform two stories tall with an attic, all the way around, except for Giselle's tower.

She had to work to keep from gaping with amazement as she realized the extent of the work that had been done.

As she drove her *vardo* around to the eastern side of the abbey, following the others, she saw (without any surprise) that an efficient system had already been worked out for dealing with wagons and livestock. *That must have been what Rosa was talking to Cody and Kellermann about last night.* A cowboy directed her where to move the *vardo* into place: close to the wall of the abbey, with just enough space for a kind of walkway between the virtual wall of wagons and the stone walls. As soon as she had it positioned to his liking, he unhitched both horses and took them away, in through a kind of tunnel through the east wing, under the second floor. She got the things she had packed this morning before they left, including her new eiderdown rolled tightly and strapped up with belts, and approached that entrance herself.

The fortress impression was even stronger when she saw that the entrance could be completely shut off by both heavy wooden doors *and* an iron portcullis.

At *both* ends.

That had never been in the design of the original abbey!

Then again, she reflected. *Dwarves are used to being able to lock up anything securely.*

The central yard of the abbey was still a garden; as it had been with the original, it was an herb and vegetable garden. But now there was a paved walkway all around the periphery, an actual stone wall around the garden itself to keep it from being trampled, and a brand new chicken coop in one corner. Someone had evidently closed the chickens up for safety while people went in and out.

The former chapel looked nothing like a religious building now, which was a relief, as she'd had a bit of unease, picturing the place as a stable. Cowboys were bringing in horses two at a time and taking them inside through a stable door in the middle of the building. She kept well out of their way, but out of curiosity, decided to go into the door in the east wing for a moment to see just what had been done there.

When she got inside, it looked like nothing so much as a stable for humans. Which, now that she thought about it, was a very good way to organize things. Most of the showfolk were used to sleeping either out in the open or several to a tent, and really didn't have much thought for privacy. This was a good way to give them each a *little* room to themselves, while at the same time making the most of the space available.

It was a single large room with a fine—huge!—iron stove at one end. At the other, of course, was the stone wall of the tunnel that went beneath the second floor. Presumably the second floor looked just like this one, but twice as big. Along each wall and down the middle were something like rows of wooden horse-stalls: plain wood reaching about seven feet high, seven feet long, and five feet wide. Each of the "stalls" contained a wooden "box" bed full of hay attached to one side, and a small table with a holder for a candle on it at the back of the stall. Some of the beds already had bedrolls and packs on them. It seemed like a very good plan for housing a lot of men in rough comfort. The stove would heat the entire room efficiently, and if the fellows didn't like the loose hay-beds, they could always sew up their own straw or hay mattresses. And meanwhile the hay certainly made a better bed than the cold, hard ground.

She decided to forego any further inspection until after she had gotten back into her own room to see if any changes had been made there. She could see a doorway at the end of this room, but rather than get in anyone's way, she decided to use the courtyard to reach the tower instead.

She was relieved to see that nothing important in the tower had changed. There was still the small kitchen on the first floor and the library on the second, although there seemed to be some changes to the kitchen she didn't trouble to examine for now. Rosa had made only the minimal addition of her own bed and some chests with her belongings on the third floor. It looked as if there was an iron stove on the hearth instead of the inefficient fireplace And on the fourth floor . . .

Everything was exactly as she had left it. With a single exception. There was another of those marvelous iron stoves. Someone had started a fire in it, and the room was delightfully warm.

I am going get some hot water very soon and have a real bath. There had been plenty of opportunities to get a good all-over wash in streams and springs when they had camped, of course, and she had taken them. And of course she could do a basin-wash in her *vardo.* But it had been . . . well, far too long since she had had a real, long, hot, soaking bath. And she had a wonderful old bathtub down there in the kitchen.

I'll bet that Rosa's used it too.

Someone had made up her bed with fresh sheets and blankets; the faint scent of lavender hung all about the bed. She tossed her new eiderdown on it, put her bags down beside it and decided to first go see about some food.

She went straight to the west wing, where Rosa had told her the kitchen was; this was when she noticed that with the exception of the east wing, which had two ground floor doors in it, all the wings had one door into the courtyard, set right into the middle of the wing. And sure enough, when she walked in the west wing door, there it was, a kitchen big enough and efficient enough to gladden the heart of the most exacting cook, in the north half of it, and benches and tables already full of hungry show folk in the south half. Presiding over it all was . . . a woman she didn't recognize. She had grey hair braided and wrapped on the top of her head and wore a black dirndl, white blouse and apron, and a black shawl cross-wrapped and tied at her waist. Her face was round, with merry eyes and a tip-tilted nose. Her cheeks were pink with the heat from the kitchen.

But as soon as the woman—who appeared to be Tante Gretchen's younger sister—turned around, it was clear that she recognized Giselle. The woman's face lit up, and she gestured to Giselle to come properly into the kitchen itself.

"You'll be Giselle," the woman said. "I'm Elfrida. Fraulein Rosamund engaged me to come take charge of the housekeeping here, since it was unlikely anyone in your company had ever done such a thing before. Also, Herr Kellermann sent many food items I do not think your cooks know how to prepare. Beets, mangel-wurzels, common things of that sort. I will show them how to deal with German food." She lowered her voice. "I, too, am an Earth Magician, although a minor one. A *kitchen-witch,* Fraulein Rosa calls me, since my powers have always been domestic. I was *most* impressed with your Mother's preservation rooms. I was able to extend them into the entire cellar, and copy them in the storage room above us. I do not think I would have been able to concoct such a work on my own."

"You sound like the answer to all prayers, Frau Elfrida," Giselle said warmly, "Since my talents are most decidedly *not* in the kitchen."

Elfrida's round face lit up with a smile, and her blue eyes shone with pleasure. "Well, you must, like the others, be starving and cold. Come get a plate and fill it up, and take care of both needs at once!"

Giselle hadn't known what to expect. It was wonderful to find that supper was to be chicken and dumplings, with a pickled beet and onion salad, fresh bread and butter, and plenty of hot coffee. She got her plate full, and went to join the others—who might not have recognized what they were about to eat, but had already tried enough native Bavarian food that they were not inclined to turn up their noses at anything that looked and smelled as good as this did. Giselle ate slowly, very glad that there would be no more performances, no more long drives in the cold, no more rising at dawn. No more rushed meals. Tonight, she would sleep as long as she liked. Then she would get the rest of her belongings from the *vardo,* move the spices to the kitchen, and . . .

I don't know. But whatever I do will have nothing *to do with performing.*

Rosa brought in the company cooks at just that moment and took them straight to Frau Elfrida. They gave her the respect any good cook does when he or she steps into the kitchen of another. In her turn, she welcomed them warmly, showed them about the place, and presumably explained where everything was and how things were done in "her" kitchen. Giselle had never had much to do with the three cooks from the show, but it appeared they were all good-tempered, and were going to get along famously with Elfrida, and that was all that mattered.

When Rosa was sure that everyone was going to get along, she cast her eyes over the tables full of hungry, tired show folk, spotted Giselle, and smiled. Since Giselle had finished eating at this point, she got up, left her dishes in the big tub of soapy water standing ready for the purpose, and joined Rosa.

"I am no mind reader, but I would risk a bet that you want a hot bath," Rosa said, chuckling. "It was the first thing I wanted when I got here."

"Oh, sweet Virgin, yes!" Giselle exclaimed. "And you can answer some of my questions while I soak."

"I started the copper warming in the little tower kitchen this morning. You should have all the water you want. And *wait* until you see the clever things the . . . builders . . . did in that kitchen!"

By now, the sun had set, and they hurried around the courtyard in the cold as more snow began to fall. It looked as if the wooden doors had been closed on the entrance, although Giselle couldn't tell if the portcullis was down. She wondered what Cody and the others had made of *that* particular facet of the abbey.

Probably they think this is a castle, and there are always iron portcullises on buildings in Germany. Certainly they had seen plenty of such things in the towns they'd played at. Almost all of them had been defensively walled towns, and most of them still had their gates and portcullises.

Now that she had the time to really look, it was evident that the dwarves had made some very important changes to the little kitchen. There was yet another iron stove, *and* a bread oven. There was a big copper boiler for heating water, and a real stone sink with a pump and drain, and the wooden bathtub had been given a drain in the bottom that let out into a grating in the floor. Giselle stared at that, and the drain from the sink. "They added *plumbing?*" she gasped.

Rosa laughed. "Yes, they did. They dug a proper cesspit for each building, including one for the stable, and built very nice *conveniences* for each building that don't stink at all! They aren't water-flushing, like the ones that the Graf has had put in, but just pour a pitcher of water down when you finish and it all goes . . . somewhere. I didn't ask for the details. I am just happy we are not having to use latrines or garderobes." She nodded at a little door off the kitchen that hadn't been there before. "It's in there, if you need it."

"Not now. What I need is a bath. I haven't had one since Freiburg. And I'm cutting my hair back, too. It's not as if it isn't going to grow again."

The bath was an old-fashioned one that allowed you to have hot water right up to your chin, and that was *exactly* what Giselle got, soaking away the bruises of the last day's travel and the grime of not having had a proper bath for two weeks. Once she had cut her hair to chest length, she washed it, setting the braids aside, since *now* she wouldn't have to worry about it falling into the wrong hands. Meanwhile, Rosa filled her in on all the details of what had been done to the abbey. "Elfrida will tell the cooks about their quarters, which are in the second floor next to the storage, so it's convenient for them," Rosa concluded. "I told Cody and Kellermann everything yesterday. Kellermann is taking care of informing the fellows who'll be living in the common quarters in the east wing, and Cody is giving the couples and families and the Pawnee the tour of their spaces. I hope the Pawnee like theirs . . . I told the dwarves to give them a stone-walled room with stone floors, so that it was as like to one of their earth-houses as we could get. It seems strange to me that people who live on the open plains would choose to make underground houses."

"Well, their homeland is not the plains, at least not for the winter," Giselle explained. "Their real home is forested hills. They've been driven out, and forced to relocate in a dry prairie area that none of them like in the least. That's why Fox wants to get a lot of money, so they can buy farm lots back where they used to live."

"Oh." Rosa shook her head. "Well, in that case, I think they will be able to make it comfortable for the winter."

"Fox, at least, is used to living with the Army in one of their forts," Giselle pointed out. "And I do *not* think any of them would care to sleep in a hide teepee in the snow!"

It was wonderful to be able to turn the spigot at the bottom of the tub and let it all run out, rather than having to bail the thing out a pail at a time until it was empty enough to turn on its side. It was wonderful to be able to change into one of her clean, warm, flannel nightgowns, bundle her damp hair under a nightcap, and climb into her own bed. Flitter had already found her way into the room, and was sitting up on a beam, dozing in the heat from the stove.

It was also oddly wonderful to hear Rosa puttering about on the floor beneath her. In fact, it was the sound of Rosa turning pages in a book that was the last thing she heard as she drifted off to sleep.

The next day was devoted to everyone getting everything they wanted for the winter out of the wagons, and then moving the wagons into the positions they'd hold until Spring, chained together. Moving her things was *her* problem; moving the wagons was the problem of the men, and she had been told so in no uncertain terms when she tried to help. For once, she wasn't inclined to argue; they were using four teams of the heaviest horses and clearly had a defined plan. Cody and the head wrangler had decided that since the wagons could not be got in under cover for the winter, the best thing to do with them would be to protect them as best as possible and use them and some lumber and tree branches to make a corral so the animals could get some time every day out in the sun.

Giselle spent the day getting all of her things out of the *vardo*, then in the small tower kitchen doing laundry. *Finally* she was able to get all of her things really clean again. Most of them she planned to pack away until spring, but this was an excellent chance to get everything that had only been dealt with sketchily properly washed. Soon drying laundry was strung back and forth across the kitchen, just as it used to be on laundry days when it had only been her and Mother here.

It was a very relaxed group that assembled for a supper of sausages, kale cooked with bacon, and fried potatoes. Rosa and Giselle went back to the tower afterward as they had last night, but tonight they were joined by Leading Fox, Cody, and Kellermann for some conversation and an impromptu game of cards. Anticipating visits of this sort, Giselle had laid in supplies in the little kitchen.

But after everyone had gone to their beds and it was long past midnight, Giselle was awakened by the wind, howling around the tower. The sounds it was making against the thick glass windows told her from long experience that this was not just wind. This was a blizzard. But there was something about it that was not quite right, something that made her come all the way awake.

She fumbled for the matches and oil lamp next to her bed and lit it. When she had turned the light up, she looked up into the rafters and saw that all of her sylph friends were up there, huddled together, looking down at her with frightened eyes.

In the next moment, she knew why they were there. This was no natural blizzard. It might have *begun* as one, but it certainly was not natural now. She sensed the magic outside, magnifying everything the storm was doing. Air Magic . . . but other things too, things she couldn't identify. The defenses that she, Rosa, Mother and the dwarves had put on this place turned it into a fortress against magic as well as against more physical attacks, but this storm was going to completely isolate them from the outside world. And from the feeling she was getting . . . that was exactly what the people steering the storm had in mind.

A light sprang up on the floor below, coming up through the stairwell. "Rosa?" she called.

"You feel it too?" Rosa replied, and her voice had steel in it. She, too, knew what this meant and she was not amused.

"Of course. I think . . . I think that watcher followed us somehow. He's not alone." She did her best to keep her voice steady.

"I'm coming up," Rosa said, and a moment later, she padded up the stairs, wrapped in a huge woolen shawl. She joined Giselle in her bed, and the two of them pulled the eiderdown around themselves. "This is an attack," she said, flatly.

"I get Air Magic, and something else," Giselle said. "The Air Magic has a bitter scent if that means anything to you."

"It means it's stolen," Rosa replied, staring at the shuttered window as if she could somehow see through it. "And I told you how magic can be stolen."

Giselle shivered.

"There's Fire Magic there too, but it's been turned to its opposite— cold. That can only be done by making a bargain with an Elemental of Cold, and none of the ones I know of are good. There's also some other magic, but it's not from an Elemental Master or even a mage. So it has to be a sorcerer or a witch. By the dark feel of it, it's all fueled by blood."

Three different kinds of magic? What had brought all this down on her head? "What do we do?" Giselle asked. "You're the one who hunts out things and destroys them, not I!"

Rosa patted her hand. "First, I promise you, whoever it is cannot get in here. Your Mother wrought even better than you thought she ever did, I put my own protections on the abbey, you already had your own in place, and you can bet that Fox is awake and reinforcing everything with *his* protections, and I very much doubt whoever is out there will be familiar with anything Fox can do. Add to that what the dwarves built in while they were rebuilding everything. The dwarves are very clever: every single opening into the walls has a warded grate of pure iron. No magic, no matter how strong, can get past magic-forged iron. It would take more than a handful of Masters to get their magic in here, it would take an army, if it could be done at all."

Giselle couldn't help it, though, she shivered. The sound of the wind outside—it was as if there were voices in it, voices howling their determination to tear down the walls and rip everything inside to bits.

"As for what we do, we wait until morning, when everyone is awake. We'll gather in the second-floor room of the tower, and we'll find a way to see *who* is out there, how many of them there are, and what they have to bring against us." Rosa clenched her jaw. "One thing I know for certain, there is *no* Earth Magic out there. So whoever is out there won't have wardings against Earth scrying."

"I thought you said you couldn't scry?" Giselle ventured.

"I said that I didn't usually do so," Rosa corrected. "I don't have the best tool for it. My obsidian plaque isn't as . . . finished . . . as I would like. But I would bet any amount of money that your Mother *did* have the tools we need, and that they will still be in the rooms that Cody is in now. The dwarves and I just locked up the cabinet that her tools and supplies were in and left it there, as it was too big to move."

"And when we find out, what will we do then?" Giselle persisted. "I—"

"It would be foolish to make plans we are only going to have to change," Rosa told her. "Now, just remember, they *cannot* get magic inside these walls. We have enough food to last the winter, if we need to. We have water from a well they cannot cut off. We need to find out how many of them there are, how powerful they are, and what their plans are. The most important thing will be to make sure that our friends in the show are not panicked by all this." At this Rosa showed her first sign of stress, rubbing her hand across her eyes. "That is the one thing that might be our undoing. I cannot do anything about that now, but as soon as Elfrida is awake—"

"Elfrida is awake now, deary," came a voice from below. "If you think anyone with magic could sleep through *this,* you are very much mistaken."

Now *Elfrida* came up the stairs, wrapped up in a woolen shawl even more voluminous than Rosa's, hair entirely covered by a frilly nightcap of monumental proportions. "Move over and give me some bed room, girls, my old bones cannot take this cold."

Giselle did more than that, she got up and stoked the stove, then came back to bed, glad that her bed was a very old one that could probably have held an entire family.

"We need to keep the others—the ones that are not the Indians, the Captain, or Herr Kellermann—from getting the notion that this is anything other than a normal storm for this part of the world, and panicking," said Rosa, once Elfrida was under the eiderdown with both of them. The sylphs were paying very close attention to what the three of them were saying; glancing up from time to time, Giselle saw their eyes shining down solemnly in the light from the lamp.

"Bless you, that will be the matter of two spells at most," the "kitchen-witch" said with conviction. "One on the oven, and the other on the salt. I'll bless the salt to drive out evil influences, so even if the bastards out there manage to get something past our defenses, anything cooked with holy salt will keep a body safe, and the Good God knows you can't bake bread without salt. And the other spell, the one I intend to put on the oven, will handle anything that's baked in it; that's all the bread, of course, and we all eat bread three times a day or more, plus all the sweets. Your friends do like their pies. I have never seen pies vanish so fast."

"Yes, but what does this other spell *do?*" Rosa said, a little impatiently.

"Keep them . . . well . . . tranquil. It'll make them a bit slow, and it isn't something I'd set under any circumstances but this, but better that the chores be done slowly, and that they maybe fall asleep over them, than that they panic." Elfrida nodded as Rosa's eyes widened. "They won't notice anything that they aren't *expecting* to see, either. I use it when I need to do something, and I don't want those who I am keeping house for to get a notion I'm unnatural."

"That must be very handy," Rosa said, envy in her voice.

"It's also dangerous. Other people outside the family will notice if the family is acting oddly, especially the man of the house, and next thing you know, people are looking for a witch in the kitchen," Elfrida replied with a frown. "I wouldn't use it now if I weren't sure no one's going to escape it. If you're worried about the beasts taking fright, we can feed them a bit of bread once a day—"

"No, I can handle the beasts. They trust me," Rosa said, and sighed. "All right. I expect that the Captain and the Indians are—"

"—are violatin' your privacy an' comin' up. Kellermann's with us," called Captain Cody from below. "Iff'n yer afraid t'be seen—"

"Oh don't be an idiot, get up here!" Rosa snapped, and soon enough, the sound of boots on the stairs heralded two of the three. Fox's footsteps could scarcely be heard, of course, because he was wearing his usual soft moccasins. They were all in pants pulled hastily over their nightshirts, and wrapped in blankets, including Fox. It seemed that when it came to sleeping in Bavarian cold, he had decided to do as the white men did, and bundle into a warm, thick, red flannel nightshirt. They all pulled chairs up to the side of the bed and huddled in them.

Rosa and Giselle took it in turns to tell them what they knew, and Elfrida added how she intended to keep the rest of the company from taking fright. When they finished, Cody and Fox exchanged a look and a wry smile. "See, now, Fox, I tol' ye the ladies woulda figgered out a short plan afore we got up here," Cody said. "Here's th' thing, though. Fox an' me, we've seen a good bit'a fightin, an' we figger this storm ain't but the beginnin'. It's got a evil feel to't. That kinda matches up with you tellin' me there's some Fire Magic mixed up with it, on'y turned t'cold. I ain't never seen that, but I heerd 'bout it, from a feller in England what recognized me as a mage." He shook his head. "That feller allowed as how he ain't *never* heerd of a Cold Elemental critter that weren't all bad, clear through. You go makin' a deal with one'a them, an' it freezes all the heart right outa ye."

"That . . . doesn't sound good," ventured Giselle.

"Yep. An' it gets worse. 'Cause I kin tell whoever's out there, if he ain't a Master, he's damn close." He picked at the edge of his blanket. "Still, Rosie, yer right. We cain't go makin' no plans without knowin' who's behind all this, how strong they are, an' maybe, iff'n we're lucky, what their plans are. An' the good news is I bet they might go guardin' 'gainst Fire, Air or Water scryin', but they ain't gonna 'gainst Earth."

"The Earth doesn't like them," Rosa muttered, after a long moment; her face was screwed up in concentration. "There is someone in this group that the Earth is powerfully revolted by."

"That there'll work in our favor." Cody leaned forward earnestly. "Rosie, I gotta say somethin', cause this ain't the first magical fight I been in. I know y'all reckon I'm a flibbertigibbet, an' maybe sometimes I am, but look here, the strongest thing we got workin' fer us right now is thet we trust each other. We gotta make sure whoever's out there cain't work on thet an' break it. Savvy?"

Rosa nodded, slowly. "Absolutely. I think . . ." She looked around at all of them. "I think we need to make a blood binding among us. Kellermann too," she added, and the impresario looked startled. "It won't take a minute. All I need is a pocketknife, a cup, and a hot coal."

"Pocketknife's here," Cody said, fishing in a pocket of his trousers and bringing one out, handing it to her.

"There's cups downstairs in the kitchen," said Giselle. "I'll get a coal."

She already had a little brazier she used for incense that required a hot coal to burn up here in her room; the sylphs loved all sorts of incense, and she had brought it in from her *vardo*. She fished a coal small enough to fit in it from the stove with the tongs and dropped it in, carrying it over to the group. Rosa had directed them to sit on the floor in a circle.

"Put the coal there," she said, pointing to the middle. As Giselle did so, and took her place in the space left vacant for her, Rosa stabbed her thumb with the smallest blade of the pocketknife and squeezed out a few drops of blood into the cup Kellermann had brought up. "Now all of you do the same, going clockwise around the circle."

They did. When the cup came back to Rosa, she took it carefully in both hands and looked at them all earnestly.

"Are we all resolved to be of one mind in this undertaking?" she asked them solemnly.

They all nodded.

"And are we all resolved that we shall let *no* difference of opinion, no perceived insult, and no grievance break our bond?"

"Yes," Giselle said firmly, prompting the others to answer likewise.

"Then in the name of the Powers of Light, in the names of the Great Ones of our Elements, and in the name of the Greatest One over all, let our good will and good hearts bind us together and let no evil tear us asunder!" Rosa intoned, holding her right hand over the cup. And when she took it away . . . the blood in the bottom was glowing as hot as the coal in the brazier.

"So let it be!" she said, prompting *all* of them to echo her exact words.

Then she poured the glowing blood over the coal.

Rosa had expected it to smell dreadful, like her hair burning. Or at least, to smell like cooked meat. But instead, the little puff of smoke when the blood hit the coal smelled . . . like incense.

"If you are expecting something dramatic," Rosa said into the long silence that followed, "I am afraid that is as dramatic as it gets."

Elfrida giggled, an unexpectedly girlish sound that made them all laugh, if a little nervously.

"It is well," said Fox. "I think we must try to sleep. There is little that can be done until morning, and we must be ready to assist Rosa in her scrying the moment that the storm drops. At that moment, our enemies will be exhausted, and we will have our best chance to work without notice."

"I think we should stand watches," said Cody. "Thet way, the second th' storm drops, th' one standin' watch kin wake 'tothers."

"I need to go to the kitchen and put the spell on the oven now, before we start the morning bread," said Elfrida. "And I will be awake at six in the morning to do the baking."

Cody pulled out his watch. "Pshaw. It's on'y two. I'll stand the watch till four, wake up Kellermann, an' he can stand till six, wake up Fox, an' he can stand till eight, an' wake me again. An when Kellermann goes t'bed he kin make sure Miz Elfrida's awake."

"How long do you think they can keep this storm going?" Fox asked Rosa.

Rosa shrugged. "Not longer than twelve hours, I think," she said.

"All right then. Back t'our beds," said Cody. "In twelve hours, for sure, we'll have more to go on."

Rosa and Giselle exchanged a wordless look. "If you three men don't mind sleeping on the floor beneath us, the three of us can sleep up here," Rosa said, and Giselle nodded.

"There should be blankets and cushions enough to make whoever isn't using the bed itself comfortable," Giselle added. "They're stowed in the linen chests. I'm sure you can find them."

"Well, I wasn't gonna ask, but I'm thinkin' that there's a right good idea," said Cody, as Fox and Kellermann nodded. "We'll do that."

"And tomorrow . . . as soon as the storm dies . . . we will find out what, exactly, we are up against, I hope." Rosa replied, getting up and getting into bed.

"Who wants the middle?" Elfrida asked, as the men went back down the stairs to make themselves as comfortable as they could.

"I would," said Giselle. The bed could easily fit five, it wasn't as if they were going to be crowded. She got in and let Elfrida take the outside. With three people in the bed it warmed quickly.

But she lay on her back, staring up at the sylphs on the rafters, unable to sleep. Listening to the storm tear at the tower, and feeling the anger, and the hate, behind it.

17

THE storm died away to nothing just after noon. By that time, everyone—except the six conspirators—had eaten two meals with food cooked in the oven, and the effects on everyone who had gorged on fresh bread and butter, baked sweet noodles, and applesauce at breakfast and baked squash, oven-roasted sausages, and roots at lunch were . . . obvious. The howling of the blizzard and the snow piling up past the windows bothered them not at all. Several made jokes about being perfectly happy to be warm and inside until spring, or about wanting to hibernate like bears. Most of them decided that once the animals were fed, there was nothing pressing enough they needed to do and elected to take a nap. The ones that remained awake might as well have elected to take a nap, since they were all settled around the stoves, bundled in shawls or blankets, discussing tobacco, food, beer, and women. Well, attempting to discuss things, since a great deal of the conversation was conducted in sleepy mono-syllables. Even the children were drowsing.

Elfrida had cooked everything *they* ate in frying pans, and they were making do with what was left of yesterday's baking. If things had not been so tense, watching the others in their little spell-haze might have been amusing, but Giselle, at least, felt as tense as a taut bowstring, and from their expressions she was sure the others felt the same. The sylphs were still terrified and there were more of them crowding up, not only in her rafters, but in the storage loft over the kitchen. From the way they were acting, it would be impossible to persuade them out.

Five gathered in Giselle's room at the top of the stairs, all the conspirators but Elfrida, who said she had nothing to contribute, and went to put similar spells of calm on the horses, cattle and buffalo. "And then I'll have to make sure the other cooks don't muddle up dinner," she explained. "Or chop off a finger, or the like. It'll take twice as long to make dinner, but better this than dealing with a lot of hysterics."

Rosa had rummaged through the cupboard of Mother's magical items, supplies, and books, and brought up a circular black plate of what looked like glass, like the one Giselle had seen in her trunk, but much more refined. "It's an obsidian mirror," Rosa explained to Giselle, as they went up the stairs to join the others. "It's just about the only way an Earth Magician can scry." Giselle examined it with curiosity; the back was still rough rock, though flat, but the stone was highly polished on the other side, and slightly concave.

"How are you going to find them?" Giselle asked, handing it back to her. They joined the others who were all sitting in a circle on the floor, as they had last night. Rosa placed the mirror in the middle, then took her own place in the circle. "They could be anywhere out there."

Rosa frowned. "I don't know," she admitted. "I suppose I'll just have to search until I find them . . . I can't think of any other way."

"You couldn't get my sylphs to budge out of the rafters," Giselle told them all. "They're terrified. I think that Air Master out there has them near hysterics."

"I have a suggestion," Fox put in. "My spirits are all birds. None of mine seemed frightened, not even at the height of the storm. I believe this Air Master does not realize that they *are* spirits of the air. I believe a raven is common enough that no one would notice it even if it ventures quite near. I will send out a raven to search for them. It will not take long."

"Oh that would be splendid!" Rosa said, her shoulders sinking a little as she sighed in relief. "If we link the raven to the mirror, we could even see and hear what it does, which would eliminate a traditional scrying spell altogether. If we can do that, a witch would not be likely to take notice."

"I reckon the less we do stuff they might know, the better off we are," Cody observed. He rubbed his hands together to warm them; despite the stove, the room was cold and all of them were draped in blankets now.

Fox closed his eyes and concentrated for a moment; there was a fluttering of wings over their heads, and a handsome, glossy raven descended from the rafters and landed next to the mirror. He seemed entirely solid and real, as did the sylphs when they wanted to fully interact with objects like ribbons. He eyed Rosa and tilted his head to the side, then looked at Fox. Fox nodded. Rosa put one hand gently on his back, cupped the other over the mirror and muttered something under her breath. When she took her hands away, the raven shook himself and uttered a thoughtful-sounding *quork*.

Fox nodded again, and the raven flew up, and *through* the roof. Just as the sylphs sometimes did, although they preferred to come and go by the windows. After all, a spirit of the air was not exactly limited by things like walls and roofs.

"It's working," said Rosa with satisfaction, and Giselle looked back down at the mirror. She felt her eyes widen, as now the concave mirror reflected a literal bird's-eye view of the snowscape below the tower, as brilliantly as if the mirror had been of the clearest, best glass, rather than obsidian. The amount of snow that had been dumped on the abbey last night was a little . . . frightening. Six feet at least, and in places it had drifted twelve feet high. She had *never* seen that much snow at once here, not in the worst of the storms that the abbey had weathered.

The raven circled the abbey, giving them all a good idea of how the snow lay about the building, then turned his attention out toward the edge of the meadow. *She* couldn't see anything that far away, but evidently the raven did. He angled out to the east, wings beating strongly, heading for the forest.

That's not where I would have gone, she thought, frowning a little. *There's nothing out that direction but thick woods.* The raven evidently knew better, however, and he must have been able to see something that was not visible to their human eyes, even looking through his in the mirror.

"He is being cautious in his approach," said Fox, calmly. "I have warned him to act like a real bird, and be very wary, as if he expected to be hunted and shot by man."

It was fascinating, and more than a little dizzying, to watch the landscape go by from a bird's point of view. He moved his head much more quickly than a human would, which was disorienting. "Fox? Can you just choose to see through his eyes?" she asked, never taking her own eyes off the mirror.

Fox looked up at her, and shook his head a little. "Not without his consent, which would be hard to gain. He is a being, just as your sylphs are, and does not care for the idea of someone else using his senses." Fox replied. Now that he was no longer playing up his heritage, he had adopted some heavy canvas trousers with suspenders in place of his leather leggings, wore long flannel underwear as virtually every one of the cowboys did, and one of the common wool flannel shirts over that, with a shawl and a blanket draped over everything. Only his long braided hair, his headband, and his features showed he was an Indian. "He does this because this is a time of exceptional need, and because this is nothing more than a reflection of what he sees, rather than a medicine-worker making use of his eyes directly."

"And I hope you let him know we are suitably grateful," Rosa said gravely. "Wait . . . he's going down into the forest."

The raven was, indeed, flying down into the forest. In a moment he was among the branches, skillfully evading them, changing directions so quickly that Giselle clutched her hands together involuntarily. If watching him fly in the open sky had been disorienting, this was very close to being nauseating. According to Mother's books an Air Master could choose to see through the eyes of any Air Elemental that would let her, but Giselle had never asked. *Seeing directly through the raven's eyes would probably have me throwing up in short order.*

Suddenly, he lofted up a bit and settled on a branch. No longer flying, he worked his way stealthily through the trees, hopping from branch to branch, staying among the evergreens where he was better hidden from sight, rather than going to the bare branches of the oaks and beeches and birches.

"Shh!" said Rosa, just as the sound of voices echoed thinly from the mirror. There were clearly several people speaking. It seemed that they had found what they were looking for!

The raven worked nearer and nearer, until at last he had a view of the speakers, seated in a camp before and below him as he hid just behind a thin screen of fir needles.

There were four people there: three men and one woman. Three were sitting around a fire; the snow was thin enough here they had been able to scrape it down to bare earth in order to get a fire going that the melting snow would not put out. One was seated in a kind of chair-sled, shrouded in blankets. Next to them was a gypsy *vardo*, one gaudily painted in the Romany manner, rather than plain as Giselle's and Rosa's had been. There was a dead horse dragged off to one side; from the look of it, it had been treated badly, and worked until it had dropped of exhaustion. It was so thin that its poor stretched-out neck was nearly flat, and every bone showed under its harsh, patchy coat. Its heavier winter coat had been rubbed off by the harness; they must never have taken it off him.

I suppose they decided that once they were here, they'd steal some of our horses, so there was no need to spare theirs.

". . . cannot get past their defenses," the woman said in tones of anger and disgust. "I tried everything! I tried the chimneys, the well, even the drains! Everything has damned forged iron and dwarven defenses on it!"

The raven hopped to another branch, hiding behind the trunk of the tree. Now he had a clear view of all of them. All were dressed in heavy, dark wool coats. Two were much older than the others. All were blond; the older man and woman had grey in their hair, yet their faces did not so much show *age* as *ill will*. The three at the fire all had a clear family resemblance; all had blue eyes, square chins, and sharp cheekbones. The youngest of those three wore a sullen look, as he glowered out from beneath furrowed brows. If it had not been for a uniform coldness to their eyes, and a cruel cast to their mouths, they would have been handsome.

"Those are never Romany," Rosa said flatly. "So where did they get that *vardo?*"

"I very much doubt they bought it," Giselle replied. She would have said more, but just then the one in the chair turned his head to say something in an undertone to the old woman, and she gasped with recognition.

It was "Johann Schmidt."

"Well, Mother, *my* servants cannot get past her defenses either," he was saying.

"What is it?" Cody asked.

"That—that's the man that—years ago—" She couldn't finish her statement, but they knew who she was talking about. "This must be his family! So that is how he escaped after he fell!"

The youngest man in the mirror snickered. "Father told you that you shouldn't have been so overconfident."

"A family!" Rosa exclaimed, and shook her head. "Of all the things I would have guessed it was never that our attackers would be a family!"

Between the family resemblance and the fact that the two younger men addressed the older couple as "Mother" and "Father," it was clear what they were dealing with now. A family of magicians. Probably "Johann" was the watcher *and* the Air Master that Giselle had sensed. And that explained . . . everything . . . about all those years ago.

"I never would have thought that bastard *had* a family," Giselle said, through clenched teeth.

"I hope you have another idea now, *brother*," growled the younger man. "All we did was seal them into a nice, cozy cave for the winter. They have all the food and drink in there that they need, aye, and firewood too, and what do we have out here? *Nothing,* that's what! We've got only enough food for a week, while they *feast* in there! We're sleeping in a cold wagon and they have warm fires and blankets and featherbeds! We haven't even got a horse to pull us out of here, because *you* said we could take theirs instead, and told us to beat it to exhaustion to get here! You swore that we'd have them out of a ruin in no time. And what do we find? A fortress! And if that isn't bad enough, you swore the bitch was without allies now that her protector was dead, and we find out there's plenty of mages in that stone vault!" His features were contorted with anger. "Just as you were oh so confident you could steal the old one's treasure all those years ago, and talked me into coming along. And then instead of sticking to *that* plan, you saw the girl and had to have her power too! And look where all that got you!"

"And this is why you are an idiot *berserker*, and not a mage, and never will be, *kleine* Dieter," the man that Giselle had known as "Johann" sneered. "You get one idea in your head, and that's all there is room for."

"Well, it's a damn good thing for you that the idea I got in my head years ago was to haul your broken carcass away from that bitch and her bitch mother, and take you to *our* mother!" Dieter shouted, standing up and clenching his fists, spittle flying from his lips. "And it's a damn good thing for you that I still serve as your legs, you crippled eunuch!"

"Sit *down,* Dieter!" the old man thundered. "Or by all the dark gods I will make you his double!" With a curse, Dieter spat in his brother's direction and sat back down, wearing a snarl.

"Obviously they were better prepared than we thought," said "Johann," as if Dieter's outburst had never happened. "That's no matter. I always have more than one plan. We have the power we got from sacrificing those filthy gypsies. That's enough to build a frost giant.

Or between us, Father and I can summon the Breath of the Ice Wurm. Or both."

"Both," said the old woman, her eyes bright with emotions that Giselle could not read. Hate? Greed? Both? "Better be safe. But we need to have that girl and whatever allies she's got in there out alive, or we'll never get their power."

"Oh, too bad you can't get her power the *proper* way, brother," sneered Dieter. "But you can't do that anymore, now, can you? You ought to let a real man have her—"

"Oh yes, a *real man* who'd kill her in his rage and let the power drain away altogether? Just like you did the *first* girl we let you have? You get no second chance, dolt." "Johann" spat into the snow. "The village must be missing its idiot with you gone."

"That's enough Johann!" the old man growled. "You're on probation yourself, here. We're only giving you a second chance at this bitch because you promised a rare fount of power from her and any of the treasure her protector left behind. So your plan had better work, or you'll be the one stretching his neck on the altar."

"You and what army will put me there, *Father?*" Johann grated back. "Even crippled, I can take you!"

This might have turned into something even more interesting than it already was, had the old woman not hissed at them. "Be quiet!" she spat. "I think I heard something!"

And with that, the vision faded away.

"What happened?" Giselle asked, stabbed with fear.

"The raven faded into the spirit world," Fox said, in reassuring tones. "A wise move, to avoid detection. They will find no trace of him. He will return to his post when he believes it is safe—or if that does not happen, at night I can send an owl. And now . . . now we know what it is we are dealing with."

"The Breath of the Ice Wurm. . . ."

They turned to Rosa, who was as white as the snow outside. "What?" Cody snapped. "What is it?"

"It's . . . cold. The very essence of cold," Rosa replied, her words laden with a fear that Giselle had never heard in her before. "It's cold so intense that it is said that even *fire* freezes. If they can direct that at us, nothing, no spell, no protection, will keep it out. And there is nothing we can do to keep ourselves warm enough in here. We'll freeze to death. That's if we're *lucky.*"

"And if we're not?" Giselle asked, her hands trembling and fear running down her spine. She had never seen Rosa at a loss before, and never, ever seen her show more than a moment of fear. To see Rosa so terrified made her insides clench with fear herself.

"And if we're not . . . they'll manage to build that Frost Giant they spoke of. It won't care about dwarven protections. It won't care about stone walls. It will just walk up to the walls and bash them down, and we'll be exposed like chickens when a bear cracks open their coop." Suddenly she put her face in her hands and began to cry. "I can't do anything about either! I don't have that kind of power! And no one I knows does!"

Giselle found herself plunged into dark despair. If *Rosa* didn't know how to handle this situation . . . what hope did they have? They didn't have a chance! And . . . not only were all her friends going to die, but the people she was closest to were going to die *horribly,* and so was she!

And in that moment, as her mind froze with terror . . . she remembered something. Something that Rosa herself had said.

When you are fighting against something or someone that is powerful in magic, and they know that you, too, are a magician, more often than not they completely forget to guard themselves against a purely physical attack. That has saved my life, and more than once.

And she heard herself speaking, calmly, before she had even consciously formed the words, before she had even *thought* past that fear. It was as if something was speaking through her, and as if Mother was once again putting a comforting arm around her shoulders.

"Well," she said, putting her hand on Rosa's shoulder, as Mother used to do for her. "Then we'll just have to kill them all before they get a chance to put their plan into motion. As you told me, they will be expecting magic to oppose them, not physical force. Simple, really."

Later she was a little appalled that she had said that out loud . . . but no one else seemed in the least shocked. Cody and Fox had even nodded in approval.

And really, what other choice did they have? It was quite clear that this was a situation of kill or be killed.

The raven evidently did not feel it was safe to come back, so after nightfall, Fox sent out an owl. It had been a long wait, but one in which they had discussed . . . a lot of plans.

"Look. 'Member when we reckoned that the strongest thing we had was *us?*" Cody finally said. "That we gotta make sure they couldn't put somethin' to drive us apart? Well, don't y'all think the other way 'round goes fer them?"

Giselle's eyes widened. "They're practically at each other's throats, all the time. And if we can get them separated . . ."

"They'll be so busy thinking of themselves, they won't come to the aid of one of the others," Rosa agreed. "What *we* have to do—"

"Is pick our ground. An' choose our opponents," Cody finished, and grinned at her.

"The most dangerous of them seems to be this Johann," Fox observed. "He may be a cripple and unable to move, but that has made him all the stronger in magic. No one will be able to approach him."

"Yes . . ." Giselle said, slowly. "But *I* don't have to."

It was already colder by the time Fox sent his owl out. And through the owl's eyes they saw there was a mound of snow in the meadow near the abbey that had not been there before. "That's the frost giant," Rosa said. "Or it will be. It will take them days to grow the thing, but they have already started the Breath of the Ice Wurm, you can tell by how much colder it is." She thought for a moment. "Actually, that can work in our favor. There will be a crust of ice on top of the snow by morning that will be thick enough to hold us."

"Yes, but how'll we move an' fight on ice?" Cody asked "I could make snowshoes iffen the snow was still soft—"

"I have just the thing," Giselle said, instantly, and ran for the rooms that had once been Mother's, where her things were still stored. She came back with two sets of ice spikes that you could strap onto your boots or shoes. "Here," she said, giving one set to Cody and one to Rosa. "You're the two that will need them."

Cody examined them with interest. "That'll do'er," he agreed. "But it'd be best iffen I kin get this bastard under the trees, where th'snow ain't so deep."

They had already picked their opponents; Cody wanted the old man, pointing out that the one advantage he had was that he had the same power, but opposite—fire against cold. "An' he'll have 'bout used his up, doin' that there frosty giant an' the ice breath. So I reckon when it comes t'fightin', 'lessen he drops them spells, he ain't gonna hev no more'n me."

And that was another point of getting their enemies separated. If none of them knew that the others were *fighting,* they'd have no reason to drop an ongoing work of Great Magic. Such a thing needed too much concentration to put into motion, and there were consequences to breaking a work of Great Magic before it had completed. The power could snap back on you. You could lose control of your Elementals.

"So, I druther hev that there Dieter, but . . ." He looked askance at Rosa. "I ain't gonna fight you fer 'im. You'll likely black my eye."

"Yes I would," Rosa said firmly. "If he's a true *berserker,* then he does more than just go battle-mad. He's a shape-shifter. And I have things to deal with a shape-shifter. You won't fit my special armor, and you don't know how to use my axe or my crossbow."

"Crossbow, mebbe. Special armor, no. An' I ain't never seen no shape-shifter." Cody cleared his throat awkwardly. "So I reckon I'll take on th' old man."

"The witch is mine." Fox's eyes glittered in a fashion that suggested he was very pleased with this. "She holds the stolen power, and perhaps the stolen souls, of too many. I shall be pleased to free it, and them."

They planned.

And then they got Elfrida to feed them a very special meal, made in her oven, and despite everything, they slept.

Fox slipped out first, swathed head to toe in a kind of oversuit that Elfrida had whipped up for him overnight out of sheets. He left in the early dawn, and if Giselle had not been watching for him, she never would have seen him against the snow. He left the mirror behind, tied to the raven, who had decided it was safe to observe again, from a distance. The witch had begun a scrying spell using a mirror of her own, presumably to keep an eye on the outside of the abbey, so that they could ambush anyone who ventured out. This was exactly what *they* wanted. In fact, their plan counted on it.

The fire had predictably died down overnight, and just as predictably, there was insufficient wood for it. Dieter, who seemed to have gotten the job of woodcutter as well as every other chore that neither his mother nor his father cared to do, was sent out, with much scolding, to fetch more. That was Rosa's signal; like Fox, she too was swathed in a garment made of a white sheet, and out she went.

When there was no sign that anyone in the camp had noticed her leaving, and the raven had determined Dieter was *well* out of earshot of the camp, no matter how much noise he made, it was Cody's turn.

And he was . . . something of a sight. He was bundled up in Mother's old woolen cape with the hood up. Over his trousers he wore a skirt. His head was so wrapped in a long scarf that nothing was visible but his eyes . . .

. . . and the two blond braids that hung down over the breast of his cape.

They were two of Giselle's braids, the hair that she had gratefully cut short when they first arrived. These, and Rosa's spell of illusion, should make him pass at a distance for her.

"I look like a durn fool," he said, voice muffled by the scarf.

"There's no one to see you but me and Kellermann," Giselle pointed out. "And Kellermann looks even sillier."

That was because Kellermann was also disguised as Giselle, with another two braids dangling over the cloak he wore. Which was Giselle's. As were the dirndl and smock, and perfume. Rosa had worked the much more difficult spell of *seeming* on him, and even to Rosa's eyes, she had to concentrate on the man she knew was under all that in order to see him. Otherwise it was like looking into a mirror.

"All right, out you go," she said, and off Cody went. There was a window in the storage above the kitchen he could just barely fit through and climb out of that would let him out onto the snow drifted to the second floor. He trudged down the stairs, and in about half an hour, the witch bit off an exclamation.

"The girl!" she spat. "The little bitch is getting away! What a time for Dieter to be cutting wood!"

"I'll get her, never fear," the old man rumbled, and got to his feet. A moment later a sort of ripple passed over him, and he seemed to disappear. "She'll never see me coming. Ha."

"She had better not. She's at full power, and *you* are—" Johann snapped.

The old man interrupted him. "I am your senior in years, wisdom *and* power, boy!" his voice snarled out of the ripple in the air. "And don't you forget it. Or cripple or not, I'll teach you that lesson all over again."

Then came the hardest part. Waiting. Waiting until they were sure that the old man was too far from their camp to call back. "All right," Giselle said, finally. "Now, Kellermann."

He was faster than Cody had been, even with the burden of a dress. It wasn't more than fifteen minutes later that the witch let out a volley of curses that practically scorched the air, and Johann, who had been watching the mirror beside her, echoed her. "It was a trick!

It was all a trick! The first one must have been the Bruderschaft hunter. *This* one is her!" The old woman looked wildly about, cursed again, and picked up a staff and a sickle. "Curse men to the darkest hells, why are they never with you when you need them?"

And with that, she scuttled off across the snow like a black spider, leaving Johann alone. She didn't even give Johann a chance to respond.

The mirror she had left beside Johann went dark, no longer controlled by the old woman. Now Johann was limited only to what he could scry . . . and it didn't appear that he knew how.

"My turn," Giselle whispered.

18

THEY had been counting on Johann not knowing how to scry, and it seemed that they had been right. Like Rosa, Giselle was wearing several layers of men's clothing and an oversized coat to fit atop all of it, although she did not have anything like Rosa's silver-lined leather "armor." And, like Fox and Rosa, she was swathed in an over-garment made of white sheets. Fox had not known how to create an "invisibility" spell, and there was no time to experiment.

Unlike the men, since she did not want to be seen, she did not try to get out though the first-floor window of the side of the abbey facing Johann's camp. Instead, she squeezed out the second-floor tower window opposite where Johann still sat; the snow had drifted up to that point and formed a steep slope downward. Making sure her chosen rifle and its little stand were securely fastened to her back, she eased herself belly-down onto the snow and pushed off.

Under other circumstances, the ride would have been exhilarating. It definitely took her breath away, and she and Mother had often made toboggan runs back when she was a child. With her heart racing, she dug in with her toes to slow herself down, and prayed she wouldn't hit anything as she catapulted down the slope, then managed to force her hurtling body into a curve that took her in the direction of Johann's camp.

Guiding herself with her hands, she used the momentum of the slide to get quite some distance closer to where her quarry sat. After she slowed and finally stopped, she kept her head down and well covered by the sheet and slowly slid herself along on her stomach, as she had done when sliding as a child. She didn't want to move too quickly; even at this distance, if Johann looked in this direction, he might notice movement. Every so often she peeked out from under the sheet to see if she could spot Johann, or the *vardo*. She saw the *vardo* first, by the splash of yellow against the white of the snow. Finally, she made out Johann; she knew him by the blue blanket he was wrapped in, a single spot of blue against the yellow and red wagon under the trees. Moving carefully so as not to dislodge her camouflaging garment, she worked her rifle off her back, eased the sheet forward, and slowly worked the rifle out until only the very tip of the barrel might be visible. Then she looked through the thing that made this rifle unique.

It had a telescope sight.

It was the only one in Cody's entire collection that did. Telescopic sights were incredibly rare, and she had been frankly astonished he had one at all when he'd shown her this summer. It was a very fine rifle to begin with, and with the scope on it . . . well, it transcended "fine." That meant that she could use it at a much greater distance than she usually shot targets. That meant that even if Johann took into consideration that she was an *expert marksman,* he would be under the impression that she would have to get close enough to him that he would see her before she could shoot him. The problem was, it only really worked within a certain range: the maximum range of the rifle itself.

Too far. He's still out of range. The blue blur in the sight told her that. Keeping her eye on the sight, she inched forward, slowly, moving carefully to minimize the chance that she would be spotted.

It seemed to take forever, and the cold seeped into her, despite all the layers between her and the snow. *Don't start shivering or you won't be able to stop,* she reminded herself. *And breathe slowly. You don't want a bit of foggy breath to escape and give you away. Let it all get caught by your scarf and the sheet.*

Her joints ached with the cold by the time she got into place. She set the little stand up and propped the rifle barrel on it; at least now she could concentrate on her magic and her aim. Then she closed her eyes, gathered up a little, little bit of Air Magic, and used it to seek out Fox's raven.

? it replied.

Yes, now, she told it.

From the forest behind where Johann sat, a black form exploded skyward, shouting out exactly four raucous alarm calls as it sped away from the *vardo* as fast as it could flap its wings.

The sound rang out across the quiet valley, sending other birds all across the valley into the sky, sounding out their own calls of alarm. In the scope, Johann merely looked annoyed.

Good, he must think something else scared the birds.

But that had been the signal for the others to stop leading their targets away and go on the attack. Hopefully, they had already chosen better ground to fight on than six feet of snow with ice on top of it.

Then, it started, and even though she was prepared for it, it still made her jump and her heart start to race uncontrollably. The noises of conflict erupted from all over the valley; the echoes made it impossible to tell how many fights there were, or where, exactly, they were happening. Male and female shouting, then one shout turning from a yell into a bestial roar. Her skin was crawling, and she clenched her teeth so hard her face ached.

Concentrate, Giselle reminded herself, and began to work her magic. She needed to create that tunnel of air . . . but she needed it to *stop* about a foot or so from him, so he wouldn't detect it. Yet.

And I'm using my magic to kill someone. No. Not just kill him. Murder him in cold blood. . . . She felt ice in the pit of her stomach, and not from the snow or the frigid air.

How would the Great Elementals feel about that? They had warned her against using her lesser allies to harm on her behalf. But what about using the magic itself? And not in self-defense, either. That was something Rosa apparently had never done; in every story she had told about destroying something, it had either pretty much been in a purely physical manner, or she had broken the renegade's magic so that his own Elementals turned on him. This, well . . . *I can't do this without magic.*

She could try, but she did not *dare* take the chance that this would fail. And to be certain, she had to use magic. She hadn't mentioned this to the others, or they might have tried to talk her out of it.

I couldn't let them do that. She watched Johann through the scope, she felt her insides twisting up with conflict. *I'm the only one that has a chance of pulling this off. And Johann* must *die, or we will find ourselves facing the Frost Giant, the Breath of the Ice Wurm, or both.* She had no doubt that Johann was conserving his magic and his strength, manipulating his parents and his brother to expend theirs on his behalf. He was the mastermind here. She had watched him prod and twist them with his words, keeping them all at each others' throats . . . but except for Dieter, never really at *his*. And the father had Dieter firmly in check. He flattered his father and mother obliquely, yet with challenge, making them prove themselves by expending themselves over and over while he sat in his chair like a spider in a web, waiting, waiting. She reckoned that if he needed to, he could continue those two terrible pieces of magic all by himself.

Is he even still a cripple? She could not be sure. It certainly suited him to be thought one right now. But he was an Air Master, so . . . it was possible he was no longer as handicapped as he once had been. Air was not noted for being able to heal, but . . .

Who knows what he has been able to coerce out of the Elementals he has in his thrall?

She was probably going to get only one chance for this shot. When she touched him with her magic, he *would* feel it. He had to be suitably distracted at that moment, so that he would not react immediately.

He was not distracted enough yet. He had expected the sounds of conflict; in fact, he was smiling a little. She realized in that moment that he *did not care* if one or more of his family fell, so long as there was at least one left. So long as *she* ended up in his hands. And the best person to take her was probably his mother. His mother was a witch, and he was probably counting on the fact that there was not a lot, magically, that even an Air *Master* could do against the knowledge and stolen powers of a witch. Witches were too unpredictable. There was no way of knowing what they had stolen, what they had learned from old books of spells, what they managed to get from pacts with Elementals or . . . other things.

It's murder him, or he murders us. She tried to rationalize it, and . . . then she realized what she was doing. There was no way of escaping what she was about to do.

I cannot rationalize it. So be it. To save my friends, I will murder. With my powers. In cold blood. And I will accept whatever comes of that.

A great calm settled over her. Her hands steadied. Her breathing steadied. And that was when Rosa's coach gun roared out over the valley.

That startled him. His head jerked in that direction. In that instant, she thrust the tube of air forward, touched it to his temple, and squeezed the trigger.

The rifle butt snapped into her shoulder. In the scope, a bright red spot blossomed at Johann's temple. And he toppled forward, out of the chair, to lie motionless in the snow.

A scream rent the air from above, and Giselle threw back the sheet and looked up to see the Thunderbird plunging toward her. She watched it come, feeling . . . still calm. *So be it*—she thought.

And then its talons skimmed a good foot above her head, and she heard a screech behind her as it hit something, and there was thunder all around her as it beat its wings to gain the sky again.

Instantly she rolled over, to see the great Elemental thundering upward with something in its talons. Some*one*. Someone screaming.

Johann's mother. The witch. The Thunderbird had caged her with its talons, holding her fast as the sickle and staff dropped from her hands to land in the snow.

The witch writhed and shrieked as the Thunderbird carried her higher and higher, until it was so high that her voice faded to nothing in the distance.

Then it let go.

The witch's screaming didn't end until she hit the snow with the same *crack* as a rifle bullet, but much louder.

Nothing could have survived that fall.

Stunned, Giselle stared, unable to move, until she realized that Fox was standing motionless beside her. How had he come up beside her without her noticing? She looked over at him and met his solemn gaze.

"Strictly speaking," he said, in a conversational tone, "It was not the Thunderbird that killed her, it was the fall. And strictly speaking, it was not your magic that killed the Air Master, it was the bullet."

"Oh," she replied. And that was all she could manage, until he took her by the elbow.

"I think we should make sure of our friends," he said.

Rosa's fight with the *berserker* had gone as she had coolly planned; Giselle read the signs in the snow and the grass when they reached her. She had ambushed him in an area of forest floor scrubbed bare by the blizzard wind. She had goaded him into shape-shifting by taunting him and staying just out of his reach. Then, once he had shifted, she had unloaded both barrels of her coach gun into him— one barrel holding a silver slug, the other silver shot. It had been a short fight. They found her calmly waiting for them, sitting on a stump, with the lacerated remains of the man-bear lying in a splatter of bloody snow at the edge of the cleared spot.

Cody they found slumped over his knees, panting heavily, while the body of Johann's father lay burning a few feet away. When he looked up at them, they could all see he'd taken a battering. One eye was swelling shut, his lip was split, and his nose was broken and bleeding.

"Mighty glad t'see y'all," he said, thickly. "Reckon I need a little he'p getting back."

"What happened?" Giselle gasped, and with Fox, ran to help him up.

"Short story. He figgered I was a-gonna challenge him to a magic-fight once he figgered out I wasn't you . . ." Cody groaned as they lifted him to his feet. "Dammit, I think he cracked m'ribs. Anyways, instead, I jest waded straight on inter him. We pounded on each other fer a while, then we heerd that witch screamin' an' he reared back, an' I reckoned I was about t'get blasted, so I did th' on'y thing I could think of. I set m'hands on fire." He shook his head. "What I didn' know was that there coat've his was oilcloth over wool. Reckon he thought he was purdy smart, bein' all waterproof in that storm. Turned out that weren't such a good ideer. He went up like a bonfire. Damndest thing I ever did see."

"You go ahead of me for a moment," Rosa ordered, looking at the forest. "I will see to cleaning up the bodies. I would rather they didn't remain here for more than another hour or so. Don't worry, it won't take me more than a few minutes to arrange. But those bodies are still reservoirs of dark magic, and we need to have them gone. Such things can spawn vengeful ghosts or turn innocent Elementals to the bad."

Giselle started to ask how Rosa intended to do that . . . then saw the look on her face, and decided not to ask. At least, not then. Maybe not ever.

The three of them headed back to the abbey, with Cody leaning on Fox, and all of them stopping when he needed to catch his breath. Rosa caught up with them when they were almost there, and told them with a curt nod that whatever it was she was doing about the bodies had been taken care of.

Giselle noticed that the spot where the mound of snow had been building—which presumably would have become the Frost Giant—had collapsed in on itself, forming a sort of concave dish. *And there goes my last worry.*

They found Kellermann waiting anxiously for them at the first floor window he and the other two men had gone out of. With much groaning and cursing, they got Cody inside, and there they left him with Giselle while they got a bench to carry him on, and a couple of the cowboys to do the carrying. Or rather, Fox and Rosa went to get the help. Kellermann vanished to get rid of his rather embarrassing "disguise."

Giselle fervently blessed Elfrida's handiwork, as the two who arrived were entirely incurious about how Cody had managed to get damaged. He stammered something about one of the broncos acting up, and they just accepted it without asking why he was wearing a strange cloak and Giselle's braids around his neck. The skirt was long gone, probably in the fight, but Giselle counted that a small cost.

Elfrida managed to get the sheets off them relatively intact, then went to work on Cody. "I'm glad your healing skills are better than mine," Rosa said, ruefully, as she divested herself of some of her layers of clothing. Unlike Giselle, she hadn't needed to borrow any. Evidently she used men's clothing quite often when she was hunting.

"That's all right, dearie. I wouldn't be of much use hunting down werewolves," Elfrida said, quite as if she dealt with battles like the one they had just been through every day. "Now, if you could just lend me a nice bit of magic, I think we can have this young fellow all right in very little time."

Giselle stripped off most of what she was wearing—it had been borrowed from Kellermann, who gathered it up and took it back to his quarters. That left her in one of her flannel shirts and the suede trousers she wore under her buckskin skirt She didn't feel at all right about leaving Cody alone, and evidently neither did Fox, so they both stayed while Elfrida and Rosa worked on him, magically and physically. When he was stripped to the waist, it was evident he had taken a wicked beating; he was black and blue from his neck to his stomach.

"I take back everything uncomplimentary I ever said about you, Captain," Rosa said, on seeing that. "I don't know too many men who could have taken the punishment you just did and still finished the fight."

"Pshaw!" Cody said, but behind his bruises, he looked pleased.

"Point is, we each did what we was supposed to. An' it all ended all right."

When Elfrida pronounced him "as fit as he was going to be without plenty of rest," she released him to go "straight to bed, and no stopping on the way," and handed Fox a bottle of brandy with instructions to "Put him into bed, put his hat on the bedpost, and have him drink until he sees two hats."

On hearing that, Cody turned, took the old woman's face in both his hands, and gave her a hearty kiss right on the lips. "Frida, you are my kind of woman! Iffen I thought you'd migrate back to Texas with me, I'd marry ya here an' now!"

Elfrida went scarlet, and laughed, sounding pleased. "You wicked boy! You could never keep up with me! I've buried two husbands, and I've no patience for training up a third! Now get along to bed with you, and I'll be up with food. If the brandy doesn't put you to sleep, my good pancakes will!"

Cody was able to travel more or less under his own power now, though he limped heavily and kept one hand pressed to his bandaged side. Kellermann met them at the door to his rooms—once Mother's—and he and Fox put him to bed, then allowed the two women in.

Giselle sighed, as she settled down in "her" old chair at Mother's hearth—much improved with one of those stoves. "I just realized how incredibly *stupid* this all was."

"How so?" Rosa asked, as Elfrida appeared with a tray of beautiful potato pancakes and applesauce. She set the tray down on Cody's lap, and he put his tumbler of brandy down beside the food, looking well pleased with himself.

"This all began because Johann and his brother heard some rumor about Mother's treasure, back when I was younger." Giselle shook her head. "If they hadn't believed such a stupid story, they'd never have come here in the first place, and none of this ever would have happened."

"Since we rid the world of four very nasty characters, I can't say I'm terribly displeased with the outcome," Rosa pointed out, dryly.

"Not to mention getting the pleasure of your company. *And* you would not have been there to help Captain Cody with the Wild West Show! But what do you mean, she didn't have any treasure? She had enough money to purchase and *abandon* that house where she lured your father. And she had enough money to support the two of you quite comfortably while she was alive. She was an Earth Master with extensive contacts with dwarves. Most of them have ways of winkling gold or gems out of the little fellows."

"Well, *I* never found any, and neither did Joachim, and we both looked," Giselle protested. "Not a copper coin or a—"

She stopped short at the odd expression on Rosa's face. "What?"

"That chest next to the chair you're sitting on," Rosa said. "What used to be in it?"

Giselle glanced at the old, beautifully carved chest of dark wood, decorated in typical Schwarzwald ornamentation. "Just my hair. Whenever mother cut it off, she'd put the braids in there. Why?"

"Because . . . when I went to pay the dwarves for their work on the abbey, the Head Workman told me that 'he'd taken the pay already from the usual place' and that 'he'd left payment for the surplus where I'd expect it.' I never looked in that chest until I went to move my things out of the room to make way for Cody. Then, it was empty."

Now Giselle was truly puzzled. "You mean, he took the payment in my *hair?* But—"

"Hush," said Rosa, and got up from her seat to run her hands around the fireplace surrounding the iron stove. And when she got to the hearthstone, she exclaimed "Aha!"

Her hands glowed a golden yellow for a moment. Then the crack around the hearthstone glowed an answering yellow.

And the hearthstone lifted up, all by itself, and shifted to one side. And there, lying in the cavity, was a stout iron box.

"I don't suppose you have a key to this, do you?" Rosa asked, as Giselle stared in astonishment.

"Mother didn't leave many keys to things, and I think they're all on the ring in my room," she replied, and without waiting for an answer, she ran to the tower and up to her room. There in a keepsake box on her mantelpiece was the key ring Mother had always worn on her belt. Giselle took it and ran back down, handing it wordlessly to Rosa as the men watched in astonishment.

Or rather, Fox and Kellermann watched in astonishment. Cody was already well on the way to seeing two hats, and just blinked in amusement.

There was only one key on it small enough to fit the lock in the top of the strongbox. Rosa put it in, and then paused.

"I think you should be the one to open this," she said. "If there is anything in there, your Mother left it to you. There might not be anything but air—but perhaps there will be a keepsake or—something."

At this point Giselle was quite past any expectations of *anything*. She hadn't expected them to get off so lightly in this fight, she hadn't expected to get off *at all* for using her powers to take down Johann. So, without really thinking much of anything, except that perhaps Mother had some letters or special books in there, she knelt down beside Rosa, turned the key and lifted the lid.

And found her breath entirely taken away. "Oh dear Virgin Mother," breathed Kellermann. Rosa could only gasp. And even Fox's eyes had gone big and round.

"What?" demanded Cody. *"What? What is it?"*

Rosa and Giselle moved aside so he could see.

"Jumpin' Jehova!" Cody gasped. *"Gold!"*

There was . . . a lot of gold. And a lot of silver too. The strongbox was almost full. If one didn't know any better, one would have been *certain* these were genuine *thalers* and *goldmarks,* from the proper German mints. But they did know better, of course. These were dwarven counterfeits, made so that their bearers could easily spend dwarven silver and gold. They were absolutely the proper weight and the proper value of precious metal, and every one had been stamped with a perfect copy of the actual mold, probably taken from brand new coins; the dwarves never did anything having to do with gold and silver shoddily. They were meticulous craftsmen. But the only "mint" these coins had ever seen were . . . well, wherever it was that dwarves had their forges and workshops.

"How?" Giselle said, finally. *"Why?"*

Rosa sucked on her lower lip. "Well, I would have to guess, but I think I'm right. Your Mother had bargains with the dwarves as many Earth Masters do, but before she brought *you* here, her bargains were nothing special. Very likely she supplied them with exceptional vegetables, and probably amazing cheese and butter, all things that dwarves do not make and cannot get enough of. The bargain was good enough to purchase an old house in a bad neighborhood and abandon it, certainly. But nothing like this. No, I think that bargain changed entirely after you came to live with her, and your hair started to grow."

Giselle wondered if she had gone mad. "What has my hair got to do with this?" she demanded.

Rosa chuckled. "Giselle . . . where, and how, is a dwarf, who is wholly and completely of Earth, going to get his hands on something so full of Air Magic as your hair? You told me yourself: sylphs and pixies play in it, all the Air Elementals love to touch it. It's as imbued with Air Magic as anything material *can* be! She'd put the cut hair in that chest, call them when she needed money, and they'd leave payment in here. That's what that dwarf meant. He'd taken their payment for all the construction they did on the abbey in the hair that had built up in that chest over the years, and left what he considered to be proper overpayment in gold and silver."

Giselle's mouth formed a silent "o." She thought about that, about how careful Mother had been when she cut it, and how the sylphs had been like cats in catnip when she burned the bits in the *vardo*. "But—what would they *use* it for?" she asked.

"Probably the strings for stringed instruments," Rosa replied, after a long moment of thought. "The dwarves are well known for their wonderful instruments, but using your hair for strings would make every instrument into a masterwork. Possibly bowstrings. Wrap it with real beaten gold and make embroidery thread? There are probably hundreds of things I can't think of because I'm not a dwarf." She closed the lid on the strongbox, because they were one and all staring at the bounty. Giselle felt as if the closing of the lid woke her from what had almost become a spell of avarice.

Now she could think again, instead of stare.

"Well," Rosa continued, still kneeling, and laying her hands in her lap. "You're rich. The treasure was real, after all. What are you going to do with it?"

All manner of ridiculous ideas flew through her head. But one stayed, lodged, and became a conviction. There was one wrong that had not yet been put right, and she actually had the power to do that.

She looked up and met Leading Fox's eyes, then Captain Cody's, then Fox's again.

"Why, it's simple," she said, quietly, suddenly flooded with joy. "I'm going to send you all home as rich as you came here to become."

It was spring before the much-shrunken company left. "We are not going to *get* out of here before all this snow melts," Leading Fox had observed, once their initial excitement had died down. "And I am told that winter travel upon the great salt water is exceedingly disagreeable and even dangerous."

Since both these things were true . . . and since the company was, quite frankly, greatly enjoying their comfort, Elfrida's cooking, and their leisure, it seemed a sensible plan. Kellermann let it be known, just about Christmas, that a second and more careful accounting had revealed to him that all the money they were saving by staying at the abbey was going to enable every man and woman to go home in the spring with tidy sums in their pockets—as much as they had expected to when they had set out from America. There would be no need for a second tour, after all. They could all go home as prosperous as they had hoped to become.

When one is told that one has not less money than one expects, but very much *more,* one is not inclined to question the accountant, or the source of the money. Only Kellermann, Cody, the girls and the Pawnee were aware that Cody, Kellermann and the Pawnee were . . . going back considerably *richer* than their wildest hopes. There would be enough to buy Cody that cattle ranch he had talked about, and enough to buy the Pawnee several thousand acres of land in their ancestral home on the Platte River in Nebraska.

And that still left Giselle with a tidy sum to take care of *her* expenses, plus a ready source of money for the future.

And now, in the lovely spring sunshine, with the meadow full of flowers and no sign that *anything* terrible had ever taken place here, she and Rosa were saying goodbye to their friends.

The cavalcade had been reduced to a few luggage and passenger wagons. No show-tent wagons, no equipment, no sideshow. They were keeping the smaller tents and camping on their way to Freiburg and the railway, then taking the rail all the way to Italy and the ship that Kellermann had booked for them. Kellermann had already disposed of all of the show equipment; a circus had come to get it a month ago.

The horses, the cattle, and the four buffalo were staying with Giselle. Even Lightning, the Wonder Horse, was staying. He had taken a liking to both Giselle and Lebkuchen, and Cody declared that he could not bear to break up such a loving couple. Truth be told, Lightning was not as young as she had thought, and she suspected Cody had both a sentimental and an utterly unsentimental reason. He didn't think Lightning had good odds of surviving a second sea voyage . . . and he was going to need good cattle-horses, not a trick horse.

Kellermann had arranged for the cart horses that they needed to take them as far as the railroad to be bought by a trusted gypsy friend at the railhead. Gypsies could always use horses for their *vardos.*

"Well," said Cody, standing beside the wagon he was going to drive. "I guess this's goodbye. Sure you don't want t'come to America? Iffen I don't make you a star, somebody sure will."

"But I don't actually want to be a star," Giselle said patiently. "The only reason I went along with the show was for the money. I didn't care for fame before, and once I got a taste of it, I cared for it even less."

Cody laughed. "Suit yerself, darlin'," he said, getting up into the wagon seat. "Like we say back home, takes all kinds. Iffen I get tired of ranchin' I might try that there vaude-ville I hear tell 'bout iffen I get too bored. Or I might hook up with Buffalo Bill. Let *him* do all the work of runnin' the show, an' I'll get me all the purdy girls. Try not t'get inta more trouble'n y'all can handle, gals. Write to me!"

"We will!" Giselle promised, and he tipped his hat to her.

"Wagons! Ho!" he shouted, and they were off. The much shorter caravan snaked out of the meadow and down to the road, while the girls watched and waved until they were gone.

"Well. Now what?" Rosa asked Giselle as they walked back to the abbey.

"Kellermann asked if he could come back," Giselle said, as two sylphs and a zephyr zoomed by her, playing a game of "chase." "He has the idea that the abbey could become a sort of lodging for young men on hiking trips through the Schwarzwald."

"That is not a bad thought," Rosa observed. "Many artists, musicians and writers go on walking tours through the Schwarzwald. They don't have much money, and they'd be perfectly happy to pay a little for a bed in one of the dormitory stalls and a meal or two from Elfrida."

"That is what Kellermann said. He also said that many artists, musicians, and writers were Elemental Magicians." She exchanged a look with Rosa.

"I think that Kellermann fancies you," said Rosa.

"I think . . . I would not discourage that," she replied, blushing. "But regardless of that, I think you are of the same mind that I am. This could be . . . perhaps another Brotherhood Lodge, of sorts?"

"And it would be a good Brotherhood Lodge in a sort of disguise, and no one questioning the coming and going of young men." Rosa looked around, at the mountains, the meadow, and finally the abbey.

"You and I still have our *vardos*. With Kellermann in charge, and Elfrida to manage housekeeping, if *we* were needed, by the Graf or by the Bruderschaft, we could go at a moment's notice."

That gave Giselle an unreasonably happy feeling. "So, you think I am up to the job of joining the Brotherhood?"

"I think we would be idiots not to ask you to join, and so does Papa Gunther. Not as a Hunt Master just yet—let's get a few more Hunt's worth of experience in you first." Rosa smiled. "But yes. And I cannot wait for you to meet Markos."

"The good werewolf?" Giselle grinned. "I shall be delighted!"

"That's excellent, because I expect him here within two days," Rosa replied, with a laugh at Giselle's expression. "Maybe sooner if he runs fast enough!"

"*You* had better run fast enough, or I shall certainly make you regret not telling me sooner!" Giselle replied. In answer, Rosa took off. Giselle gave her a head start.

"Run, Rosamund von Schwartzwald!" she cried, then called up Flitter, Luna, and Sparrow. "Go get her, my friends," she said, "And make sure there is not a hair on her head that is not in tangles when you do!"

Giggling madly, the sylphs dashed after Rosa. With the wind in her own hair, she paused for a moment to take a long look around.

Somewhere there might be someone who is happier than my friends and I are today, she thought. *But . . . I doubt it.*

Then she laughed, and ran after Rosa.